Entwined Realms

VOLUME ONE

DANIELLE MONSCH

Romantic Geek Publishing

ENTWINED REALMS VOLUME ONE (AN ENTWINED REALMS COMPILATION)
Copyright © 2014 Danielle Monsch

E-book ISBN 978-1-938593-22-2
Print book ISBN 978-1-938593-23-9

Publication Date: October 2014

Content Editor: Gwen Hayes (Stone Guardian) Anna Alexander (Stone Embrace) Rhonda Helms (The Cage King)
Line Editor: Jessa Slade
Copy Editor: Eilis Flynn
Cover Design: Nathalia Suellen

Interior format by The Killion Group
http://thekilliongroupinc.com

DEDICATION

To you, The Readers. This series exists because of you. As someone who is still new to this business, you have supported me beyond anything I could ever have expected.
THANK YOU!

TABLE OF CONTENTS

BOOKS BY DANIELLE MONSCH

Entwined Realms
Modern-Day Fantasy, where Sword & Sorcery and Romance Meet
There are no Dragons…are there?

Stone Guardian – *From the Shadows He Watches Over Her*
Stone Embrace – *In the New Realms, Love can be the Most Dangerous Battle of All…*
The Cage King – *He Will Claim Victory*
The Rooftop – *Only the Stars as Witness*

Fairy Tales & Ever Afters
Slightly Twisted and Very Sassy takes on Fairy Tales

Loving a Fairy Godmother – *Don't Fairy Godmothers deserve a little lovin' too?*
Loving an Ugly Beast – *Can't an Ugly Beast get a little lovin' here?*
Loving a Prince Charming – *When you are Prince Charming, everyone wants a little lovin' from you.*

Pleasure Chronicles
Sexy Sci-Fi about Warrior Women and the Alpha Males who love them

Pleasure Satellite – *To the Strongest goes Everything…*

And want to know whenever a New Book is Released?

DANIELLE MONSCH ANNOUNCEMENT LIST!

STONE GUARDIAN

CHAPTER ONE

Jack Miller aimed his shotgun at the monster's grey-skinned head and pulled the trigger. Green sludge and bits of bone and flesh splattered through the air to land on the street, the gory aftermath releasing a noxious, sulfurous odor.

Shit! His head whipped around, on search for others. He'd hoped to avoid these creatures, but his luck was overall fucked today. The noise would bring more monsters, more death. There was no further advantage to keep creeping around in shadows. It was time to haul ass.

After the earthquake an hour earlier, the streets now resembled pieces of a jigsaw puzzle strewn around. A car wouldn't make it three feet. Shotgun reloaded, he took off through the jagged mess, years of trail running keeping him upright.

A low undertone of anguish surrounded him, cries from people needing help, unable to escape their stone prisons. He didn't pause. *I'm getting my wife. I'm sorry, but you're on your own.*

His Lauren, who he had last seen rubbing her nine months pregnant belly, giving him that crooked smile at his panicked question, "Is it time to go to the hospital? Should we call Ana to get the boys?"

She had waved him out the door in the peaceful morning light saying there was still time, she would start to take care of things, now go be a good cop and let the captain know paternity leave was about to take their best detective away.

Six hours after she kissed him goodbye, Jack stepped into his standard public-servant-worn office, on return from a jail run. His own cell phone out of commission due to a run-in with a perp, he reached for the desk phone to call Lauren and see how she was feeling when the phone rang. He picked it up. "Detective Miller."

"Yes, is this the husband of Lauren Miller?"

Jack's skin goose-bumped at the detachment in that voice, as practiced as any cop who worked homicide for twenty years. It took two tries to swallow and relax his throat enough to speak. "I'm Lauren's husband."

"Detective, this is County General. Your wife has been admitted, and I'm afraid that an emergency situation has devel-"

The ground buckled and twisted and threw him against the wall. The building creaked and groaned, the high-pitched crack of shattering glass sharp in his ears.

The floor still moved. He struggled to regain his footing and watched the earthquake tear through the city from his third-story view. Buildings wrenched from the earth, cars tossed through the air, glass shattered in visible streams. Outside a maelstrom of loud, crashing noise accompanied by the acrid smell of smoke and burning gasoline.

As the destruction continued outside another change took place. Nothing physical signaled this wreckage, but against his skin was scraping, surging, scratching, a changing of air and atmosphere – something shaking up his guts, fucking with him down to the bone and beyond.

Wrongness. Jack locked his knees and leaned against the scarred-wooden desk. Acid surged up his throat and he kept swallowing hard against the urge to keel over and vomit.

"CODE 999! CODE 999!"

Moments later a volley of gunfire sounded outside. A stampede of footsteps pounded past his door. The precinct charged into crisis mode.

Jack stepped into the swarm of cops heading for the munitions locker. The sergeant handed out weapons, only taking enough notice to make sure he was handing to a cop. "Don't forget the sting grenades," Sarge called out as officers suited up in Kevlar, riot gear, and automatic weapons.

Running to the front of the station, Jack heard screams, then a horrified *"What the fuck are those?"*

Disbelief stopped Jack dead as he exited the station and looked what was coming down the road.

Dear God...

The rookie behind him plowed hard into his back. It didn't knock him over, but it shook him out of the daze.

Training took over, and as he drew his gun and began firing, he catalogued the monsters descriptions. Humanoid features, heights 6'5" to 7'5", built like weightlifters. Grey-green skin, with overlarge heads and features misshapen like they'd been pummeled thirteen rounds in the ring. Jaws shoved forward with tusks protruding upward like ivory knives.

They were every nightmare had by every little boy made flesh.

They carried swords and axes and bows as though they had stepped out of a medieval exhibit. The metal surfaces gleamed in the late afternoon sun, the glint menace personified as it shone in his eyes.

The bullets of the .45s weren't doing enough damage. Jack shouted behind him, "Get me a shotgun!"

Cops fired while several monsters broke into a run and ran at them in a full-frontal assault.

Gun empty, Jack looked around for a weapon. A sword lay on the ground. Not seeing any other options, he picked it up.

The fucker was heavier than any bat he'd ever swung. One creature ran to mow him down, and at the last moment Jack went down to his knees, swinging the sword at the creature's thigh.

The sword sliced clean through, severing leg from body. The creature fell forward and hit the ground with a hard thud. Before it could move, Jack drove the sword straight down into the creature's chest where a human's heart would be.

It worked. The creature exhaled in a death gasp. Jack pulled the sword out and again faced the fray.

"Detective, here!" called a voice, a shotgun thrust into Jack's hands the moment he turned toward it. The gun settled against him in familiar comfort.

With several officers now firing shotguns and automatics the monsters were taking damage at a good rate. As their body count rose the largest of the monsters – who stayed toward the rear during the attack – threw his head back and released a high-pitched primal scream. The monsters turned from the station and retreated deeper into the city.

Retreated toward the hospital.

Oh God...

The bark of the captain's voice overwhelmed the confusion. He took charge and centered the group of cops, breaking them into large teams to start search and rescue.

Jack stormed to the older man's side. "Captain, my wife's at the hospital, I've got to get to her."

The older man shook his head, dismissing Jack without even bothering to look at him. "Not happening. In case you failed to notice, we are in a state of emergency. We have a disaster plan to follow, and we're sticking to it."

Jack's hands curled into fists. Fear and anger and worry urged him to strike out against anything that stood between him and Lauren. This man was an obstacle to be eliminated. "My wife needs me."

As if he could sense the younger man's thoughts, the captain took a protective step back. "Those things ran into the city, straight in the direction of the hospital. It is unsafe to go there when we have no idea what the hell we are facing." Turning toward other officers, the captain continued, "We need to start canvassing the surrounding areas, get survivors out and to safety. Miller, I want you to take your men and scour zone D. Direct everyone back to the safe haven."

A firm hand on his shoulder prevented Jack from damaging both the captain and his career, a hand that belonged to his partner Hector Torres. Jack nodded at Hector's unspoken command, saying nothing as the plans were finalized. Weapons were distributed, boundaries were gone over, and one by one the groups went.

After his group had cleared the precinct, Jack turned to Hector. "Torres-" he began, but the older Hispanic man shook his head, stopping the words.

"I know, Miller, you're heading to the hospital. I'm surprised you lasted this long. Ana called me, she has the boys and they're heading to safety now. Lauren asked her to come get them before she went to the hospital. You worry about your wife."

"Thanks, man."

Hector shrugged, black humor that spoke of long years on the force coming out as he responded, "Hope you make it back alive."

"Just take care of my boys." And Jack left to face the nightmares between him and Lauren.

The bite of autumn air froze his lungs as Jack continued his jog, shotgun at his side. Several monsters appeared, searching the area.

Damn, they heard that last gunshot.

One monster spotted him, pointing in his direction and leading the other creatures toward him.

Jack started shooting. He was hitting his targets with the accuracy born out of long hours at the gun range, but too soon the last round was fired.

Dropping the useless shotgun to the ground, he pulled out the large bowie knife from his waistband.

A howl rolled through the darkening night – deeper and fiercer than any howl he'd ever encountered on the ranch growing up. Jack should have been pissing his pants in terror, but right now was only numbness, too much seen and felt and dealt with today.

Bursting from the ruined buildings came the biggest wolves he had ever seen, big as shit. Except they weren't wolves, they looked like wolves mixed with human. Some ran on two legs, some on all four. Broad barrel chests and long arms and legs thick with muscle, fur stuck out in stiff tufts, ears pointed and alert atop their skulls, short snouts that gleamed white, sharp teeth.

Werewolves? Are these werewolves?

They ran at the grey-skinned monsters, jumping from great distances to snap at the monsters faces and throats, claws leaving deep gouges and drawing out more green blood and viscous matter.

Creatures that only should exist in big-budget horror films fought each other. Even as blood and bodies marked the streets, he could only look on with a detached fascination.

Three of the wolven creatures broke away from the back and ran for Jack, and the numbness fled before a spike of adrenaline. Sweat beaded at the base of his neck and marked a trail down his back. He brought his blade up.

The werewolf in front was much larger than the other two. The closer they got the clearer the details were. Jack could start marking where they must have sustained wounds. The smallest one had the worst, a deep gouge on its face that still bled.

They stopped, all upright. Dark brown fur was absorbed by skin, snouts shortened to form a humanoid nose and mouth, claws became hands. In moments, a human man with shaggy dark blond hair and yellow eyes stood before him. The two smaller ones were both male, a teen and a prepubescent, with features so similar to the adult they had to be family.

The adult stared him down, those yellow eyes unwavering as they appraised Jack. "I would appreciate it if you lowered your blade," the now man said, motioning with his chin to the knife in Jack's hand.

These creatures could kill him with little difficulty. As loath as he was to give up any weapon, it would be nothing but stupidity to keep it out and antagonize the creature. Jack opened his mouth, and words he didn't plan tumbled out. "How is this real?"

Battle cries sounded in the background as the werewolf spoke. "I do not know. What I have been told is our realms have collided."

"*Collided*? What do you mean, *realms*?"

"I mean your world is not my world. Yet somehow, they have become one."

Jack looked to the battle still waging, the werewolves winning over the other monsters. "What are those things?"

"Orcs. They are our enemies."

"And humans?"

The werewolf studied him with the palest yellow eyes he had ever seen. "Humans exist on my world. Most were allies. We will see if the humans on this world will be considered the same. For the moment I am willing to give you the benefit of the doubt. We will fight the orcs so the humans of this area will be safe."

The orcs were retreating. The werewolves still in battle followed, and all the monsters dispersed toward the city's edge.

Jack wasn't going to follow to see how it played out. Right now only Lauren mattered. "Thank you for saving me."

The werewolf nodded. "Perhaps in the future, you will return the favor," he said, turning back into his other form, the young ones following his lead. All three took off in the direction of the sounds of battle, and Jack went the opposite way, toward his wife.

The double doors of the hospital entrance were in sight when a great flapping sounded overhead, air gusting around him like a mini-tornado, whipping up debris in great chunks.

Around him the late afternoon sun disappeared, leaving shadow and darkness. Jack looked up.

Fucking hell.

This can't be.

Am I...?

Crazy. Have to be crazy.

Dra-

Dear Lord, please,

Dragon?

Help us...

It was straight from every fairy tale ever told. Enormous enough to block the sun. A wingspan easily three times that of the largest plane he'd ever seen. A long neck and an even longer tail.

It passed over him, lost to his sight within moments.

Sensation returned to his limbs. Only then did the throb of his palms and the ache in his knees make themselves known, where concrete shards sliced into his hands and ripped out the knees of his trousers to bloody the skin underneath. His legs throbbed as he rose.

No. Compartmentalize. Later. He'd think on it later. Now he had to get into that fucking hospital.

Ignoring shouts to keep out, he bounded up the steps to the sixth-floor maternity ward, leaping over rock and broken steps that littered his path.

The front desk of the maternity ward was empty and the automatic doors were open. Here the earthquake had done enough damage to twist walls and leave chunks of tile lying about. Power was on, but it was dim – back-up generator only. It was safe enough to keep the patients here, but it was clear the ward was in crisis mode. With no one to stop him, he ran down the hall. "Lauren! Lauren!"

A nurse ran out of one of the rooms in front of him. "Sir, you need to stop! We are trying to keep everyone calm."

"I'm looking for my wife. What room is Lauren Miller in?"

A stillness stole over the nurse's form except her shoulders, which pushed back in quick movement. "Lauren Miller?" she asked, but it was stalling disguised as a question, something a cop saw and heard on a daily basis. Tendrils of fear Jack had not experienced even when faced with those monsters only minutes before uncurled from his belly, his skin growing chilled as they wormed their way to the surface.

"Where is my wife?" he asked, advancing on the younger woman.

The nurse would not look him in the eye, her throat working in nervousness, and his skin went from chilled to sub-zero. "Sir, you need to wait here. I need to get my supervisor…"

"Where's my wife?" he screamed, grabbing the young woman by the shoulders and shaking her.

"That's enough." The voice was a whip, cracking through the air. He turned to behold a battle-axe of a woman, late sixties, built broad and strong with a face that told she had seen much and overcame it all. "Let the girl go."

"I want my wife! *Where is Lauren Miller?*"

The older woman walked to him, no fear in her as she grabbed his hands and peeled them away from the girl's shoulders, her focus such he could not look away from her. She said to no one in particular, "Bring Mr. Miller a wet cloth to wipe down and a scrub shirt."

The squeak of shoes at his side told him someone was following her orders. Wet cloth was thrust into his hands and habit had his body moving even as his thoughts were centered on his wife. As soon as he pulled the clean top over his head, he said, "Please, my wife, where is she?"

There. That flash of compassion in her eyes, that fucking flash that every cop and doctor and nurse displayed when they were about to tell you your life was over. He backed away from her, shaking his head. "No. No, no, no."

She was ruthless in her efficiency. "Mr. Miller, I'm sorry to tell you that your wife died today. There were complications. The baby was born as the earthquake started and we lost power, and in the chaos we couldn't do what was necessary to save her life."

No.

No no no nononono nonononononononononononononononono

It was the hand on his cheek, the living warmth of another human that brought him to awareness, the realization the litany was not in his head but coming out of his mouth. He grabbed her wrist. "Let me see my wife. Take me to my wife!"

"No Mr. Miller." The nurse's eyes were steady on him. Not breaking eye contact, she called out, "Sarah, bring the baby."

A young woman approached, sidling up to the older woman and angling her body away from his. With unhurried movement, the nurse disentangled her wrist from his grasp, twisting to take the bundled infant from Sarah.

She put the baby to his chest. Long practice had him grabbing the precious bundle before his brain caught the significance of the moment. "This is your daughter, Mr. Miller."

Daughter. He had wanted a baby girl so badly, had prayed for her every night. *Lord, you've blessed me with my boys and I'm grateful for them. But if you could, I'd love a little girl. I want her to be like my Lauren.*

"Daughter..."

"Did you know you were having a little girl, Mr. Miller?"

He shook his head. "No. Lauren wanted it to be a surprise, Lauren..." and he choked, because Lauren should be here answering these questions, about how she refused to find out, because she said, *I'm not going to let anyone make a big deal if this baby is a girl or act all sad for us if it's another boy. You and me, Jack Miller, we make the best babies in this world, and boy or girl, that's how it is.*

"How many other children do you have, Mr. Miller?"

The question brought his attention back to the battle-axe, and he blinked several times to focus on her.

"I know you have others. The way you hold that baby speaks of a lot of experience."

"Four. Four boys."

"So you have four boys, and now you have a little girl to protect as well. I'm sorry about your loss, but you can't be carrying on any more. You've got too much responsibility on your shoulders and you need to be strong for them."

An electric current passed between them, empathy between two survivors who knew there was a path ahead they needed to take, and their loved ones would have to wait a little while before they were reunited. He straightened his back and brought his daughter up to his chest, laying her little head over his heart. "Yes, ma'am."

The nurse gave a decisive nod and turned back to the hospital personnel behind her, issuing orders as she marched down the hall.

His daughter started to snuffle, so he brought her head up higher onto his shoulder, bouncing lightly to calm her. He looked down, seeing the curve of baby cheek, smelling the baby soft smell only newborns possessed, bringing peace even when the world around them was falling apart. "Don't worry, baby. You're safe now. Daddy is here and will always protect you, I promise."

His little girl. He hoped she would have her mother's coloring, especially those cornflower blue eyes. He hoped she had her mother's kind heart and strong spirit and loving compassion...

He squeezed his eyes shut, holding the tears back. None of that now. There were other things to do.

Like a name. He and Lauren hadn't chosen one for a girl. Mostly because Lauren didn't really believe they were going to have a girl, but also because she hadn't wanted to use his choice.

We can't name our daughter that, Jack. I know you love it, but it sounds too much like my name. I don't want people thinking I'm so egotistical I need my little girl to remind everyone who her momma is.

Lauren, my love, my life, your little girl will be as amazing as you are, and she'll be proud to let everyone know who her momma is.

Jack Miller, don't try to sweet talk me. Jack... -stop that! You letch!

Jack... Jack... I love you...

He rubbed his cheek over the downy soft skin of his little girl's head. "Your name is Larissa, little girl. I know it fits you, and I think your momma would agree."

Later, and soon, he'd have the outside to deal with. Later was telling four boys they no longer had a momma who would love and care for them. Later was dealing with a world that went to hell and figuring out how to bring it back. Later. But now, there was only this moment with his precious baby girl.

Welcome to our family, Larissa Joy.

CHAPTER TWO

26 years later

She is connected to the future of your Clan. Guard her well.
Three months.

Three months he stood sentry, crouched in the shadows of the building across from her.

Three months he watched, waiting for her importance to become clear, to explain why she was brought into his life.

Three months she consumed his every waking moment.

She was in the living room, picking up the clutter which accumulated over the day. She danced as she went about her task, her hips moving in sinuous rhythm to the song heard through the open door of her balcony – the beat heavy, the female singer's voice soft and alluring and darkly sexual.

The fingers of his right hand curled, claws raking over his palm.

The autumn night had taken on the crispness that spoke of winter arriving soon. Humans were more sensitive to temperature than his kind, but the cold seemed not to bother her. After finishing her task, she walked out on the balcony and sat on the metal chair that stood flush with the outside wall. The thin sweater she wore offered little protection from the chill but she made no move to go back inside. She wrapped her arms around her waist and stretched long legs in front of her, crossing them at the ankles.

He burrowed deeper into the shadows, more habit than fear she would notice him.

Her long hair spilled behind her, a color he had only seen once before when he flew over a wheat field on a blinding summer day. Her face contained no harsh lines. It was all soft curves, heart-shaped with the fullest mouth, one that made her appear to always be on the verge of pouting. Her body was ripe, her sweater and jeans tight over lush curves.

She was so innocent to the dangers of this world, so unprepared to deal with any danger. Why did her Clan let her live away from them? They must know how exposed she left herself, what a tempting target she made. Her father had been a fool to let her leave the safety of his house.

Her phone rang. She took it from her pants pocket. Her side of the conversation was loud in the still evening. "Hello? Dad, hi."

After several moments her laughter rang out, light and airy and free. Tension eased from him, the bunched muscles in his back loosening. Her face was animated, enjoyment evident as she talked with her father. She confused him, but in this one thing they were the same – absolute loyalty to their Clan.

Then she groaned. "I'm going to be grading papers. I told you Mrs. Wajkowski's appendix burst, right? Well, the substitute they brought in is overwhelmed and I volunteered to help her out."

She would never refuse anything her family asked of her, so she tried to get them to rescind their invitations when she didn't like the request. What now was her father asking of her?

She rubbed the back of her neck, the motion causing her chest to thrust out, bringing the neckline of her sweater a fraction lower. "No, I don't think I've had the pleasure of meeting Nick yet, and I'm sure he's a very nice guy."

Now the reason for the invitation became clear. Her father often tried to match her with suitable mates, though without success thus far. They were too forward in their attentions. None crossed the line with her, but one had frightened her with his disregard for her words and the way he towered over her. That man would never go near her again.

"Can't any of the brothers fill out the poker game? Make it all precinct guys?" she asked, but her defeated tone told him she would be going to her father's home tonight. She snorted at something her father said, saying in return, "Are you trying to tell me you happened to schedule all four on the Friday night shift and not a soul said anything to you?"

Whatever her father said caused her to roll her eyes, but she responded as expected. "Okay, Dad, I'll be over a little later. I have a few things to do first, so you'll have to survive a little while without me." A beat of time. "I'm always cute, and no, I'm not changing into a skirt." A few more moments of her father speaking, then with exasperation on her features, she said, "Love you Dad, buh-bye."

She hung up the phone, a long sigh escaping. She stood up and stretched her arms, the movement lifting the sweater so the silky skin of her stomach was visible and the material bunched in such a way that it showed a generous expanse of breast.

He ran his palm over his mouth, the bite of fang on flesh hard enough to draw a thin line of blood.

She lowered her arms and leaned on the railing, her gaze coming to meet his.

Discomposure thrilled through him, alighting down his spine. Could she see him? Time hung for a moment, his puff of visible breath going still in the air as though it too waited for the answer.

She gave a final sigh and entered her apartment to get ready for her journey.

12

Relief and an odd disappointment skittered through his mind before sense reasserted itself. Of course she could not see him. No one as unobservant as she could ever hope to glimpse one of his kind.

The odd ache in his chest was back. The ache that started the night he realized he had only one more week with her, and it was time to get back to his life, his responsibilities, his Clan. Three months he had sworn to watch over her, and now he was free to never again take up this sentry, never again place her safety before his Clan, never again look upon her face.

Never see her again...

She finished her preparations and left her apartment.

He would now need to follow her to her father's house. It was harder to hide there, more chance of discovery, but there was no choice. She would not be allowed to leave his protection as long as he watched, not even to exchange it for the protection of her family. They were human guardians, yes, but he trusted her to no one else.

He watched the front entrance for her exit. It took only moments before she emerged from the building and went toward the side street where her car waited for her.

The wind changed. With the shift the smell assailed him. Decomposition, death, rotting flesh and decay.

Zombies.

Larissa...

This hard pit in his stomach, this weakness in his limbs, this ice in his veins that threatened to stop his heart – this was unknown. Never, not even as a fledgling warrior, had he been so powerless.

Rage, though, rage was a familiar companion, and the rage he welcomed, let it engulf these other sensations and bury them deep. A white and blinding wave overwhelmed all in its path and directed itself at those that would hurt what was his to protect.

They dare come after her?

They dare?

A bellow clawed its way from his throat. He ran the length of the roof and with a snap of his wings, he plummeted toward his enemies.

Her brothers were going to kill her. No way around it, she was a marked woman.

Subtle Dad wasn't. Sad thing was, her father wasn't the hairiest matchmaker she had ever seen. That honor belonged to her third-grade teacher, Mrs. Donovan, who had tried to match up every single father in her class with her unmarried daughter. Even her widowed father hadn't been able to escape the madness.

But Dad could scheme with the best of them. Would he really force all her brothers to work the despised Friday night shift so he could set up his daughter on a blind date?

Why yes, yes he would.

Larissa gave a loud exhale as she left the safety of her building and marched forth to yet another set-up. The coffee shop across the street was still open and Larissa faltered, a hot chocolate calling her name. No, better not. If she didn't hurry, her brothers would come to carry her bodily to wherever this Nick was, not unlike the traditional virgin sacrifice.

They really hated working the Friday night shifts.

Not that she wanted to go. It had been tough to leave the little haven of her apartment tonight. The night was crystal clear with a moon so bright and big she might have had a chance of touching it. The air was crisp and fragrant with the scent of the dampened oak leaves carpeting all the once-green, grassy areas.

And there was the presence of her phantom companion. It had to be her family's paranoia about her living alone catching up to her, but these last couple months she had been living with a constant presence. Maybe if the feeling scared her she would be more wary, but she was comfortable with this companion. It was protective in its watchfulness, a dark energy against those who would hurt her while it wrapped her in safety. She felt safer these last months than she had even when she had lived at home.

A snort of laughter spilled out as she imagined Dad's indignant expression if she ever told him that. Maybe a hint or two she should rethink the whole coming-back-home-to-live thing.

Enough with the flights of fancy. There were plans to make. Okay, poker. Another set-up sure, but maybe Nick would be nice. He couldn't be worse than Anthony, he of the love obsession with his abs, who pulled up his shirt four separate times to try to convince her to touch the muscle mass. Or there was Ben, who took her to the steak and seafood restaurant and ate and drank everything in sight while she ordered salad, then proceeded to split the check with her.

And then there was Leonard.

Yeah, Dad didn't do too well with choosing Leonard.

Still, he hadn't been *so* horrific, and she was a tad ashamed of the momentary glee that rushed through hers the next day when Dad told her Leonard's car had been mysteriously crushed.

Besides, if it worked out with Nick, she would be spared her brothers' accusing glares during Saturday dinner when she told them that, once again, there had been no spark and no chance for further romance.

So, reframe this whole set-up situation. She didn't want to go over to Dad's, but there was always a chance it could turn out to be a real blessing.

Larissa breathed in the autumn night air, taking in great lungfuls as she moved toward her car. There were no better nights than these, when the leaves were changing colors and the bite in the air made every breath a pleasure-pain mix.

And then her breath stopped, frozen in her chest as every muscle in her body froze when a roar sounded through the empty streets, the unholy sound moving ever closer.

CHAPTER THREE

Larissa's mouth went dry, her palms dampening in spite of the chilled night. She looked up to find the source of that inhuman sound.

What was that? This was a protected area – humans-only. The magical wards had been recast only last month with the specific purpose to fend off any non-human race or species.

The low hum of voices brought her attention back down to the street. Three bodies moved toward her. Probably male, judging by the taller height and broader shoulders, but she couldn't be sure. They wore hoods to hide their faces, and their jackets hid any shape of the upper torso. She had seen similar groupings many times at the high school she taught at. Still, they seemed… -wrong. Their bodies were at odd angles, their steps uneven, more akin to a series of lurches rather than the awkward gaits of adolescents or the surer steps of adult males.

If it feels wrong, run. Even before the echo of Dad's oft-repeated advice faded, she had turned away from the group and was sprinting back to her car.

Their steps quickened behind her, faster than their shuffling led her to believe. It took mere seconds for her to feel a brush of fingertips against the back of her coat. Adrenaline surged, fueling her muscles, and she shot forward.

She turned the corner to see three other men in front of her. Skidding to a stop she swiveled on the ball of her foot, turning to go the opposite direction, but found that the three who had been trailing her had already come out of the side street and now surrounded her.

Her heart beat double-time, a staccato that urged flight, but no avenue was open. The men had formed a loose circle, blocking any escape, and several more beings coming from various directions. All she could do was stand there.

The wash of tears clouded her vision. Images of Dad, of her brothers, of school and Olivia and even her damned stuffed giraffe she had since kindergarten.

They bore down on her, their heads still covered by hoods. Thin hands with a skeletal appearance reached out for her, the faint whiff of decay around them, like meat that had been left out.

She wrapped her arms around herself, hunched over, bracing against that first touch.

The primal scream ripped through the air again, closer this time. A mountain of a man with wings descended from the sky.

He landed on the street before her with such force the pavement under her feet shook. No, he wasn't a man. Stone-grey skin, black hair, and those huge wings, but before she could get a better look, the creature advanced on the things that surrounded her.

The hooded men turned their attention to the creature. One of them rushed forward, but the creature picked him up by the front of the hoodie with one hand and threw the man against the building, the impact causing the hood to fall away and reveal his face.

One eye bounced against its cheek, only a ligament keeping the eye attached, while on the opposite side of the face the skin of its jaw was gone and the white bone underneath visible. Its nose was half chewed away and the remaining skin was bloated and pus filled.

Larissa screamed, covering her eyes in against the *wrongness*.

Zombies? Zombies here? No, not in the protected zone, it couldn't be. Things like these weren't allowed to be here.

Zombies meant…

Zombies meant…

"This is not happening, this is not happening, this is not happening…" But it was, and Larissa clenched her jaw hard to stop the flow of unconscious words. What would Dad say, what would Dad say?

Always be aware of your surroundings, kiddo.

Larissa forced her hands away from her face and watched as the zombies brought out knives and flung themselves at the creature. He towered over the zombies, but for something as big as he was, the creature was graceful, dodging the weapons while he used his wings, hands, and tail to fight off his enemies.

The creature ripped off one zombie's arm and threw him against the wall. The zombie hit hard and tumbled to the ground, the severed arm landing a few feet away. The zombie rose and grabbed the arm, pushing it back against the socket. As Larissa watched, the flesh mended together, and once again the zombie had use of the arm.

It flung itself back into the battle. This time the winged creature tore off its head before he threw the body away. There was no more movement after that.

There had to be at least fifty zombies swarming the creature. They were so engrossed in their fight they had forgotten about her.

Move! Run away!

A sharp zing raced through her body and broke the frozen panic that engulfed her. Let the monsters fight between themselves – she needed to get to her car.

Her car was on the other side of a nearby alleyway, and after a quick look around confirmed nothing was near her, she ran full speed toward the alley. As she neared the entrance something grabbed her ankle.

Larissa put her hands out to protect her face as she fell. Her wrist throbbed and the pressure she put on it to push herself up caused it to give way under her. She flipped over onto her back, but before she could try to stand again a zombie loomed above, milky eyes intent on her.

She used the heels of her hands and feet in an effort to push herself away from the zombie, but it reached down and grabbed the front of her jacket. He lifted her as if she weighed nothing and she dangled a good foot above the street. Larissa punched his arm, but for something disintegrating before her eyes, she couldn't make him move even a millimeter.

She looked for a weapon, anything that would help, but instead caught sight of movement out of the corner of her eye. Shadows moved like spilled ink over the ground toward the wall. They crept up the wall, fanning out. From the middle of this darkness, from the solid wall of the alleyway, a new man emerged.

He was shadow made flesh, his eyes and hair purest black, his body fuzzy as if the shadows still clung to his skin like a dark cloud. In each hand he held a curved sword.

The zombie jerked its head to look back, but before he could complete the action the shadow man moved and held up his hand, the streetlight glittering on the metal of the blade as it arced down and beheaded the zombie holding her.

With the loss of its head, the zombie crashed to the ground. Larissa fell those inches she had been held aloft but managed to keep her feet under her and stumbled against the building for support.

The shadow warrior came toward her. His eyes met hers for the briefest moment before commotion at the alleyway's entrance drew his gaze. With both swords aloft, he went to meet the zombies coming after her.

Sudden pressure on her arm. She turned, screaming and slapping her hands at whatever was behind her.

It was a woman, long red hair vibrant under the street lights. She blocked Larissa's flailing arms and ineffectual swats. "We're getting you out of here," she said, and grabbed Larissa's wrist to lead her out of the alleyway.

Before they could do so, the other end of the alleyway was crowded by more zombies. "Keep back," the woman ordered, pushing Larissa to the side.

The woman reached behind her shoulder and pulled free the longest sword Larissa had ever seen. It looked as tall as the woman and half as wide, but she hefted it in her hand as though it weighed no more than a kitchen knife.

The large sword took on a red glow. As though in response, scrolls of fire appeared on the woman's bare arm. They settled into her skin, winding their way up to her shoulder to disappear underneath the black leather vest she wore, muted flame under flesh. Sword in hand, she ran toward the zombies blocking the path.

Trapped. But across the alley was a door on that building's side. If by some luck it was unlocked maybe Larissa could get away from all this madness. She took one step forward when something fell from the sky in front of her.

The winged creature stood before her, his massive body blocking her exit. He reached down and grabbed her around the waist.

No, no, I was so close!

"Let me go!" she screamed, raking her nails against his bare chest in an effort to wound him, his skin so hard it was as though her nails slid against stone. If she hurt him he gave no sign. He put one arm under her knees and held her bridal style tight against him. He spread his wings, the wingspan massive.

She looked back at the shadow warrior. He had finished with the zombies, swords still in the air as if he had swung his last killing strokes. His head turned toward her as she was pulled into the air, the creature taking flight with her.

Soft words were spoken into her ear. "I will not harm you, little human. Hold onto me. I will protect you."

The creature could speak. His voice was deep and soothing and gentle and so at odds with his appearance. That voice, combined with her fear of falling, overrode any other considerations. She circled her arms around his thick neck for some semblance of stability and safety and held tight as the creature flew her into the waiting night.

CHAPTER FOUR

They had been flying – what… thirty minutes? Three hours? – when they arrived at an expansive keep nestled within a jagged mountain range. From this angle she noticed several multi-story towers rising from the stone, but the design was so clever the keep had to be near invisible most of the time.

They set down on the top of the highest tower, the landing so skilled only the slightest bounce let her know they were on solid ground.

She was in shock – she had to be. It was the only explanation for why she was not crying or cursing her luck, the creature, her father, card games, and anything else that led her to leave her apartment in the first place. The calmness infusing her now felt unnatural, ready to shatter with the first application of force.

Still, she'd take whatever advantage she could get right now. Maybe the calm would hold, at least long enough to discover why she had been taken.

Be reasonable. Friendly. The first rule of negotiation her dad taught her was to find out what the other person wanted and figure out a way you could convince them you'd be able to supply it. That, and always be realistic about what was going on.

Well, here were the ugly facts. She had no mad-ninja-skillz to rely on and her family didn't know where she was. *She* didn't know where she was. The only way she was leaving was if this creature allowed it.

The creature was looking at her and made no move to put her down. Should she look at him? Would he take that as aggression? During the flight she hadn't looked at him and instead kept her gaze fixed on the hollow at the base of his throat. His neck was thick and led into heavily muscled shoulders, and his body gave off so much heat he might be able to be substitute for the furnace of a small home. She hadn't gotten cold as they flew.

There was no other option. She needed to try to communicate, and communication couldn't happen if she didn't look at him.

She muttered a quick prayer in case any gods were wandering around. None appeared, so what choice but to get on with this? *Steady on, girl*. One deep breath, two, and then her gaze met his.

Midnight black eyes under a prominent brow bone. The planes of his face were nothing but hard angles, his chin a square slab. It was as if he had been chiseled out of stone, his face displaying none of the roundness of flesh.

He was studying her as much as she was studying him. He didn't have any eyebrows, but his brow bone came together to form a little furrow between his eyes.

He seemed approachable, no negative emotion on his face she could detect. No time like the present to find out her fate. "Why have you brought me here?"

Those eyebrows drew even closer together at her question. Did her words confuse him? Unless she had been hallucinating, he had spoken English to her.

Before he made any sign that he would answer she heard movement behind her, the same *thwup* that had marked his landing. She turned to see a good dozen creatures like him, every single gaze locked on her as though she was wearing a homing beacon.

Calm, I need you to hang on. Don't leave me now.

A female pushed away from the others and walked until inches from Larissa, one clawed hand coming to rest on her hip. Her features were a fraction softer than the male's, her body the stuff of comic books – outrageous curves framed with sleek muscle. About her she had an aura Larissa recognized from every cop she had ever met. It was confidence and authority mixed with a good dose of *Don't fuck with me.*

This female would never be pathetic enough to huddle in an alleyway screaming or freeze in terror. Larissa's eyes flicked away.

"Terak, what is this?" asked the female, in an offhand way that was supposed to indicate you really weren't interested in the answer.

Terak, huh? Always good to know your kidnapper's name.

Larissa's attention went back to the female, but as she met those eyes her throat tightened. Her earlier tone was a lie, because the female creature in front of her looked as though she were debating on how many strips of flesh she could cut from Larissa with those claws.

What had she done to earn this ire? None of the others displayed hostility.

Earlier she hadn't wanted to be taken for an impromptu flying trip, but her kidnapper wouldn't let her out of his grasp. Now when she had a psycho female in front of her and really didn't want leave the relative safety of his arms, of course Terak chose to put her down. His wings folded in, settling over his shoulders like the fall of a cape.

"What should we do with her?" the female creature continued. "Shall I take her to the dungeon?"

A dungeon? Whips and chains and iron maidens dungeon? That was what Terak planned for her? Bile rose in her throat when he answered from behind her, "No Valry, she is not a prisoner."

Valry was not happy with that, if the further flattening of her already non-existent lips was any indication. Nope, nope, no matter what, Larissa was not going to ever be alone with this female.

Valry's anger radiated off her in waves while the other Clan members showed only curiosity. The mood was not censorious but Terak hated that he had no answers to give. They might be uncertain on what happened to bring about this unprecedented incident, but their confusion could not match his own.

He had turned from his fight with the zombies to see his little human in the grasp of the female Guild member. He knew the Guild would not harm her, but they would take her somewhere he could not follow. A haze settled over his vision.

Once she was in his arms instinct took over. He brought her to where none would dare touch her without his permission.

She took a step back to put distance between herself and Valry, a move that illustrated his little human was no fool. She came close enough that her hair brushed across his wings. His gaze slid over her form. Small but constant tremors were shaking her frame, and his chest went concave.

She was unused to battle, and not only had she faced zombies this night but had been taken from her home against her will. Fear, tension, and fatigue were riding her hard.

And instead of sheltering her, he placed her in front of his people with no explanation, making her unsure if her fight was over.

Though he knew his Clan – Valry – was studying his every move, he could not let her suffer any further. He picked her up, hearing her small gasp from his unexpected movement. His mouth to her ear, his words meant for her alone, he said, "You are safe here, little human. I vow it. None will harm you."

He pulled back enough to study her eyes. The cornflower blue absorbed him, drowning out the knowledge that his Clan standing feet away or the words of the Oracle that had brought them together. All these months watching her, the one question he could not answer was the color of her eyes.

Terak thought he had imagined every shade possible, but he had been wrong. This shade of blue – soft and warm, the color pure throughout – he had not conceived of, but now that he beheld them, he could think of no more perfect color for her.

The rustling of wings brought his attention back to his people. Valry's hands were clenched into tight fists. He would have to deal with her later, but for now his first responsibility lay in providing for the woman in his arms.

His gaze on his Clan, Terak said, "This woman is guest, not enemy." Ignoring the questioning eyes of his people, he continued, "Are all patrols back?"

Malek, his second-in-command, came forward. "All but two."

"Which patrols?"

"Over the vampire stronghold."

Terak nodded. "We will speak of it later," he said. With no further words of explanation and the human held tight in his arms again, he turned to descend the stairway that led into the tower.

Everything was grey – walls, stairs, ceilings. Maybe the creatures kept it that way so they could camouflage themselves if something attacked them here. If it weren't for his hair and the black pants he wore, the creature holding her would have disappeared into his surroundings.

The creature took her through the tower and into the body of the castle. After a lot of stairs, twists, and turns with nothing to look at but miles of utilitarian grey stone, they came to a room that held the biggest collection of books Larissa had ever seen.

The room was two, maybe three stories tall, and from floor to ceiling were nothing but shelves lined with books. Rich splashes of blue, burgundy, brown and green delighted her color-starved eyes. Several couches in a muted tan fabric and a large fireplace in the middle of the back wall were the only other decorations in the room.

The creature set her on her feet again. She stepped back a few paces, gauging his reaction as she moved away.

He did not try to keep her near and let her roam as she wished. With the speed of the night's events, Larissa hadn't had the chance to study him. She took advantage of this quiet interlude to do so now.

His wings appeared leathery, and though they were currently draped over his shoulders, she remembered the full wingspan well enough that she was sure it equaled his nearly seven feet in height. He had a tail, the tip of which currently rested beside his booted foot. He was thick with muscle, every part of his body defined. His arms seemed the size of support beams, his legs thick as oaks, and his clawed hands looked as if he could encircle her waist in them.

Outside of the wings, tail, and claws that tipped his fingers, his features overall were almost human, just a little – *more*. A little sharper, a little harder, a little bigger.

And almost...*beautiful*, in a rough-hewn, alien way.

He called her a guest and hadn't yet tried to harm her. She owed him an acknowledgment of what he had done for her. "Thank you for saving my life."

His eyes widened in surprise at her words, as if gratitude was the last thing he ever expected to receive. He inclined his head a fraction. "You are welcome," he said in those deep tones that relaxed her against her will.

"Your name is Terak?"

"Yes."

"I assume from your conversation-" Larissa waved her hand toward the ceiling, "-with the others, you are the leader here?"

"I am."

"So can you tell me what you are?"

His head tilted as he studied her. "You do not know?"

"I'm a human who lives in a human-only city. I know elves have pointy ears and dwarves are easy to trip over. Too much beyond that, I'm at a loss."

The question unsettled him, if the way he broke off from her gaze and stared into the blazing fire was any indication. "I am a gargoyle," he said at last, tension in the rigid set of his shoulders.

There was a time when Larissa had wanted to learn about the other races, before she realized why her father carried such stress at the mention of any creature that had appeared since the Great Collision and set aside any curiosity in favor of pleasing her father. She only knew the big ones – dwarves, elves, werewolves... vampires. Still, for the first time since she was little, Larissa wished she had read some books on the sly and spent a little more time learning about the new races.

Terak's tension had not abated, so he must be expecting a negative reaction. She could understand why. Gargoyles were a fearsome race if tonight was anything to go by. What human wouldn't be terrified of them?

"What were you doing in the city?" *And why didn't the wards keep you out?* she mentally added.

His body relaxed, maybe because she didn't react to the gargoyle revelation by screaming or something. He turned to face her. "My Clan is... friendless... in this world. We rely only on ourselves for survival. To that end, we patrol all areas to keep aware of the happenings of this world, even those places that are forbidden to us."

It made sense. She could see her father doing the exact same thing under similar circumstances. The whole *friendless* business, though, *not* a good omen. Was it because they feared other races, or other races feared them? From tonight's goings-on, she was a firm follower of the second camp. Still didn't explain the wards, but she wasn't stupid enough to bring that up to him. That was a question purely for when she was safe back at home.

"So why did you save me? Why did you bring me here?" The next question stuck in her throat. Swallowing a few times to work saliva into her mouth, she formed the question she dreaded asking. "Am I going to be allowed to go home?"

Her voice cracked on the last word. Terak made a brief move toward her before seeming to reconsider. "You will be returned home. I swear it."

Damn tears. She didn't want them to fall, not now, not when she wasn't sure she could stop them once they started. Larissa scrubbed her eyes with the back of her hand. "Please take me home then."

"Not yet. We have much to discuss."

"Discuss what?" Her voice rose several decibels. Larissa stopped for a moment, taking deep breaths. He said he was going to take her home, but that didn't mean she was home yet. Best to remember that. "Sorry. I don't understand what we need to talk about. I thank you for saving me, but what else is there?"

Terak made a motion to one of the couches, an order to sit disguised as polite concern. Larissa obeyed.

He opened his mouth, then hesitated. "May I know your name?"

"Oh." Surprise at his words lit through her, the normalcy of the question releasing some of the tension pitted in her stomach. "Larissa. Larissa Miller."

"Larissa," he said, and she wanted to close her eyes and listen to him repeat those three syllables on an endless loop. "Why were you attacked by the zombies?"

"I don't know."

"You don't know?"

There wasn't any disbelief in his voice – none that she could detect, anyway – but there was still something in the spacing of the words that made it clear he didn't fully believe her. "No, I don't know. It was probably some random occurrence, though they shouldn't have been able to get into the city." *Like you* was added in her head, but once again, self-preservation kept her from speaking those words aloud.

"It wasn't a random occurrence." His voice carried absolute conviction.

"And how would you know?"

Once again that small hesitation before he spoke. "In the past, my Clan has had dealings with necromancers."

Zombies meant...

Necromancers. The word she been avoiding all night was now spoken, drifting through the air on icy currents. The sound alone had her rubbing her arms for warmth. "Dealings, huh?" she asked, more in avoidance than actual interest. She didn't want to talk about them, didn't even want to *think* about their existence, not while an image of one eyeball hanging out of its socket waited behind her eyelids.

"While I claim no intimate knowledge, I know enough to say the zombies I fought tonight were created by a master necromancer. Masters of that level do not make mistakes." He crouched before her then, so close she could reach out and stroke his face. "Are you involved with the necromancers?"

"What? No! Gods no, never!" She jumped up from the couch as though she could run away from the words. "*Necromancers?* They're... no, just no."

"Then why did the zombies target you?"

Maybe that was why he brought her here, thinking she was somehow connected with necromancers. "Listen, I don't deal with anything like that. I'm a history teacher. I work, tutor kids, and the most exciting thing I do is play card games with my dad on the weekend – that's where I was headed tonight when all this started. I was in the wrong place at the wrong time. Somehow those things got past the city's security and went after me."

She shook her head. It couldn't be real, zombies attacking her. Her? She was always the good kid. While her brothers had given their dad many grey hairs over the years, she never got into fights or broke curfew or lied about who she was hanging around with. How does someone like that get attacked by zombies? Why would they come after her?

Why would they touch her?

Hold her?

Trap her?

An eye hanging out of its socket…

From far away a long, keening sob.

And Larissa realized…

…the sob came from her.

Her body betrayed her, legs giving out, limbs trembling and twisting and the hard inward jerk of torso to protect her, the curl that would shelter from the outside world, outside pain. Teeth chattered with an echo that resonated through skull, through bone, through marrow.

Weightless. A second of air. A second of vulnerability. A second of alone.

Then warmth seeped into her skin, burrowing into damaged spaces, replacing danger with safety, shame with forgiveness. She was immobile against an immovable surface, but as long as she could bask in that warmth she didn't fear her imprisonment. The smell of newly cracked stone washed over her, an unknown language sounded, spoken in a deep, resonant tone that promised protection.

The shaking eased, the sobs stuttered and hiccupped their last, and she opened her eyes to find her fingers digging into Terak's chest, his leathery wings curled around her, holding her close to him.

The hard planes and grey tone to his skin gave the impression of cold, but his body was a furnace, a warm blanket on a winter day. His skin was firm but supple, the texture inviting her to stroke where her fingers lay against him.

She nuzzled deeper into him when awareness of her situation slammed through her. Cloaking herself with the trailing ends of her dignity she straightened and leaned back.

The first attempt to get away from him was unsuccessful, his arms still tight around her. Clearing her throat, she looked up at him, glancing at his wings when his gaze met hers. "Thank you, but I'm fine now. You can let go."

He followed her gaze, his brows coming together once again. The wings opened and he set her down.

CHAPTER FIVE

He had wrapped her in his wings.

Disbelief coursed through Terak's system as the little human stepped away and went to look over the books.

He had wrapped her in his wings.

Her hair was tangled, its usual smoothness lost to the exertions of the night. She appeared so defenseless at that moment he wanted to cradle her against him again, tell her that nothing like this night would ever touch her in the future.

He had wrapped her in his wings.

She was so soft, so fragile, she could never be a true threat to him. With no threat, there was no consequence to keeping her close. That could be the only reason his wings had come around her. That and no other.

He settled his wings around his shoulders, the softness of her lingering on the membranes.

She glanced at him, a faint tremble still on her lips. Pushing her hair behind her ear, she went to sit back down on the couch.

She is connected to the future of your Clan. Guard her well.

Three months ago the Oracle had come to them unannounced as few beings would dare. She had given little more than that cryptic message. Any questions were ignored, and she left their stronghold unconcerned how her words would be taken.

He was unused to taking orders from anyone, but he could not shake the need to discover why the Oracle had sought him out and placed this human woman into his care.

Larissa Miller was nothing like he expected. She was as ill-suited to his world as any being in existence. Instead of a woman wielding magic or sword, he beheld a woman who was petted and protected by her family. She was uninterested in the world outside of the safe confines of the human-only city. Nothing about her spoke of darkness or subterfuge.

All these months watching her, and before this night he had come to believe the Oracle had made a mistake.

Why had she been attacked? It was not a mistake, no matter what she claimed. He needed to unravel this mystery. Somehow she was connected to his Clan, and until he understood the reason for the Oracle's intervention he would not separate from her.

Before he could speak her voice rang out. "I need to call my father."

"Why?"

The line of her mouth turned mulish, her look equal parts confusion and annoyance. "He's expecting me, and I need to tell him what happened. He's a cop. He'll want to investigate."

That could not happen. If her father interfered, she would be lost to him. "He is human."

Her arms crossed over her chest. "My father is a good cop, human or not. You shouldn't be so quick to dismiss his abilities just because he doesn't have wings."

She was insulted on behalf of her Clan and would not let him say anything to degrade them. The last of the trembling stopped as her chin went high, and he much preferred the fire that lit her eyes to the trembling that engulfed her earlier.

Diplomacy had never been one of his strengths, but he must tread carefully here. He needed her to accept her family could not protect her but not feel as though he were dismissing their abilities. "It matters not how skilled your father is in solving human matters. These are enemies he has no hope of prevailing against. Has he ever fought a necromancer?"

Her lips tightened, but she answered honest. "No."

He stopped himself from pursuing the conversation and let her think on those words. He asked, "You truly do not know why the zombies attacked you?"

Defiance crossed her features, and for one moment he thought she would once again ask to talk to her father. Instead she seemed to reconsider, because she drew a deep breath and answered instead, "I understand what you are saying about how the necromancers work, but there is some mistake. There is nothing about me that would interest anyone. I'm as ordinary as they come and *I know nothing*. All I want is to go back to my life."

She was either the most accomplished liar he had ever encountered or she was telling the truth. He wasn't sure which of those options he wanted to believe. "Your wants do not change reality. A necromancer is after you. Yes, one is," he repeated, adding volume in case she tried to voice her denial, but while she did not vocalize her disagreement she did start shaking her head. "You do not know why, but you have caught the attention of a necromancer. This is an enemy you can in no way fight."

"My dad…"

She would not listen to reason, so bluntness was his only hope of convincing her. "If you involve your father, you will be responsible for his death. Are you prepared to bury him in hopes of proving me wrong?"

All color leeched out of her face, his words penetrating her stubbornness. If anything could change her mind, it would be the protection of her Clan.

She rose from the couch, her movements stiff and jerky. She walked over to the fireplace and stood in front of it, staring down at the flames. The firelight illuminated her hair, creating a glow around her soft face. "What are you suggesting?"

He walked to her until he stood an arm's distance away, not crowding her, but forcing her to deal with his presence. "Let me and my Clan protect you while we discover why you have been targeted. We can fight this enemy, your father cannot."

Her head jerked toward him, eyebrows furrowing together and a suspicious cast crossing her features. "Why would you want to do that? Even if you're right, why do you care I'm being targeted?"

This question he was not prepared for. Of course she would want details. She was naïve and protected, but his little human was not stupid or blindly trusting.

A heavy knock interrupted the moment. Never had he been more grateful for one of the constant interruptions on his time. He opened the door to see Malek. "Yes?"

Malek spoke in low tones. "The Council requires your presence."

News of the human's arrival had spread quickly it seemed. He said, "I will be out momentarily," and shut the door.

Larissa was watching him with undisguised interest. He said, "I find I must go and talk with my Council."

"Can I go home now?"

"I wish to finish our discussion first. This will only be a few minutes. I will not let it take any longer than that." He gave a small bow. "Excuse me."

"Wait." She held out her hand to him. "My father is expecting me. If I'm not there soon, he'll start searching for me. I promise I won't say anything about tonight. I don't want him to worry."

It was a reasonable request. "I will have a phone brought so you may contact him."

With those words, she smiled at him. "Thank you."

He had seen her smile many times, but never like this, never so close. Worry and tiredness still lined her features, but the smile created a radiance the firelight could never replicate.

Another knock brought Terak back to awareness. "Excuse me," he repeated and left the room.

Malek was waiting, along with another warrior. "Have a phone waiting for me when I get back," he told the younger warrior. As he and Malek turned and walked down the corridor to the Council Chamber, he asked Malek, "What news?"

"Word of your guest has spread throughout the Clan and not all are happy she is here. She is the one the Oracle told you of, is she not?"

"Who else would she be?"

The displeasure Terak was feeling must have announced itself in his voice, for Malek lowered his head. "I live and die for you, *Mennak*. Please do not mistake my observations for censure."

Malek did not deserve misplaced ire heaped upon him. Terak said, "Forgive me. I find I do not like being summoned like a youngling."

Malek nodded, accepting the apology. "Your absences these last months have emboldened the Council."

"They are my councillors, not my wardens." That they assumed they could summon him with a moment's notice meant they were bolder than Terak had suspected. That would be put to rights tonight. "Who is fueling tonight's displeasure?"

"Valry."

Of course. His future *Meyla* had hated his watching over the human from the first, had fought against the Clan acting on the Oracle's prediction. And now she presumed she could openly go against his decisions.

That also needed to be put to rights.

Terak entered the Council Chamber, a large room with a round table and thirteen seats surrounding it. He did not bother to go to his seat. Krikus, the eldest member of the Council, rose and spoke. "*Mennak-*"

"I have only a few moments, so all here will listen well," Terak interrupted, projecting his authority and banked anger into the tone. The members quieted in their seats. "You seem to forget who is leader here, though you still call me *Mennak*. Let me remind you. You do not summon me. You may seek my presence, you may ask for my decision, but never again shall you summon me. Is this understood, or are any here demanding challenge?"

Most lowered their heads and refused to look at Terak. Krikus held his hand up in apology. "We never wish to insult you, *Mennak*. But this news about the human was so unexpected, we needed to know the situation."

"You only need know your *Mennak* has the situation under control. Any explanations will come when I deem them necessary."

Krikus lowered his head. "If you wish for our counsel, we are always at your service."

"And I do wish your counsel," Terak said. His point had been made, now peace had to be restored. He did not want seeds of resentment and suspicion taking root because of this night. "There is a new development with the human. She was attacked by zombies tonight."

An explosion of sound circled the table as the Council talked among themselves. Terak held up his hand for silence. "I do not yet know what it means, but I do know we cannot leave the human unguarded. We must remain with her."

"Is she in league with necromancers?"

"No." Of that Terak was sure. "All of the information we have collected on her both by watching her and by other means, nothing hints at that. They hunt her for an unknown reason, and we must protect her until all these threads are untangled and the reason of her importance is clear."

Nalith rose. He was new to the Council, joining after the death of his father. While Terak had enjoyed the father's counsel, Nalith was discord and whispered poison in the shadows of the night. "*Mennak*," he began, his tone as far from respectful as it could be while still remaining civil. "This is foolish. We had agreed to three months of guarding the human, long enough to decide how she could be of interest to the Clan. It is clear she has no importance to us. The Oracle's pronouncement is nothing more than a powerful being bored enough that she wishes to cause mayhem among other races. It is not an unknown situation."

A couple Council members gave half-nods at Nalith's words, though none would speak aloud after Terak's earlier rebuke.

"While I do not disagree about the chaos the gods cause, it matters little in this situation. She was attacked in the agreed-upon time frame, and we will determine if this is what the Oracle alluded to before we leave the human." Nalith's jaw clenched and he sat. Terak continued, "We will watch the human. We will meet tomorrow at first light and continue this discussion. Now, I must go. Until the morrow."

Krikus nodded. "Agreed." The other Council members nodded, though Terak could not tell those who were displaying their true feelings from those who did not wish to anger him any further.

Terak left and headed back to Larissa. He needed to speak to Valry as well, but that he would leave to later. Larissa had been alone long enough.

The young warrior was holding a phone when Terak approached the door. He took the phone and entered the room.

Larissa was still by the fire, looking into the flame as though all answers could be found there. She looked up when the door, first focusing on his face, then on the small black phone held in his hand.

He held it out to her and she walked as fast as she could without running to grab the phone from him.

While she dialed the number and said, "Dad," into the receiver, Terak pondered the schism within his Clan, the one even now Nalith and Valry were working to exploit – between those who wished to have contact with the outside world versus those who wished to remain as they had always been, self-sufficient and without any outside encumbrances save for favors owed them.

Encumbrances this one human woman exemplified.

And as she said, "Yes, Dad, I owe you big. Promise, next time I'm there... Yes, Dad, with a skirt and make-up," Terak knew how to answer her question and convince her that he should be allowed to stay at her side.

CHAPTER SIX

It hadn't been this hard to part with a phone since she was fourteen and had been waiting for Jared Thompson to ask her to junior prom, but as Terak held out a massive hand, Larissa placed the shiny black rectangle there without any outward sign of her struggle.

"I was able to convince Dad not to send out a search party by promising to be there for brunch tomorrow," she said, aware even as the words were leaving her mouth that such a blatant warning would do nothing more than amuse the gargoyle in front of her.

Thankfully he didn't laugh, though she could swear a ghost of a smile played on his lips. Instead he said, "You will be there, do not worry."

The reassurance beat back the fear that had begun creeping through her while he was gone. She nodded toward the door. "It must be hard to be in charge, people always needing you for something."

"It is my duty and my role to fulfill."

He said that without any boast or pridefulness. It was a statement of fact, his calling made into words. "How are you the leader? Were you elected?"

"My father was leader. At his death, I took his place."

"So you are a king?"

"Not quite." He went to the couch in front of the fireplace and sat down. There was a natural elegance about him, so at odds with the warrior exterior. His wings folded around him with enough of an opening to allow her to still see his hands and chest. "While leadership is passed down through a bloodline, the *Mennak* must also be the strongest. Any gargoyle may issue challenge to claim the title."

"*Mennak?*"

"The title of the leader."

"What kind of challenge?"

He didn't answer, not in words, but the way the question made his eyes flicker from hers answered it anyway. Before the Collision, the Magic Realm was closely related to Earth's medieval feudal societies. She knew that as a fact found in books and as lectures written in chalk, but it never impressed itself upon her as deeply as right now.

Terak rose then. He motioned around the room. "These books contain histories created by gargoyles of all the races, dating back tens of thousands of years from the Magic Realm, information that can only be found in this one room. They are observations, studies of outsiders looking in. There are very few interactions between my people and those of the outside world. Gargoyles have long kept ourselves apart from the other races. But with the Great Collision, many of my people wish to experience the New Realm not as outsiders, but as part of the fabric of this new world."

"It's a worthy goal," Larissa said, not sure where he was going with this.

"It is hard to let go of millennia of suspicions – on both sides – but it must start somewhere. Perhaps the first step needed is a gargoyle helping a human woman escape from necromancers. Let us watch over you as a first step."

So he was back to talking about guarding her. "You did that tonight. Why take it further?"

"Necromancers are an enemy of my people as well. Whatever plan you are part of can bring no good to anyone of this world. Not your people, nor mine."

What if he was right? As terrifying as the night had been, there was comfort in the knowledge it was a case of horrific timing, an event that would never be repeated.

But if she had been targeted? If it was not some random woman on the street, but *her* they had been waiting for?

She plopped onto the couch, no strength left in her legs to hold her up. She looked at Terak, his sculpted face taking on a pinched expression of worry as he watched her. "You're wrong," she said, the tiny voice coming from her mouth sounding nothing like her.

He came to kneel before her. "I hope I am," he said, putting one hand on the couch beside her leg. "But if I am not, I want to be there to protect you."

Memory struck her, bringing to mind another question. "The woman and man from tonight, the ones who were also fighting the zombies – do you know who they are?"

"Yes. They are members of the Guild."

The Guild. She had never heard of them. "Are they good guys?"

There was a considering pause before he answered. "They are protectors."

"Of humans?"

"Of anyone the necromancers target."

His words were very measured, and no way she was getting the whole story here. "You sound like you don't like them."

"Our history together is too complex to explore this late at night. Though we are not enemies, there have been clashes."

Probably not the only moment in gargoyle history where a personality conflict occurred. "Fair enough. But you said they were protectors. What about going to them and letting them protect me? They're supposed to protect humans, right?" And they seemed to be human themselves. Well, at least one of them did. Sorta.

Onyx eyes locked on to her, not allowing Larissa to look away. "They will protect you. They will protect you by locking you up in a room and allowing no one to come near you until they discover what use the necromancers have for you."

His eyes were too dark, too direct. Larissa looked away, the flickering shadows over a millennia of knowledge drawing her attention.

Did this night have to keep getting worse? What were her options here?

If he was telling the truth, then trying to contact the Guild would amount to jail time. Any self-respecting cop's kid had a healthy loathing at the thought of jail. And really, did she know anything more about them than she did the gargoyles?

Nope, she knew exactly the same about both groups – a big old zilch.

She should have... she should have learned. She could have done it without upsetting dad, and if she had bothered, and maybe she would know what decision to make. She had wanted to once, why didn't it occur to her she was allowed to change her mind and go back to it?

Hindsight and all that. It didn't change the now, and in the now, the only organization she could trust would be the police.

But she didn't want her father involved in this. He could not know what was going on, not yet.

He would disagree with her, in loud and vehement tones. If he ever found out she was hiding tonight from him, he'd ream her up one side of the block and down the other, then proceed to tan her hide as he hadn't done since she was a little girl.

He wouldn't understand. He would be hurt that she didn't come to him.

But... Larissa clenched her teeth hard against the image of the zombie that pushed itself to the front of her mind. She wouldn't cry again. That was done with.

But she didn't want him pitted against those creatures and that magic, that strength. He was a fighter through and through, but he wasn't a young man anymore, and Dad had already gone through one war with the creatures brought here by the Great Collision, a battle that had cost him dearly. She never wanted him to go through that again.

Besides, if she was right – *and I am right* – this was a mistake. This was random. Bringing her father in on it would only cause problems for her. Dad would move her back to the family house in two seconds flat, the brothers carting her back kicking and screaming if that was what it took.

As much as she loved her father, she didn't want that. She'd been gone from home not even a year. She didn't want to lose her hard-won freedom.

Larissa focused again on Terak. His eyes were still steady on her, his jaw set as he waited to counter her next argument.

What she needed was time, time to figure out what was going on and somehow come up with a solution.

"How would you protect me?"

That jaw relaxed a fraction at her words. No doubt he considered the battle won. "You will go about your life and we will be near."

"You expect me to go into the grocery store with my gargoyle bodyguard?"

And there it was again, that tiny curl to his lips that disappeared almost before it registered. She seemed to amuse him. "You will never know we are there. You will only see us should another attack occur."

She didn't see how it was possible something as big and alien as a gargoyle could hide in the city, but Terak radiated conviction. He absolutely believed she would never know they were near.

Which meant entering the city was not a one-time event or something he thought of as dangerous.

Which meant the wards – those magical barriers in which she had placed absolute trust and belief in for all these years – were worthless.

She got up, walking past the bookshelves, trying to ease the unsettled sensation in her stomach. All her life the wards had been an absolute – never worry about the outside races, the wards will keep them out. Had it always been a lie?

With a delicate touch she stroked the spine of a very old binding, breathing deep the scent of wondrous decay that always accompanied large libraries. The familiar and much-loved perfume helped release some of the tension holding fast in her shoulders, her arms, her back. One worry at a time. Right now, it was getting back home. "I won't know you're there?" she verified, taking up their conversation.

He leaned forward a fraction. "No, you will not."

Larissa gave a small laugh, rubbing the back of her neck as she returned to the couch. "It has to be the exhaustion, but I'm going to agree to this." Before he could say anything she added, "As long as we have a few ground rules."

While his face remained impassive, Larissa noticed the tip of his tail twitched. *Interesting.* She filed that away for future reference and went on. "First, we need a time limit. I don't want to be an eighty-year-old granny wondering if a gargoyle is following me."

"A year," said Terak.

"I was thinking more along the lines of a month."

Terak shook his head. "Necromancers are immortal. They can afford patience. One month is nothing to them. They will want to give you time to forget this and let down your guard."

She sighed. He had a point. "Two months."

"A year."

"Three months."

"A year."

"You haven't had much experience with negotiation, have you?"

His head tilted, as though even the thought was foreign and without precedent. "Most follow my orders without question."

That's right. He was the leader here. "Then let me be clear," she said. "There is no way I'm agreeing to a year. Six months you can follow me around. After that, when there are no more attacks and you see how boring my life is, no more bodyguards. Agreed?"

There it was, another tail twitch, but his voice was steady when he replied, "Agreed. Six months. But when another attack does happen, we will renegotiate the time frame."

"I'm beginning to think you're kind of hoping I get jumped."

"Not at all. I know this enemy and am preparing for battle instead of living in a dream world."

Was that snark? Did he just snark at her? With that theater-actor voice and impassive face it was hard to tell, but she'd lay odds it was snark. Still, he was agreeing so far, so she didn't comment and pressed on. "Rule two, I don't want Valry to be one of my bodyguards."

Forget his former impassiveness. Shock was now writ large across his face. "Valry?"

"Yes, the female gargoyle from the roof. I do not want her ever to guard me. Never ever. If it's a choice between her and no one, you go with no one. Agreed?"

"Agreed," he said quickly. Too quickly. Her gut was right then. Joy.

"Third and final. If you're right about all this – and that's a big if – and you find something out about why I was targeted, you have to share with me. No handling things on your own. No plans without me knowing about them."

"Why do you desire this?"

One thing this night taught her beyond all doubt – all males were lunkheads, all of them. She recognized that *protect the poor helpless girl and don't worry her little wee head* tone. "I'm not stupid. I'm not going to run into a situation I have no business being in to show no one can boss me around. I'm not a warrior and tonight made that clear in large neon signage. But I deserve to know about events that concern me and help make the decisions on how to handle them."

His jaw tightened as he considered her words. He really didn't want to agree, she knew that like she knew her own name. But this was a deal-breaker.

He must have seen that determination in her face because he exhaled deeply. "Agreed. I will share all knowledge with you. *However*, if we find ourselves in battle, my words are absolute. You may not question my orders, you will obey."

"That's fair." Larissa rose from the couch, holding her hand out to him. "I think we have a deal then."

He rose as well, looking at her hand as if he had never seen the appendage before. "This is what humans call a *handshake*?"

"Oh, I'm sorry." It had been pure reflex to hold out her hand. She hadn't considered it an unusual motion. Then again, not like she had much experience with any other race. "I wasn't thinking…"

She started to pull her hand away, but before it moved even an inch Terak engulfed her hand with his.

His skin was warm, callouses and scars marking every inch resting against her palm. Up close his claws were more like mini-curved daggers.

"This is how humans become allies?" His voice had softened, the timbre dropping a few registers until it was a rough brush against her spine, and she fought the unexpected shiver, the first of the night that had nothing to do with fear.

"Yes."

"Then make no mistake, little human. You are under my protection now, and I protect what is mine."

CHAPTER SEVEN

The *whoosh* of students running past her in the hallways, the slamming of lockers, the girls talking about their hair and clothes and make-up and the boys talking about the girls – all welcome signs of normalcy to Larissa as she made her way to the first class of the morning.

The bell rang moments before she entered the door. "Okay everyone. Settle down and take your seats," Larissa said as she headed toward her desk, placing her messenger bag on the chair and taking out graded papers and lesson plans.

Juvenile grumbling, paper rustling, and feet shuffling met Larissa's words. The mood was not a shiny happy one.

Ah yes, what senior in high school didn't love being up this early, especially on a Monday morning with only a few weeks until vacation. It was about time to petition for hazard pay.

Larissa handed out papers and accepted homework, answered some questions and shushed Jason Evans after he let out a wolf whistle when she passed. All in all, a normal Monday, making the events of this weekend seem even more surreal.

Necromancers after her? No, no.

A gargoyle protector? What an insane notion.

"Now," said Larissa, coming to stand in front of the room. "We are going to get into a favorite topic for most. We are going to discuss the Great Collision."

As expected, a hush fell over the room. No student could keep up the façade of indifference when the topic of the Great Collision came up, reason *numero uno* she always saved it for Mondays. "Twenty-six years ago, probably the most momentous moment in history outside of the actual creation of life occurred. I'll let your science teachers explain the theories behind why it happened, parallel dimensions and quarks and neutrons and all that good stuff. That's not for my discussion here."

"You trying to tell us you weren't a science genius, Miss Miller?"

Ah, Jason Evans, star quarterback and all around smart-ass. Class would not be the same if he didn't inject his *too cool for school* attitude into her lectures at least once a day. "Science is wonderful, Mr. Evans. I do admit, though, I never had the head for it. That doesn't mean you shouldn't ask

Mr. Patel to go into details for you. Anyway, the Great Collision. In layman's terms…"

"Dummy terms!" Jason interjected.

"Layman's terms," Larissa continued on, not bothering to waste breath to engage him. "Our universe is composed of multiple dimensions, also sometimes called realms. How many is still a question the scientific community is grappling with, but that has no bearing here. What matters for our discussion is two of these realms collided. One realm was very similar to what you see around you every day – skyscrapers, cars, computers, cell phones – but humans were the only sentient race and no magic existed. I'm sure many of your parents have already told you stories about the good old days."

Groans sounded then, followed by tales of parental misconduct. Larissa let it go for a few moments before bringing attention back to her. "The other realm was a realm of sword and sorcery. Elves and dwarves existed there, as well as countless other races and magical creatures. For simplicity, we have come to label these dimensions the Human Realm and the Magic Realm, though humans did exist in the Magic Realm. The difference is they weren't the only sentient race."

A hand rose at the back of the class. "Miss Miller, my mom told me we used to use oil and electricity for power, not magic."

Larissa nodded. "That is true. In the Great Collision, the Human Realm absorbed the Magic Realm. Earth is the same physically as it was before the collision. What changed is now Earth can sustain magic, which was not possible before. Once the chaos from the collision began to settle, wizards and mages were able to figure out how to supply our energy needs magically."

"What's the difference between a wizard and a mage?" a female voice interrupted. Taneasha Jackson reminded Larissa of herself at a younger age, too smart by half and surrounded by family who protected her to the point of suffocation. The young woman was more likely to be found in a library than at any of the school events.

"Good question," said Larissa. "A wizard is someone who channels magic through spells and items. A mage is someone with an inborn gift for magic and channels magic from themselves. Mages are much rarer and more powerful, but they usually are more limited. They have a gift for a certain type of magic and can only create spells that use that classification of magic. Different classifications include transmutation, illusion, conjuration-"

"Necromancy. Are we going to talk about necromancers?" asked Jason, in a sly voice with a little too much enthusiasm backing it.

"Not as much as you probably want," Larissa said. Not at all, if she had a choice. *An eye hanging out of its socket*, and she rubbed the heel of her palm against her forehead as if the motion could erase the image. "Why are you not supposed to be so excited over necromancers?"

In the tone of someone who is humoring you and wants you to know it, Jason said, "They derive their power from death."

"Exactly," said Larissa.

"But all the girls love vampires, and I'd look hot with red eyes," Jason said, causing some girls to giggle and smile in his direction.

"Yes, well, while all vampires are necromancers, not every necromancer is a vampire. Only the strongest of necromancers become true vampires."

Jason leaned back in his seat, a satisfied smirk on his face. "Gives me something to work for, then I'd have an eternity with the ladies." The guys all started high-fiving amid themselves, and Larissa shushed them before the words got too far out of hand.

Taneasha spoke again. "I want to learn more about the fantastical creatures that we thought were myths until they appeared after the Collision. I really want to see a unicorn one day."

"Ever see any, Miss Miller?" asked a voice from the back.

Not until three days ago. "No, I've lived in the city all my life and never traveled outside of it." Maybe it was time for that to change, though.

Another male voice from the back said, "Unicorns are too girly. I want to see gryphons, basilisks, dragons, stuff like that."

And from the doorway came the response, the voice a smooth feminine growl. "There are no dragons."

Larissa hadn't heard the door open and turned to question why someone was interrupting her class.

The textbook Larissa was holding slipped from nerveless fingers, causing a sharp crack as the second silence of the morning fell over the classroom.

In the open doorway stood the redheaded woman from Friday night, her gaze locked on Larissa as she leaned against the frame, her arms and legs crossed in what would have been a relaxed posture for anyone else, but on this woman it seemed more akin to leashed watchfulness.

The woman continued, "Dragons were as much myth in the Magic Realm as in ours, disappointing as that seems." She smiled then, the barest trace of a dimple in her grin. "Or maybe not. Having a dragon fly overhead would not be my idea of a good time."

She was the very definition of an Amazon – taller than some men with broad shoulders and long limbs displaying muscle, but her evident strength only highlighted how very feminine she was. She had classic features most women would kill for and hourglass curves her musculature enhanced.

A higher-pitched feminine grunt came from behind the redhead, and the redhead shifted as she glanced behind her. "Move your ass, Fallon. I want to see her. I missed all the excitement, remember?"

"If you quit poking me, I will," the redheaded woman said to whoever was back there, and took several steps into the room.

Larissa gaped as she beheld the person coming in behind the amazon.

The other woman was short. Very short. So short even the platform heels on her shoes only brought her to average height. She was wearing an elaborate jade green kimono – except unlike a traditional kimono, this woman's skirt ended mid-thigh – with matching jade hair styled in three rolls and piled so high it added an extra half-foot of height to the woman.

It was hard to tell what age or ethnicity the woman was under her dramatic kabuki make-up. Best guess, early-to-mid-twenties, and Asian but mixed with some European ancestry.

The unnatural quiet the class had been under broke. With one voice, her students started calling out questions – about the women, what they were doing here, why did they want to talk to Miss Miller?

"Quiet," the woman called Fallon said, her voice level but her tone absolute, and in a situation Larissa had never before experienced, her class shut up as they were told. "Miss Miller, I have some questions for you. Please step outside with me."

The small Asian woman sat on Larissa's desk, crossing her legs once she was settled. "It might have sounded like a request, but it really wasn't." She flicked her fingers at Larissa in a dismissive gesture. "You need to go. I'll stay with the kiddies."

Sure enough, the redhead didn't look like she was moving, and Larissa didn't want to have this conversation in front of her students. Stifling a sigh, she said, "Class, talk quietly among yourselves for a few minutes. I'll be right back."

There was an empty classroom a few rooms down. Larissa went in, not bothering with politeness to allow Fallon to enter first. The redhead followed, though not before her eyes scanned the room. Classic tactical maneuver. No cop in the world ever entered anywhere before getting the lay of the land.

The woman didn't crowd Larissa, but her unwavering gaze and unvoiced suspicions made breathing a tad difficult, like wearing a shirt with a constrictive collar. It was so different from how she felt with the gargoyle, where toward the end their interactions edged into the companionable.

Larissa cleared her throat, ready to start this inquisition. "How did you know where to find me, or who I am? Who are you, for that matter?"

"Me? I'm Fallon, and the monochromatic midget currently alone with your students is Laire. We're part of a group that protects the city."

Larissa crossed her arms. "If that's true, why didn't I know you existed before today? If you know about me, then you know my dad's the chief of police, and he's never mentioned you."

Fallon's lips twitched, though if the tic was irritation or amusement Larissa couldn't guess. The woman's features were neutral as she studied Larissa. "Why would you expect *daddy* to tell you? From what we can gather, it would be the opposite."

The *zing* brought a flush of heat to the back of Larissa's neck, but she pressed her lips together to keep from responding. This woman wasn't going to provoke her into anything, if that was indeed her plan. And the bit of embarrassment didn't mask the fact Fallon neither confirmed nor denied that Dad knew about them. If this whole protection business was the truth, that meant either her dad had kept this from her – and given his standard *modus operandi* that wouldn't be a shock – or this group was very, very secret.

And if a very, very secret group told you about their existence...

"Oh gods, you're going to kidnap me now, aren't you?"

The corner of Fallon's lip quirked at Larissa's outburst, that shadow of a dimple again emerging. "Your students saw you walk out of a room with me. It would be kind of stupid for me to grab you and run."

"You could make them forget. Who knows what kind of magic you can perform."

"I don't do magic. I turn your attention back to Friday night and the big-ass sword I was carrying. My job is to run and swing."

Larissa wanted nothing more than to lay her head on the desk and close her eyes until the woman disappeared. Unfortunately, there was no chance Fallon would cooperate. "What do you want from me?"

Fallon walked over and crouched in front of her, bringing them to eye level. "What happened Friday?"

"I don't know. You tell me. You were there so you obviously knew what was going to happen."

Annoyance reflected in Fallon's features. "You would think I should have been told the reason I was there, but no, the meddling bitch who sent me doesn't believe in giving anyone details. She thinks it's enough to send you on your way." By the end Fallon's eyes were narrow slits and murder was written over her face.

Not anxious to step on this particular minefield, Larissa still had to ask. "What about afterward? Couldn't you get any information from the zombies?"

"No. No information from that path." Fallon's tone was a stop sign, telling Larissa no questions asked would be answered.

Larissa swiveled in the chair and stood, needing space. "I don't know why the zombies were there. I wasn't even supposed to go out that night. It was a spur of the moment decision to join my dad's poker game. I think it was a coincidence, nothing more."

Fallon stood as well, and Larissa conceded that Fallon rising to her full height was a much more impressive movement than she could ever pull off. "What about the gargoyle?" Fallon asked.

"What about him?" Good, no cracks in her vocals. Learning to deflect her father's questions was paying off in unexpected ways.

Fallon's eyebrow arched. "He flew away with you. You were gone for a considerable length of time. Are you telling me that happens to you every day?"

"Of course not. I don't know why he was there either. He flew me away, and I guess when he decided it was safe, he brought me back?"

"That simple?"

"Well, at the time it wasn't! At the time I was scared to death. Actually, I'm still sleeping with my lights on. But I don't know what to tell you when I have no clue why what happened on Friday night... happened. Zombies attacked, you appeared, the gargoyle appeared. The more time that passes, the more it becomes a blur in my head, which is good, because I want to forget it!"

Fallon stared at her as though she were a bug under a microscope. Breathing as she did in her yoga class, Larissa quieted her mind, quieted her body. She would not give away anything. No matter what assurances Fallon gave, the little warning bell in the back of her skull was still sounding an alert.

Fallon's body relaxed, the signal to Larissa that she won this round. At least she wouldn't be kidnapped again right now, but Larissa didn't need the thinning of Fallon's mouth to tell her that the amazon was not yet finished with her. "By all means, you know nothing and the gargoyle flew you around for a couple hours before taking you home. Why, it almost sounds romantic."

"I need to get back to my class now."

"Of course Who am I to deprive those poor children of their education? Then again, Laire is probably educating them beyond their wildest dreams." Fallon went to the door and opened it, then turned and motioned for Larissa to precede her out.

Larissa entered her classroom to find her students scribbling notes with a frenetic intensity, their expressions sharpened as they seldom were for any of her lectures.

Then she heard the Asian woman speak.

"Yes, I do realize men who have an orc ancestor tend to be really ugly, but that's why they invented paper bags. Trust me, as long as a guy knows he's getting some, he'll wear a pink bunny costume if that's what's needed to seal the deal. What matters here and what you need to remember is guys who have some orc in them are hung like nobody's business. If you like your men large and dominating, make a beeline for them."

"What about elves?" called a male student.

"Elves are ridiculously high maintenance. If that's fine with you, the key to elves is the ears and the back. Sure, they like the other areas fine, but if you want to make one a little puddle of goo, spend ten minutes massaging their back. It's practically a sure thing after that."

"What are you telling my students?" While Larissa's squeaky tone may not have been what one would call commanding, it did stop the small woman from talking.

"I was answering questions. They are woefully unprepared to enter the real world," Laire said, turning back to a student in the front with her hand up.

"I think that's enough question and answer. Let's go," said Fallon, a quick movement of her head signaling the other woman to get off the desk.

"But Fallon, they need educated. You wouldn't believe the misconceptions they had about how to have sex with a shifter."

Fallon walked over to the desk and grabbed the woman's ear, walking toward the door without waiting to see if Laire was on her feet yet. "Ow, Fallon, ow! Let go, I'm coming, I'm coming!"

"Goodbye, Miss Miller," Fallon said. Larissa didn't have to be a mind reader to see the *for now* Fallon mentally added onto the end of that sentence.

Fallon walked toward the door, pulling the smaller woman behind her. "I knew I should have brought Aislynn," Fallon said as they left the classroom.

Laire's snort was loud and clear, though her voice was fading as they walked away from the classroom. "Good idea to bring an elf among hormonal high school seniors. Do you really think Ais wants to be the jerk-off fantasy of the graduating class... OWWWWWWW!"

"So I hear there was much excitement in your class this morning." Olivia Berry took her usual seat across from Larissa in the teacher's lounge, leaning forward as though she'd be able to get the full scoop faster that way.

"That's one way to put it," Larissa agreed, not looking up from the book she was reading. It was always nice when Olivia went crazy over good gossip, a situation not to be rushed.

Olivia didn't even try at uninterested. "Tell me all or I'll seduce one of your brothers and give you the play by play."

The full body shudder overtook Larissa before she could stop it. "Eww. Don't even talk about that."

"Michael is seriously hot..."

"Fine, I'll talk! Just stay away from the male members of my family."

Olivia settled down, smug radiating from every pore. "So who were your guests? I won't even tell you the official version of the story, it's too much BS to believe."

"Why are you such a conspiracy theorist? Maybe the official story is the real story." Olivia said nothing, just blinked once, twice, three times. Larissa sighed. "So here's what happened. I was attacked over the weekend..."

Olivia's face lost its maniacal interest, replaced by pure concern. She grabbed Larissa's hand. "Are you okay?"

"Yeah, I am, I am," Larissa reassured her, squeezing Olivia's hand. "I was attacked by zombies."

"Zombies!" Olivia's voice ricocheted in the empty room.

"Shh!" Larissa admonished, looking around to verify they were indeed alone. "I'd rather not everyone know, thank you."

Olivia leaned closer, her voice lowering. "Are you kidding me? Zombies?"

"Yeah, zombies. And those two who visited me wanted to know why."

Olivia's body shook as if in preparation for the answer. "And why were you?"

"I have no idea."

Disbelief was as evident on Olivia's face as it had been on both Terak's and Fallon's. "You have no idea?"

"None. I think it was an accident and they attacked the wrong woman, but everyone around me seems determined to believe I was attacked on purpose."

Olivia pulled back then, angling away from Larissa, her hand smoothing her brown curls back. "It seems likely that attack was on purpose. Necromancers don't make many mistakes."

"And what would you know about necromancers?" This was new. Olivia had never expressed any personal knowledge of the other races before.

Olivia shrugged, the movement the height of nonchalance. "Only what everyone else knows. Mages that powerful probably don't make mistakes." Changing the subject, she motioned to the book Larissa had open. "What's that? Going to teach gargoyles?"

It was Larissa's turn to shrug. This part she didn't want to mention to Olivia. "After my attack, I thought it would be a good idea to be a little more concerned with the other races. They seemed interesting."

Olivia studied the picture, tapping the gargoyle illustration with one long red nail. "I would have chosen another race to start with. Outside of necromancers, I can't think of any creature I'd want to meet less."

"Why do you say that?"

"Because, if they had nothing to hide, they'd be part of the world among all the other creatures. Hell, you can even find necromancer clubs in certain areas."

Which was disturbing, but considering how vampires had been romanticized and fetishized in the Human Realm before the collision, the fact those clubs existed wasn't as shocking as it should have been. "Maybe they're afraid. It can't be easy to enter the world when you've always shunned it before."

"Well, yeah, or maybe they are as evil as the necromancers but don't have that dark, sexy-charm swagger to cover their deviousness."

Deviousness. There was no word she could think of less right to describe Terak. No, he wasn't telling her everything, but it seemed to come from a place of protection, not slyness.

Then again, she could be fooling herself.

"Olivia, have you ever left the city?"

"Why, are you thinking of taking a long weekend or something? Your dad would flip."

"No, it's just..." Larissa looked down at the picture again. "I'm starting to think about what I don't know. It never occurred to me before, but the attack has me thinking about things."

The bell rang, and Olivia stood. "I have class next period, so I've got to get going. If you need to talk, I'll be free tonight."

Larissa shook her head. "I'm fine. Really."

Olivia looked dubious, but nodded. "If you change your mind, give me a call."

When she left, Larissa stared at the drawing in the book, at the large wings and sharp claws. The picture was terrifying, yet it was not nearly as impressive as seeing the creatures in moving flesh.

Emulating Olivia, she stroked the snarling face on the picture. Terrifying, yes, but she couldn't quite remember ever feeling so warm as when she had been enfolded in Terak's wings.

Larissa looked out the window. Was a gargoyle nearby, watching her? The sun was shining, a light wind whipping the occasional leaf past the glass. How could a gargoyle exist on a day like today? They belonged to the night, to full moons and dark clouds and the wind howling through trees.

They certainly didn't get involved with people like her, boring people with a too-stifling family and a regular job. She had no money problems, no social life... hell, she hadn't even had a steady boyfriend yet. Growing up, the brothers had scared off anyone who they didn't think was good enough for their baby sister, and then Dad took over with the matchmaking. Her big weekend plans involved playing cards with her family.

How sad was that?

How could someone like her attract the attention of necromancers? Or gargoyles?

Stubborn gargoyles who don't listen to reason and take over your life even though they may be next in line for the *Ultimate Evil* award.

Why couldn't she have been saved by an elf?

CHAPTER EIGHT

When going back to your childhood home, there is that one perfect moment. It's the moment where, as you grab the door knob and start turning, memories jumble across your mind like the spill of photographs from a box, quick and cluttered and all of them so damned good you wish you could crawl inside one.

"Baby sister! Get your ass in here, you're letting the cold air in."

And then a male member of the family opens his mouth and reminds you why you moved out.

"Bite me there, Steven. How can you pretend to be this big, bad cop if two seconds in the wind has you whining?"

Her third oldest brother came over from the couch and enveloped her in a hug, which he used to maneuver her out of the doorway and then closed the door with his foot. "So, you missed Friday night, huh?"

Leave it to Steven to bulldoze over any pleasantries and get straight to what concerned him.

"I do have a life outside of this house."

"You were tutoring a student."

After he let go, she shrugged out of her coat and hung it in the closet. Larissa said, "Teaching is not a job, it's my life's calling. I read that on a greeting card somewhere."

She walked toward the kitchen, the hub of activity in their house, with Steven following. "Your life's calling is condemning us to the crap shifts."

"Don't blame me. I don't set your schedule."

"You're right, the chief does."

"Do I hear you complaining out there again, boy?" came the call from the kitchen.

Larissa stepped into the kitchen to see her father at the stove and her other brothers Gary, Michael, and Christopher sitting at the black granite island. She crossed the wood floor and gave her father a kiss on the cheek. "Hi Daddy."

"Pumpkin." Going grey dark-brown hair and a non-ironic mustache on a slightly chubby but still very handsome face, Jack Miller was in his element, stirring a pot of simmering chili and surrounded by his kids. "How was work?"

"Went fine. You didn't tell me we were having chili, I would have made some salsa and cornbread."

"I had Michael bring some. You can set the table."

The brothers jumped up and began their respective chores. Before her stomach had the chance to start growling, the table was set and everyone dug into their food, her dad on one end, her on the other, and two brothers on each side.

"So, baby sis, your television still on the fritz?" asked Gary, youngest of all the boys and the one who tortured her most while they were growing up.

Larissa sighed. "I haven't had a chance to bring it in to the shop yet."

"How did you manage to break this one?" asked Steven.

Jack snorted before taking a long drink from his bottle of beer. "Why is it I have four boys but whenever anything broke around here, it was always the fault of my baby girl?"

She couldn't help it she had a black thumb, only instead of killing plants, she killed all their electronics. Four rambunctious older brothers, but when something broke in the house, all eyes turned to her. "I had to do something to stand out from the pack. At least I never almost burned the house down, or snuck boys in by having them climb in the third-story window."

This time Michael snorted. The oldest, Michael was the only one who inherited their father's coloring of dark brown hair and eyes while she and the other brothers favored their mom. He also inherited their father's stubborn streak and overdeveloped sense of responsibility, leading to the nickname *Dad Two* while they were growing up. "No boy would ever have dared climb through your window, Ris. Remember when you hit puberty? Dad started to clean his guns on the front porch."

"Hell yes, I did. You look like your mother, who was only the most beautiful woman to ever be born. I saw her for the first time when she was sixteen and I was seventeen and I remember exactly what I wished I could be doing to her. No way any little punk was going to think those things about my daughter."

"Dad!" Larissa protested.

"Well, it's true."

Any parent could embarrass their kids during the teenage years, but only a true virtuoso could embarrass them into their twenties and beyond.

She opened her mouth to force out some sort of retort – what, she didn't know – but her dad's focus wasn't on her. He was looking to the left of her, where a picture of Lauren Miller hung on the wall, frozen forever in the prime of her life.

Guilt, thick and familiar, churned through her body and soured every cell it enveloped. Even after all these years her father's love for her mother was undimmed. It was the stuff of fairy tales, but because of her the fairy tale was cut short.

Her, and the Great Collision.

And now she was going to stir up bad memories, talk about things they avoided in this house. Gods knew she didn't want to hurt him, but she couldn't think of who else to talk to.

Larissa kept her head down and mouth full for the rest of the meal, letting the brothers talk. The meal was winding down; spoons clinked against flatware and a good portion of the side dishes were gone. It was now or never to start asking questions.

She wiped her damp palms against the legs of her jeans and began. "Dad, do you know what would happen if the city was ever attacked?"

Her father paused in bringing the cornbread to his mouth. "What do you mean?"

"Attacked. Like by a group of wizards, or some magical creature, or whatever."

Jack waved his spoon in the air, dismissing the possibility without words. "We've got wards to protect us."

If only you knew the folly of that statement. "But what if the wards failed?"

"They wouldn't. Believe me, we go through a lot every year to get them renewed."

Had she really been this complacent that she never thought to think beyond these answers before? Why did it take getting attacked to ask these questions? A five-year-old wouldn't accept these types of simplistic answers, but she had, all of her life. "Isn't there a back-up plan?"

The lines bracketing Jack's mouth went from charming to hardened as his lips thinned. "Baby girl, what's this about?"

Her father's tone roughened, taking on that edge that said to anyone who knew Jack Miller they should back off.

Dad hated talking about anything to do with the New Realms, and Larissa hated to bring this up to him. In any other situation, she'd be shutting her mouth right now.

But the wards had failed, and there was a secret group of protectors of the city. Would this info be a surprise to Dad, or was withholding this information another of the ways Jack Miller protected his family, most specifically her? Larissa's hands went up in supplication and she continued. "I'm curious. I got asked in class today about it and I realized I had no idea what the answer was. I figured it was something I should probably know."

"Well, there's nothing to worry about. The wards have held for over twenty years. They're not going to fail."

Her father dug into what was left of his chili, his signal that this discussion was at an end. Larissa rubbed the back of her neck. "Are there any exceptions to who can get past the wards or when?"

The spoon dropped from Jack's hand, a loud *clank* resounding through the room, and the tension from the brothers was now palpable as they looked between her and Dad. "Larissa Joy, where is this coming from?"

His anger kindled a similar blaze in her. She wasn't being unfair in her questions, and he needed to stop treating her as though she were eight. "I'm asking reasonable questions and you aren't giving me any answers. Wards are magical barriers. So what happens if the wizard who set them is incompetent, or has been blackmailed or bought off? And magic is dispelled all the time. But you sit there and act like none of these are a possibility, that I shouldn't concern myself over it."

Her dad gripped the edge of the table with one hand, the knuckles white. "It's several wizards casting several layers of spells that takes months out of every year to renew and strengthen. It's not someone showing up and waving a wand. And in my house I'll be shown respect, young lady."

"Then don't treat my questions as annoyances. You're the chief of police, Dad. You need to have some back-up plans in place, unless you want to find yourself in the middle of another disaster and have more people die..." Her voice trailed off as her brain caught up to her words. "Dad, I'm sorry."

Jack Miller took a deep breath. He pushed himself away from the table and stood. He was every day his age at this moment, older than Larissa had ever seen him. Without a word he left the dining room.

Awkward silence hung over the table for a beat of time, then by wordless agreement Gary, Steven, and Christopher got up and left to follow their father, leaving her alone with Michael.

Michael's eyes were narrowed on her, the deep brown burning with laser intensity. "Michael-"

"What was that about, Ris?"

The words hit her ear, but the vibration was wrong, unexpected. This wasn't Michael chiding her about upsetting Dad, at least not completely. Michael was in cop-mode, and he was *never* in cop-mode with her.

Does he know about Friday?

Her fingers went icy. *No. He can't. Dad doesn't know.*

Because if Dad knew, he would have been on her doorstep dragging her out of the apartment. No way around that. Dad didn't know, and he was the guy in charge.

So why was Michael looking at her as he would a suspect at the station?

It wasn't until right now, when the half-formed thought of telling Michael was discarded, that she realized she was even thinking of it. She deflected. "I went a little far, Michael, but I'm teaching the Great Collision and it came up and it's a valid point. The question stuck with me."

"Are you sure that's it? Anything else bothering you?"

His eyes didn't lose their laser focus, and she really needed to leave and think things through. "I'm-" she licked her lips, buying herself a few seconds. "I'm sorry I upset Dad. I think I need to go home. Things have somehow derailed, and me leaving is a good idea."

He placed his hands on the table, readying himself to get up. "I'll drive you."

She placed her hand over his, stopping him. "That's silly, Michael. My car is here, I haven't drunk any alcohol. A little fresh air and I'll be fine."

Michael looked dubious but didn't stop her as she grabbed up her coat and bag. She opened the door, slinging her purse over her shoulder, "Tell

Dad I'll give him a call tomorrow and I love him." Without waiting for an answer, she went outside.

This was more complicated by the minute. Dad didn't know anything but Michael might? Impossible.

Impossible.

Just as impossible as a gargoyle protector.

Just as impossible as zombies coming after her.

Just as impossible as necromancers waiting for the chance to grab her again.

Instead of taking her usual back-alley shortcut home, Larissa kept to the well-travelled streets.

CHAPTER NINE

Once again, Terak was on the roof of the opposite building and watched the little human through her glass doors. This time, though, she was aware of him, or aware someone was watching her. She kept pacing to the window, looking out, retreating into her home, only to repeat the process moments later.

After doing this several times, her head snapped up and her spine straightened, as though she had come to a decision. She again began to move toward the windows, but this time, instead of stopping there, she continued to the glass doors that led to her balcony and opened them. Stepping out onto the balcony, she waved her arms in wide arcs through the air.

He neither saw nor sensed any threat to her. Uncertainty kept him still, a sensation unknown to him before she entered his life.

After several moments of waving she brought her arms down and around herself, hugging her body against the cold. Her lips tightened, and she went back inside.

She could not wish his company, could she? She fought hard against any guards, so why would she seek him out?

But she kept looking out the window, her attention never leaving the balcony for more than a few minutes.

Standing, he snapped his wings in preparation, leaping in the air and gliding the short distance to her.

She heard his landing. Within moments she scrambled from her inner rooms toward the balcony door. Her eyes widened when she saw him. "It's you."

Did she not wish to see him again? They had parted on as pleasant of terms as possible considering the circumstances of their initial meeting. His shoulders went back as he braced himself. "Does this upset you?"

"Oh." She shook her head, the action appearing as a way to clear her mind than a motion of the negative. "I'm sorry, that sounded so rude. I didn't mean anything by that. I wasn't expecting you though."

"Why?"

She motioned at him. "You are the leader. I never expected you would be on guard duty."

Her words were intelligent, as under any other circumstances he would not be. Still, best she not know that. "A leader who views himself above any task is setting a poor example for his people."

The nod she gave was little more than humoring him, if the flattened twist of her mouth was honest in revealing her true thoughts. Still, she did not question him any further, and that was the outcome he desired. She asked instead, "Does this mean I'm going to see you often?"

Yes, but she did not need to know the truth at this time. "In the beginning only a handful of warriors will watch you as I search for information. I will be among them."

"Oh," she muttered, though he doubted she meant the word to be audible. She licked her lips, a nervous gesture. She looked around her apartment. "I'm sorry. I'm forgetting my manners. Would you like something to drink or eat? I mean, I don't know what gargoyles eat..."

The words trailed off and she was studying him again, her eyes stopping and lingering on the expanse of his chest, bare as his kind rarely wore shirts. The hint of a blush swept her cheeks, the color of springtime roses, which suited her pale hair and sky eyes.

"Water would be fine. As long as the glass is not delicate, I will be able to use it."

Relief washed over her features as her gaze met his again. "Not a problem. Please sit."

She motioned to the lone couch and walked into the adjoining kitchen area. Her apartment was small enough that the kitchen was readily visible from the living area, her graceful movements always in his view.

She brought the water, handing it to him. After drinking a sip, he put the cup down. "Your hospitality is gracious, so please forgive me when I ask if there was a reason you invited me in?"

Chagrin danced across her features before a smile crossed her lips. He easily saw her as a little girl, caught in her naughtiness by her father but trying to charm him from giving any deserved punishment. "I wanted to talk. I needed to ask some more questions."

"I am always willing to answer your questions, but I feel uneasy here. I am more effective as a guardian if I observe you from afar. I am more aware of the surrounding areas and can prevent anyone from getting near you."

Larissa took the seat across from him, drinking from her own water glass before answering. "And here I thought bodyguards always wanted to be closer to the people they were protecting."

He never had, not until her. "Gargoyles are not used to anyone wanting them near."

The wind howled past the glass, creating a haunting backdrop to their conversation. He missed the play of firelight over her skin. She was a creature of light. Sunlight or firelight, it did not matter. She should be bathed in radiance.

Her eyes were direct on his, proof that his memory was correct and he hadn't been imagining how bright and clear and true the blue was. "I still don't think I need a babysitter, but I'd prefer that whenever possible, you are close to me. It feels too weird to know someone is out there watching me when I can't see them." Her eyes flicked over his frame and before they shied from him they deepened in color to reflect a twilight sky. "But only you. No offense to anyone else."

Strange, his throat was tight. He swallowed before speaking. "If that is your wish, I will do so when possible."

She nodded, her fingers tangling together as she lost herself to her own thoughts. Then she let out a chuckle, the sound resigned humor. "Can my life get any stranger?"

No answer was needed, and she rose to pace the length of her living area again.

Movement seemed to calm her. Both at the keep and now here in her own home, her movements started frantic, mellowing as her body burned the negative emotion from her.

Once she reached calm, she turned her attention back to him. "A member of the Guild came to my school today. Well, I should say two of them. The redheaded woman I saw Friday night and an Asian woman."

"Yes," he said.

"My dad," she took a deep breath, uncertainty coating her words. "I don't think my dad knows about them."

"He may not. Or he might not know the extent of their influence. They would not bother him over the daily dealings of crime in this city. That is not their concern. Their concern is the battle with the necromancers."

"But my dad is chief of police. He's not some bumbling civilian – his whole life is dedicated to protecting this city. How could he not know that there are these people with all these powers waiting in the shadows?" Her voice rose and her fingers wound together, almost violent in how they twisted around themselves.

He stood, taking her hands in his. He eased them apart, massaging the soft digits. "What exactly upsets you so?"

She turned her head away, not meeting his gaze. "I've been thrust into some new dimension where up is down and everything I've given complete faith to is worthless. I've blindly trusted my dad and the system, and it's all a lie. Right now, whether I'm being targeted or not seems almost immaterial."

He stroked her forearm, willing her with his touch to relax. In small increments she did so, growing more pliant under his fingers. "Because your father does not know about the existence of a group who have long guarded their privacy is not a reason to start doubting him. Your father is a good man and a good protector. Your city could not be in better hands."

"I don't-" She backed away, but her movements had gentled, the tension gone. "I don't mean Dad. Not completely. But the wards are a lie. Zombies got past, you," she said, motioning at him as she paced, "Got past. My predictable life is turning into a minefield."

"And I am here to help you, little human. I do not wish you to carry this burden alone."

Her eyes locked onto his and he could not turn away from the hurt in them. "I believe that, but I also believe that is not the only reason. If you weren't also helping yourself somehow, I'm not sure you would be here right now."

She was withdrawing from him, even more than that first night, and being allowed to continue in her life was hanging on these next few moments. "And you are right, little human. Though I will admit to admiring your bravery, if I did not believe more forces were at play I would not be here."

"Bravery?" Shock colored her words, disbelief written over her face. "What have I done that's so brave? I froze. If you hadn't come, I would have stood there as those zombies tore me apart, doing nothing but screaming as I died. And after standing there like a log watching them attack you, I turned and ran."

"You did not know you could trust me not to hurt you."

She slashed her arm as though it were a sword, cutting through the air at her side. "Don't try to make excuses for me."

Terak stopped her pacing and brought her to stand with him. He cupped her face, that beautiful face that did not flinch as his clawed fingers came into contact. "I make no excuses. You are not a warrior. You are a scholar, one who cares for and nurtures younglings. That you did not act as a hardened soldier who has lived with death is not a reason to call yourself a coward. You feel shame because you ran, but I see that as only strength. You were strong enough to not let the horrific sights around you paralyze you until the battle was over. You broke away. Many can never do that."

She looked at him in wonderment. Fat, lazy tears started to roll down her cheek, burying themselves in the collar of her sweater.

His wings half closed around them as he used the pad of his thumb to wipe away her tears. "You confuse me, little human."

"How so?" she asked, her voice not much above a whisper. She closed her eyes and leaned into his palm, letting the weight of her head rest in his hands.

"Most beings I have known feel they are more important than reality dictates. You, though, you seem to not realize how special you truly are."

Her smile was small, quiet, but it suited this intimacy. "You seem to know a lot about me for having known me a weekend."

The warning from her words tested the mood, but did not shatter it. He must not misspeak. She could not know how long he had been part of her life. "My father once said that once you learn how to see people, it takes only a moment to truly know them. Everything after that moment is details and happy memories."

One of her hands covered his. "Your father sounds like a wise man."

"No son alive who loves his father would ever say otherwise."

Her eyes opened then. The tiny lines around them had eased and the sheen of tears was now absent. They were back to the bright sky color that had his heart beating a little faster as they stared into his. "And what would you say?"

He bowed his head, images of his father and mother from a time long ago dancing in his memory. A time before the Collision, when they had all been free of the burdens of this new reality, his father gathering his mother up and spinning her around, only to bring her in and kiss her, the sight embarrassing him, yet warming something in his chest as he beheld it. "My father was the wisest of gargoyles."

Terak moved his hands into her hair, pushing the blond strands off her face with gentle strokes. He continued, "My father would have enjoyed meeting your father. From what I have heard, they were very alike."

"You know about my father?" she asked, curiosity sparking her eyes and dampening the last of the pain that remained there.

"I am leader of my Clan. It is my job to know of all beings whose decisions could affect the balance of this world. Your father is one such man. He is well respected, and though he issues no decrees, his words are taken seriously by those who do."

Pride lit her features, her smile going wide and free. "Yeah, that's my dad."

The intimacy of their situation hit him then, his hands buried in her hair while his wings surrounded them, protected them in their own universe. Her own gaze held no discomfort yet, but it would in moments.

It was better to back away, remove himself from her space. He forced fingers that did not wish to unwind from the strands of hair. He backed away.

He shifted his gaze away and focused on her home, to give them both a moment to recover. The room was warm, blue walls and white furniture and a hint of everlasting summer. It suited her.

The title of the book on the table caught his eye and he reached down to grab it. From the corner of his eye he viewed Larissa as she made a lunge to grab the book from him before she stopped herself.

"*History of Gargoyles*," he intoned, reading the title. "I have never read this work. Is it any good?"

He turned his attention back to her to see her little chin raised. "I'm not going to apologize for trying to learn about you."

Of course she shouldn't. He would have not respected her as much if she took everything on faith. "I would not expect you to. A scholar always seeks more information."

Her eyes still held their earlier warmth, though a small shadow entered them. "There is not a lot of information out there, and what little there is, it's... mixed."

Here he needed to tread carefully. Her hesitation over the last word spoke volumes. He wanted to keep the level of camaraderie they had developed. "I do not know what the volume contains, but I can say with certainty that we are not as bad as many stories would have you believe."

Her fingers ran over the cover of the volume, which featured a gargoyle in battle mode. "If gargoyles don't deserve the bad press, why do you have so much of it?"

"Separation and isolation creates fear and mistrust, on both sides."

"Which is why you want to start living in the world?"

"Yes."

"But not all your people do, isn't that what you told me?" The shadow was growing larger.

He waved his hand over the cover, and need to make her understand struck him with the force of a warhammer. He didn't want her to look on him with fear. He didn't want to lose the closeness they were developing. He wanted to be able to touch her face again. "Stories like this tell only one side. They never speak to the many betrayals gargoyles suffered at the hands of other races. My people do need to move on, but many cannot forget the past, a past where they learned that they can only depend on other gargoyles, lessons learned with blood and fire. They have learned that other races would destroy us if they got the chance." He sat across from her, not wanting to force her to keep looking up at him. "But we must move forward now, not forgetting those lessons, but not letting them control us either. We no longer live in the Magic Realm, and I need your help to accomplish what I want."

The shadow was gone. Her eyes now held only curiosity, the question in them not on his trustworthiness but on the worthiness of his plan. "Spell it out for me. What exactly is it you want?"

"I want what every leader wants. I want to protect my Clan. My people have been in flux since the Great Collision. I want to bring calm and prosperity and peace to my people. I want us to be able to move in this world without fearing or bringing fear to others."

She motioned to the book with the gargoyle drawn to inspire fear. "And you believe helping me will help you achieve that goal? That it will change centuries of mistrust on both sides?"

"It is only a first step, but yes, it is a valuable first step, one that will set my people on that desired path. While the outcome is not guaranteed, I can only hope so."

She studied the book still in his hand. Reaching for it, her fingers brushed his as she took the book from his hand, soft and warm and gentle, the sensation sparking nerves and tendons in ways not even the fiercest of battles had ever caused. There was a split-second pause, a hesitation before she drew away and left him bereft. Without a word she went into her kitchen and tossed the book into the trash, the look she gave him almost defiant, as though she was waiting for him to comment.

When no words came from him she changed from defiant to bashful, pink once again dusting her skin while her hand reached up to rub the back of her neck. She cleared her throat. "Bringing the conversation back to my school crashers, Fallon said something rather interesting to me."

"I do not doubt that. What did she say?"

Larissa started giggling, sweet, nervous sounds that she covered by placing her hand over her mouth. She was as adorable as any youngling at that moment, her shining eyes still visible beneath half-closed lids and her cheekbones rounded in mirth. Something in him loosened at the sight, freeing space in him that let air travel easier and deeper, as though now was the first time he knew what it was to truly breathe unencumbered. "She is a very intimidating woman when you are up close and personal."

Perhaps a diplomatic meeting with the Guild was in order. He did not wish Larissa to fear in the place that should be her sanctuary. "Do not feel cowardly for thinking that. Most warriors would rather run than face Fallon in battle."

"Have you ever fought her?" she asked, stark interest in her tone.

"No, and while I would if I had no choice, I would never wish to. What did she say?"

"Well, like you," Larissa said, giving him a pointed look, "she didn't seem to believe me when I said I had no idea why I was attacked by zombies. I then asked her why she didn't know what was going on. Obviously, she had some information if she was there waiting. And she had the funniest look of annoyance come over her face. She said some meddling bitch sent her to my place that night and didn't have the courtesy to tell her why she was there. Would you have any idea who she meant?"

There was only one being who could possibly cause that reaction in a warrior of Fallon's caliber. "My guess would be the Oracle."

"The Oracle? *THE* Oracle?"

"As far as I know, there is only one."

Larissa's mouth hung open for a moment. "The Oracle," she repeated. "I've heard about her, but...wow."

She is connected to the future of your Clan. Guard her well.

"I don't understand," Larissa continued. "If the Oracle is involved, why didn't she just tell them who was behind this and what they want me for?"

"Yes, it would be nice if she were something other than inscrutable."

"Have you ever met her?"

No, he would not tell.

His protection of her was all that mattered. There was no reason to inform her of the Oracle's visit which started his interest in her, or the months he watched over her without her knowledge. He would not risk their fragile relationship over the truth.

There was no reason then for this gnawing sensation that crawled through his insides with sharp teeth, eager to tear into his flesh and let him bleed.

None.

"No, I have not."

A clock chimed in the background, bringing Larissa's head up. "It's later than I thought. I need to get to bed." She seemed to become unsure again, the same uncertainty that colored those first minutes. "Thank you for coming in and answering some questions. And thank you for..." here she colored again, her eyes softening at the memory that played behind them. "Thank you for everything you said to me tonight. I might not want what is happening, but I'm grateful to have you helping me."

His wings flickered, and for the first time in his life he had to hold them steady against him. "I would not have you afraid if I can prevent it."

Her hands were twisting together lightly, broadcasting her nervousness in the next question. "Is there some way I can contact you if I need to speak with you again?"

"I will be around often."

"Yes, but unless you want me jumping up and down on the balcony and hoping you are on guard duty to answer, I was thinking there had to be an easier method of communication."

With rare exception he was the only one who watched her. Her worry was for naught, but to not scare her he said, "You may ask any gargoyle any question. They have been given orders to keep you apprised."

"Thank you for thinking to order that, but," and here she licked her lips again, a pink and glistening temptation amidst silken hair and fathomless eyes. If he had not so much experience listening to those around him even as his concentration was directed elsewhere, he would have missed her next words. "I like talking to you."

Warmth lit up his chest, inappropriate and all-consuming. Clearing his throat, he gave a gruff nod and stepped back toward the balcony. "I will bring something the next time I guard you."

"Good. I guess I should see you out then." She stepped out with him onto the balcony. "Try to get some rest."

"I shall."

She looked down, pushing her long hair behind her ear in a nervous gesture. "Next time you come, you don't have to wait for an invitation. I wouldn't mind if I saw you knocking on the door." Without waiting to see his reaction to those words, she entered her home, turning off lights as she made her way to her bedroom.

Terak leaned against the wall. If he quieted his breathing he could hear her going about her nightly rituals, hear the splash of water and the soft music she used as a background noise to lull her to sleep.

Did he imagine it, or could he hear the graze of her shirt as it slipped from her shoulders and fell to her feet? The rasp of the pull of a zipper, and then those nimble little fingers tugging the coarse denim over the lushness of her hips, over the round swell of her backside, down those long legs.

His groan resounded through the otherwise quiet night.

CHAPTER TEN

Running in the middle of the day sucked.

Early morning, great. Early evening, even better. In the middle of the day, she was a little too much white girl to enjoy the sun beating hard down at her.

It must not be an issue for gargoyles. It wasn't as though they were pasty like her, and the odds were good sunburn was an unknown to them.

That in a nutshell was why she had not been able to convince Terak to let her run at her usual times. He look mystified she would equate something as insignificant as turning as red as a lobster to the possible danger from attack, and since she would be safest from attacks in the middle of the day, that was when she would run. So sayeth from on high.

Damn stubborn gargoyle. The only thing she had to fear was heatstroke.

It was a gorgeous day, and in good news for her skin, there was a decent amount of cloud cover, though not enough to lose the cheer of the day. She was running on her favorite trail through the largest wooded park to be enjoyed while still within the city's limits. She might not have left the city, but darned if she didn't feel like she was in her own woodland habitat.

Two men came from behind and sped past her, both at a pace much faster than her own ten-minute mile time. One turned and ran backward for a couple of moments, smiling and winking at her before turning around and catching up with his friend.

Ha, ha! Still got it. Nice to know she could get a glance or two, being an old maid and all.

Up ahead a tall woman in a red running bra and matching spandex shorts came running toward them, jogging in the other direction. Both men slowed as they stared at her, eventually tripping over each other's feet.

Larissa half expected to see their tongues in that mass of body parts. The men righted themselves and took off at top speed to finish their run.

Her own oversize shirt and baggy shorts were a hell of a lot more comfortable than that red number. Who put lace edging on anything you were supposed to exercise in? That had to chafe.

Who cared what those guys thought anyway. Neither of them were built. Compared to Terak they were pubescent boys, and no doubt Terak could bench press both of them with his tail.

Terak...urgh.

The last two weeks were the most disturbing of her life, and yes, she was including the week when she first got her period. She had been attacked by zombies, kidnapped by a gargoyle, had both a brother and a best friend who were acting suspicious, and a father who was still upset at her for asking questions about the security of the city.

And she had a gargoyle protector she was starting to care about, maybe even like.

Out of all the above, that last one kicked her hardest in the solar plexus.

He had wings. And a tail. *A tail.*

How the hell did this happen? Stockholm syndrome? Some power dynamic because she was the helpless little woman and he was the big, powerful gargoyle?

No, it was because of his chest. No male should have a chest like that, and he never wore a shirt. Never, like they offended him or something. Maybe she should be grateful that at least he wore pants.

No, she shouldn't be.

Yes, she should.

Well...

Back to chests. Terak's was so broad it might take *hours* to explore every inch exposed. And that chest tapered to that stomach, which was not a six-pack but an eight-pack. What human had an eight-pack? How could a human guy compete?

Gargoyles were very unfair to humans. Maybe she wasn't right to help them become friendly with other races. All the other females of the various species would jump them on sight.

But if any of them jumped on Terak, she'd have to tear the female's hair out. To protect inter-races relationships.

Was inter-races a word? Well, it was now.

Sweat soaked hair fell into her eyes, and Larissa pushed the damp tendrils that clung to her forehead back into the mass of hair knotted on top of her head.

Heatstroke. Had to be heatstroke causing these freaking thoughts. No matter how much Terak complained, she was never running in the afternoon again.

Up ahead was the most delightful part of the run, a steep incline that always made her swear she would give up running every time she crested it. Turning up the volume, she forged ahead.

The scream rent the air, the sound of feminine terror stopping her cold. Instinct had her turning before her brain could warn her it was a bad idea.

A woman, the one in the skimpy running gear, six feet in the air and grabbed around the throat by...

Oh dear *gods*...

Orcs.

Why hadn't she fought her dad harder about the wards? But this... how was she to know this could happen? Orcs in the park, backlit by a hazy sun during an afternoon run where she should be safe.

Her hands hung there, cold, numb. Her mouth opened, she knew it was open, but no sound was coming out.

Orcs.

"Not her."

They spoke? Those monstrous creatures could *speak*?

And then one of them locked eyes with her. He threw his head back and roared, the guttural noise flaying her exposed nerves. The rest of the orcs turned their attention to him. He proceeded to point at her.

"Her!"

By the gods, me?

No.

No.

Are you involved with the necromancers?

But she wasn't. Never, she'd never had anything to do with them.

This couldn't be happening.

Orcs, larger even than Terak, their greenish skin oozing and oily, their heads misshapen, like someone used their skulls for batting practice.

A dozen orcs now chasing after her.

She was running, she was running even though she didn't remember turning from them, branches flicking over her skin as she crashed through the wooded area. The ground vibrated from the force of the running creatures, creating an uneven surface under her feet.

"*Terak!*" she screamed. She hadn't seen him during the run, but he had to be here. He had to be. He promised he'd protect her and Terak, Terak would always keep his promises.

She tore through the forest, bramble and brush scraping against her body with every step. Heavy footsteps were so close, the clang of metal and the rhythm of their stride gaining.

This couldn't be happening. She was a nobody, a nothing. This couldn't be happening.

A primal scream sounded from above and powerful relief surged through her body, stopping her in her tracks as she looked for him.

Terak.

He was here. She was safe.

Terak's arm emerged from the foliage up above. He grabbed the tallest orc and brought him into the air, wrenching his neck so hard to one side that Larissa heard the crack of bones.

The orc stopped moving, and Terak threw the body far away, then dropped to the ground and grabbed another orc, his clawed hands ripping into its chest through the metal casing.

The other orcs turned to Terak, all but one. One orc still had her in his sights. He shouldered through the others surrounding him, coming straight at her. Terak turned from the orc he was fighting to launch himself at that one, preventing it from getting any nearer to her.

That move left his back unguarded, and another orc took advantage, taking its sword and slicing through Terak's wing.

Terak made no sound or movement to indicate he had been struck with a sword. He never stopped fighting the orc in front of him, keeping it from getting near her.

She could get away. Now, while their attention was on Terak, she could run to her car on the other side of the wood and escape.

An eye hanging from its socket.

She had stood there, waiting for the zombies to grab her.

If Terak hadn't been there, she would be dead. Afterward he held her in his wings as she cried and he called her brave.

I don't want to die.

I don't want to die and I don't know what to do.

But I never want to be that person in the alley again.

There had to be something she could do beyond run away in her car.

Her car...

She didn't have a weapon but she had two thousand pounds of magic-fortified metal at her disposal. Could an orc survive being run over?

Only one way to find out.

Larissa ran to the vehicle. Her fingers shook as she turned the key in the ignition, but the car started readily. Snapping on her seat belt she jammed down on the gas pedal, then spinning the wheel so hard tires squealed.

Her massive SUV took the grass easily, the bumps and dips rocking her in her seat. The trees were spaced apart far enough that the car was able to drive through the openings.

The fight was in front of her. Several orc bodies littered the ground, but three orcs still fought Terak. Terak was holding his own, but his chest and arms were swathed in large splashes of red and one wing was useless, the torn skin flapping in the wind.

Larissa pressed hard on the gas pedal, aiming the car at the two orcs farthest from Terak.

The orcs responded a second too late to the sound of an approaching car, lifting their heads as the car rammed into them. She rolled over them, sickening thumps and crunches that had her stomach begging to lose its contents. She clenched her teeth against the urge to vomit.

One hand appeared from underneath and landed on her hood, and the face and shoulders of one orc came into view.

Ahead was a thick line of trees. Pressing down on the accelerator, her body went tight, bracing for the expected impact as she headed straight for them.

She closed her eyes before they hit.

The airbag deployed at impact, pressed into her face so she couldn't breathe, her nose flattened and her chest punched concave. The wait for it to deflate was eternity, but she pushed at it, speeding up the process the best she could.

She turned the key, and thank gods the car started again. She put the car in reverse and made her way back to Terak.

No more orcs were left alive. Terak had more wounds than before, blood streaming over a good portion of his body. He was erect but kept falling to his knees.

She parked and rushed to his side. His right side seemed the least injured, so she propped herself under that arm to help him toward the car. "Your wing," she said, though it wasn't as if he needed her to point out the obvious. There was no way he could fly.

What were they going to do? He wasn't allowed within city limits. If they were caught driving in the city the authorities would take him into custody. Her too, but what would happen to her wasn't the worry. If he was jailed the other gargoyles would attack to free him, stomping on the possibility of a peaceful coexistence.

It had *Disaster of Epic Proportions* stamped all over it.

Maybe it was time to call her father. He would be furious, but he would help Terak escape, considering the gargoyle had saved her life. Of course, she would have to tell him what was going on, and her father would lock her up before she finished telling him about that first night.

But she couldn't see an alternative. Terak needed medical attention and she couldn't risk a fight between human and gargoyles. She owed Terak that and much more.

"Terak, I'm going to call my father. I think he'll help us. At the very least we need to get you to a hospital."

"No hospital," said the gargoyle, sweat beading his forehead. "No father."

"I'm not a nurse. You're wounded and in no shape to fly or fight, and if a gargoyle is seen within city limits, they'll take you into custody."

"No father," he repeated, breathing rapid, his voice reedy. He was going to pass out soon. She could convince him after she had him in the car, and she needed to get him there before he passed out. There would be no way she could handle his weight by herself.

As she got him settled into the passenger seat there was a buzzing underneath her hand, a vibration so small she didn't bother to look as it was occurring, focusing instead on the belt buckle. She turned to Terak…

… And reared back, hitting her head on the inside of the car, the pain bringing tears to her eyes.

Larissa's eyes slid shut as her hands grasped the newly formed bump. Maybe she had seen wrong, but her eyes opened, and no, she hadn't been seeing things.

Instead of a gargoyle sitting in her passenger seat, now there was a human male – bare-chested and bloody, with black hair and stone-grey eyes.

"Say nothing," he said.

Then he fainted.

CHAPTER ELEVEN

Human.
Human.
Human.

The words beat through her head with the same rhythm as her heart, which was currently doing double-time since she was carting two hundred and fifty pounds of a gargoyle-turned-human through her bedroom door.

The bed lay before her, smooth sheets and fluffed-up pillows, and it might as well have been a mile away. "Terak?" she asked, but a pained groan was his only response. He was fading out of consciousness fast, and there was no way she could pick him up if he crashed to the floor.

No way around it.

"I'm sorry, I'm sorry, I'm sorry," she muttered as she hefted his arm away from her and all but knocked him onto the bed.

He upgraded from a groan to a yelp as his battered body collided with the mattress. "I'm so sorry," she said again and again, the words on repeat as the maneuvering began to get him fully situated.

Finally he was settled and the growly sounds diminished to only a few every minute. Larissa pushed her hair back from her face with both hands. A rising tide of panic was coursing through her body, starting low in her stomach and rising up her chest.

No. That nonsense needed to stop. Panic was not allowed until after she got her gargoyle back.

Breathe in through the nose, out through the mouth. Do it again. After this is over you better be prepared, Double Mocha Fudge Ripple, because you are going down.

First she had to get Terak bandaged up. The first-aid kit was under the sink, so well-stocked a hospital could borrow it in an emergency. Only nurses appreciated a fully loaded first-aid kit more than a cop's kid.

Kit, check. She turned on the water and let it run for a few moments to warm up, then let a plastic basin fill while she grabbed a few washcloths.

Terak gave a loud groan. She scooped up everything she needed and hustled back into the bedroom. The items were placed around her on the floor as she took stock of Terak's injuries. Her goal was to bandage him up enough that when her next gargoyle protector came on duty, that gargoyle could then take Terak home, where his own people could heal him. Gods, please let him heal enough that a hospital visit wouldn't be necessary. He might look human now, but who knew if he was as human on the inside? He might have extra organs or something that would give him away. And that was assuming they could actually survive the trip out the building to the car.

Car! *Crap!*

Since her gargoyle-turned-human protector had been bleeding out over her seat on the drive here, it was understandable little things like orc parts possibly caught in the bumper or a front end that had held a strong resemblance to an accordion were overlooked.

No way could she leave Terak, and anyway taking the SUV to Cliff, the mechanic who usually worked on her car, was out. He'd be on the phone to her father in three seconds flat. Any body shop would, all of them by law were supposed to report anything suspicious.

Right now what was needed was a friend who'd dump it somewhere and could be trusted to not blab, and only one person fit that description.

On the second ring the woman on the other end of the phone answered, and before she could finish her "Hello?" Larissa started talking. "Olivia, I'm in trouble. Help me."

Olivia's tone was soothing. "Calm down, sweetie. Of course I'll help you. What is going on?"

Thank gods for Olivia. "I need you to take my car away and not ask any questions."

Confusion burned through Olivia's tone. "Take your car? To do what?"

And now came the hard part. "I was chased by orcs. I had to slam into one to escape and now my car is messed up. Please, Olivia, I need you to come get it and hide it somewhere."

There was a long silence on the other end. Before Larissa hung up to dial again, Olivia spoke. "I know someone. I'll get your car fixed for you. Don't worry, there won't be any questions."

Olivia's voice was calm and low and apprehension skittered the length of Larissa's spine at her friend's words. This was not what she expected when she picked up that phone. "You... *know* someone? Olivia, what are you talking about?"

"You said no questions, I'm going to say the same to you. We are going to have a nice long talk later, but right now, where is your car?"

"On the south side of the building."

"It's taken care of. Don't worry and I'll call you tomorrow." And Olivia hung up.

Were there any more surprises ready to drop down on her head? If so, a little advance notice would be welcome, because the nice people at the mental hospital might give her a discount rate after a certain number of shocks to the system.

Terak was still on the bed, his breathing not as labored as it had been. Picking up a washcloth, she ran it over his flesh, now a sun-kissed tone instead of stone grey. He slept through her ministrations.

The wounds across his abdomen looked the worst. Cleaning them would reveal whether she could wait with him here or she'd have to brave the hospital.

The washcloth cleared the blood away and a small giggle erupted from her throat.

Relief caused some weird reactions, but after everything that happened today, a little giggle was a nice surprise. The wounds weren't as bad as all that blood suggested. He still needed to be seen by a healer, but cleaning and wrapping the wounds would suffice for now. Her gargoyle was going to be fine.

He was going to be fine, and the relief flooding through her system left her light-headed in its wake. She closed her eyes tight for a moment to regain equilibrium before opening them to continue with the cleaning.

Through all wiping and bandaging he stayed asleep, even the groans becoming less frequent. And now, was that...*a snore?*

Some bodyguard.

His face was gentler now, softer. It wasn't the human features that caused the change, though that helped. Asleep, he lost the worry and the authority he always carried otherwise.

Not that the human features were bad to look at. The gargoyle made a damn fine-looking human. That had been obvious from the first moment he shifted, but it seemed impolite to ogle someone when they needed medical attention.

His chest was done, now his...pants.

Oh dear gods, she had to take off his pants.

Did gargoyles wear underwear?

Did they need to? Did gargoyle males have the same equipment...?

No. That was not what mature, adult women thought when taking care of an injured male. That response was more in line with pubescent males who hid the girlie mags they stole from their dads under their mattresses. She was above such thoughts.

She grabbed a towel and laid it across his pelvis. Eyes on his face, she reached under the towel to lay her hands at his waist, his skin as warm as a human as it was as a gargoyle. She inched fabric down, slow and gentle in deference to wounds both known and yet undiscovered.

The whole process to remove Terak's pants took less than a minute, and at the end of it she was breathing as heavily as she did after running a 5K.

She cleared her throat, embarrassment warring with the crazy, inappropriate thoughts that had somehow become embedded in her brain this last week. She was taking care of him, and that was why she was running her hands over his legs. There were a few scrapes and bruises, but his legs were fine. Well, not *fine* like that. No, wait, they were...

She rapped her forehead a few times. This was ridiculous when she was even a stuttering fool within her own brain.

A little more washing, a few more bandages, and a patched-up, human-looking gargoyle was now in her bed. "When you wake up, we are having a serious talk. Like about gargoyle emergency contacts, and this whole *turning human* thing."

If he was awake he wasn't admitting to it. His eyes stayed closed and his breathing stayed even.

Her warrior.

Without her bidding a smile curled in the corner of her mouth. Yeah, he was. He had been amazing, ferocious and unstoppable. He took on those orcs without hesitation, all to protect her.

She leaned back against the wall and slid down until her butt hit the floor. She could still see him from this angle, that human face displaying no signs of distress.

What did she have to do now? Car was taken care of, and the list of questions she was going to be asking Olivia tomorrow could be made later. Olivia *knew* people. When had she started *knowing* people, people who could fix a car filled with orc parts and not blink?

Later. Much, much later.

Blood. Maybe cleaning up any blood trail would be a good idea, yes?

Thirty minutes later, any signs she had hauled a bleeding guy around were taken care of, thankfully without any neighbors catching her in the middle of clean-up duty. The sheets and towels would need to be trashed, but other than that no worries.

Terak was still resting when she went to check on him. His breathing was easier and his color better than it had been when she left.

Pulling one of the bandages away from his chest she looked, then looked again, doing a double-take. "Oh holy *hell*."

He said no hospital and it wasn't him being a stubborn male. He was healing on his own. What had been a good-sized gash was now half the depth and width it had been when she had cleaned it.

It wasn't that she had misjudged the severity of his wounds at the park. It was that they had already begun to heal in the time that it took to get to the apartment.

Huh. So gargoyles could shift into human form, and they healed in no time flat. Handy gifts, those.

Larissa kneeled down beside him and smoothed his hair back from his forehead. The human hair was finer than the coarse gargoyle strands, but it was the same deep black. No fever, just warm, perfect skin. "Do you think next time you can share the important info that will keep me from worrying *before* you faint?" No answer, but his breaths were deep and regular without a hint of pain in them. She sighed. "You're lucky you saved my life today, or you'd be in for a serious talking to."

As she stood, splotches of red on her once blue T-shirt caught her eye. Oh, *ew*. Blood and sweat and dirt and who knew what else were all down the front of her clothing. And her hair was still damp with sweat. And her legs had stuff streaked on them that she didn't even want to identify.

Terak was still sleeping comfortably. A quick shower wouldn't hurt.

The hot water pounded her from above, working into sore muscles in a painfully pleasurable way. She had entered academia and not followed her dad and brothers into law enforcement for a reason. She was not cut out for all this physical stuff.

After tossing on some comfy pajamas and giving her hair a quick towel dry, she went back to the bedroom, where Terak had flipped over and was now on his stomach, his face at the edge of the bed and his arm hanging over the side of the mattress.

He had been so frightening and alien that first night, a monster who had grabbed her against her will. Now here he was, undeniably human, and there was such a strong physical resemblance between man and gargoyle that it seemed ridiculous she'd ever thought gargoyles were scary-looking.

Larissa smoothed the blankets over him since he was in danger of losing the towel with his maneuverings. Would he be embarrassed waking up without his pants? An embarrassed Terak – now that expression would be worth checking out.

She left the room and headed for the balcony. She never asked about the schedule on who watched over her when, so she didn't know when the next gargoyle would arrive. After five minutes of doing the arm-waving trick and no one showing up, she went back inside.

Someone would figure it out eventually, and it wasn't like Terak was in danger anymore.

She entered the living room, glancing at the clock. Dinnertime. Her stomach let out a low roar that would be highly embarrassing if anyone else would have been around to hear it.

Well, she was hungry, and everything that could be done was done. No sense starving while she waited.

The television caught her eye as she wandered to the kitchen. Sigh. It would be nice to have a television that worked, and she needed to make a note to call a repairman tomorrow.

What was being reported on? Was the city in panic? How was her dad going to respond to the news that the wards were broken?

Speaking of Dad, why wasn't her phone ringing off the hook? As soon as an orc invasion was reported, her father should have made a beeline to the apartment and proceeded to try to grab her up and bring her home.

Strange. Maybe not the strangest incident of the day, but strange.

She made a turkey on rye. It was nice to do something as normal as make food after the last few hours. Normal was severely underrated, and if her life ever went back to normal, she would never take it for granted again.

Normal was not a gargoyle who had the ability to shift into human form. Human.

It had been so crazy today she hadn't considered how important this was, but this... this was big. How the zombies and orcs had gotten past the wards was still a question, but this ability was probably the way gargoyles were able to enter the city and pass the wards that guarded it – presuming the other gargoyles had this same ability. Only a human was supposed to be able to walk past them, and right now Terak was certainly human, at least on the outside.

Think of the implications. So many spells, especially protection spells, relied on that one designator. *Human.* An enemy who could bypass them at will, especially a race as powerful as the gargoyles – that would scare a whole lot of people.

Alone and unarmed, Terak had fought a band of orcs. He had been hurt, and yes, she helped, but none of that changed the fact he alone killed over a dozen of some of the most feared fighters in this world.

Gargoyles were not to be underestimated.

A hard knock sounded against the door.

CHAPTER TWELVE

Surprise visitors had to be bad news. *Terak...*

Several loud thumps sounded in a row, as though the person on the other side were hitting the door with the side of their fist. "Ris, open up. Now."

Michael, using his patented *I'm the eldest and with Dad gone I'm in charge* voice.

Her brother the cop, who never came over without calling first.

As tempting as not opening that door was, that wasn't an option. Michael would kick it down in a heartbeat – any of the family would. And if she objected in any way, shape, or form or threatened parts of their anatomy, she would be met with a shrug and an insincere apology, and left with the full knowledge they would do it again if they felt it necessary.

With no other choice unless she wanted this to become a full-scale incident, she opened the door. "Michael, what are you doing here?"

He walked in before she had a chance to fully block the entrance or voice an excuse on why this was not a good time to visit, which translated meant he was not going to be leaving until whatever had brought him over was wrapped up to his satisfaction.

She shut the door with a quiet click. Michael wasn't yelling – not yet, at least – and it would be best to do everything possible to keep things quiet and prevent Terak from waking up during their little family chat.

Overprotective gargoyle versus overprotective big brother. That was a match-up she had no interest in seeing anytime soon.

Michael's eyes wandered her apartment, not in casual interest but in a hard sweep, searching out any hidden secret or concealed clue.

He was looking at her place with cop's eyes, and there went any hope that this was a friendly visit.

He'd never used the sweep on her before. He once joked this was the only place he could relax and not be a cop. Something had sent him here.

So what did he know, and how did he know it? If he knew she was at the park, where were the drawn weapons, and where were the other brothers and her father? And why wasn't he asking about the gargoyle sighted in the park? And if he was here only because there was an orc attack in the city, why wasn't he ushering her out of the apartment and straight to Dad's?

Nothing was adding up. This needed to be played casual, at least until she had a better idea of what her brother knew. "Michael, what are you doing here?"

"You went to the park today?" It was question and statement mixed together, a tactic used by cops where they were asking you a question, but in the words it was implied they already knew what was going on.

Keep up the confusion act. "Actually, I did. I went running this morning."

His voice was curt, not letting her sentence die before he asked the next question. "Did you see anything while there?"

"Yeah, lots of trees and two men ogling this one woman who was wearing red running lingerie."

"Anything else?"

In their usual conversations, now would be the time she would get annoyed with her big brother and start acting huffy. Crossing her arms and cocking her hip to one side, she added a touch of annoyance into her tone. "What's this about?"

Michael's eyes were cold and calculating. In that gaze, he was weighing whatever he knew in his head against what he had seen from her today.

Her brother was deciding if he could trust her. He was deciding if she was his baby sister, or if she was responsible for a wrong he needed to set right.

Damn, this hurt. And the worst of it was, he was right. He was right to question her and act as though she was some bum he grabbed from the street, because right now, right this minute, for the first time in her life, she was lying to him. Not a fib, not a stall for more time, but a lie.

A big lie. A lie over something that mattered.

End this now.

Maybe that would be best. This situation was spiraling out of control. If today proved anything, it was that the zombie incident was not a mistake. Something was hunting her for whatever reason. What were the choices? Have a gargoyle sleeping under her bed all her life?

End this now. Confess everything and throw herself on Dad's mercy, then come up with a plan on where to go from here. He'd be mad as hell, no doubt about it, but that didn't change the fact they would do anything to protect her.

And Terak?

What would they do to Terak?

What would they do to the gargoyle who had been protecting her all this time, the being she had begun to call her friend? He fought and bled for her. He laughed with her. He snarked at her.

He called her brave and she knew, to the center of her soul she knew, he meant it.

Even if they didn't do anything to him, coming clean to Michael would mean the end of her relationship with Terak.

They would force her to let him go.

Michael's eyes were still indecisive.

Larissa raised her eyebrows at him. "Well, I'm waiting. What has you coming over here in such a snit? Couldn't you at least call me first and warn me you had attitude to spare?"

Michael relaxed, the signal that he had put his suspicions aside. He put his hand out to her, something between his fingers that he was giving her. It was her driver's license. "Did I leave this at Dad's?"

"It was found today at the park. There was an incident and I happened to notice it near the scene."

So that's what had started this. "What happened at the park?" *No, I'm not going to move back and live with Dad. No, I don't care if there was an orc attack...*

He shook his head. "Sorry, I can't give any details of an ongoing inves…Ris, you all right?"

It was a good thing she tripped and fell to the floor, otherwise Michael couldn't have missed the shock that had streaked through her body and had to be evident on her face, and he would have known she'd been lying earlier.

The zombies had disintegrated – at least, that's what she assumed was the reason the earlier attack was undetected. But the orcs? That was destruction on a large scale, and their bodies didn't disintegrate. They were in large heaps, bloody and broken bodies littering a little-used section of a public park. That couldn't be hidden.

Could it?

And if someone did have the ability to hide it? Who? And why would they?

What the hell was Michael part of?

She needed answers, but right now Michael needed to leave. There was still another large male she had to take care of. She picked herself off the floor and used her palms to dust off her legs. "One of these days I'll become graceful, you'll see," she said, picking the threads of a long-running family joke.

Michael fell into the rhythm. "The day that happens is the day I'll trust you with my computer."

"You'd be lucky if I broke that thing. There's old technology, and then there is technology that has seniors laughing at you for owning it." She walked into the kitchen and picked up her sandwich. "Well it was nice seeing you, and thanks for bringing back my ID. If that's all, I'm kind of busy. I'll see you this weekend."

He didn't take the hint, which was the usual for Michael. While he was no longer in full cop-mode, speculation was still clear on his face. "What are you busy with?"

Why couldn't her family be the type that avoided each other except the holidays? "Michael, quit treating me like a kid. I'm allowed to have a life and I don't have to run every decision by you."

"Who gave you that wrong information?" His eyes narrowed. "What are you hiding from me?"

A noise brought both of their gazes to the door of her bedroom.

Terak appeared in the doorway, the towel around his waist the only covering over his naked body.

CHAPTER THIRTEEN

Warm honeysuckle drifted around him, tease and temptation. Just like her, sweet and comforting and sensual, she was able to ease his tension with a touch of her hand or have him hard and wanting with a glance of those eyes.

She had been delectable, her long legs bare and the sunlight exposing the multiple hues of blond in her hair.

A coppery tang worked its way past the honeysuckle. No, this should never touch her. It was his duty to protect her from necromancers, and from orcs...

Late afternoon sunlight filtered through his eyelids as he cracked them. Slow and steady, he forced his eyes open.

He was on a bed. Blue walls surrounded him, and on top of the furniture were feminine bottles and potions.

Larissa's bedroom.

Images were creeping back, the fuzziness of sleep giving way to the clarity of memory. Orcs were often allies of the necromancers but they were not slaves. If they were there on behalf of the same masters as the zombies, the necromancers must have agreed to a very high price.

Also, they were able to pass the wards, a situation that was very different from the zombies getting into the city. Zombies were once human. It would take powerful magic to confuse the wards enough to let the zombies through, but it was not outside the abilities of a master necromancer.

Orcs, though – orcs should have been impossible.

If the wards were completely useless, Larissa was in greater danger than ever, and a new plan for her protection needed to be drawn up.

But what? She would not agree to stay at the keep until the danger had passed. Indeed, he used that very suggestion to sway her away from the Guild.

And that was if she was still willing to let him guard her, now that she knew...

She knew!

He jerked from the bed, his half-healed injuries tearing anew at the sudden movement.

She knew. No.

No.

Had any of his Clan appeared? No, no one was to be here until the middle of the night. None would have come and seen him... human.

On unsteady legs he went to the bathroom. In the mirror was undeniable evidence, the face that of a human male. Larissa knew that he could shift into a human form.

From their earliest history, there was only one absolute rule held by his race - if any outsider discovered that gargoyles could shift, the outsider was to be executed at once.

His clawless hands fisted against the white tile of the sink. He would be dead if she had not entered the battle. Instead of running for safety she had appeared to aid him in battle, as fierce as any goddess of war. She had taken him home, cared for him, nursed him. And he was to repay that with death?

No, no harm would ever come to his little human. She would never be hurt, even if he had to battle his own Clan for her life.

But the Clan's secrets must be protected. How could he ensure that?

Rubbing his hand over his face, he pushed back from the mirror.

There was nothing to be done now. It was time for more practical considerations, and later, he would reflect more upon how to contain the situation.

He took off the bandages and stepped into the shower, the hot water getting the last of the blood from this day's battle. There was very little that had been missed. Larissa had done well bathing him and tending to his wounds.

His hand stilled in washing his hair. He had been naked in that bed.

Larissa had stripped away his clothes. She had caressed his body with those soft little hands.

Did she like what she saw? What she *felt*?

His cock hardened, becoming as heavy and as stiff as the stone statues his kind resembled.

She would have been above him, leaning over him to tend to his wounds. She would have nibbled on her lower lip, as she often did when she concentrated, leaving it pink and swollen and glistening.

He palmed his cock, rubbing it with slow movements. Her little tongue would have come out to swipe over her lower lip after she had finished nibbling it, the way he wanted it to swipe over his body. He wanted her to peel the clothing from his body not because of injuries, but because she needed to know the taste and feel of him. She would get on her knees in front of him-

Voices.

His hand stopped. He tilted his head for clearer sound.

Larissa, and one other.

A *male* other.

The growl echoed through the shower stall. He grabbed a towel to cover his body and exited the room.

If the man threatened her, he was dead.

If the man was a rival for her, he would wish he was never born.

As he entered her living room, the two humans sensed his presence. Larissa's eyes widened while the male's narrowed, and the grinding of the man's teeth was sharp in Terak's ears.

The male was her brother, the only dark-haired one among the boys. She was not dealing with a male who desired her.

Larissa's mouth parted in surprise. Her hair was damp from a recent shower of her own, and she wore a shirt that hung off her shoulder, as if she had risen from the soft bed he had awoken in.

Her eyes locked with his, wide and blue and bright. The slope of her shoulder enticed him, invited him to nuzzle her, follow the curve of her skin wherever it led him.

She swallowed hard, her hand coming up to cover her bare shoulder, her thumb brushing the skin of her neck as he wanted to do.

The energy from her brother grew so dark Terak turned his gaze to the human male. He was murderous, his body tensed in preparation for a fight.

Larissa seemed to sense her brother's mood, for she broke from his gaze to turn to her brother. For a few long moments debate was clear on her features, a questioning on what to do next.

Then her chin came up, that little signal of defiance that often wrung a groan of frustration from him even as every cell filled with pride at the sight.

She walked over to stand in front of him. Sliding her hands up his chest, she stood on her toes to brush a kiss over his mouth, the pink lips softer than anything he had ever experienced before. "Baby, this is my brother, and we're having a sibling discussion. Why don't you wait in the other room and we'll be done in a moment."

Thank goodness Terak had done as she requested.

Of course, she still had a pissed older brother to deal with.

"Ris, who was that?"

Her hands went to her hips, an instinctive reaction when her brother used that tone on her. "You don't get to lecture me, Michael."

He stomped over to her, his eyes ablaze. "*I* don't get to say anything when my baby sister is obviously sleeping with some guy she never even introduced to the family?"

She poked him in the chest to get him to back up. "*Your* baby sister is twenty-six years old and lives on her own! Do I stomp over to your house to see what kind of hussy you are shacking up with?"

"We aren't talking about me!"

"Well, we aren't talking about me, either! My sex life is none of your concern."

He groaned, putting his hands up over her ears like he could block the words. "I don't want to hear my little sister use that word again."

"Grow up. You're the one trying to insinuate yourself into my life. Don't act like you can't handle it."

They eyed each other, both refusing to back down. Hands on hips, he said, "This isn't right."

Realization struck Larissa and she looked down to see her stance mirroring her brother's. They really were a lot alike.

Of course they were. They were family.

Larissa drew a deep breath, releasing the tension. She walked up to him and patted his chest, causing her brother to drop his hands to his sides. "I love all you guys. More than that, I like you all, and your approval means so much to me. But don't you feel it too? That sometimes it's too much, that you need a break from the family and their expectations, that you need your own life and freedom? Michael, you had to, you're the one who left us first."

Her brother's gaze slid across the floor, taking in her words. Her brother had been gone for eight years in the military, the only family member who left the neighborhood.

Her father had been so proud of his boy, talking to everyone about how his son had signed up, but Larissa saw it in him, the constant worry, the dread that gave him an ulcer and had him eating antacids like candy.

None of the rest of them ever left after that.

And Larissa would swear that the happiest she had ever seen her father was when Michael announced he was coming back and joining the police force.

"Larissa, is it serious with this guy?" Time to proceed with caution. If her brother thought Terak was trying to take advantage of her, he would go into the other room and dangle her guest off the balcony.

He wouldn't drop Terak though.

Probably.

"I'm not sure what we have together yet. I do know he's special to me. And I know, even if we separate, I will never regret him."

He sighed, rubbing the back of his neck, and Larissa knew she won. "Baby sister, you're killing me. Dad's going to scent I'm hiding something and he's going to make my life hell."

She gave him a hug. "Thank you."

He returned the hug, but then grabbed her by the shoulders and set her back from him, looking deep into her eyes. "You have a little time, but only a little. Figure out what you want, then either move on or the family has to meet him."

He sighed again, moving toward the door. "At least this will stop Dad from putting us all on Friday shift so he can introduce you to another guy."

The door closed. One male taken care of. Now the other to deal with.

CHAPTER FOURTEEN

Terak was leaning against the wall, his arms crossed over his chest, waiting for her return.

At least he put his pants back on. As tattered as they were, it was still a lot easier on her respiratory system seeing him in those versus the white towel.

She put her hands up, a signal to please let her talk before any yelling started. "I didn't call him. He found my ID at the park when they were investigating the attack. I'm lucky it was him, otherwise there would have been a whole squadron of cops at my door."

His features were a shade different, softened into human lines, but the intensity of his eyes and set of his mouth was pure Terak. She'd recognize both no matter what else changed. "I know this. I am curious why you did not tell him about me?"

"Why would I? The whole reason I agreed to your people guarding me was so that I didn't get my family involved in this mess. Running to them would kind of defeat the purpose."

He started shaking his head, his arms coming to his sides as he propelled himself away from the wall. "Why did you not tell your brother about my abilities, that the human male in front of him is in reality a gargoyle?"

There was a strange tension in Terak, his usual intensity magnified. He was waiting for her answer, his now-clawless hands clenching and unclenching at his sides. The question of whether she should be scared popped into her head, but she pushed it away. Nothing about him scared her. What he was...was...hopeful. "Why would you even ask that? This is your secret. I would never tell anyone about this."

Terak challenged her, that deep voice still the same in this form. "He is a protector of the human world. Information on your enemies is what any protector would wish."

Before she could stop herself, her hands went to her hips. "There is nothing I want less than to get into another fight with a stubborn male who is trying to drive me crazy. Now, I don't know what's going on in that human-looking gargoyle head of yours, but quit it. You saved me multiple times. We've fought together. More than that, I consider you a friend, and I trust you. I would never betray a secret I discovered from my friend."

Terak reeled back as if someone hit him. "You would call me a friend?"

He looked so adorable and bewildered, and while the smile curling her lips couldn't be stopped, there was a pang in her chest over what this male's life was like that the thought of someone calling him friend elicited a reaction like this. "Shocking, huh? Kind of surprised me to. Maybe that kind of stuff only becomes apparent when you're watching someone bleed and praying he doesn't die."

His face held wonderment. It was if he received a rare gift, something he always wanted but never thought he would get for himself. His gaze roamed over her face, like he was committing everything in this moment to memory.

"So," Larissa said, wanting to stop the awkwardness creeping through her skin, "how does this work? You look pretty healed up, I'd say. Does this mean you are healed as a gargoyle? Your wing was torn pretty bad."

He shifted. Strange, this big, bad secret, but it bordered on anti-climactic seeing it in action. He went out of focus – only for a second – and then became the other form. If Larissa took a long blink she would have missed it.

She walked behind him to check his wing, stroking her hand over the membrane. It felt like leather, but that soft, luxurious leather, the kind where a jacket would cost most people's yearly salary.

Her hand traveled to the frame. Even this was warm, his body heat coming through. The muscles bunched under her hand as she took in the area where the frame met his back. This body was that of a warrior. He was hard, perfectly formed. This body was her salvation, her sword and shield in a world that made no sense.

Tiny tremors rippled under her fingertips as she stroked down his muscles. Which shook, her hand or his back?

Her thumb brushed over the tiny hollow in his back that separated his wings. She leaned closer, breathing in his smell as she did that night where he held her in his arms. She'd been so scared that the sensation of flying was a blur. She couldn't remember if she enjoyed it, even on a subconscious level. Would he take her flying again if she asked?

Adding more pressure, she ran her thumb down the strong curve of his spine

Would he let her follow it with her tongue?

Larissa pushed back even as her mouth parted to make the thought a reality.

Sleep, that was the ticket. She needed a break from this day in the worst way. Sleep would be good. Sleep would get her emotions back in line. Clearing her throat, she said, "You look completely healed. I'm not a nurse though, so you should have one of your people look at it."

His muscles still trembled where she had caressed him. His lips still carried the warmth of hers. Her scent filled his nostrils.

This woman was consuming him, bit by bit. She was becoming the reason and the reward of his existence, and if he did not shield himself, everything he did not have to give would belong to her.

He turned and brought her back into his sight. She was so appealing standing there, the over-large shirt hanging from her frame, her hair still damp and laying along her back.

Her hands were twisting together in a nervous fashion, her pupils dilated, darkening her eyes to the color of the stormy sea.

Once he had boasted to a group of young warriors that he could withstand any torture. The woman before him made him realize the fool he had been.

She forced her hands apart, a deliberate relaxation. She was trying to bring normalcy back to their interactions. "So, gargoyles can shift, huh?"

He hung onto the safety line she provided, willing to walk away from whatever edge they had been traveling. "We have hidden it for a very long time. In the distant past other races knew. In return for our trust, we received death."

Her eyes widened. "Your allies turned on you? How did they succeed?" She paused, then in a mutter meant for her own ears more than his, said, "I've seen you guys in battle. I'm not sure anyone could win against you."

Pride swept through him at her assessment of his skills. "We are more vulnerable in our human form. We are stronger than humans, but nowhere near the power of our gargoyle forms. We foolishly let others know of this weakness."

His thoughts drifted off into memories until he was a boy at a fire, listening to the weathered elder tell the darkest moment of their race, the only story that ever brought him to his knees.

Soft skin cradled his face, breaking the memory. Larissa was before him, her warm eyes pleading for him to confide in her, promising him she would be strong enough for them both. "What happened?"

"There was a great celebration. Gargoyles were invited, including the children and the elderly. We were asked to come in our human guises. We did."

His eyes closed and his head bowed. He did not want to finish the story. Not because he did not want to relive the elder's words as she warned them all on that firelit night to never trust an outsider again, but because he wished Larissa to never be exposed to the depths of depravity some were capable of.

Those soft hands slid around his neck, pulling him down into her arms. She buried her face into his neck. He leaned into the silk of her hair, pulling in breath after breath of her beloved scent.

"I'll never tell," she said, low tones that still displayed the steel of her will. "I swear to you, I'll never tell."

He wrapped his arms around the little human and into her hands, he placed the fate of his people.

They stayed still for long moments before Larissa broke the contact. "I'm sorry you are in this position. I realize now how hard this is for you, making the decision between staying separate and entering this new world."

"I wish," he paused, the words stopping on his tongue. Uncertainty was not something he shared with others. The leader must be invulnerable. Still, she was not a member of the Clan. His doubts would not be held against him. "I hope that those who do not agree with my decision to help you will understand when this is over. They are so intent on never being vulnerable again that they lose all the possibility that this world can offer. But then I remember what has come before when we opened ourselves up, and I wonder if I am the naïve fool many call me behind my back."

"Terak, you are not a fool. You are a great leader, one who cares for his people more than he cares for himself. Your instincts will not steer you wrong."

"There are many of my Clan who do not possess your surety." He backed away from her, the weakness that demanded he take her in his arms becoming stronger the longer he was near her. "I owe you a debt. You protected me."

She snorted, the tiny sound adorable to his ears. "Well, you protected me. I say that makes us even. Or if you argue it, I'm probably still in your debt with your two life-saving rescues against my one. Besides, it's a moot point. The way I see us, we are now allies trying to figure out what is going on."

"You now accept that you are in danger?"

She sighed. "Guess I have no choice, do I? When a bunch of zombies and orcs come after you, it's kind of hard to argue that it is one giant mistake."

The teasing words came to him, another impulse he rarely experienced before entering her world. But though his first inclination was to swallow them, instead he freed them, directing them toward her. "I do not know, little human. You seem to have a great gift for arguing any situation."

Her eyes widened. Were his words not received as they were meant? Perhaps...

And a huge smile broke out on her face, the effect that of the sun escaping from a dark grey sky. "Is that so, oh Great Leader? I'm honored that you noticed my wondrous skills in that area."

He pushed back, gentle, not wanting to end their ease with each other. "I am sure the most silver-tongued of all elves could not argue more effectively than you."

"That's because no elf grew up with my family."

He had nothing to add, so he stayed silent, letting the playfulness rest peacefully between them.

She spoke again. "How do we discover why they are after me? I acknowledge that they are after me, but it doesn't change the fact that I don't know why I have been singled out." She ran her hands over her arms, the playfulness fading from her features to be replaced with a fearful uncertainty. "I'm scared."

He did not dare touch her again, but he projected every ounce of his strength into his voice. "No matter who your enemy is, I will protect you."

CHAPTER FIFTEEN

"Why don't they call this place '*Goths R Us*' and be done with it? And seriously? Red velvet? Even I wouldn't go there."

Fallon didn't waste the movement it would have taken to look down at the mouthy mage. Goth overload was an apt description of the vampire club. Black and red was the color scheme of everyone and everything, the haze of smoke beneath the dim lights could have been from the multitude of clove cigarettes or a few more nefarious drugs of choice, and with the attire on display, there was a good chance a leather-and-lace factory nearby had been robbed.

"And considering all the places you have gone, Laire, that is a statement." She scanned the contours and corners from where they stood at the entrance. Invitation or not, this place was dangerous. Life-ending dangerous. Soul-stealing dangerous. Invitation or not, there was no letting down her guard. "Besides, do you really expect us to defer to your color judgment? Bubblegum pink? Why?"

A vision in leg warmers and a miniskirt, Laire pushed back her feathered, pink-tipped hair. "Just because you can't understand color, don't try to bring me down. Black should be an accent, not your whole color palette. I'd almost say you fit right in here among the groupies."

"Bite your tongue."

"No thanks, I don't want a horde of suckers descending on me if I drew blood. And you," Laire said, turning to the man who rounded out their spectacularly *not*-happy-to-be-here trio. "You need to up your act as well."

"Hey, I do blue." His dark blond hair was a shaggy mess that hung over his forehead, almost covering yellow eyes but not hiding the scar that ran down the right side of his face into his well-trimmed beard.

"Wulver, blue jeans every day are as bad as Fallon's forever black. I do not give you a pass."

"But jeans do good things for my tushie." He turned his back to Laire, raising the lumberjack overshirt with one hand while pointing at his derriere with the other. "See? Proof right there. Why mess with perfection?"

Laire ogled him a touch longer than necessary before giving her nod. "You win. That is a great butt, truly a class by itself."

"Thank you."

"Before Laire comes up with a reason why we should start removing clothes to prove some theory, I got a question." Fallon said. "Can we teleport out of here if this turns ugly?"

"Nope, our only hope will be for you to swing your sword, Wulver to fang out, and me to set everything on fire...*Ooh!* Liquor," And Laire turned away to scamper to the bar.

"Laire, get back here! You do *not* drink before we meet with our mortal enemy." Not even a stutter-step to indicate she heard. Fallon's head fell forward, the annoyance-and-more-annoyance mixture swirling through her synapses so familiar when dealing with Laire. She turned to Wulver. "Can't you control her?"

Wulver snorted. "Can you?"

"You are the boss."

"Like that's ever worked."

They went over to Laire who was pounding on the bar. "Hey! Walking blood bank, I need some service."

The bartender, a woman was in her mid-twenties, was beautiful, of course, because vampires would surround themselves with nothing else. She kept to the red-and-black theme in her tight corset and red lips. Her expression was a mixture of disdain and horror – but to be fair that was how most people looked at Laire's outfits. "I don't think you belong here."

Laire plopped down on the barstool. "And I'm supposed to care about the opinion of someone who drools over corpses? Your implants have more sense than you do. Get me a boilermaker."

The woman's nostrils flared, which probably hurt when you took into account all those piercings. Still, she started to fill the order. Laire called after her, "And hurry. Who knows when we're going to be interrupted, and I want my drink."

"What are you, an alkie?" Fallon stood to the left of the mage while Wulver sat on the right.

"You are the one who said I needed to be pleasant to a suckhead and not start a war. Don't harsh my means of achieving it."

The music was low, played more to enhance the dark, sensual mood than as a main attraction. The majority of beings here were human, though a few elves and a couple of nymphs were visible in the crowd. All of them beautiful and most of them women.

So where was their host?

Fallon extended her senses for the magical signatures. There by the far wall, a pulse of necromantic magic. And another in the middle of the dance floor. Neither were strong, acolytes monitoring the outer club or other low-level duties.

She extended further, discarding the signatures of the weaklings. They would pose no threat if she needed to kill them to escape. Stronger here and there, but not yet, not quite...

Tendrils vibrating with a heavy thrum of magic wrapped around her senses, caressing down the length until it reached her body. Without her shields it would have engulfed her and demanded she kneel in its wake, shudder with despair, degradation…desire.

Reign.

A big tankard was placed in front of Laire, leaving the mage clasping her hands in childish display and with a gleeful, "Sweet! I was afraid all they would have was absinthe or shit like that."

Wulver was on the stool next to Laire, leaning back so his thick forearms rested behind him on the bar, the movement stretching his blue T-shirt tight across his chest. "I know we're on time. How long do you think before they notice us?"

Fallon catalogued all eyes on them from both living and dead. "Oh, they've noticed us. But Reign wouldn't be Reign if he didn't exert his authority."

Wulver nodded. He tried to appear nonchalant, unconcerned, but he failed so spectacularly the passersby were giving him looks of pity. Not unexpected, since there were few things bossman hated more than being surrounded by suckheads.

Then he tensed, his gaze fixed on the far end of the bar. "What's this?"

Laire turned to look. She straightened in her seat, her hand going to fix her hair. "Oh, he's cute!"

"Sure is. Too bad he's up for sale to the highest bidder," Fallon said, taking in the V-shaped torso and long legs of the man at the end of the bar.

"For sale?" parroted Laire, and damned if she didn't reach for her purse.

"Give me that." Fallon grabbed the purse and threw it to Wulver, who threw it behind him. "Please tell me you recognize the most in-demand mercenary in the business."

"Why, did we have a drunken one-night stand you forgot to tell me about?"

The jeans and T-shirt combo marked the man as much an outsider as they were. Anyone without training would buy the good-ole-boy obliviousness he projected – if good-ole-boys had thick black tribal tattoos running over large chunks of exposed skin and long black hair with dyed-red streaks in it – but the defined lines of his body were a little too tense, his stance too close to battle-ready for those used to war to mistake this man as a non-threat.

Motioning toward the end of the bar, Fallon said, "Since we're waiting for Reign anyway, I'm heading over and saying hi, maybe ask him about a certain rumor we've heard."

Wulver nodded, while Laire asked, "Can I come too and get his number?"

"I'm going to say no."

When she was only a step away he called out, "Fancy meeting you here, Dragon Slayer. Hanging with vampires…seems I should have given the stories I heard a little more consideration."

Leaning against the bar so her sword hand was free, Fallon said, "I was wondering why I'm seeing you here as well, Merc. I never took you for a guy who was interested in the lace and tights crowd. Searching for a new personal style?"

"No, not me. Only male elves can pull that off."

"So why are you here?"

His shrug was perfect nonchalance, the movement hiking the shirt from his waistband and giving a quick glance of muscled torso. "Blood banks are legal under the treaty between the Seven Houses. No reason why I shouldn't be here."

"No, no reason. Meeting anyone special?"

He smiled at her, a deep dimple appearing with the movement. "Why? You looking for a date? While I'm flattered, I tend to like the ladies a little darker-haired and darker-skinned. However, I might know the perfect guy for you."

"You are sweet to be so concerned over my love life, but I've decided only to date guys who have bigger swords than me."

"I can see how that limits your dating pool."

Reign would send for them any minute, and Merc wouldn't meet with his client, not now that he'd seen them. So when he reached again for his drink, Fallon placed her hand over the glass.

His fingers folded into a strike form, but there were no further signs of aggression as he took her in and awaited her next move. Fallon said, "I'm not interested in a fight. I want to give a friendly warning. You've always been under our watch, but you've never done anything stupid enough to warrant being placed on our shit list. I advise you not to change that habit now."

His smile held the same level of friendliness as a shark's. "Whatever could you mean?"

"I've heard things about a spellbook and an auction run by a certain facilitator. Ring any bells?"

"Not a one. But if I hear anything, I'm coming straight to you."

He was good – impossible to read and giving nothing away. Such a waste he hadn't joined them when he was invited. "Appreciate that. Think about what I said. I'd hate for us to end up on opposite sides."

Merc grabbed his shot glass from the table. After saluting her, he brought it to his lips and drank the contents down, the strong column of his throat advertising the liquid's path. "I find I'm a little tired. If you'll excuse me." With that, he left.

Wulver's eyes were on her as Fallon made her way back. He gave a small shake of his head, indicating he didn't want to talk about it yet. Yeah, probably best not to discuss their business around here.

Moments after Merc walked out of the club, a vampire walked through the crowd and toward their little group. While his necromantic energy was unmistakable, his eyes were not red. So not a true vampire, merely one of the serving boys.

One who had overestimated his power, the poor deluded bastard, because instead of stopping some distance away he came to stand right before the three of them. Holding out his hand, he said, "I need your sword."

Laire snorted into her drink while Wulver's chuckles sounded on Fallon's other side. Smartasses. Fallon really didn't want to deal with baby vamp right now. Going to see Reign was never an activity that put her in a happy mood, and if Reign was tempting her into a fight by sending some fool into her path, it was a ploy that had a good chance of working. "Everyone needs my sword sweet-cheeks, but I'm the only one who's going to be holding it. Now run along, because I'm not supposed to fight anyone tonight."

The vampire's eyes narrowed. His lip curled, flashing a hint of fang. "You will give me your sword, or I will beat your insolence out of you."

Laire laughed so hard she proceeded to fall off the chair. Through the slightly-screechy, slightly-snorty display, she managed to eke out, "He's killing me here. Tell him to stop."

The vampire was young and wanted to start a fight. Fallon was feeling charitable enough to give it to him, but if she started one, Kyo would scold Laire, and Laire would mope for a week, and all in all, it wasn't worth it. Besides, she could turn this around and work it to her advantage, maybe get out of this damned meeting. "Tenro goes where I go. I'm either admitted to Reign with my sword, or I leave."

Wulver's low, "Don't even think it, Fallon," squashed that plan. Damn.

"Master Reign, human. Do not take such liberties with his name."

Laire had calmed down from her laughing fit enough she could stand by her chair again. At the vamp's words she piped up. "Trust us, junior. Reign wants nothing more than for her to take liberties with him."

Before Fallon could smack Laire, a bald, dark-skinned man appeared behind the young vampire. Sleek and elegant, he was all smooth lines, from his expensive suit complete with tie and cufflinks to the well-trimmed mustache and goatee. He bowed. "Lady Fallon, please forgive your treatment. I am here to escort you to Master Reign."

The young vampire voiced his displeasure. "But the human has a sword."

The man's gaze beat into the young vampire, and the vamp shrank from it. The man spoke. "Listen well. Whenever Lady Fallon appears, you are to immediately bring her to our Master. Do you understand?"

The vampire bowed and scurried away, escaping the anger emanating from the suited man. The man's almost-black eyes focused on Fallon, deliberate in his exclusion of Laire and Wulver. "My apologies, Lady Fallon. If you and your guests will come this way."

Wulver looked at her with a *told you* expression. Letting loose her sigh only in her own mind, Fallon took the lead and followed the man.

Laire spoke low at her side. "Who is that?"

"Zemar. He's Reign's personal bodyguard."

"But he's human?"

"I have no idea what he is."

Zemar led them to the back of the club, where a well-hidden door awaited them and opened to a hellish wonderland. The outer club Outside was decadent, but in here, in this room, it was the first level of Dante's Hell. Everywhere was flesh and pain and degradation and underneath it all, the copper tang of blood, oppressive and inescapable.

Wulver's energy flared and Fallon turned back to see his eyes brighten and turn translucent in the dim light. She put her hand on his arm, his skin shuddering under her palm.

It was unfair that Kyo sent Wulver instead of coming himself. None of them liked being here, but a place like this was special torture for Wulver. But he was here, and none of them could be weak in front of an enemy. Fallon's fingertips bit harder into Wulver's forearm in wordless demand, and he blinked, his eyes back to their normal yellow the next time they met hers.

They followed Zemar, passing scenes of damaged carnality on all sides. One woman was flat on a table, her legs spread wide as a man pounded into her with inhuman strength. Two vampires hovered over her chest, biting her breasts as she screamed out her pleasure. Another corner held a woman being whipped. With each stroke, vampires would come to lick the trickling blood off her back.

The back of the room had a wide set of stairs that led to the second floor, an open space that overlooked the cavernous club area. Here the gothic scheme morphed into chrome-and-glass and clean minimal lines.

A large, luxurious white couch spanned one end of the back wall to the other. A dozen beings sat on the couch – all but one a woman, all of them otherworldly beautiful, all laughing as though they weren't part of a nightmare. Blood and alcohol lined the table in front of them, as well as other stimulants that guaranteed they wouldn't have to live with their conscience for yet another night.

In the middle was the lone male. Physically, he appeared to be a human man in his mid-twenties. Impeccable grooming and stylish dark good looks, and an old-world manner evident even though he was doing nothing save sitting on the couch. Ungodly beautiful, with a square jaw and thick brows over deep-set blood-red eyes, nicely formed mouth and a straight Roman nose.

He had a woman on each side, both of them stroking and nuzzling him. He paid them no mind.

His eyes sought and stayed fast on Fallon, roaming the contours of her face, her body, the marking so intense it was almost physical. "Fallon."

Fallon swallowed, caught in that gaze. Inside her was a shifting, a growl, a warning to leave that she ignored. She inclined her head in acknowledgment. "Reign."

Reign murmured, "It's been a long time."

Wulver stepped in front of her, protecting her and partially blocking her from Reign's gaze. "Vampire Reign, thank you for seeing us."

"Wulver." Not bothering with any courtesy, Reign turned his attention toward the male of the group. Reign's voice was deep, cultured, giving even ugly words an elegance they did not otherwise deserve. "Make no mistake, I granted this meeting as it was a personal request from Fallon."

"We appreciate it no matter the circumstances. We can only hold the peace as long as all stay within the boundaries that were agreed on after the Great Collision. This protects both your interests and ours."

"Not that you have any boundaries, huh?" Laire piped in, gesturing to the many scenes behind her.

Reign's attention turned to Laire for the first time of the evening. "Everything done here is consensual, as was agreed upon in those long-ago talks and sealed by each leader of the Seven Houses, *including* Kyo. Blood is life, and we agreed not to seek it out from unwilling sources as long as willing sources were not stopped from seeking us."

Laire looked like she wanted to say something else, but Wulver raised his hand in signal to stop. Wulver's voice rang out, no diplomacy left in his tone. "There was a zombie attack in the protected zone two nights ago. Do you know anything about that?"

"No."

Wulver waited a beat, but when Reign said nothing else, Wulver continued. "This attack was done by a master. The zombies were not created by someone new to the craft."

Reign shrugged, the movement more eloquent then it deserved to be. "No master under my control had anything to do with the attack. My people know the rules. I'm sure you have studied them for magical brands – use those."

"The zombies disintegrated once they were no longer functional. As I said, they were not created by a novice."

Reign made a dismissive gesture. "My magical kin are not exactly unionized. I control those under me. I do not ask what others do."

Wulver's back was a mass of knotted muscle, but his voice was even as he continued. "There was also an orc attack in the city. Would you know anything about that? Orcs would never be able to get in the city on their own, and they would have no reason to do this without someone bargaining with them."

"I'm afraid I do not. Is there anything else before you go?"

Laire made a great display of looking over her nails, saying in an offhand manner, "No surprise you suckheads are so weak you can't keep tabs on one another."

"Would you like to see how weak I am, Battle Mage? Do you truly believe I fear your little fireballs?"

Reign began to rise and Wulver began to growl. This was going FUBAR fast.

Fallon sidestepped Wulver, only the inches of the table separating her from Reign. She kept her hands down, away from her sword. "The only one here you should fear is me. I told you long ago, *I'm* the one to separate your soul from your body."

Reign's full attention was on her, those blood eyes as light as she'd ever seen. He reached toward her, the smooth skin of his fingertips grazing over her forehead while his thumb made sure, short strokes over her cheekbone, the strokes coming ever nearer her mouth.

She didn't object. Her gaze stayed locked with his and her hands stayed at her side. With a slow, deliberate movement, he pushed his hand into the fall of her hair, wrapping a thick strand around his fingers and wrist. His voice dropped, deepening as he spoke words meant for her. "I love your hair. The color of blood at its most fragrant and powerful."

The light tug on the strands didn't hurt. Instead it sensitized her. The swirl of color in his eyes was myriad shades of red reflected and magnified. "You should let go now," she said, low even tones that matched his own.

The corner of that edible mouth lifted, baring a fang. "Never." He pulled her closer, keeping to that edge of discomfort that never crossed into pain. "Stay by my side."

She ghosted her mouth across the air over his, one inch all the space that separated them, that he could feel the warm, moist puff of her breath a certainty. Her voice held a low, breathy undertone she had never heard come from her lips. "Never."

He gazed down at her through heavy-lidded eyes, the pull on her hair now a welcome pain that did nothing to break her away from him.

Wulver's voice came from behind her, tones that spoke of barely leashed violence. "Is there anything you wish to tell us about the zombie attack? If not, my people and I will take our leave."

Reign's lips thinned, the muscle in the corner of his jaw betraying itself with a small tic. His hand clenched in her hair, his greedy gaze roamed her face once more, lingering over each square inch of her skin.

Then he pulled back into himself, cloaking himself with decorum. He unwound her hair from his hand, sitting down on the couch. In moments the two women were back at his side. "I know nothing about the zombies. Good luck in finding their maker."

Fallon turned to step down from the platform, Reign's voice following her. "You are welcome anytime, Fallon, but please do not invite your friends again." Without stopping she walked toward the exit, the shift in air currents preceding Wulver and Laire as they followed her.

Once they were in the car, Laire spoke. "That was productive."

"To be expected," Fallon said. "We knew talking with him was a longshot at best."

Laire pursed her lips, studying Fallon with an intensity rare outside of a shoe sale. "Vampire boy is a little too touchy-feely with you, and you aren't afraid of getting in his space. You sure you two never dated?"

Leave it to Laire to start awkward conversations at completely the wrong time. "Are you serious?"

Laire shrugged. "He may be the scourge of all the realms, but there is no denying undead boy is damn, *damn* fine."

"So you think ultimate evil necromancer is my type?"

"I'd be really thrilled to find out you had a type. It's not like I see you dating right now. Or ever."

"Why is everyone suddenly worried about my dating habits?"

Thank the gods Wulver had the sense to interrupt this line of questioning. He directed a question to Fallon. "What information on the teacher?"

"Tec hasn't found any info that would suggest why she's targeted. The only interesting pieces of trivia we found are she was born the day of the Great Collision, and big brother isn't as finished with the military as his family thinks he is."

"What about fangwhipped?" Laire asked, bringing her hand in front of her mouth and using the first two fingers to mimic fangs.

"Who are you, vampire bunny? And no. There is no sign of it."

"Laire," interrupted Wulver. "What about her birth? If she was born around the time of the Collision, could that have affected her?"

"I would normally say yes. There were large amounts of wild magic, and a new life would be very susceptible to any effects. But by twenty-six she would have manifested any magical abilities."

"I want you to keep researching that angle. It's a long shot, but that's a hell of a coincidence." Wulver turned back to Fallon. "And Terak? Why is he so interested in her, and are we any closer to discovering how he and all the other races have gotten into the city?"

"No and no. We have all of our own people going over each ward individually, so hopefully we'll know about that soon. But as for Terak," Fallon's hand did a quick triple-beat against her leg, an outward sign of frustration. "I don't know why he was there, and I don't like it, especially since I don't have much more faith in gargoyles than I do necromancers. Right now sucks, because all we're doing is sitting on our hands waiting for something to break."

Wulver smirked at her. As glad as Fallon was to see him relaxed again after getting out of the blood bank, it wasn't pleasant to have all the relieved energy directed at her, peeving her off when she was already in a sour mood. "Then be glad you have Merc to take care of in the meantime until something pans out. Any word on the Dream Crafter?"

"None yet, but she can't hide forever."

"And Rhaum?"

"He's being his usual inscrutable self and making a crazy request as payment. I agreed to it. We need her. Merc is too good and has too many defenses against any of our other means to get to him. I wouldn't want to go against him unless I had no other choice."

"But has he committed to guarding the spellbook? He's never done a job for anyone evil."

"No, but he's going to." Fallon looked out the window, the occasional streetlight only deepening the gloom of the road in front of them. "And we both know why."

CHAPTER SIXTEEN

Knocks on the door tended not to mean good news these days, but Larissa rose to answer anyway.

Olivia stood there, carrying take-out bags with the name of a nearby Thai restaurant and emitted an amazing smell that started Larissa's stomach growling. "I come bearing gifts to make up for not calling ahead."

Larissa jerked her head. "You're in. I'll grab some plates."

After food had been dished out and wine had been poured, the women retired to the couch to start their feast. "So," Olivia began, "your car will be ready in two days. My friend was impressed by the damage you did."

Larissa swallowed a spring roll. "Thanks. I was rather impressed to have caused it."

"You know there was never any mention of an orc attack in the news, right?" Olivia waited until Larissa nodded to continue. "What is going on?"

Taking a swig of wine – fake courage at its finest – Larissa said, "Does this mean you are going to tell me how you know someone who'll fix a car full of orc splatter?"

Without answering, Olivia stood up and walked toward the kitchen. "Olivia?"

Opening the refrigerator door, she held up a couple more bottles of wine. "With all the stories we are going to be telling tonight, I think we're going to need these."

Larissa lifted her glass. "Top me up."

After wine was poured and they were once again settled, Larissa started. "I have no idea what's going on. None. Zilch. I'm as in the dark as I was after I was attacked by zombies. The only difference is I know now that it wasn't an accident. I am the target of all this."

Olivia tilted her head, disbelief written all over her face. "How can you not have a clue? These people… this isn't tiny, this isn't a scrap of information you might have stumbled across in a book or the wrong person crossing your path."

That was the same question on endless loop since she accepted the attacks were meant for her. Frustration beat a strong rhythm through her head and had her digging her toes into the carpet. "Believe me, if I had ever done anything that might be causing this, I'd be confessing it in the town square, in front of Dad and whoever else might be watching. I don't want any of this."

"Speaking of dad," and Olivia ran her hand through her brunette curls, the aftereffect a tousled look most women paid salons big bucks for. "Could this have something to do with him or one of your brothers? Have you talked to them at all about this?"

"No."

"Why?"

Larissa ran her hand through her own hair. Through long experience she knew the look was nowhere near as flattering as Olivia had achieved with the same motion. "Because Dad can't help me, and if I bring him into this, I'm going to get him killed. You know how he is, how my brothers are."

Narrowed-eyed disbelief met that statement. "Maybe – *maybe* – you can justify not telling the family when you thought it was a mistake or a one-off. But now, it's wrong to keep them out of this."

Larissa quelled the urge to squirm like a seven-year-old under the Olivia's look. "If I go to Dad, he's going to lock me down. I won't be allowed out of the house."

"Yeah, that's horrible, having a family love you that much. What was I thinking?"

The urge to squirm morphed into an urge to hang her head in shame under the harsh tone. It wasn't something they talked about, but Olivia had been abandoned when she was little and had been on her own most of her life. Though she never voiced the thought aloud, Larissa was sure one of the reasons Olivia hung out with her was to be able to experience a tight-knit family.

"You're right. I am a lucky woman to have these people back me up. They would put their own lives on the line to protect me." Larissa kneaded the back of her neck, her fingernails scraping the sensitive skin there. How to make Olivia understand? "Would you give up your freedom for prison? A wonderful prison, one with amazing people and great food and lots of love within its walls, but still a prison."

Olivia wasn't about to be placated. "You have no clue what a prison is like, or being on your own."

"No, but I do know what it's like to suffocate because no one around will let you breathe. No matter how loud you yell, or what you say, it's always a pat on the head and they send you down the path they want you to take, no matter what your wishes are." Larissa placed her hand on Olivia's forearm, forcing the brunette to look at her. "I was a good daughter, and I did what was expected of me, and you know what? I'm happy I did. I don't have any regrets, because I love my family and I love my life. But if I go to Dad now, I will never have another moment in my life where I am not under his thumb, and he'll justify every second by saying he's protecting me. And I love him enough that I'll let him do it, because the only other option is to lose him, and I can't abide that thought."

Olivia covered Larissa's hand with her own. "So you're saying family is a little overrated?"

Larissa smiled, though she couldn't quite manage the laugh Olivia was angling for. "I'm saying my family has to stay in the dark, at least for a short while. I'm not yet at the point where I have no other choice except to inform them and take the consequences."

Olivia squeezed Larissa's hand before letting go, and Larissa removed her hand from Olivia's forearm. "How are you going to protect yourself? You are the only one of the Miller clan who doesn't know at least three martial arts and can shoot a gnat from a mile away."

If only she could blame her father clinging to outdated gender roles for that fact. Reality was Larissa never had any interest in learning any of those things, no matter how much Dad tried to get her involved. She preferred spending her time in the library, always had. It was still her favorite hangout. "I have someone looking out for me."

Not good. Olivia's eyes widened a fraction, then took on a gleam of devious speculation. "Oh you do? Who would this paragon be, and why have you never mentioned him to me before?"

How to explain Terak in terms that would not have Olivia salivating and asking ever more uncomfortable questions? "He saved me from the zombies, and said he wanted to protect me."

"Did he have a hand in getting you away from the orcs?"

"Yes."

"And you've never mentioned him before because...?"

"He's... shy."

Olivia leaned closer, practically climbing on top of her. "Who is he?"

"I can't tell you."

"Why not?"

"Olivia!" Olivia took that as her cue to back away, though still within pouncing distance. "It's a secret."

"I thought we weren't having any more secrets."

"That's right," confirmed Larissa. "No more hiding my secrets. That doesn't mean I can tell secrets entrusted to me."

"He's trustworthy, you're sure?"

You would call me a friend? "Yeah, I'm sure."

Olivia nodded. "You're covered in the bodyguard department, good news. Now, how are you going to figure out the whys and wherefores of what's happening on your own?"

Larissa reached over and grabbed Olivia's hand. "I'm not on my own. I've got you."

"Fat chance. We get chased by orcs, I'm tripping you and running the other direction." But Olivia twined her fingers with Larissa's, giving a reassuring squeeze.

And now came the part of the evening where Olivia had to answer a few questions. "Since you know people, do you think you know anyone who can help me figure this out?"

Olivia's gaze became distant as she considered. "I think I do. But he's a hard one to get hold of, and he isn't a certainty. He's got his own demons chasing after him."

"Figuratively or literally?" Larissa asked. Olivia rolled her eyes but didn't answer the question. "I'd be grateful if you can try to get him, even if he isn't a certainty."

"I will. I'll put in a call when I get home."

"Thank you." Eyeing her wineglass, Larissa refilled it and took a long drink. She'd probably need it for this portion of the evening. "Just how do you know people?"

To her credit, Olivia didn't pretend ignorance. "You know me. I talk to everyone."

Olivia certainly did that. It was talent and gift rolled together, the way she was able to bond with anyone no matter their background. Within minutes, she went from stranger to beloved family friend. "Why didn't you tell me?"

"Why would I have?" Olivia's face held a hint of censure. "Before this happened to you, you were content to live far away from any of the New Realms. It wasn't a part of my life that I thought you would enjoy. Maybe I didn't think you'd approve of it."

"I wouldn't have approved or disapproved, I just wouldn't have been interested in it. That sort of dovetails back to our previous discussion about being surrounded by a loving family who think they know best for you, being in a prison that isn't really a prison."

An *o* of surprise formed across Olivia's mouth. A shading of understanding crossed her face as she closed her mouth, bowing her head slightly. "Sorry."

"Yeah." The wine was more than half gone by this point, but despite being a lightweight when it came to alcohol, Larissa wasn't affected by the hazy happiness that usually accompanied consumption. "Don't worry about it. Honestly, I didn't realize I was in a prison of my own making until recently."

"And now?"

Larissa drained the last of the wine in her glass. "Jailbreak."

CHAPTER SEVENTEEN

Larissa leaned on her balcony railing, looking toward the sky. Olivia had left twenty minutes before following a lot of food and a lot of conversation that didn't revolve around the crazy turn her life had taken recently.

It had been a great reminder of normalcy, but now she wanted to speak with Terak.

She hadn't seen him since the day of the orc battle. He said he would be gone for a few days to fulfill his responsibilities at home, then had flown away.

Should she call out, maybe wave her arms like she had done the first day?

Her reverie was interrupted by Terak dropping beside her.

"Terak!" she cried, her hand going over her heart. "You scared me!" That was what one called an understatement. These days a stray leaf was enough to get her jumping.

"My apologies," he replied, but that deep voice didn't quite convey that sentiment. He sounded far away, his mind and thoughts in another place and another conversation.

Leader of a Clan. She watched over one hundred students on a regular basis and sometimes she wanted to explode at the end of the day. To know a whole race depended on your every decision? She added a note of teasing to her voice, to let him know no harm done. "If my life keeps up at this pace, I'm going to have a heart attack by the time I'm thirty." She took a deep breath, trying to settle her racing pulse, when a thought struck. "Do gargoyles age like humans?"

He turned his attention to her, finally shaking off whatever shackles he arrived with. "Yes, our lifespans are quite similar."

She motioned to his wings. "But you guys have that cool healing power."

His brow bone arched above his right eye. No fair, even without eyebrows he could do the eyebrow arch. Why could she never manage that? "Cool?" And she might be wrong, but there sounded like a hint of tease underlining his words, the same tone he used after he had been healed.

She crossed her arms over her chest. "Are you asking me what it means, or are you questioning my choice of outdated slang?"

He mirrored her body language, though watching those massive arms stretch over his impressive chest made her heart pound in a way that had nothing to do with fright. "You are a teacher. Do you not know the new slang by listening to them?"

"No, kids only speak new slang when they don't want you to know what they're talking about. They use the classics around us old people." She motioned to his wing again before returning to her arms crossed position. "Healing factor?"

Instead of his usual almost smile she got the real thing, small and quick and unexpected and it wasn't until her lungs told her to bring in some oxygen that she remembered – breathing, it was a good thing. "I am glad you approve of it, though I do not think of it as cool, more as necessity. You need every advantage in battle."

She nodded. "Understood. I'm still going with cool."

"You do that." Damn, she really liked that teasing note in his voice. It was rusty, hesitant, and she held close the thought that it might be because he used it with no one else but her. He continued, "I have a gift for you."

"A gift?" Her inner seven-year-old was jumping up and down with excitement. "What did you get me? It wasn't necessary."

"This gift is practical, not celebratory, but as you requested it, I wished you to get it as soon as it was ready."

Into her hand he placed a small silver ball with an unknown script etched into the casing. "What's this?"

"A way to contact me. Hold it in your hands and think my name, and I will answer you."

"We'll be able to talk telepathically?" Wow, this was... this was... Yes, everything ran on magic these days – from cars to telephones – but in the city, people tried to minimize that as much as possible. They used magic only for the necessities, and they never used it in such a way that it was obvious magic was responsible for what was going on.

This was something she'd never had before. Pure magic, and a being who encouraged her to use it.

"Yes. No matter where I am in this world, I will hear your call, and I will answer."

Her fingers curled around the silver ball, so tight the mysterious script might have imprinted itself into her skin. "Thank you so much."

"Do not thank me. It is a selfish gift."

"Selfish?"

His midnight gaze locked with hers. "Now I will always be able to talk with you."

Didn't gargoyle men know you couldn't say that to a human woman? Not if you didn't want her to lose her ability to think and definitely not if you wanted to keep any kind of emotional distance.

Human men needed to explain the basics to him. A *How to Deal with Women* summit. Nothing would bond the races faster.

But this gift also meant another obligation on him, on top of the thousands of obligations he was answerable to every day of his life. And as amazing as this feeling was, she didn't want to experience it if all he received on his side was the look of burden he had arrived with tonight. Pulling herself away from his gaze, she motioned to the empty expanse of horizon before them. "It's a gorgeous night. Don't you get tired of watching over me? There must be other things you could be doing."

"Would you wish another to watch over you?"

Maybe it was her wishful thinking, but she could swear she heard the barest trace of hurt underlining the words. She put her hand over his forearm, an echo of what had happened with Olivia earlier tonight. "No, I'm glad it's you, I really am. I worry that if you keep up watching me, your people will suffer."

He didn't cover her hand with his, but he did lean close enough to her that they could share a breath. "I am gratified that you worry over my people, but they are able to function without my presence for this period of time."

"But not for long, not if you are a good leader. And I know you are a good leader."

He stepped even closer, and his wings half-closed around her, blocking her peripheral vision. "You do?"

"You have this way about you. I've seen it before." She bit her tongue to stop any more words from flowing out with what else she thought – that he was good and honorable and walked the edge of humorlessness in his determination to make every right decision. "Anyway, all I meant is that I know you make your people proud. You can't waste all your time watching over me."

"It is not a waste, little human. It could never be a waste. We have shed blood together, have shared secrets and held them honorably. You are my comrade in arms, and my friend. I would not have anything harm you."

Yes, she should request that summit immediately, because this night was turning her into a puddle of emotional goo.

His wings flared, and she held onto that to pull herself out of this emotional morass she was falling into. "Do you like flying?"

It took him a moment to orient himself to the new thread of conversation. "Like it? How do you mean?"

"Well, I guess flying for you is like running for humans, right?" After his nod, she continued. "Some humans hate running and will never do it. Some force themselves to do it, but there is no joy in the act. And some humans love to run. Which is it with you and flying?"

"I have never thought on it." His eyelids lowered, bringing his eyelashes into relief against his skin. No eyebrows, but yes to eyelashes. Hair on his head but none on his chest or arms. In this form, did he still have hair in his private regions?

The split second after that thought crossed her brain – *Damn you, Id!* – the most intense heat in the history of the blush raced over her skin, from her cheeks to her forehead and down her neck to the top of her chest.

His eyelids raised and his brows furrowed the moment he saw her face. "Are you well? You appear overheated."

"I'm fine, really hot all of a sudden." One hand pulled her hair away from her face while the other fanned away. "No worries. You were saying about flying?"

He glanced around to see if he could ascertain the cause of her reaction. Thank gods there was no way that could happen. Not finding anything, he turned back to her, answering her question. "There is a freedom in flying that I can find nowhere else. I am away from my obligations and only answerable to the elements."

"Sounds like you fall into the *love* category, then."

He considered some more before giving a final, decisive nod. "That is a fair way to put it. I cannot disagree."

She was going to ask. Worst that could happen, he would say no.

Best that could happen, he would say yes and she would be cradled against the large expanse of chest, breathing in the smell of newly cracked stone as she saw the world as he experienced it every day, his deep voice low, intimate breaths against her ear as he kept her close so his words weren't lost on the wind.

On second thought, maybe that was the worst that could happen.

She was going to ask anyway.

"Terak?"

It would take mere moments to reach over and cradle her heated cheek in his palm. His claws curled, eager to experience the feel of her warm flesh. A deeper blush than he had ever seen on her, apparent even in the dark of the moonlit night.

So appealing, his little human. She spoke words of duty to him, her certainty of his leadership flinging open passageways to deep caverns, shining light on hidden doubts and tenacious worries.

And after the comfort brought by her declaration, she immediately caused discomfort to throb through his body by the lift of her hair and the curve of her neck.

To follow that blush as far down as it goes, and then to go further...

Her eyes were luminous in the moonlight, a warmth even in the midst of the coldest night.

"Yes?"

"I-" She broke off, letting her arms down so her hair fell around her face. She licked her full lips, a nervous gesture he was growing familiar with, coming to loathe as he could not follow where that pink little tongue led. "Remember that first night?"

The first night? "Impossible to forget."

"True." Her smile held for long moments, not a product of nervousness but of fondness. While he thought on it with a certain amount of pleasure as well, he never dared hope she shared the sentiment. "That was the first time I ever flew."

"Not even in one of the human machines?" He could see no pleasure in flying if it was in one of those contraptions. Where was the pleasure without the wind on a face or the force of wings slicing through air? No, it would only be good as a means of transportation.

She shook her head. "No. My only family lives here, and my father said there was no reason to go elsewhere."

He had never thought to ask her, afterwards. Understandable. While at the end of that first night a cautious truce had been declared, she had been a far way from trusting him and he wished to make no mistakes that would change that. "Did you enjoy it?"

"That's the thing. There was so much going on, and I couldn't see beyond my own fear and then later my exhaustion. But I think I might under other circumstances." She reached out to touch his wing but caught herself, bringing her arm back with a jerk. "Would it be possible for us to go flying another time?"

To have her in his arms. To cuddle her generous body against his and have her arms wrapped around his neck, her warm breath rhythmic against his neck. "I would enjoy that very much."

"You would?" She let out a small, audible breath, and it was only now when she let it go he saw the nervousness interwoven throughout this entire conversation. "So would I."

So appealing... "Why not now?"

"Really?" She looked around, though what she thought she would see he did not know. "Are you sure it would be okay?"

He held out his hand. "Come, little human. Let me show you your city from above."

She stared at it for long moments, and as she looked, he began to see the appendage as it looked from her point of view. Did the sharp claws frighten her? Did the grey skin bring her distress?

She laid her small, soft hand in his and her gaze showed no distress when it met his, only excitement at this new adventure.

He came to stand in front of her, taking in those miraculous blue eyes. He bent to accommodate her smaller frame. "Wrap your arms around my neck," and the words were a rumble, coming out from part of him he dare not explore.

She was hesitant, her fingers first resting on his collarbone before moving over the planes of his shoulders to twine around the curve of his neck.

His arms snaked around her, one over the long curve of her torso to rest at the small of her back, the other curling under her lush thighs.

With a sharp exhale that had nothing to do with physical exertion, he brought her fully against him.

The movement brought their faces within a beat of space. Larissa's gaze darted to his mouth.

Terak flung himself from the building. He heard Larissa's sharp inhale as they plummeted and then her small, relieved gasp as the wind caught under his wings ringing in his ears.

He went as low as he dared over the city, but after a few moments she shook her head. "I have no desire to see the city, so don't tempt fate over being caught. I want to fly."

As though to emphasize her words she nestled her head into the valley between his neck and shoulder, a placement that would give her limited visibility but allowed him the full experience of her body against his.

He took her outside of the city. He flew high, the chill in the air biting into even his skin. He went low, where there was the chance of feeling the scrape of foliage.

She egged him on with her sounds and her sighs. She laughed and she screeched, and at one point she stretched her neck out and tilted her head, her hair a banner behind them.

"I can see why you love this. I do, too."

The pleasure from those words was out of proportion to their importance.

She leaned up, her eyes on the sky. "Gods, look at that sky. It's amazing. You can't see a sky like that in the city."

"Why have you never traveled outside?"

She was quiet, her exhale forceful. Finally, she said, "Dad never had much use for the New Realms, but I could never blame him for that. My mom died in the Great Collision."

"I am sorry."

"I..." she exhaled, and from her weighted pause he knew this was the part that was hardest for her to share. "She died giving birth to me. There were complications during the birth, and in the chaos after the collision the hospital was overwhelmed. Probably any other day she would have survived, but I chose to make my appearance in the world right then."

She looked up at the sky again, and her eyes held a sheen that told of tears. The burden she carried was palpable, the blame she accepted immutable and undeserved. There would be future days to tell her this guilt was misplaced, but now was the time to be quiet and listen to her story.

"Dad never blamed me," she said, looking up at him with the defense of her father. "He never spoke about it much, except to say how much Mom loved me, and he knew she was happy, because she finally got her little girl. When I turned twelve I tried to combine my birthday with a memorial for her. Dad wouldn't have it. He said there were other days and other ways to show we loved and honored Mom. My birthday was a celebration that I'd been brought into this world."

"Your father is a good man."

"My dad's the best." Her eyes shone with pride. "My whole family is. I couldn't have had better if I had been able to order them to my specifications. Well, except for the over-protectiveness."

"Overprotective? Your father makes my Clan look permissive by comparison."

She laughed. "You got that right. It's probably one of the reasons I came to enjoy history so much – I got to investigate actions and ask questions and actually have them answered." She took another deep breath, her mouth turning inward. "I can't blame my dad too much, though. He was a cop during the Great Collision. Now that I'm older and realize how horrible the first few months were, and then the uncertainty the following couple years... I can't blame him. He did his best to care for and protect us while the world was going crazy and had taken his wife away from him."

"That is all any of us can do, they best we can under the circumstances we are given."

She nodded. Her fingers were curling themselves in his hair. The unconscious stroking soothed him, the intimacy of the act yet another chain binding him to her. "What about your parents? What were they like?"

The air shifted around him, its currents disturbed. He tightened his grip on her, pulling her close, so close her face smashed into his neck. "Terak, what's wrong?"

From the left it whizzed by them, clipping his wing enough to throw him to the side until he righted himself.

"Terak?" and all pleasure was gone from her tone.

It came down from above several yards in front of him, far enough away that he could pull himself short and hover there, his wings flapping to keep them steady in the air.

A small human woman, with Asian features and hair such a blinding color of blue it hurt his eyes. "Boo."

CHAPTER EIGHTEEN

"Like I said, romantic. Can I call them or what?"

They landed some twenty feet away from the waiting group in a cleared section of woodland, far outside the city limits. It was Fallon who had called out to them, that giant sword strapped to her back, with the same combo of black leather-ish clothes, though this time she wore a coat that fell to the ground. Laire was standing to the right of the swordswoman, her outfit tonight a neon-blue ode-to-naughty Alice in Wonderland ensemble, full of lace and Victorian trappings, but if she bent over, Larissa was sure any underwear would be exposed to the world.

If she wore underwear.

Shaking off *that* thought, Larissa turned her attention to the third and final member of the gang. Her breath hitched as she beheld the newest woman, the same wonderment she experienced moments ago as she flew in Terak's arms spreading through her now.

This woman's height was average, but nothing else about her could be described that way. Her pale blue eyes glowed against the light tan of her skin and her long silky hair was so black it had a blue sheen in the moonlight. Her face had an appealing pixie-ish quality, but Larissa could tell nothing about her body, which was hidden underneath a long brown cloak.

A gust of wind ruffled her hair, giving a glimpse of a long neck, delicate jaw, and pointed ears.

Pointed ears. "You're an elf, aren't you?"

The woman inclined her head. "I am Aislynn." Her voice held the clear luster of ringing bells.

Being in front of an elf must not have had the same sense of awe for Terak, if his clenched jaw and the tight lines of his body were anything to go by. He said, "What is it you wish, Dragon Slayer?"

Dragon Slayer. In reaction to his words Fallon held herself even straighter. Why would he call her Dragon Slayer?

Fallon said, "I make no move against you or yours, Clan Leader of the Gargoyles, but I wish to talk to this woman. She is a human who lives in the city, and thus is under my protection."

"I saved her. Therefore, she is mine." Terak's voice pitched low while his clawed hands flexed, and while it held warning for the women in front of them, for Larissa it sparked a heat that spiraled through her torso and down the length of her body.

"Is that so? Shall we take it before the Seven Houses to hear their verdict?"

Terak held himself still, but his anger was palpable. "Beware casting your fate in that direction. Do not think my Clan powerless."

Enough of this. Whether this was jockeying for some kind of position or they really thought they could argue about her as if she was a lost pet, it was over now. "Don't talk about me as if I'm not even here," Larissa said, meeting the eyes of each of the women before turning a quick glance toward Terak. "I'll decide who I'm going to talk with and when, and flying out of nowhere and then hitting us with these intimidation tactics isn't going to endear you to me."

Aislynn came forward, bowing slightly. "Forgive Fallon. She is so single-minded she forgets to show any manners."

"Hey!"

Aislynn continued, not sparing the swordswoman as much as a glance. "We have not detained you for any fight-"

"Speak for yourself, Ais."

Aislynn rolled her eyes heavenward but showed no other sign that she heard Fallon behind her. "-But we must ask you questions. The appearance of the orcs signals an escalation. We must discover the reason behind this."

How had they connected her? Was this a shot in the dark? "I don't know what you're talking about."

Fallon started looking around her, quick movements of her head in all directions. Laire was watching her teammate with a puzzled expression on her face. "What are you doing?"

"Looking for a brick wall to hit my head against. I'm sure I'd have more luck with it than with her. You know, Teach, you might want to stop and think for a moment. Do you really believe Terak is the only one watching you now? How do you think we were able to plan this little get together?"

Oh gods, why hadn't she thought about that before? These people knew everything about her. Why wouldn't they also be watching her? She had been so focused on Terak...

A warm, calloused palm met hers, and Terak's large hand squeezed, snapping her out of her daze. She raised her face to his. His dark eyes reassured her.

She squeezed back, and was rewarded with that almost smile.

Aislynn took another step forward and spoke not to Larissa, but to Terak. "Clan Leader of the Gargoyles, while we may not be allies, we are not enemies. Our goal is a common one, to protect this woman. Everything we have done has been with that purpose."

"And how would you do this?" Terak inquired of the elf, his voice stilted but no longer furious. "You have not protected her thus far."

"We have tried. We would have protected her had you not that first night." Terak tilted his head as if acknowledging the elf's words, but didn't speak himself. Aislynn continued, "We ask to be brought into your confidence. We may have information that you do not, as you may also have information unknown to us. We wish to protect this woman. We wish to protect the Realms. We wish to defeat the necromancers. Surely these commonalities outweigh our differences."

A play of emotions crossed Terak's face as he kept his gaze steady on Aislynn. Larissa wasn't sure what she thought about what was being proposed, but there was no doubt in her mind that the elf had been brought here as the peacemaker and dealmaker. The other two women deferred to her, keeping silent as she talked to Terak. Larissa would place money that wasn't a common occurrence.

Decision sharpened Terak's expression, and he looked not at the elf, but at Fallon. "And which of these goals is your priority?"

Fallon's head tilted, assessing Terak. "Why do you ask? Isn't it enough they are goals we share?"

"No." Terak's baritone was laced with finality. "Only when there is no conflict can there be truce. We are not the same, Dragon Slayer. Even if you could bring yourself to lie and tell me otherwise, we both know the truth."

What was he talking about? But even before the echo of the words faded Laire's expression turned serious in a way Larissa never would have believed possible. She reached out her arms in front of her, fingers splayed wide, and with a quick movement flung her arms out to the side.

Around them dozens of floating spheres appeared, bright white with a core of black through the middle. Laire clenched her hands into quick fists, and the spheres exploded in balls of flame. "We need to leave," Laire said, but before she could be made, she jerked and fell forward as if someone punched her in the stomach, though no one was near.

Fallon was at her side in two quick steps, grabbing the mage's arm and helping her straighten. "What's happening?"

A howl sounded, far away, and then a legion of answering howls, growls and almost-human screams of such menace that Larissa's blood turned to sludge and flowed through her veins, weighing down her limbs and making fleeing impossible. Terak wrapped his arms around her, bending to speak into her ear. "Calm, little human. I will protect you. Have I failed you yet?"

No. No, never.

My sword and my shield.

She wrapped her arms around him, returning the embrace. "Sorry about the momentary freak out. I'm good now."

From behind her Fallon's voice ground out, "Laire, what's going on?"

With a final squeeze, Larissa let go of Terak and turned back to the group of women. They were standing in a close circle. Laire looked recovered from whatever had attacked her. "Someone was watching her," she said, nodding toward Larissa. "When I destroyed their little spies, they must have decided to send something after us."

"Let's get out of here."

Laire shook her head, looking up to the sky. "Magic barrier, which means they have a mage and there is no flying out of here."

Fallon turned to the elf. "Ais-"

Before Fallon could finish, Aislynn ran past them toward a large outcropping of rocks, jumping onto the largest of them with a grace and an athleticism no human could ever match. She peered into the dark, the full moon only giving a little help in illuminating their surroundings. Within seconds she called down, "Direwolves, ridden by goblins. We have a battalion of them coming fast. I see bows, so expect to become target practice."

"Ais, a volley as soon as they're in range." Aislynn must have been expecting this order, because even before Fallon stopped talking she threw her cloak off, revealing a bow and a quiver of arrows. She grabbed the bow and an arrow, putting them together and getting into a firing position, all with such speed that Larissa couldn't tell what was happening as it occurred, only filling in the blanks once Aislynn was still and prepared for battle.

Fallon turned to Laire. "Why didn't they arrive closer to us? Why that far away?"

Laire twirled a finger around a curl of blue hair. "Don't know. It would be impossible to teleport that many with pinpoint accuracy, but they should have gotten closer than what they are."

"Maybe there is something wrong with their mage, or maybe they only have a wizard. Any feel on what we're dealing with?"

Laire's eyes...*swirled*. There was no other word to explain it. Her eyes lost color and iris and became a violent mass of movement. "Defensive magic specialist. And yes, only a wizard. Male. And young. Each of them has a personal shield spell, so Ais's arrows won't do jack and damage will be minimal until it's dispelled." Her lips tightened, hard anger on her face. "Who do they think I am, sending a pansy-ass like that against me?"

Fallon patted Laire's shoulder, a *there-there* motion. "I don't think they knew we'd be waiting when they prepared this trap. But for you, we'll send his head back to them with a note to not insult you again. Does that make you feel better?"

Laire gave a long, theatrical sigh. "I don't know, maybe."

"Think on it." Fallon turned, the full weight of her gaze back on Larissa. "We have a battalion of direwolves – and a wizard – running around the exact area you are in. Care to reassess that whole *I don't know what you're talking about* line of crap?"

They deserved something. She wasn't sure of their exact motives and didn't fully trust them, but they were about to fight to save her life. "I don't know why they are after me. If I ever find out I will tell you, but right now I do not know."

Fallon's one eyebrow arched, the swift look of surprise crossing her face before it morphed into a speculative cast. She turned to Laire, who shrugged and said, "I believe her."

"Hell of it is, I believe her too." Fallon drew a deep breath. "We found the ward that allowed the orcs and zombies to get in. It was set by a powerful wizard who has since disappeared. He was thought to be above reproach, so the standard triple-check wasn't done. Of course, that doesn't explain how *you've* gotten into the city," Fallon finished, giving Terak a pointed glare.

"No, it doesn't," he agreed, and said nothing more.

Fallon unsheathed her massive sword, a faint glow coming from under her coat, no doubt that same scrolling that Larissa beheld that first night. "Well Gargoyle, do we fight each other, or do we fight what is coming to meet us?"

"This night I will fight at your side." Terak turned to Larissa. "Stay near the mage. She will protect you."

He was a great warrior. She had seen it herself. That didn't change this hollow ache inside her. It was unnecessary, but she had to say it. She had to know she said it, a charm that would protect him. It had to. "Terak, be careful."

"I will be." He gently pushed her toward Laire, holding the mage's attention with a hard glare. "If she dies, Battle Mage, until my last breath, I will dedicate every moment of my life to the destruction of your world."

For once, Laire was not the smartass Larissa expected. Giving a perfect bow, she answered, "I will protect her, Clan Leader of the Gargoyles."

Fallon broke in. "Now that we got the mushy stuff out of the way, let's go meet us some goblins." She turned to Laire. "Shield Larissa. Don't worry about the rest of us. Break the wizard so we can cut through the army."

"Understood," said Laire. She grabbed Larissa's hand, bringing her over to a nearby wall. "Sit on that stone wall. I'm putting a barrier around you."

"A barrier?"

"A magic shield. It will keep the bad guys out."

Larissa sat. The Asian woman made a motion as if she were clutching a ball in her hands, then pushed out toward Larissa.

Nothing happened. Larissa looked around her, but nothing was different. "Is it working?"

Laire yelled out, "Aislynn, help me here."

The elf turned and shot an arrow right at Larissa, the point heading straight for her forehead. It came closer and closer and-

And it stopped dead, falling to the ground several feet away, as if it had bumped into something solid.

"There's your proof," Laire said. "So don't do anything stupid like try to run out. It wouldn't work anyway, you'd only hit the barrier, but those things hurt like hell if you run into them full speed."

"I won't."

"They're in range!" Aislynn started firing arrows again, this time at the upcoming army. They were still far enough away that they looked like little more than black dots in the distance, but the elf called out, "Laire was right about the shield spell, the arrows are bouncing. Laire, you need to do something."

"Working on it," called out Laire. What it looked like she was doing was working on her statue-mimicry skills. She stood stock still, her hand held out toward the open field with her thumb perpendicular to the ground and her first and middle finger curled above it, the other two fingers pressed against her palm.

Her body might have been still, but sweat was beading on the skin of her forehead and neck, the same way it would for most people who were in the middle of intense physical exertion.

"How long?" Fallon asked.

"Don't know. He's good."

Fallon smirked. "Are you saying some pansy-ass is getting the best of our mage?"

"Instead of flirting with me, why don't you swing your little sword and hit a couple of them? Just because they have a shield over them doesn't mean they would like it if they were batted around like a baseball."

"Good idea." Fallon turned to Terak. "You might not be able to fly up high, Gargoyle. Doesn't mean you can't fly at all, and a shield won't prevent them from being picked up and thrown from their mounts."

Terak looked back at Larissa. She smiled at him, with what she hoped was a reassuring smile. "You saw the arrow bounce. Out of everyone here, I'm the safest. If you think meeting them is the best way to end this, you need to leave me here."

He nodded. "I will make this as quick as possible."

"I know."

Terak's wings snapped out to their full wingspan. He ran a few steps then took off into the air, his battle cry quieting the wolves coming toward them and even Fallon looked a little in awe as she said, "That's impressive."

They were arriving fast, what only moments before looked like black dots were now fully formed silhouettes of small creatures riding atop vicious-looking canines.

Terak reached the army. Some must have seen him coming, because she heard the ping of fired arrows at him. He didn't react as if he had been hit, but in the past no matter how beaten up he was he never stopped fighting. He swooped down, grabbing some of the creatures and lifting them into the air. He flew high and dropped them down. Once they hit the ground, they didn't get back up.

Fallon was right. Whatever shielding was on them wasn't helping against Terak.

Arrows were flying at them now. Aislynn hid in cracks in the stone outcropping, while Fallon stepped in front of Laire and drove her sword into the ground. "Tenro, *shield*," whispered the swordswoman, and the sword glowed. The volley of arrows that should have hit her and the mage instead disappeared into the light emitted by the sword.

Laire never moved a muscle throughout any of this.

Terak was swooping in and out of the army, grabbing as he did. The goblins waved their swords at him, but he never stopped.

The direwolves were closing in fast, close enough now that the moonlight glinted off rows of teeth a shark would be jealous of. Fallon pulled her sword out of the ground and started toward the incoming army, her movements fast but deliberate, her sword out straight at her side.

Laire yelled out, "Aislynn, fifty degrees, eye level, four-hundred feet. On my mark!"

Aislynn got into firing stance, holding still despite the arrows falling around her.

"Now!"

Aislynn fired, the arrow disappearing within the army.

"You got him!" Laire yelled, glee in her voice. "Rock on!"

Aislynn began to fire into the throng. Wolves howled in pain and fell to the side, knocking over those closest to them and causing chain reactions of wolves and goblins falling atop each other.

The voices of the goblins rose, words indistinct but confusion and panic clear in the sound. Laire brought her hands together and flung them out, and a ball of fire fifteen feet in diameter hurled through the air and smashed into the advancing creatures.

Screams rent the air, burnt flesh and ash swirling in the currents and reaching Larissa even through the barrier.

"Laire, how much spell power do you have left?" Aislynn asked, still firing arrows into the fray.

"Not much. I wanted to make sure the wizard was out of the equation for good."

"Then keep it in reserve. We'll be okay without it."

How much. That's right, wizards and mages could only do so much magic a day, the strength of the caster being the deciding factor on how much they cast and how strong those spells would be. Larissa looked over towards the Asian woman. So Laire either wasn't very strong or this was the end of a very busy day for her.

Fallon had arrived in front of the advancing direwolves. The animals snarled and hurled themselves at her, as if they were delighted they finally had an enemy in front of them to tear into.

She swung her sword and cut through a half dozen of them, their blood flying through the sky in splatters as thick as paint. She whirled, the battle becoming a dance, the wolves and the goblins her partners in a death waltz.

The three warriors were swift and sure, their movements as choreographed as any on stage. They weaved and they jumped, making graceful arcs with their bodies and their weapons.

The bodies of the dead were piling up, lying across the once-empty landscape. Thank gods it was dark enough that the small details were not visible, like the pools of blood and the strewn body parts such a display must leave behind.

Finally, few enough of the army remained that Terak landed, battling now with claws and wings. A direwolf lunged for him, but Terak tore through the creature's throat, slicing through it with his claws. The goblin riding on it tried to stab Terak, but he grabbed the sword with his other hand, impaling the goblin on its own blade.

The mad rush was now over and those remaining were more precise, taking their time and studying Terak and Fallon.

Terak's wings flared, his clawed hands coming up before him, blood dripping from the ends. "You think you can come here and take what is *mine*? Go now, go and tell your masters that the woman is under my protection. Tell them that no one will ever touch her, and anyone who comes. Against. Me. Will. *Die!*"

He was a god of vengeance, a demon arising from the night to destroy everything in his path. The direwolves bent before his final roar, their heads dropping and their ears flattening against their heads. The goblins cowered as well. A handful turned away at that point, racing back into the night.

"Cowards. Like the necromancers aren't going to kill them for failing." Aislynn's approach was silent and Larissa jumped when she heard the voice. "Laire, drop the shield. It's over."

The mage did as requested, and the elf came to sit on the wall beside Larissa.

Laire came back as well, sitting on Larissa's other side. "Aren't you two going to help finish this?" Larissa asked.

"What, and mess up my hair?" Laire's hand went to plump up her ringlets. "Heck no. Besides, Fallon loves this shit."

Larissa's attention went to Terak first, but he had finished with the creatures near him. She turned to Fallon to see the woman bring her sword on an upstroke and slice both a direwolf and the goblin riding it in two.

There was something amazing watching Fallon wield her sword, the arc of metal and the sureness of movement the woman displayed, slicing through her enemies without pause. A brutal, bloody beauty. As if she read Larissa's mind – and who knew, maybe she did – Laire sighed in admiration. "Watching that woman, it's like *damn*."

Aislynn nodded in agreement.

One final move, one final death of an enemy at her hands, and Fallon landed on the ground before them, her hand and one knee resting on soil, her sword held high in the air, surrounded by the dead. She rose, slow and sure, a goddess of war demanding her beaten, ravaged due, leaving no space untouched with her eyes as she circled and surveyed the battlefield.

Satisfied with what she saw, Fallon turned to the three of them sitting on the wall. "And that is how you do it! You may bow before me now, peons."

To Aislynn and Larissa, Laire said, "And then she opens her mouth, and all wonderment vanishes."

Aislynn nodded in agreement.

CHAPTER NINETEEN

"Are you ashamed that you're with me?"

They were in her home now, and these were the first words Larissa had spoken since the end of battle. After their enemy was defeated, Terak had gathered her close and flew away, not giving the Guild members time to respond. She said nothing and cuddled close, burying herself in his arms.

"What?" Why would she ever think that?

She shrugged, the movement jerky, her shoulder half-hunched inward. "I'm useless. I sit on a wall surrounded by a magic barrier while Aislynn fires an arrow a second and Fallon slices through an army."

He despised the beaten note that threaded her voice. "I would never be ashamed to be at your side. And you must stop comparing yourself to them. The world needs its warriors and it needs its peacemakers. You have experienced too much war these last weeks. It has you questioning your worth." Why did the one woman he wished to keep far away from the brutal reality of this world find herself always buried in yet another battle?

Larissa unfurled her body and looked at him. Instead of fear or loathing clouding her gaze, he saw warmth.

Thankfulness.

Admiration.

"I know you're right. No one can be all things." She shrugged, her mouth flattening. "I never cared about fighting or... any of that. When I was a kid, I never wanted to play cops and robbers, though it was the only game my brothers *would* play. Too violent and I didn't like all the fighting. I just wanted to read."

"So you didn't play with your siblings?" That didn't seem to fit with the closeness he had witnessed between the siblings.

"Oh no, they forced me to play. They always made me the robber and would cuff me, though Dad said never to play with his handcuffs. Joke was on them, though." She lifted her arm until her hand was in his line of vision and rotated her wrists. "Double-jointed. No matter how tight they made the cuffs, I could get out. Made them so mad."

Her fondness for her siblings banished the last lingering traces of any self-doubt. Her eyes brightened with memory and glee before she banked both, her gaze now holding a question. "Back to tonight. You called Fallon *Dragon Slayer*. What did you mean by that?"

"Her sword, Tenro, is a sacred weapon and known as the Slayer of Dragons."

"But I thought dragons didn't exist – never existed – even in the Magic Realm." His face must have betrayed his feelings because Larissa's own eyebrows drew together and she asked in a hesitant voice, "Did they?"

"I have never seen any true record of their existence," he conceded, letting the full weight of his misgivings play into his tone.

Her face still held the same hesitance. "But…?"

"But I cannot forget something my father once said. He said with all the terrible creatures we have that are real, why would anyone create the myth of the dragon? And if dragons are even half as powerful as they are portrayed, would it be any true test for them to disappear without a trace if they so wished?" Though he could only hope his father was wrong, and that dragons never existed, or if they did, they would stay far gone.

"What are the Seven Houses?"

It took a beat of time to follow the change in topic. "Where did you hear that?"

"When Fallon started threatening you. She asked if she should let the Seven Houses sort it out."

"Ah." Now he remembered. "They are connected to the New Realms."

Larissa's gaze went unfocused. "I remember when I was little and first heard the term *New Realms*. I thought that to get to those places, you needed to go through some magical door. For a long time, I opened every closet door in every house I entered." Her gaze sharpened again as she came back to the present. "I was so disappointed when I found out it was just a term for the governments and lands of the different races. What's the importance of the Seven Houses? I'm positive I've never heard that name before."

"They are a shadow council which wields much power in the New Realms. They deal with matters outside the purview of any single race."

"Any humans on this council?"

"Yes, one, though I do not know her name or status within the human world. The leader of the Guild is another member."

"The Guild have their hands in lots of places, don't they?" Larissa asked, though her tone made clear the question was rhetorical. She continued with barely a pause. "Why have this council? I thought the various races all kept their own ways of government, just as the human governments remained as they were from before the Great Collision."

"The Seven Houses have always existed. When you have a threat such as the necromancers, you must have a governing body that can answer that threat."

"And the gods? The Oracle? Where do they fit into this?"

"They are all powerful beings outside of all. They have their own agendas, would that we knew them. Never doubt that there are always deeper powers and deeper secrets at play."

She wrinkled her nose, and he stifled the urge to lean down and nuzzle it with his own. "Have I ever mentioned I hate cloak-and-dagger stuff? I don't even watch spy movies on TV."

"I am sorry this has been brought into your life."

She looked at him again, and to his surprise a brilliant smile dominated her face. "Have I ever told you that our dates have been some of the most exciting and eventful of my life?"

"Dates?" he asked. While not a custom gargoyles engaged in, he did know the meaning of the word. What she meant by that phrase interested him.

When hearing the word repeated to her, Larissa's cheeks went scarlet. Ducking her head, she said, "I was kidding, being humorous. Trying to lighten things up."

She was curled against him in her attempt to not be seen, her soft warmth a balm after the fierce battle. He could offer her nothing less and met her attempts at normalcy with his own. "I was thinking on how our next date could go. Maybe we should fight a cave troll."

She looked up at him. Her face was still red, but her eyes shone with laughter. "Only a cave troll? I demand that we go to the top and meet a necromancer."

Terak shook his head. "I am afraid that is too advanced for you. I'm willing to show you a wraith, but no more than that."

She was smiling, and... Terak stopped.

He was smiling.

He was smiling and laughing and teasing the woman in his arms.

What's more, he hadn't put her down. They had been in her apartment for fully five minutes, and never had he the desire to let her go.

"Terak, what's wrong?"

What could he say?

I would give everything to you if you always look at me with those eyes.

A *thwup* sounded on the balcony, and Terak turned to face their intruder. Valry stood there, her gaze held by how he cradled Larissa against him.

Anger surged through him, anger at the interruption, and anger at the reminder of his responsibilities. "Valry, what is the meaning of this?"

She strolled in, undaunted and unstoppable. "We were alerted to the battle tonight. When I heard of it, I had to make sure you were unhurt."

"You were told never to come here."

"My need to know my Intended was safe overrode all other concerns."

"*Intended?*" Larissa's voice cut through the words Terak was about to speak. He looked down at her, still cradled in his arms. Her eyebrows drew close together, and there was a shadowing, a hesitance in her eyes that he had not seen since the first night they had met. "What does that mean, *Intended?*"

Valry's voice was quick, malicious. "I believe you humans call it an engagement. Lord Terak and I are to be mated."

Larissa's eyes were wide and round and hurt. "You're going to marry her?"

Terak began to shake his head, and it took force of will to stop the movement.

Larissa started to look around. "I feel much better now. You can let me down."

In reaction to her words his fingers gripped harder, disobeying the command from his brain to follow her order. He forced himself to let her go.

She continued, not meeting his eyes. "Once again I seem to owe you my life. Thank you for saving me. But I'm very tired right now. Would you please excuse me?" She turned and walked into her bedroom, closing the door behind her without a backwards glance.

Terak left, leaving Valry to follow him. He did not wish to bring her to the perch he had spent so many nights watching over Larissa, so instead he brought her to another, further away but still with a view of his little human's abode.

He wasted no time after they had landed. "Why did you say such a thing?"

"Why would I not? She asked a question and I answered it honest. Why are you upset she knows you are promised to another?"

"Part of protection is having her comfortable with me. I do not wish her to feel uncomfortable."

Valry studied him, a hard look in her eyes. "Why would she care about our customs?"

He would not let himself be baited. "It matters not. You have defied my wishes, the wishes of your *Mennak*."

Her claws ripped through the air in fury, her mouth in a snarl. "I am talking as your future mate! Why is she allowed more liberty with you than the female who will bear your young?"

"I am your lord first, your mate second, always."

"And would you say the same to your human, Terak?" Her tone was disgusted, filled with her contempt of anything that was not gargoyle.

...which of these goals is your priority?

My priority will forever be her.

A human whom his Clan would never accept.

He must bring the Clan together. They were too fractured now, stresses from both within and without crushing them.

To be a leader meant sacrifice. His sacrifice was staring at him with hard eyes.

No, his sacrifice lay on soft blue sheets within blue walls with a halo of gold always surrounding her.

The anger left him. Weariness, bone-deep and aging, settled in. He looked at Valry, and whatever she saw had her reeling back. "We will be mated, Valry. You will bear my young and stand by my side. But never forget this – I mate you only out of duty. You knew this from the first as I never hid my motives, and you accepted them. So do not now or ever pretend to be an injured party, and never ask again which has the most importance to me. The answer will always be the Clan. Now, do you wish to be released from our Intention?"

She shook her head, mute before him.

"Return to the keep. Never come here again."

She left without a word, and once she was out of sight Terak flew to his usual spot. As he watched over his little human he allowed himself one brief moment never to be repeated, a moment to imagine a life without sacrifice.

Why was she so shocked that Terak was engaged?

Larissa rolled over onto her side. Though only moments before she willed her eyes not to look at the time, the little buggers betrayed her. *2:43*.

Terak was going to be married.

Larissa flung the covers aside and sat up. Screw this. If she was going to be up, she was going to watch a movie and eat some ice cream.

She strode into the living room and picked up the remote.

Click.

And then she remembered her television was on the fritz.

The remote fell from her hand and she collapsed back in the couch with a heavy sigh. With all the commotion of the last few weeks, getting a wizard out here to recalibrate it had been nowhere on her list of priorities.

Now she had no television and no ice cream. Sure, she could go to the refrigerator and eat the ice cream, but then she wouldn't be a woman who was eating ice cream because she wanted a snack with her late time viewing.

No, she would then be a woman who was eating ice cream after hearing a guy she knew had a girlfriend.

No, make that an Intended.

Larissa rubbed the back of her neck, trying to ease the tense muscles she found there.

Why the hell would she be upset over this?

She took a deep breath, a slow and forceful inhalation to expand her lungs and clear out the cobwebs.

Okay, she had gotten used to having Terak around and had some proprietary feelings where he was concerned. He'd saved her several times over, so it was understandable and natural. Anybody would react the same.

And tonight, he had stood between her and an army, a warrior whom demons bowed before, and said *mine*.

The shiver raced up her spine at the memory. It was said on a harsh growl, claws and blood entwined in his promise. Only death awaited anyone who challenged him.

Mine.

She owed him her life. She owed him so much.

Mine.

That was it. It was gratitude mixed with shock and the closeness you can only feel with someone when you have faced death with them.

There was nothing else to this insomnia.
She'd feel better tomorrow.
And she'd call the repairman.

CHAPTER TWENTY

The ringing phone awoke Larissa. Even as she reached for the phone she looked at the time. *4:59.* If someone wasn't dead, they were going to be. "Hello?"

"Sweetie." Olivia's voice was soft on the other end. "You have to wake up."

"Says who? What's going on, Olivia?"

"The person who I said might help? He wants to see you, and he wants to do it now. I'll pick you up in twenty minutes."

Olivia's words wound through Larissa's mind three times before she realized the implication. "I'll be ready – wait, Olivia," she said before the other woman could hang up.

"What?"

"People are watching me."

"My friend already assumed that. I've got it covered. Just be waiting in the lobby."

"I'll be there," said Larissa, hanging up the phone even as she went to her bureau for shirt and pants.

Gods, it would be so good to get some answers. If she knew the why, maybe Terak...

Terak.

His name brought her up short. What should she do? Who knew if he was guarding her? Maybe he left with his *In-ten-ded.*

She winced. Who knew her subconscious could be so bitchy?

Larissa sat down on the bed, wasting time she didn't have but needing a minute. If she had gotten two hours of sleep she was lucky, and even that short time was filled with unremembered but unsettling dreams, the type that sour your mood the next day even when you can't remember a single detail about them.

This needed to be put to rest inside her, fast. She didn't have the luxury of acting all junior high school, pouting because the boy she liked didn't like her back and taking it out on the world.

She liked Terak.

There. She admitted it. Damned junior high.

Maybe more than like, or within easy distance of that thought. But even if he didn't have an Intended – not like that was a small issue – they still could never be together. He was a leader who was dragging his Clan into this new world and dealing with the consequences of those actions. And she was a human who once this was finished would go back to teaching kids and pretending everything outside the city gates didn't exist.

Right?

No.

No. It was loud and clear and certain. No, she wouldn't be going back to that life.

She could picture clear as day the look on her dad's face as he worried over Michael, the only child who had ever left the nest.

Larissa loved her father, but for the first time, the thought of that look wasn't enough to have her backing down.

No, when this was over, it was time to explore this world, to learn all the things she wanted to learn but denied herself out of the fear of hurting her father. It was time to make her place. It was time to cut the strings and leave the nest. She fooled herself in thinking moving out of the house was the only step she needed to take to make that happen, but she wouldn't make that mistake again.

A lightness hollowed out her chest, and she couldn't breathe deep enough to fill it. Tears and laughter were threatening in equal measure, and it would be really nice if her mind would choose a more appropriate time to make known these little revelations. She had ten minutes before she had to leave to meet someone who might know what's going on.

Which brought her back to Terak.

And any more revelations would be for later. Right now, she would leave it at she needed him near and by her side. He was the only one she could trust.

Dressed, teeth and hair brushed, shoes on with five minutes to spare, she went out to the balcony, waving her arms and jumping up and down. If he wasn't near the silver ball was stashed in her pocket and she'd call him on the road.

Within moments Terak landed in front of her. Relief and a whole slew of emotions she threw into her mental lockbox ran through her. "You're here."

"Where else would I be?"

"I have some news. My friend Olivia knows someone she thinks might be able to help us. She called me and is on her way here to pick me up."

Terak stilled, his claws flexing at this unexpected piece of news. Damn, she should have told him about this possibility earlier, but so much had happened and she forgot all about it. "Who is she taking you to see?"

Larissa shook her head. "I have no clue. Olivia wouldn't say, but from what I gather he is a difficult man to talk to. He's in hiding from something, I don't know what."

Terak was already shaking his head. "I do not like this. I do not want you going to an unknown."

She wasn't thrilled about the thought either. She was still shaky from earlier – both of the night's surprises. There was nothing to be done though. "In this case, I don't think we have a choice. The chance to learn something supersedes the fact we're flying blind."

Terak snarled, but Larissa paid it no mind. It was aimed at the situation, not her. "This Olivia, you are sure she is trustworthy?"

Talk about echoes in conversation. Larissa could only answer the same way she had earlier. "Yes, I'm sure. Of course, I don't know him so I'm not trusting him. That's why I want you to come with me."

Surprise crossed his features. "You are not going to fight me on this?"

"Remember when I told you I'm not stupid and won't go into situations alone I have no business in to try to prove something? This is what we call a case in point. But you can't come as a gargoyle. You are going to need to switch into human form." Terak's mouth tightened and his tail twitched. Time for some charm. "You can protect me, I know you can, no matter what form you wear. And you can switch if it becomes necessary. But like you said, we're walking into an unknown, and they don't need to know I have a gargoyle watching over me. The less information we give them the better. So please, trust me?"

In his human form, Terak rode in the backseat of the car as it traveled outside of the city limits. Larissa was at his side and her friend Olivia drove the vehicle. Olivia kept glancing at him via the rearview mirror, but didn't say anything about the man who had unexpectedly joined them.

He wore a shirt that belonged to one of Larissa's brothers. It was small, but not so much that he could not move in it. He wished that one of her brothers had left their human weapons at her home. He flexed his hand, despising the flimsy fingernails where claws should be. Yes, he could change, but what if those moments were the ones that decided Larissa's fate?

They stopped in front of a large building, no decoration on the outside and no other buildings around it. It was a unique location, giving the impression of being completely insular, but in reality only minutes away from the bustle of the outer metropolis.

Upon entering, Larissa exclaimed, "I was not expecting this from the outside."

He believed humans called this a "bar", a gathering place for celebrations. But even without personal experience, he could see this was a place the very powerful and important would inhabit. Everything gleamed in rich tones and sumptuous fabrics, and one could almost feel the wealth that had gone into creating it.

"Right on time."

Terak zeroed in on the voice that came from a door on the side. It was a human adult male, but he stood no taller than a youngling who had not yet reached majority. His brown hair hung in a careless fashion around his face, but his green eyes did not project carelessness – they were lit with intelligence and an edge that Terak ground his teeth against, and he fought his instinct to step closer to Larissa. He would give away nothing to this man.

Olivia motioned between everyone. "Rhaum, this is my friend Larissa and her friend, Terak."

Rhaum's eyes flickered between them. "Pleasure to meet you both."

"Where is Simon?"

Rhaum answered Olivia's question with a movement of his head, motioning to stairs across from them.

"Thanks," said Olivia. Turning to them, she said, "Let's go."

Terak's impression of wealth only intensified as they walked up the stairs and toward a hidden room in the corner. This was an important place, and that man – Rhaum – was not one to be disregarded.

Olivia reached the door first, opening it and going inside. When Larissa made to follow, Terak held her back, placing her behind him. Her mouth tightened but she did not gainsay him.

He edged in by only scant inches, enough to take in the room and the lone male inhabitant.

"What trickery is this?" Olivia had betrayed them. He would tear her limb from limb to inflict the same hurt upon her she had visited upon Larissa.

"No! No, I promise, it's not what you think!" Olivia's wails were entwined with Larissa's scared, confused words behind him. "Terak? Terak! What's happening, *please*."

"So you know what I am, do you?"

The male's steady, even voice cut through the confusion. He didn't look up. Instead, his concentration was on the vials and beakers before him, all filled with a multitude of bubbling and colorful concoctions.

Terak felt Larissa's chin graze his arm as she looked around him into the room. She gasped, and he knew then she saw the man as well. His skin was sallow with a flaky appearance. His hair was thinning, dandruff thick on his scalp. He was thin but bloated.

He looked up from a purple concoction, zeroing in on Larissa. "Hello, young lady. Do you understand your protector's worry now?"

Terak knew she nodded by the scrape of her chin against his arm. "You're a zombie, aren't you?"

"Manner of speaking," Simon said. "Most zombies don't have their original thoughts left and were created to mindlessly follow the orders of their master. That was not the case for me, which is why I'm not aligned with bad guys and am hanging here."

Larissa was pushing against Terak, without words telling him to let her in the room. Olivia was standing on the side, her eyes begging him to believe this was not a trap.

He had thought he had prepared for every possible situation, but this…this was beyond his comprehension. Before him was an abomination, the culmination of a necromancer's lust for death and destruction. He spoke to the creature. "Why would they create one such as you? I have never heard of any like you before."

Simon had already turned back to his bubbling tubes. He was studying one of them, making notes. "They turned me because I am a being of exceptional brilliance."

Larissa gave a small laugh behind him. "Not exactly modest."

"I'm a man of science. I deal in truth, not obfuscation." Simon finished his notes, then after lowering the heat on the tube, turned his attention back to them. "That truth was why they made me undead in the first place. Cancer would have killed me within six months and they didn't want to lose me."

"Who is your master?" Terak asked.

"Don't have one."

"Do not lie to me, creature. All of your kind has a master."

Simon shook his head as a teacher would at an unruly student. "I don't lie. A necromancer created me, yes, but he is not my master. No one controls me."

"I have never heard of such a thing."

"Yes, well, weren't you the one who said you never heard of anything like me before?" The zombie motioned toward Larissa. "Can the young woman come in now? I understand she has questions for me."

There was a poke in his ribs, no doubt from Larissa's finger. She did indeed want to enter. With ill will he let her enter, but when she made a move to stand in front of him he held his arm to the side, not letting her any further than his side. Again she gave that small huff, but she stayed put.

He might be willing to accept this was not a trap, but he would not let her nearer. No matter what the creature believed, a necromancer created him and a necromancer would always be master to him. "Why would a necromancer create one that had free will? It is counter to their interests."

The zombie shrugged. "I'm a man of science and I don't know the intricacies of necromantic magic. My understanding is if they had imprinted me, I would have lost my genius and been useless to them."

"Then why are you not with your creator now?"

"As my free will and my genius remained, so did my morality. I may be a zombie, but I am in all other ways still the human male who existed before the Great Collision." He motioned to himself with a sweep of his arm down the front of his body, and for the first time Terak detected emotion, a flicker of disgust at what was beheld. "Do you think I want others to become this? The necromancers to win? No, not at all. I want them defeated."

"If they are defeated, you will cease to exist." Cruel words, but truth. How would the zombie react?

The creature took the news as calmly as one would a situation that peace had been made with long ago. "I should have died seven years ago. Even if I expire this moment, I've gotten more than my share."

Larissa's hand touched Terak's shoulder, giving his arm a small caress. "Do you know anything that can help me?"

Simon shook his head. "I don't know any specifics about you. I've been away from them too long. But I do know what their ultimate goal is, and with what Olivia has told me, I have to assume somehow you are mixed up in that."

"Ultimate goal? You mean beyond the usual of bringing death and mayhem wherever they go?"

Simon's face showed no response to Larissa's attempt at levity. "They want to rip the Human Realm and the Magic Realm apart."

"Impossible," Terak breathed, unable to stop his head from shaking, unable to stop his body from backing away even as the gasps from both Olivia and Larissa sounded in his ears. "You speak of the impossible. The realms are forever entwined. All the great mages have proclaimed it."

Simon's eyes bore into his. "The realms can't be separated in a way that won't involve carnage and destruction on a scale unparalleled in the history of either realm. When has that ever been a deterrent to a necromancer?"

Terak thought back to the First Council after the Great Collision, where various leaders came together to understand how to proceed. His father had journeyed forth against the advice of many in the Clan, bringing him and his mother. He remembered how one – an elf? – asked if it was possible the realms could ever be separated.

The mage hesitated, then replied, "No spell is impossible, only the conditions that surround it."

It was double-speak at the time, a way to say no without appearing less powerful, and he and his father, as well as the cadre of leaders, paid no mind to those words. But if this creature was correct? He asked, "This separation of the realms? What would happen exactly?"

Simon shook his head. "I don't know any specifics. I know we are entering a short period of time where it will be possible to rip the realms apart – planets in alignment and other mystical happenings. If they are able to make this happen, the Human Realm will be destroyed while the Magic Realm will revert to the way it was before."

Larissa's hand went to her throat. "The Human Realm will be destroyed?"

Simon nodded. "Since the Human Realm is dominant, it would take the brunt of the destructive force and become the Realm sacrifice required. Anyone who was originally from the Human Realm would die with it. Those who have been born since the Great Collision it's less clear. With as complex a spell as we are talking about, I doubt any magic user truly understands the full impact."

"And me? You think them coming after me is somehow related to this?" Larissa's tone held the fear and uncertainty of a child who had lost sight of her family and was now alone amid a large, uncaring throng of adults. Anyone observing be damned. Terak took the step needed to be situated behind her and wrapped her in his arms, bringing her close to his body. She leaned back into him, her arms circling his own.

If Simon took any special notice of the display he didn't let on. Instead his attention turned back to his beakers, one of which looked to be on the verge of bubbling over. He went to it, saying over his shoulder, "I don't see how you could be connected. There is nothing I've heard about you that makes me understand why they would pick you as a target. At the same time, this is what they have been planning for since the Realms first collided, and considering the effort and the risks they are taking to collect you, I see no other possibility that explains their interest."

In the thickness of the ensuing silence, only the zombie appeared to not be troubled by dark and heavy thoughts. Olivia shook off her own worries first, and she smiled at the zombie, small and trembling, but warmth still evident in it. "Thank you for seeing us, Simon."

"Anything for you." It was the first spark of human feeling the zombie had exhibited, this response to the dark-haired woman. She was important to him, though in what way Terak could not fathom. Simon then turned to Larissa. "Young lady, I can't press this upon you enough. If you are somehow connected to this, they will stop at nothing to get to you. This is all they exist for. They want their world the way it once was. They hate this new reality. They still have power, but not the complete domination and utter subservience they enjoyed in the other realm. They want it back, and will do anything to get it."

CHAPTER TWENTY-ONE

Back in the car, Terak watched as Larissa continued to absorb the information. She was pale, almost as pale as the abomination, and her arms were wrapped around her stomach as though it were the only way to keep herself from flying apart.

Olivia looked into the rear view mirror. "Larissa? You okay, sweetie?"

She was anything but okay, but the question brought some strength back to her. She straightened in the seat. "You know a zombie, Olivia. A sentient *zombie*."

Olivia's eyes went back to the road. "I never planned for that. I kept getting introduced to more and more people, and the more people I talked to, the deeper I got sucked into the politics and the backstage goings-on. Believe me, right now I really wish I didn't know so much. This shit with the necromancers…I could happily have lived in ignorance."

"Yeah," Larissa said. She absently started to pick at her fingernails as she looked out the window.

"Are we still friends?"

Larissa's head jerked at that statement. "Of course we are. You've stood behind me since all this started. Why would I leave you after you've put yourself in danger helping me?"

Olivia's shoulders relaxed at the sincerity in Larissa's tone. "What are you going to tell your family?"

Larissa shook her head. "I'm not quite sure where to go with this yet."

Olivia laughed, a harsh sound. "I got you. Right now I'm so messed up I can't remember how to diagram a sentence. My kids are going to eat me up and spit me out."

"Jason Evans will be king for the day. I hope the school is still standing tomorrow." Both women laughed, a call to move beyond fear and back to normalcy.

After the laughter died down, Larissa breathed deep. "Thank you again for setting up this meeting. So please don't think me ungrateful when I say I wish he had been a little more helpful. I'm still no closer to knowing why they are targeting *me*, and that's what I was hoping to find out."

Olivia smiled, and Terak saw mischief in her features. "Well, if you weren't here with a fine-looking man who happened to be in your bedroom at five in the morning, I would have said it was because you were a virgin."

"Olivia!"

Larissa's scandalized tone was barely heard over the sudden pounding in Terak's ears.

She was untouched?

"I'm just saying…" Olivia didn't even try to hide her smirk.

"Well, don't!"

Yes, her father was protective, but from what he knew of humans, they did not reserve sexual intimacy solely for their mates. She was old enough that not having a lover would be unusual.

Larissa refused to look at him, her face scarlet and muttering under her breath on how she would take revenge on Olivia.

It was still early morning when they arrived back at her apartment, but late enough that she would have awoken already to get ready for her day. Larissa motioned toward the balcony. "Thank you for coming with me, but I need to get started-"

"Is what Olivia said true?" he broke in, no finesse in his words. He needed to know, now.

Her face flamed immediately, but Larissa pretended ignorance. "What are you talking about?"

"Are you untouched?"

Larissa turned to walk into her room. "My…sexual life…has nothing to do with what is occurring."

He came before her, not letting her escape into her bedroom. "You say that you can think of no reason why the necromancers are targeting you. There is no overt reason, but there is some reason. They have gone to extraordinary lengths to apprehend you. No possibility can be overlooked."

Larissa would not look him in the eye, instead tried to step around him. When she failed in her quest, she went still, looking down at the floor. Finally, she said, "Yes."

Yes. How could one small word have such power over him, delivering a punch greater than any enemy who ever came before him? He worked saliva into his now-dry mouth to speak, feigning a calmness his heartbeats would easily belie. "Why does this embarrass you?"

She shrugged, still looking at the floor. "People usually don't discuss their sexual history, or their complete lack thereof. And most people my age don't have a complete lack thereof."

The defensiveness in her tone hurt something in him. He did not like her feeling she was inadequate in any way. "I do not know the ways of humans, but while virginity is not held sacred, most of my Clan do not engage in sexual acts with anyone before they take a mate."

That brought Larissa's head up, her interest in the subject easily read on her face. "Really? Why is that?"

"Vulnerability."

Larissa's eyebrows creased. "I don't understand."

"A gargoyle is vulnerable during intimacy. There would be no better time for an enemy to strike."

Her lips twisted, a smile that couldn't quite form. "If that wasn't so sad, there is a pithy comment in that statement."

He reached out and smoothed back her hair. "What statement?"

"Your people have trust issues."

"I have never denied this."

She laughed a little, but her eyes widened, her lush mouth opening in surprise. "Wait. So does this mean you are…?"

She let the question hang, but what she was asking was clear. "I have never had a lover. I am as you are."

"Oh." She cleared her throat, her head once again hanging down, her gaze on the ground. Then without lifting her head, her eyes came back to his. "Valry?"

"No."

Now her head lifted. "But you two are engag – I mean, Intended."

"Yes. It is my duty to mate with her. As the strongest female, she will protect the Clan well, and any young we have will have the strength to protect the Clan in the future."

Her eyebrows furrowed. "Wait, you don't love Valry, but you're going to marry her?"

"I must do what is best for my Clan, and my Clan will prosper with Valry as my mate."

Larissa shook her head, though she seemed not aware of the movement. "You can't be serious. Life isn't worth living if you're not with the one you love."

"Humans can live with such fanciful notions. As leader, I am allowed no such luxury."

"That's bull!" The exclamation was a surprise, as was the finger that poked him in the chest. "I understand you are under pressures I can't comprehend, but there is nothing strong or noble about picking a female you don't love as your wife. It's a cowardly way out."

"Cowardly?" He had never been described that way in his life. He was the leader of the greatest warriors of this realm, and this little human would call him a coward? "Watch your words."

"Oh, I am!" Her eyes were blazing, and in her anger she seemed to grow in size. "Only a coward would marry someone he doesn't love. You know why? Because love is the ultimate vulnerability. It can put you on your knees and destroy parts of you that will never function again when it's gone. A coward couldn't handle that, so they would instead marry someone that could never happen with."

"What would you have me do? Would you have me defy tradition and the will of my people?"

"Yes! Isn't that the point of being here with me, to bring your people away from what they know to something better? Be with someone you love." Her eyes were bright, shining with the ferocity of her belief while she spoke of love and cowardice.

"You do not understand."

"Then make me understand. Make me understand why you would be with a female you don't love when there is a female in front of you who..."

She faltered, her hand going over her mouth and stopping any more words from coming forth.

A female in front of him. A female who was warm and loving and brave and so damn desirable his teeth ached in want of her. "Make you understand, little human? How can I make you understand something that becomes less clear to me every time I am near you?"

He picked her up by her waist, bringing her to eye level. Before the question in her eyes could translate to words, he leaned down, pressing his mouth to hers.

Her lips were soft, as soft as he'd imagined those rare moments he was away from her. Even then, she was as much a part of him as when she was in his sight. There was never a moment he was free of her.

She didn't respond as he moved his lips over hers. Maybe this was not correct. It was perfect to him, but...

Thought left as her mouth opened under his, pressing against him to push closer. Her tongue slipped past his lips, a tentative touch against his own.

Her tongue was becoming bolder, tangling with his in long strokes. He raised one hand to grasp her hair, slanting her head so he could dive deeper into that warmth.

Her arms wound around his shoulders, her own fingers digging into hair as her body writhed against him. Gods, that body, that soft, sensual body was draining the strength from his. He leaned her against the wall, bodies now tight together. Her chest was against his, her nipples such hard points he felt them through the cloth that separated their bodies.

She moved against him with that sinuous grace he had seen so many nights from a distance, the movements slow and sensuous and reducing him to a mindless beast.

He wanted her skin. He wanted her naked. He wanted his mouth on every inch of her – her breasts, her stomach, that valley between her thighs.

Especially there. He wanted to live there. He wanted to wring every ounce of pleasure from her body, and once he did, he wanted to do it again. And again. And again.

She pulled her mouth from his, her eyes wide and shocked as she looked down at him. She opened her mouth, closed it. Opened her mouth again, licked her lips, closed her mouth.

He looked at her mouth and a vibration rolled through his chest. That mouth was far sweeter and softer than any dream had promised.

"I..." She had gotten her voice back, though shock colored her tone. "School. My kids. I need to go."

He let her go and backed away before he convinced himself of the wisdom of taking her back into his arms. With a bow, he returned to his gargoyle form and leapt from the window.

CHAPTER TWENTY-TWO

"Miss Miller? You're about a million miles away today,"

"Huh?" Larissa looked up to see half of her first-period students staring at her. "What?"

Jason Evans sighed. "You might consider making all your classes study periods today. You keep zoning in and out."

Damn it! Stupid gargoyle. No, no fair blaming Terak for her inability to do her job. The fault lay squarely with her and her hormones. "Thank you, Jason. I'll take that under advisement. Any other questions before class ends?"

Jason spoke. "You never answered my question. If the necromancers are such bad guys, why didn't everyone band together to destroy them?"

Every day Jason somehow brought up either necromancers or vampires. Older teachers told her there was one kid every year who fixated on them, but Jason didn't fit the mold. He was the golden boy, an athletic genius who was adored around the school, not some emo kid who had no other way of expressing dissatisfaction with their lot in life than by thumbing their nose at society's conventions and openly embracing something everyone else feared. "Necromancers are very powerful, so it's not that easy to fight them. Plus there is due process to consider."

Jason shrugged. "Or maybe everyone makes them out to be the bad guys to keep all the attention on them and away from the other races."

The intensity in Jason's eyes, the set of his shoulders and the line of his mouth, had warning bells clanging in uncomfortable cacophony. When had this unhealthy fascination begun again? "Jason, while I am not one who swallows the party line completely, trying to make necromancers in any way good is a bit of a stretch."

"And I think we're only being given one side of the story," Jason argued back, his arms crossed over his chest with typical teenage mulishness.

The minute bell rang, saving Larissa from this conversation. "Okay, everybody, no homework tonight, but review the last few chapters. Big hint here – expect a pop quiz."

Disgruntled voices followed that announcement as the kids grabbed their items and left. Jason went against the tide and came over to her desk.

Before he could say anything she took the initiative. "Jason, you're entitled to your opinion, but you're not going to convince me otherwise."

He smiled, the earlier intensity gone. "No, I understand, Miss Miller. I was actually going to ask you something else. Would you be my sponsor for the upcoming fall carnival? I want to do a dunking booth. "

"An oldie but goodie – I approve. Who would be the one dunked?"

"You, of course."

Of course. When *don't* the students want to dunk the teacher? "Ah. Silly me for asking."

"Maybe we can meet up after school today so I can show you my designs and go over a few ideas I had. How about we meet in the gym?"

The gym, which was a separate building from the school and would be very empty after classes were done for the day. Goosebumps rose across the back of her neck. "I'm busy after school. Seventh-period study hall, why don't you meet me in the teacher's lounge?

"C'mon, Miss Miller, it will only take fifteen minutes, and I need you in the gym so you can see what I've done so far. We've been keeping all the supplies in the back." The wheedling tone was in direct contrast to that intense look that had once again entered his eyes.

"Sorry, I can't. Let's plan it for next Tuesday, I'll meet you then." *Like hell I will.*

His lips thinned for a long moment and his eyes grew stormy. But he came back to himself and all traces of anger at her pronouncement disappeared. "Sure, next Tuesday. But let me know if you have an opening before then. I'm really eager to get on this design." He turned and left the classroom as other students came filing in.

Jason Evans, all-star quarterback and the golden boy of the school, who was unnaturally fixated on necromancers and was doing his best to get her someplace alone.

This needed to end, because either she was starting to jump at shadows or those evil creatures were coming at her through her kids, and like hell she'd let them near her kids.

For the first time since she finished the student side of high school and began the educator side, the final bell ringing brought sweet, sweet relief and thankfulness that the day was done. She was out of the building before most of her students, her little yellow loaner car tearing up the asphalt to get her home. Once home, she closed the curtains tight, hoping that would discourage any knocks from her gargoyle guardian.

She was being a coward. Fully admitted it, would sign a note to that effect. But what else could she do after that kiss…

That kiss.

Gods.

Never had anything like that happened in her life, that flint-to-wood inferno that exploded the moment his lips touched hers. If that was what happened when you called a male a coward, it was something that needed to happen a lot more often.

Every millimeter of his skin branded hers and demanded she press closer, and she wanted to do nothing except obey. There had never been anyone else who had ever caused that reaction, that desperation to have him trapped in the most intimate embrace she could hold him in.

It would have been the most perfect moment of her life, except he was the member of another race, she'd just called him a coward, and he was engaged.

She didn't mess up often, but when she did, she went big.

The memory brought the 20/20 cringe. Somehow at the time it made sense, she was saving him from a stupid mistake – never mind it was self-serving bunk.

Gargoyles were hardly alone in their philosophy of strength, and not everyone was meant to have the fairy tale that her parents did. Even her parents hadn't had the fairy tale. Reality needed to be acknowledged.

But he was the one who kissed her. He cradled her in his arms and held her tight and made her feel so cherished. If he didn't return her feelings, if he was at peace with his people's traditions, then none of that would have happened. Right?

A knock sounded on the door. No, not a knock. Several heavy thumps and a loud, "Damn it, Ris, open this gods damned door now!"

Couldn't she have one day alone to mope and obsess? After checking the peephole and seeing it was indeed family, Larissa pulled the door open, fixing in place a scowl that would signal her extreme displeasure. "What do you want, Michael?"

He pushed past her, kicking the door closed with his foot. "Don't you dare lie to me. What are you involved in?"

Oh, he did not. It didn't matter if he had eight inches and a hundred pounds on her, like hell she was letting him get away with this bullying. "You might want to stop with the attitude right now and back off. I don't know what you mean."

Michael was pacing, his hands running in his hair as he talked, the way all the males of her family acted when they were upset. "You aren't going to throw me off that easily. I'm fucking mad as hell I let myself become so wrapped up in seeing that guy in your apartment that I forgot myself the first time and let you talk me out of what my gut was saying."

"Nothing was left unfinished the last time."

"Red running lingerie."

The out-of-the-blue statement jarred her. "What are you talking about?" she asked, the volume lower than before.

"The woman in red running lingerie, that's what you said you saw at the park. Except how could you have seen the woman who had barely started her run when she was grabbed by the orcs if you weren't there at the same time? And where is your car? Shall I tell you what lot it's in and what the current shape is, because I made a point to find it when I realized it *disappeared* the same day as the attack!"

He tried to tower over her but she wasn't having it, stepping forward to make him break away. "What orc attack, Michael? The orc attack that was never reported on the news and there is no police record of? You might be on the force, but being the chief of police's daughter has its own set of advantages. Don't think I can't find things out."

"Why the hell did you go behind my back?"

"*That's* all you have to say to me? You come here full of righteous indignation while you are hiding all sorts of crap from me, and when called on it you get huffy because I was a little underhanded in finding things out? I'm not playing that. You either come clean or you can get out."

He raked his hand through his hair, creating chaos in the formerly smooth strands. "This isn't about me."

Really? He thought he could play that with her? "It sure as hell *is* about you! It's about the fact that I don't know what's what in this world anymore, and even those closest to me have secrets I would never have imagined. So you tell me, Michael – does Dad know? Whatever you're involved in, does he know about it?"

Muscles ticked in his jaw as he contemplated her, anger still within easy reach but banked at the moment. "Are we coming clean with each other?"

She sat on the couch in front of him, crossing her arms. "You tell me."

The drumming of his fingers made a staccato against his jean-clad leg. He lowered his head as if in defeat. When he brought it up all heat was gone from his gaze. "I wasn't in the military, not like you think."

The world shifted beneath her feet, a roller-coaster sensation she didn't expect and didn't want. "That isn't funny."

"Not meant to be." He shook his head, coming to sit beside her on the couch. "In basic training, I was recruited for a Special Forces-type team."

"You mean like the SEALS?"

"I mean..." He trailed off. The late afternoon sun came through the window, casting half of him in shadow and making his features a little starker, a little harsher. "There are a lot of dangers in this world. Humans can't completely place our protection under the control of members of other races. We need to keep a hand in things ourselves."

"The Seven Houses," she muttered, and was rewarded with his surprised jump.

"You really do know a lot of things." He picked at his pants leg. "We're not enemies and this isn't about trying to start trouble, but yeah, we can't leave things entirely to the Seven Houses or the other races' governments. We need to remain strong on our own, and I was part of a group whose job is to protect us."

"Why are you telling this to me now?"

He took a deep breath, his face filling with sorrow. "I've never left it. I'm still part of that Special Forces team."

She jumped up, away from him. If he slapped her it would have shocked her less. "You're a cop, Michael. You're a cop with Dad and the bros."

"I came back because it was part of my cover." He looked up at her, his eyes tired, haunted. "I'm not a cop, I'm undercover. I'm sorry, Ris."

Her father… "Does Daddy know?"

Michael shook his head, his eyes breaking away from hers.

"This would kill him." She rubbed her hand against her upper arm, trying to warm herself against this sudden cold. "He'd never recover from this."

"I know." Flat, blunt, taking full responsibility for the damage.

"Then why?"

He stood then, his posture not showing any further apology. "Same reason you're keeping secrets now. To protect him. To protect all of us. All I ever wanted is my family to be safe. Dad buries his head in the sand. I don't blame him, and I never want to force him to do otherwise, but I knew I had to do things differently."

When put like that, she couldn't argue. Everything he said was true, and wasn't that why she had gone against what she knew her father would have wanted? Having your own thoughts spoken aloud by someone else made it really hard to remain mad at them.

"Your turn. What are you involved with?"

Tiredness hit her like a sledgehammer. These last twenty-four hours had been hell, and she wasn't out of the woods yet. She wanted to sleep and process, but Michael wouldn't let this go, not until he knew everything. "How did you know, and don't tell me lingerie girl – you pieced that together after the fact."

His eyes narrowed and became cop's eyes, questioning and searching out the truth. "A woman named Fallon came to visit me. She said you would recognize her name."

If she lived a thousand years, Larissa was pretty sure she'd never forget Fallon. "What did she have to say?"

"She didn't give me any details. She said she had more information about the attacks for you and your guardian, and gave me directions of where to bring you tonight if you wanted to meet." The pacing started again. "Who does she mean, *guardian*? The man in your apartment?"

"Yes, he's been protecting me."

"And what have you needed protection from?"

She didn't want to say it. She didn't want Michael to become part of this nightmare. But he had told his secrets, and that was the deal. "Necromancers."

Michael's knees buckled before he righted himself. "Fuck no, fuck no…*Necromancers*, Ris? You don't know what they can do, the horrors I've seen…" He grabbed her hand, pulling her closer. "You're sure?"

His terror was bringing her own back, batting down walls she'd been using to keep it contained. She had to get away or she would be curled up on the floor. She pulled her hand from his, wiping it over her face as she nodded, the only answer he was going to receive.

He stayed still for several moments, looking lost, his hands clenching at his sides. A word floated through the air. "Why?"

She would give anything to fully know the answer to that question. "They're going to use me to somehow rip the Human Realm and the Magic Realm apart and return the Magic Realm back to how it was before."

If Michael was unhappily stunned at the prior mention of necromancers, he was poleaxed at this latest revelation. "Impossible," he whispered, the slice of sound low and haunted.

She said nothing and let him come to terms with this newest revelation in his own time. When he came out of his stupor, his eyes were a laser focus on her. "This Fallon, she's from the Guild, isn't she? Fuck, I should have known."

He didn't sound happy about this new bit of knowledge. "You know of the Guild?"

"Not because I want to. I've been very happy that I haven't had any run-ins with them this far in life, though I guess that's changing now."

"What did you think of her?"

He didn't hesitate. "That she's scary as hell and you'd be ten shades of stupid to mess with her." He took a few moments then, and she saw protective older brother fade to be replaced by cool cop logic. "That doesn't mean you shouldn't meet up with her and see if you can learn something, as long as you have your back-up guardian – who, by the way, you haven't fully explained yet."

"I can't explain him."

Michael narrowed his eyes at her. "Larissa..."

She held up a finger in warning. "Don't take that tone with me. I can tell you my secrets, but I won't betray those who have been protecting me all this time. I would be dead several times over if it wasn't for the man you saw. He's been by my side throughout all of this."

Michael's hands slipped into the back pockets of his jeans. "I'm sorry you didn't feel like you could have come to me, to the family."

"It's not that I couldn't, it's that I wouldn't. Protection, right? If something had happened to any of you because of me...it was easier to risk myself alone."

He came over and enveloped her in a giant hug, squeezing her so hard she was lifted a few inches off the ground. "Never again. No matter what, you come to us."

"No." She pushed away from him. "I still don't want Dad to know, and I have others to protect me, people more qualified than Dad or the other bros."

She could see the war behind his eyes at that statement, but after long moments he nodded. "Yeah. I hear you."

"Thanks."

He looked around the room, taking in the family photographs that lined her walls. "So what now, Miss Hear-Me-Roar?"

She smacked his arm, a giggle escaping. Gods, it felt good to laugh again, even such a small sound. "I need to see Fallon. It's time we all laid our cards face up, because cloak-and-dagger is not my thing, and if the Guild can help, I want to meet with them." Jason's face flashed before her, the weird intense look in his eyes as disturbing in memory as it was in person. "This might be affecting people close to me. It needs to end, no matter how unsure I am about my possible allies."

"I agree. I'll talk to my superiors and see if I can bring my people into it." He took a strand of her hair, curling it around his finger and pulling slightly, like he did when she was little. "We'll figure this out. I'll pick you up tonight and we'll see what this Fallon has to say."

"You'll pick up me and Terak."

"Terak? That's the guy's name?" Michael's mouth thinned and turned down. "You sure you still want him if I'm with you?"

I can't do this without Terak. The response almost leapt from her throat before she tamped it down. Probably best not to go into that minefield with her brother. It was an area she wasn't sure how to handle yet, so discussion with her brothers – all of whom had less than enthusiastic responses to any male who had ever gotten close to her – was strictly a no-go. "It would feel weird if I didn't bring him with me, like a betrayal. He's been through every step with me."

"When I see this guy again, I'm going to shake his hand and thank him for taking care of you."

"Aw, Michael, that's so sweet-"

"And then I'm beating the crap out of him for being naked in your apartment."

Men were stupid. It was all she could come up with most days. Change of subject. "What time are you going to pick us up?"

"Seven."

"We'll be ready."

He leaned down and kissed the top of her head. "Love you, baby sister. No matter what else, you have to remember that."

"I always know that."

When Michael was gone she went to the balcony and did her patented wave and dance, which had always worked in the past to get Terak's attention.

No Terak. Not then and not for the next several minutes.

The image of that little silver ball popped up. Yes, thank gods Terak had the foresight to get it. Going into the bedroom and opening the top drawer of her nightstand, the silver ball was where she left it, safely stored in a velvet bag in the corner.

All right, hold it tight and start speaking in your head. *Terak. Terak, I need you. Can you hear me? Fallon wants to meet with us tonight, and I need you here.*

Thirty minutes later she had a pounding headache and not heard a word from her erstwhile gargoyle.

The next two hours were spent between going to the balcony and trying to use the silver ball, but Terak never arrived at her side.

This couldn't be about the kiss, could it?

Did he hate himself?

Did he hate her?

Maybe he felt guilt. It didn't matter if he wasn't in love with his fiancée. The fact was he was engaged to marry one woman while he kissed another. She wouldn't like him if he was the type of male who thought so little of his promises and responsibilities.

Whatever the reason, he wasn't here, and Michael was arriving in five minutes for their meeting with the Guild.

This meeting had to happen. Working with the Guild was her best bet of finding out the information needed. She wasn't going to let necromancers use her to destroy this world, and she needed to protect her kids and anyone else close to her the necromancers might use to get to her.

Terak would hate that she left without him, but there was no choice.

It was time for her to step up.

Michael arrived at seven sharp. A smile plastered on her face and her hands stuffed into the pockets of her slacks to hide the shaking, she said with all the false confidence she could muster, "Let's go meet with the Guild."

CHAPTER TWENTY-THREE

Michael drove to the town hall, parking in the back. There were no other cars around, and all the lights had somehow stopped functioning, making the parking lot pitch-black. Nice touch.

"This way," Michael said, guiding her toward the emergency exit. No alarms went off as they opened the door. He led her to the elevators, and they went up to the fourth floor where the meeting rooms were. They walked three doors down into the only lighted office.

Fallon and Laire were waiting, tonight's outfit of choice for the mage a lime-green catsuit. Maybe she was colorblind. Or someone who really hated her bought all her outfits.

Fallon nodded. "Thank you for coming. Did your bodyguard decide to take the night off?"

Larissa might want a truce with the Guild, but that didn't mean she was going to become best buds and tell them everything. "Terak has other duties, as you well know. Besides, considering how *tense* conversations can become, I thought it might be best to leave him out of it."

Fallon nodded again. "I hear you. That's fine by me. In fact, it makes my life lots easier."

Warning bells went off at Fallon's words and the smug way she held herself. *This was a mistake.* Larissa shouldn't have come here without Terak. "Tell me what you wanted to tell me, and then I need to go."

"Sorry, not going to happen."

"What the-" Michael's voice cut-off and Larissa turned. The shadow man from that first night was emerging from the wall, at least his torso was, the rest of his body still hidden. He wrapped his arms around Michael and pulled, taking Michael...

...through the wall.

"Michael!"

She ran to the wall and beat on it, but it was unyielding. "Michael!"

"He's safe, I promise," and Fallon was there in front of her. Larissa shrank back, but the wall was solid behind her, not allowing any more movement. "Sorry, Teach. You need to come with us now. The time of pussy-footing around is over."

Laire's voice popped up. "Is that what pussy-footing means? Why was I thinking it was something sexual?"

"Just read from the scroll." Fallon sounded like an annoyed instructor during last period instead of someone in the midst of a kidnapping.

Laire huffed, but brought out a parchment sheet. Larissa recognized it from pictures in her lecture books. It was a magic scroll, which gave a magic user the ability to cast spells they normally couldn't. There were several conditions to be able to use one, not the least of which was the magic user had to be a powerful caster – the book said only ten percent of casters were powerful enough to make any use of scrolls.

"What are you going to do to me?" Larissa hated that she couldn't keep the tremor entirely out of her voice.

"You are going unconscious. This is the easiest way," and even as Fallon explained, Larissa could hear Laire chanting in some strange language, a mixture of smooth vowels and guttural consonants.

Laire finished.

Nothing happened.

"Laire," and Fallon's annoyed voice was now ratcheted up several notches.

Laire was looking at the scroll with confusion plain on her heavily made-up face. "I have never had a scroll not work before. It's a beginner spell – there should be no way they could mess it up."

Larissa made a break for it, sprinting past the women, but as she stepped out the door someone picked her up, giving her body a hard squeeze. Even as she struggled a blindfold was placed over her eyes and ropes wrapped around her body.

"Hard way it is."

It was an interrogation room – big and white, with a long table and two chairs in the middle, a couple spare bulbs hanging overhead, and one wall consisting of what was undoubtedly a two-way mirror.

Larissa sat on one of those chairs, looking toward the mirror. She wasn't going to throw anything, not until she had a living, breathing target. Those mirrors were notoriously hard to break.

Fallon and Laire walked into the room. Well, more accurately, Fallon glided in, her balance centered on the balls of her feet. In contrast, Laire was wearing six-inch stilettos and was doing a hurried shuffle to keep up.

They stopped in front of the mirror. Fallon never so much as glanced at her reflection and leaned back against it. Laire was the opposite, leaning close to the mirror fix her make-up and slick on a very shiny gloss on her lips.

"My brother?" Larissa asked. Keep it cool. She could do that.

"He's perfectly fine," Fallon answered. "He's back at his home right now without so much as a hair out of place, though *very* pissed over what happened. He's calling his commanding officers even now."

Several moments of silence followed. *"Why?"* So much for playing it cool. The word exploded out of Larissa. "Why am I here? Why did you kidnap me? You said we were meeting to talk, and I *trusted* you."

"Told you we should have waited for Aislynn," said the tiny mage to Fallon, still looking at herself in the mirror.

Fallon's jaw tightened. She probably wasn't the one often engaged in diplomacy, and the peeved look on her face told Larissa everything she needed to know about how Fallon felt being put in that position. Fallon said, "This was necessary. You are in a lot of danger and we had no other way to keep you safe."

"Don't try to sell me that crap. You're mad that I didn't play your game, and you decided to change the rules."

"It was necessary," Fallon repeated. Her sword kept peeking out from behind her head, a deadly reminder of what she could do. Well, she might be counting on that to help her out, but fat chance. This woman's intimidation tactics weren't working today.

Larissa put as much scorn in her voice as she could. "Keep telling yourself that if it helps you sleep at night, though I can't imagine anything could."

Laire, in the process of adding more eye shadow, spoke to Fallon then. "You aren't helping the situation."

Fallon turned, narrowing her eyes. "I notice you aren't speaking to her."

"I'm smart enough to recognize my weaknesses. I don't do that empathy shit. That's Ais's department."

As if in answer to their words, the elf came through the door, followed by a man Larissa had not seen before. Overlong dark blond hair and deep-set yellow eyes, and a scar that ran from the bridge of his nose below his cheekbone to end somewhere under a close cropped beard. He wore blue jeans and an open flannel shirt over a T-shirt.

He came to sit in front of her. "I'm Wulver," he said, smart enough not to offer his hand when his advance caused an involuntary flinch on Larissa's part. "I'm leader here."

Fallon was still standing with her back to the mirror, not reacting to those words at all. Larissa pointed to her. "I thought that was her, the way she acts."

He smiled but refused to be drawn in by her words. It was a nice smile, his teeth white and sharp.

Maybe a little too sharp.

No, no she was not going to ask. There was enough on her plate right now without wondering if the guy in front of her was a human or not.

Guess the human. That might make a neat game.

Well, he said he was boss. It gave her someone else to yell at. "Since you are in charge and not her, I'm assuming it was your order that brought me here?"

He nodded. His eyes did hold some compassion, but something in the set of his shoulders, the way he carried himself, all told that while he might be sorry she was so upset, he felt no remorse in grabbing her and bringing her here against her will. "I'm sorry it was done this way, but with that last attack, we decided it was too dangerous for you to be free any longer."

That was an interesting way to put it. "Who's this *we* if you are the leader?"

Once again, he didn't answer her question, the compassion in his eyes morphing into something harder. He said instead, "We want your stay to be enjoyable. Is there anything we can bring you?"

"A nail file."

"Sure. Any nail polish? May I suggest red? It's a personal thing, but I prefer when women stick with the classics." He smiled again, and in that grin she saw the easy charm he possessed and could project when he wanted to. That might be the secret why he ran things, because in moments she was half under his spell, imprisonment be darned.

Enough of that. Charm wasn't going to get her home. "How long are you going to keep me here?"

His grin faded, and her stomach sank to the soles of her feet. "You must understand how much danger you're in-"

"How long?" she repeated.

He leaned back in the chair, trying to project nonchalance but failing. "Until you're safe."

She crossed her arms and directed at him her hardest stare, the one that kept even her most unruly student in line. It didn't do anything to free her, but she got some satisfaction in using it. "Meaning you're keeping me here indefinitely, unless you know why I've been targeted and are only holding me here until you get your man – well, necromancer. Is that the case?"

"There are things going on-"

Screw this. She was here against her will, but she was here, and she was going to get some gods damned answers right *now*. "How are they going to use me to rip the realms apart?"

Wulver jerked, and she'd bet money he rarely looked as surprised as he did right now. He looked at Fallon. Her brows were lifted slightly, the lines of her face softened from their usual intensity. She shook her head.

He turned back to her. "You've learned a lot in a relatively short period of time."

"Did you think I was sitting on my butt waiting for the zombies to eat my brains?"

Laire turned away from the mirror. "It's not really true that zombies eat brains, it's an urban legend...*mrph*."

The impromptu lesson was finished when Fallon clapped her hand over Laire's mouth. Wanting to move the conversation forward before any possible explosion between the two could take place, Larissa said, "So why me?"

Wulver settled in the chair, the smile and charm fading as weariness settled over his features. He half-opened his mouth before closing it, his gaze shifting away for a bare moment. His confusion was tangible. "We've searched and dug and researched and watched, but there is nothing about you that tells us what is going on."

That was not telling her anything she didn't already know. She pressed on. "Do you know how the spell works that the necromancers would use?"

"It isn't one spell. There is a final spell that would need to be cast at the end – the one that rips the realms asunder. That one doesn't change, but before that spell can be cast, certain requirements must be met. The problem we have is there are a lot of ways and a lot of roads to get things ready for that spell." Wulver's jaw tightened, and certainty once again infused his demeanor. "Bottom line is you are in danger. We still don't know why you've been targeted, and all the paths we've traveled thus far have led to dead ends. With you here, maybe together we can figure this out. Isn't that why you were going to meet us tonight, to get some answers?"

"Yes, by talking and working together, *not* to be treated like a criminal. I came to you in good faith, to answer questions and open up my life to you so we could get answers together. But now I'm in jail and while you can take your sweet time figuring out what's going on, my life will be in shambles. Isn't that special?"

"I promise I'll get you home as soon as possible."

"Forgive me for saying that your promises don't mean squat."

He drew in a deep breath, his eyes searching hers, as though he was trying to figure out how she worked, at least enough to say something that would have her agreeing to stay by her own free will.

The door creaked and opened and a man entered. He had curly ginger hair with sideburns and was wearing jeans and scuffed up tennis shoes, with a grey T-shirt under a battered dark brown leather jacket. He walked over to Wulver, leaning close and whispering into the leader's ear.

Wulver's eyebrows furrowed and he stared at ginger boy. Ginger's mouth turned down and he nodded, then left the room.

Laire, Fallon, and Aislynn looked on with curiosity. Not a sliver of sound reached Larissa, but from the way Wulver's mouth tightened and his eyes narrowed, she knew he didn't like what he heard.

His eyes settled back on her. "For having the cleanest record I've ever seen, a whole lot of people want to meet you. What is your secret?"

"Wulver," Fallon called. "What's going on?"

Yes please, what the hell is happening now?

Wulver sighed. He closed his eyes and scrunched up his face, the way people do when they're expecting an explosion. "The Oracle has summoned her."

"*Ah, hell no!*" Fallon said, and Larissa flinched. Wulver really could have warned her about the volume Fallon could achieve, at least given her some ear plugs. "What do you mean *summon*? We only just got her to the safety of the compound."

Wulver stood, facing the swordswoman. "The Oracle commands that Larissa be brought to her at moonrise."

"The Oracle can also feel the backside of my boot."

Anyone who irritated Fallon that much couldn't be all bad. This might be fun. And hey, she was an Oracle – hence the name. Maybe answers would finally be forthcoming.

Larissa stood, looking to Wulver. "Can she tell me why all this has been happening to me? Is that why she wants to see me?"

Wulver didn't look like he believed that was a possibility, but after a moment he plastered on a smile and said, "I don't know why you've been called, but yes, the Oracle may give you some answers."

"Wouldn't count on it," Fallon muttered.

Wulver pinned his gaze on Fallon, command and authority in his bearing. Yes, this man was leader here. "She is to go to the Oracle." *Do you understand?* was unsaid, but Larissa felt it.

Fallon crossed her arms, slouching back against the mirror. "Yeah, got it."

Wulver left the room. The second the door closed after him Laire started jumping, a huge smile on her face and her body shaking in repressed excitement. "I'll go, I'll go, I'll go! You don't even like the Oracle. Let me."

Before the first words were out of Laire's mouth, Fallon started to shake her head, and as soon as the green-haired woman took a breath, Fallon used it as her opportunity to say, "No way."

"Please please *please*."

"Let me rephrase. No way in the four hells."

Laire stopped jumping, a small pout coming to her lips. How she had been able to prevent an ankle fracture on those spikes, Larissa didn't know. "Why not?"

"Because if they have an orgy going on, you'll want to join. And if they don't have an orgy going on, you'll want to start one. I'll take Aislynn with me." Fallon looked over at Larissa. "Congratulations. You are about to do something many mortals dream about but few get to experience. You're about to meet the Oracle."

CHAPTER TWENTY-FOUR

The acolyte was a young elf male, no more than hundred years old. His hair was shorn in the way of all those newly pledged to their necromancer master while the scar pattern on his chest denoted who his master was to those that knew the code. His eyes gleamed with a feral and fierce devotion, one the gargoyles had yet to crack.

Terak stood before him as he had the last several hours. "I ask again, why are you here trespassing on our lands? Your master knows my kind is resistant to your magic, so it is not in his best interest to court the wrath of gargoyles."

The high-pitched giggle teetered on the edge of sanity. "Perhaps my Master knows he has nothing to fear from a gargoyle obsessed with a worthless human woman. Tell me, Gargoyle, is what's between her legs so unique that you let it take you away from your Clan?"

There was nothing Terak wanted more than to feel flesh shred beneath his claws, but long training kept him still. This was the most the acolyte had offered all day. There would be time for vengeance later. Now there were only answers to be found. "Not so worthless. You have been unstoppable in your quest for her. Why should only necromancers possess that type of power?"

For the first time, a gleam of intelligent cunning peeked out from behind the madness. "You don't even know her secret."

"I know you want her so badly you go against the Guild to collect her. What else do I need to know to realize her worth?" Only when the words were spoken did Terak realize their truth. He had been so focused on the necromancers and the new knowledge of their ultimate plan he never considered all the other avenues where danger now lurked. She was a prize of great worth. His stomach wrenched hard at all the ways she could be now used to further various interests.

"Our source never indicated you felt this way."

Source?

Betrayal.

A gargoyle was in league with this evil, feeding them information. Who? In exchange for what? He pushed the bitter burn away to think on later. To the acolyte he said, "I am *Mennak*. I am answerable to no one, and your master is pitiable if he does not know even that about my kind."

The acolyte made no reaction to the offense. Instead, his mad smile gleamed brighter. "Only time will tell us if your words are true, gargoyle. We should like to see you prove them."

And a gut-deep realization spread through Terak that he would get no more from the acolyte, no matter the methods he used.

Malek waited outside the thick cell doors. "Does anyone else know he is here?" Terak asked once he cleared the prison. Malek had been the one to find the acolyte, and had come straight to Terak.

"No, just as you ordered."

"You heard what the creature insinuated?" Terak wanted his second-in-command to gainsay him, to tell him he was wrong in thinking one of their kind turned on them.

Instead, Malek nodded. "I wish I did not believe it, but it makes sense."

Terak placed a hand on his shoulder. "At this moment, I trust only you. Keep watch on the grounds. With the capture of the acolyte, the necromancer may try to force a meeting with the betrayer."

Terak headed for his chambers, but was waylaid by Krikus. "There is an issue with the human woman," the old councilor said without preamble.

Cold, sick fear spread through his stomach. "Is she hurt?" and even he could hear the terror the tone held.

"She was captured by the Guild. We do not know where they hold her."

A powerful relief hit so hard he was dizzy, and he almost embarrassed himself with the need to lean against the wall. Instead, he forced his legs to stiffen and hold his weight upright.

His first instinct was to pursue her, to gather warriors and fight. But even if he knew where she was held, he could not leave. His Clan was in danger, and he needed to find the threat within. With the Guild she was safe.

Later, the Guild would pay for taking her. Now, they were the best option to keep her protected.

To Krikus, Terak said, "Send out our scouts to be on the lookout for her. As soon as she is found, they are to send word. We will take her back…

…by battle if necessary."

"You would betray me, Valry?"

She had arrived to her meeting with the accursed vampire with her shoulders squared and her head high, but now, as she saw Terak step from behind several rocks and Malek at his side, her body hunched over, losing her usual arrogance.

She reached out, beseeching. "This is not betrayal. I would never betray you. Everything I have done was so our people can become great again." She motioned to the vampire who was still several feet away. "He is here to offer a bargain."

"Which means you do not believe us great now, under my leadership and the leadership of my father. If that is the case, I wonder then why you would *not* betray me."

"You are a great leader, but you are blinded by a utopian vision of living in this world as equals among the other races, but they will never accept us. We must always live separate, and they must know our strength so they will never come against us!"

It should hurt more, the female with whom he had once meant to mate aligning herself with a man with the blood-red eyes, a mark of a true vampire and necromancer. It should tear at his chest, drive him to howl at the moon and claw the dirt around him.

And he did feel that, but for another female. Larissa was apart from him and the ache in his chest would not abate. He could not lean over and pull her toward him. He could not see her little chin lifting as she fought him or those blue eyes laughing and inviting him to share in her joy. All he could not do was tearing at him, pulling him apart at the seams.

He would get her back, and if the Guild fought him, he'd destroy them all.

The only emotion he could spare for Valry was anger, anger that she was keeping him from finding Larissa.

Betrayal or not, perhaps some good could come of this night if he could discover why it was Larissa these beings were obsessed with. Terak turned to the vampire. "What is your name?"

The vampire cocked his head in surprise. "You would speak to me, Terak, Clan Leader of the Gargoyles?"

"I would be a fool to not listen to your words now that you are here before me. Valry spoke of a bargain. Tell me what it is."

"I am Garof."

"And who is your master?"

"That does not concern you, Clan Leader. That knowledge will not affect the words I speak. I hope my lack of answer will not stop you from listening to my other words."

Terak inclined his head. Vampires never gave the name of their Master; it had been a desperate attempt, nothing more. "I will listen to your words. What actions I will take based upon them is not guaranteed."

"My people want the woman. She is needed for a spell."

"She is needed to rip the Realms apart, this I know." Terak watched the vampire closely, but to the vampire's credit, the only sign this might have been a surprise was an extra-long blink. "How would she accomplish such a task? Why her?"

Garof shook his head. "You do not need to know the specifics. What I am willing to divulge is that we need her and her alone. To possess her we would be willing to pay a very high price."

What did the vampire think to offer? "How high?"

"Since you know the ultimate purpose the woman would serve, you will understand when I say this. Once we return the Magic Realm to its former state, we will have gargoyles rule over all, second only to the necromancers."

They would never quit hunting her.

As Valry gasped and even Malek let out a grunt of surprise, this knowledge pounded through Terak. She would never be safe again. There was nothing he could do to blunt their interest. With his words and his covetous gaze, the vampire showed how much they desired her.

For him to stay with her was to put his Clan in the direct path of the necromancers. They would go from neutral parties to fierce enemies.

But to walk away from her was as good as handing her over to them.

She was sunshine. She was light and laughter and the key to a part of him that had sat, unused and rusty, since his mother had died. She was gentleness that surrounded a will of steel, and a fierce protectiveness to her family and her students and whoever else she considered her Clan.

She kept the secrets of a gargoyle and had fought to save him. She told him her secrets and let him wipe away her tears.

Calm descended, thick and complete.

She was his heart, his life, and he would forever protect her. Whatever he needed to do, whatever he needed to give up, he would keep her at his side and ally with whomever he must, as long as she was safe.

The vampire was watching him with careful eyes. This channel had to remain open, for the hope of future information. "What if the spell does not work? What will you give that will serve my people here, in this realm?"

The vampire looked surprised. "The Magic Realm will once again exist, Clan Leader."

"Do not talk to me of certainties. Yes, the Magic Realm may once again exist, but I will not make my people an enemy of several powerful Houses on that hope. I want to know what I will receive should this not come to pass."

"I would need to talk to my Master and ask him what he would wish to give." Garof nodded at Valry. "I will contact the female in our usual manner when I have a response for you."

"You speak of this one?" Terak grabbed Valry's wing and flung her toward Malek who caught and bound her.

"Terak, *no*. How can you do this, when you yourself are talking to the vampire?" She struggled against Malek's hold. "Let me go."

"This one," said Terak, ignoring Valry's pleas, "has betrayed her *Mennak* and kept secrets that might have placed my Clan in danger. Look at this female tonight and remember her face, Vampire, for you will never see it in the flesh again."

Garof smiled. "I have high expectations for our future conversation, Gargoyle. I will be in contact with you."

The vampire disappeared, teleporting away in less than a blink of time.

Valry cried as they flew back to the keep, struggling against the ropes that bound her. They landed among several warriors. Terak ignored the questioning gazes on him and told Malek, "Lock her away." Malek nodded and led her to the dungeons.

Before anyone could voice their questions, a cry of "*Mennak!*" sounded through the crowd. A warrior broke through and stood before Terak.

"What is it?" Terak asked.

"The warrior Fallon has been seen in the Wilderness with two other females entering the Oracle's domain. The one who spotted them wasn't certain who the other females were, but one of the females had blonde hair."

There was no need to hear anymore. Terak leapt from the parapet, letting the rage and adrenaline that had been banked to come to the fore and fuel him.

It was time to meet Fallon.

CHAPTER TWENTY-FIVE

For the first time in her life, Larissa found herself in the area known as the Wilderness. Several miles from the city, it was a mini-city in its own right, except here you could find any race, any beast, or any magic.

Too dangerous, Dad had said when he forbade her or her brothers to ever go here, with the creatures that had only become known in the last few decades mingling with the humans who didn't feel the need to separate themselves from everything new the realms offered.

The building they pulled in front of was a dark-brown brick box, but the line of beings outside of the building was a sight from Larissa's wildest imaginings – neo-hippie fairies, elves in leather corsets and collars, dwarven drag queens, and even the occasional humanoid beast in a business suit.

Fallon and Aislynn rode in the front of the car, Aislynn driving. Car, what a laugh. Tank was more like it, everything thick and dark. Safe and suffocating.

From the vantage point of the middle seat and observing in the rearview mirror, Larissa watched as Fallon's expression got progressively darker throughout the trip, until now when it was near thunderous. "Should I be scared about meeting the Oracle?" She hated that she had to ask, making her appear weaker than she already felt.

Aislynn looked back and gave a reassuring smile. "Don't mind Fallon. She has issues with this place."

Fallon's lip curled. "Oh, of all the beings in that place, I'm the one with issues?"

"We're expected," Aislynn said, pointing toward the door.

"Fine, fine." Fallon looked back. "Stay with us, don't drink anything, and roll your eyes at whatever the bitch says."

"Fallon!"

Fallon didn't respond to Aislynn. She got out of the car and waited until Aislynn and Larissa lined behind her. Once they were ready, Fallon walked across the street, aggression projecting from every line of her body.

At either side of the entrance were two giants. Literal giants. They had to be about nine feet tall, both bald with grey-tinged skin. They were big and blocky, and Larissa didn't want to be anywhere near them.

Aislynn must have seen the question in her face because she leaned down. "Stone giants," she explained. "Not full-blooded though. That's why they're so small."

Larissa nodded, not sure what she could add to that.

Beside the stone giants was a man. He was human, unless excessive greasiness was a special characteristic of one of the new races. He was in charge of admittance – allowing entrance at his whim, denying those who seemed to have a problem with him putting his hand under their skirts. Anyone who voiced disappointment was given a look by one of the giants, after which they slunk away.

As they walked toward the door, something that looked like a cherub with a mustache zoomed around them. When he saw Fallon, a small scream erupted from him and he headed for the door, waving chubby arms. "Boss, she's here!"

Fallon approached, her gaze focused entirely on the greasy man. Aislynn was on lookout, taking in their surroundings and the people around them.

They stopped in front of the giants, ignoring the loud complaints of those in line they jumped in front of. Fallon said, "Seemus, nice to see you at the door today."

The oily man's lips pressed together, his eyes giving a slow rake over Fallon's body in an obvious and distasteful show of dominance. It might have worked if he wasn't noticeably shorter than the swordswoman. "You've been summoned, I assume?"

"Would I be here otherwise?"

"You have to leave the sword," Seemus said, taking a step back between the two stone giants, getting out of Fallon's reach while allowing the giants a clear path to her.

Fallon eyed the two giants and snorted. They did not like this probably rare display of fearlessness, for both brought themselves to their full height in preparation for a fight. Fallon took a step closer. "Tenro goes where I go, and as I've been summoned, I'm going inside."

Seemus made a small motion with his hand and stepped back even farther inside the doorway. "I'm afraid my orders are very specific. No weapons ever. You need to go now, and tell Wulver to send someone more respectful."

"Which means you are denying me?" Fallon asked, and smiled. Larissa had seen rabid dogs snarl with more warmth. "After the day I've had, that is excellent news."

The stone giants took a step forward.

Inside the club, the silvery curtains that separated the front doorway from the club entrance billowed inward as Seemus crashed between them. He landed on the edge of the dance floor, out cold. If any of the beings noticed, it didn't stop them from dancing.

Fallon came through the door, stepping on Seemus's body as she entered. Aislynn was a little gentler, stepping over the unconscious man and directing Larissa to do the same.

Aislynn kept a hand on her elbow, but that pressure was nothing in comparison to all the other stimuli. Breathing wasn't the best idea here, as thick smoke and the earthy, sharp smells of herbs and spices – even money most were of a narcotic nature – clogged her sinuses. The lights went from too bright to deepest dark and back again in seconds, not letting eyes adjust. Underneath the too-loud music were snippets of conversation in dozens of languages, with most of them not in a human dialect.

Fallon led the way, her gait steady and sure as she made a path toward the back of the club, seeming not to take in any of the sights, though how she could be immune to the sight of the tall elf in a tuxedo dancing with the short, bearded dwarf in a wedding dress was a mystery.

What kind of place was this?

Better question, what kind of woman was this Oracle?

Fallon reached the back and flung aside a set of dark silk curtains to reveal a door. Without knocking, she opened it and stepped inside

It was *1001 Nights* in live action. Everyone here wore body-baring, jewel-toned outfits right out of a harem scene.

By the heat suffusing her face, Larissa knew she was sporting a mighty blush. Their actions belonged in a harem, people all around engaging in acts of hedonism that would make the most jaded courtesan blush.

Dear gods, I never knew a man could do that. I need to find another cuss-out when some guy makes me really mad...

"So *why the hell* did we need to come here to you?"

Fallon's pissed-off voice knocked through Larissa's shock. It took a few moments to focus on the swordswoman, standing a few feet away from a teal blue settee that adorned the middle of the room. The settee was surrounded by men and women, all of them tall and lithe and so beautiful Larissa had to check the urge to smooth her hair and clothes in their presence. The way Fallon stood blocked the person she was talking to.

A few steps closer, and the face of the Oracle came into view.

She looked human to Larissa's eyes – and it wasn't as if she was wearing a lot of clothing to hide any parts that might not be – but her coloring could best be described as *dipped in gold*. Velvety brown skin, thick dark hair, near-black eyes, but all held a deep golden sheen that was as beautiful as it was unusual. The woman was beyond stunning.

The Oracle said nothing at Fallon's outburst. The men and women surrounding her paid no attention to the swordswoman. They kept massaging the Oracle, the oil they used smelling sickly-sweet to Larissa's overworked nasal passages. When the Oracle tilted her head back, a man took the opportunity to lean in and press his lips to the hollow of her throat.

After long moments that had Fallon growing more agitated by the second, the Oracle finally spoke. "Oh, Fallon, you're here."

It looked like Fallon was tensing to attack the woman, but before she could, Aislynn sidled alongside her and grabbed her shoulder. "Let me take over now," she said to the redhead. Fallon's eyes still blazed, but she nodded, taking a step back.

Aislynn kneeled in front of the Oracle. "Great Oracle, we have come as requested."

The Oracle's attention was still on Fallon. She smiled, a lift of her lips designed to irritate. "You see, Fallon, this is how I should be approached. Watch and learn."

Fallon ground her teeth together and bent forward, her sword hand giving a little jerk.

Without turning, Aislynn lifted her hand and motioned Fallon to stay back. This scene or some variation thereof had to be a popular one.

The Oracle turned her attention to the elf and graced her with a blinding smile. The Oracle was a beautiful woman, but when she smiled she transformed into otherworldly. "Dearest Aislynn, it is so good to see you."

"It is always an honor to be in your presence," Aislynn replied. The words were said with the perfect balance of sincerity and warmth, and what should have sounded forced and phony became a lovely sentiment.

That dark-gold gaze turned toward Larissa. "Larissa Miller," the Oracle said. She had a rich, cultured voice, and Larissa straightened at the sound of it, half-remembered lessons in manners taking over. The Oracle smiled, and damned if it didn't look like she heard Larissa's thoughts. "It is lovely to meet you. You wouldn't believe how many people have you in the center of their minds right now."

Only one male mattered, the rest could go hang. "That's lovely, though I don't know why I deserve the sentiment. Would you have any clue why I'm suddenly so popular?"

The Oracle's smile was smug and a touch superior. Fallon's reactions were making more sense. "Now, now, I didn't bring you here to talk shop. You'll find out soon enough. Besides, your popularity has brought Terak into your life. How does it feel to be under the protection of a gargoyle? Have you become friends, or perhaps something more?"

She was the Oracle, so she probably knew everything that happened and everything that was going to happen. Fine, it was another piece of crazy Larissa needed to get used to. That didn't mean the first time she spoke of her feelings aloud it was going to be to this woman. Instead Larissa said, "Terak is a good protector. He's kept me safe while still trying to let me have my life."

One of the Oracle's female attendants rubbed oil into her bare feet. The Oracle made a little hum of pleasure, but still kept on with the conversation. "And yet he didn't protect you from being taken by Fallon."

"That was my fault. I was the one stupid enough to trust *her*," Larissa finished, using her thumb to point over at Fallon. Fallon looked supremely unconcerned. "And I walked right into a trap."

"Yes, Fallon is quite adept at deceptions with the right coaching, *aren't you*?" Fallon might have tried to make a hand gesture at that statement, but if she did, Aislynn was able to hide it quite well.

The Oracle stood, a lithe, graceful movement. She reached out to Larissa. "Come here, I have a gift for you."

No, Larissa really didn't want a gift from this woman, other than the gift of telling her exactly why a bunch of undead were after her. But the way all eyes were watching her, she probably didn't have the luxury of refusing at this moment, so she stepped forward. The Oracle took her hand, the dark skin soft and the touch delicate.

"I think," began the Oracle, "you enjoy being with the gargoyle more than you are letting on. But I understand a woman does not like giving up her secrets, especially before she knows what's going within the mind of a thick-headed male. You don't need to say anymore. I wish to give you this."

The Oracle handed her a small, leather bound booklet, about as thick as a pamphlet, and said, "You are a teacher, yes?"

It was nice of the Oracle to phrase things in the form of a question and let people feel they were imparting information. "Yes, I am."

"Excellent. I know teachers value learning, and this book has very valuable information on gargoyles. If Terak remains part of your life, this you'll want to know."

Larissa weighed it in her hand. "This is a very light history."

The Oracle arched one fine brow. "Why would I bother with that? This, my dear, is about how gargoyles mate."

Huh. So this was what dumbfounded felt like.

"Trust me, read that book. You'll like what you learn." The Oracle stepped back, though she didn't sit on the settee again. She looked at the elf. "Oh, and Aislynn? I need you to tell Fallon something."

"Yes, Oracle?" Aislynn answered, acting like it wasn't unusual to be receiving messages for a woman not two feet away.

The Oracle smiled, full of mischief and torment. "Tell her to get her sword ready. They're coming through the door."

Fallon bared her teeth even as she reached back and grabbed her sword. In a fluid movement she turned and ran, coming within a few feet of the doorway as the walls exploded.

This time the revelers were disturbed. Screams rent the air as a mass of bodies started running away from the chaos. Aislynn grabbed Larissa's arm, and displaying more strength than such an ethereal woman should ever possess, picked her up and toward a wall in the back.

"*Protect the Oracle,*" came shouts from all around. The men and women, so languid moments ago, now held the same warrior postures of Fallon and Aislynn.

In the confusion, Larissa was thrown hard against a wall. Pain radiated through her back where she was hit, but it was manageable. She put down her hands against the wall to push away, only to feel a doorknob, thank gods. One turn confirmed it wasn't locked. It opened into an alleyway. One side was blocked off, so there was only one way to go.

Once she was at the end of the alley she glanced in both directions. Several blocks down on the right was lots of traffic and wandering beings.

After one last look behind her to make sure no one had followed, she took off.

After several blocks of running the sidewalks became crowded. If it weren't for the mix of races she had never seen outside of books, it could have been any night on the town, with revelers searching for the next bar or club. She still stood out a little with her casual clothing and too quick breathing, but if ever there was a moment to celebrate being on the shorter side height wise it was now.

Head down, she walked fast and straight. Find a phone and call Michael. He'd be able to get to her. Piece of cake, though it would be a little easier if her ears weren't still buzzing from the earlier club noise.

A hand wrapped around her mouth and pulled her into an alleyway.

CHAPTER TWENTY-SIX

Larissa's nails dug into the arm holding her as she kicked backwards. Another hand closed around her middle and a low buzz of sound started near her ear, gradually turning into words. "Calm, little human. You are safe."

She relaxed. That voice, that deep baritone meant safety. She withdrew her nails. The arms loosened enough that she could move, and she turned to face Terak.

"Thank gods." She threw herself against him with such force his body rocked back. She wrapped her arms around his neck, hugging him with all the strength in her body.

There was no hesitation as he returned the gesture. He brought her tight against him, his arms steel bands as they closed around her. His mouth rained small kisses against her temple. "You are safe. I have you. You are safe and they will never touch you again."

His wings flapped, taking them up into the air.

"I was so scared." Gods, his smell was so clean, warm and heady and such an amazing contrast from inside the club. *This* was what she wanted to be surrounded with. How could any drug be more potent than Terak close and warm and all hers?

His breath puffed across her ear and his lips never quite left her skin. "I would never stop searching for you, *never*. If I had to make war with the Guild for your safety, they would all be laid before me. I will never be separated from you."

They traveled in silence then, though Terak kept her close. As they approached her apartment, Terak's mood began to change. His relief was being replaced by silence and stillness. Once they entered the apartment the transformation was complete, as anger charged through every inch of his body. He was so tight she was almost surprised he wasn't vibrating.

He let her down, folding his wings around himself with a snap. He circled her, taking her in. "You left without me and my protection."

The words and tone were flat, but they held such anger he may as well been screaming for the knot they caused in her stomach.

"Terak." She took a cautious step toward him, holding out her hand the way she would to a growling junkyard dog. He stopped circling, and that was a good-enough sign to touch him, to rub his arm, plea and apology mixed together in the gesture. "I tried contacting you several times over two hours. I swear I did. I jumped on the balcony and I used that little silver ball you gave me, but neither worked. I didn't know what else to do."

"I never received any message. The ball is foolproof, it should have reached me." He shook his head. "It does not matter. You should not have gone! It was foolishness to leave." The flatness was now gone, and the walls vibrated with his anger.

"I had to!" He could be mad, but she wasn't going to be talked to like she was eight. "They lied and said the meeting was going to be an exchange of information. I never expected to be kidnapped, and I had my brother with me, so I wasn't alone. I had to take a chance to find out if they knew anything to help."

He made a sound of dismissal, wiping away her words with the swipe of his arm as he stomped away from her. "I told you not to trust the Guild, and I told you to never leave without me. You disobeyed my instructions. It is pure luck I was able to find you as quickly as I did."

"Excuse me?" Now he was pushing it. "If you were so worried, then you shouldn't have disappeared on me. I wasn't the one who ran away after kissing someone senseless!"

"I…" He straightened, wrapping himself in his usual dignity. "I did not run away."

"Sure seemed like that to me. For weeks every time I turned around I tripped over you, and then suddenly we share a kiss and you are nowhere to be found? What would you call that if not running away?"

"It was not running away. I needed to think upon the events of the last few days."

"Yeah, including how you kissed me."

"It was…it was…" He looked defeated. "Do you regret it?"

Talk about turning it around. Now she was on the defensive, looking into eyes filled with pain and hope. She pushed her hair back, ducking her head. "I wouldn't say I regretted it," and she really shouldn't mumble like that, because she didn't want him to ask her to repeat what she said.

"Then what would you say?" he asked, his eyes sharpening.

"I'm…not unhappy it happened."

"Does that mean you are happy it occurred?"

Wasn't this leading the witness? Oh right, they weren't in court. "I would have preferred other circumstances."

"Such as?"

"Such as you not being engaged." Ha! There, couldn't argue with that one.

"Valry and I are no longer Intended."

Back the truck up. "What? When… How? Really?" Eloquence, thy name is Larissa Miller.

He studied her for several moments, and then he smiled.

He smiled.

A full-blown grin such as she had never seen on him. Happiness *radiated* from him in a way she'd never experienced before, and how was she supposed to respond when the sight was frying the synapses in her brain?

He advanced, walking toward her with a predatory grace he'd never displayed before. "You seem pleased by that news."

Who was this gargoyle? He had always been reserved, almost courtly in his bearing before, not this magnetic, determined animal stalking his prey. And by his direct stare, there was no doubt that his prey was her.

Since he was advancing, what else could she do but back up? "I need more details before I decide how I feel."

"What type of details, little human?"

"The usual — what happened, any chance of reconciliation, are you returning the engagement gifts?" Her back hit the wall and he was leaning over her, not allowing her any more movement.

He studied her, his eyes intense, almost scary in how focused they were on her. "What do you feel, Larissa?" and gods knew, she would admit to about anything if it meant that he kept saying her name in that exact voice.

She didn't know why he was no longer engaged, whether it was because of her words or some other reason. But it was time to move forward. If these last few weeks – hell, last few hours – had taught her anything, it was life was uncertain, and you needed to grab hold of the chances you were given, all the outside forces be damned.

His alien, beautiful face was right by hers, every line and plane as familiar as her own. A face she dreamed of belonging to a male she longed for. She reached up, stroking her finger over the grey skin. "I don't regret a moment of what's happened to me, because I found you in the middle of it all."

His head reared back inches, shock and hope and gratitude mixed together in his expression. He cupped her face, tilting her head back. His lips were warm with the right pressure, demanding she open to him without bullying her on it.

This was connection, soul-deep and scary in how right it was. His wings came around her, wrapping her in an embrace more consuming than any that only consisted of arms. Those wings brought them together, sinking skin into skin, and even that wasn't nearly close enough.

"Your lips are so soft," he said, pulling back the tiniest bit, as if parting hurt him. "All of you is so soft."

He didn't take her mouth again, but pressed his lips against the underside of her chin. With exquisite leisure he made his way down the side of her throat, only moving further after every inch had been explored.

She groaned. "Terak, what are you doing to me?"

He loved her breathy voice. He loved everything about her, but he especially loved she was now in his arms. "Do not humans enjoy this?" He licked her pulse point, the texture of her skin under his tongue a wonderful sensation. "Or this? Shall I tell you what gargoyles enjoy, little human? What a male will do when he has a female in his arms that he has dreamed about since the first moment he saw her?"

Her breathless *"Show me"* almost dropped him to his knees. Instead, he stepped back and pulled her shirt from her pants, ripping the front and scattering buttons. "I hurt every time I left you. You had me wanting, and it felt as if I would never be at ease again."

Her smile had an edge. She liked the torment she had put him through. "I need to make that up to you."

His clawed fingers traced the edge of lace on her bra. It was blue, the same blue of her eyes, and it offered her up to his mouth those plump, mouth -watering mounds. "Wearing this, *Meyja*, is apology enough."

He leaned down, his tongue tracing the edge of the lace. Her head fell backwards, offering him access to what he desired. "I love your tongue. I love how warm you are." She shook her head, as though trying to clear it. "What does *Meyja* mean?"

Coward he might be, but he wasn't ready to tell her yet. He could not chance her feelings not being the same as his, or worse, that they were, but she could not go against her family to accept him. "I will tell you after we defeat our enemy. This way you will have something pleasant to obsess over in the coming days."

Her frown told him what she thought of that, but there were ways to distract her. He stroked his claws over her stomach to her waistband and pulled the pants down her long legs.

She stood before him, bare except her undergarments. He needed to bury his face between her legs, let her taste dance on his tongue. She was warm and sweet and he needed her more than the air he breathed.

He picked her up, coming to his feet and carrying her to her bedroom. "Terak?" she asked, but stopped when he put her down on the bed.

"Shh, *Meyja*. Let me do this. I need you."

He nuzzled her through her blue panties, her little coils of hair crushing beneath his nose as he breathed deep her intoxicating fragrance.

His tongue came out and pushed against her through her panties. She groaned, wrapping her hands in his hair and holding on as if it was her only source of stability. "Oh gods yes, I do love that tongue."

He pulled the underwear to the side, and swiped his tongue over her bare sex.

Her cries dimly registered in his ears. She was pink and perfect, sweet with an undercurrent of tang.

Very much how she was in all other ways.

He wanted to take his time, bring her satisfaction over and over. His tongue moved on her and brought a long, keening cry to her lips. "Terak! Please."

"Please what?"

"I want to come. I want to come when it isn't my own hand bringing me satisfaction."

The thought of her touching herself flashed through his mind and he growled. She would do that for him one day soon.

But not now. Now she would come because of his tongue.

The little nub at the top of her sex was glistening, beckoning him. He surrounded it with his mouth, giving gentle pulls that had her gasping.

"Yes, Terak. Like that."

He pulled a little harder.

"I was wrong before. Just like that."

He smiled, and then went to work. She had the most decadent taste he had ever experienced, water after having survived crossing the desert.

The muscles in her thighs jumped under his hand, giving proof to her excitement. Her groans grew in volume, begging him to finish it.

Finally she keened, her back arching as the tremors against his tongue spoke of her climax.

Her body was pulsing in aftershock, the ripples driving him insane, because he wanted his cock inside her to experience it that way. He wanted to be deep inside her. He wanted to come in her as she clenched around him, marking her with his seed. Marking her as his woman in body as she had been in mind since the first moment he had seen her.

Her fingers uncurled from his hair, and she laughed. "I hope I didn't pull out any hair."

"A small loss considering what I have been given this night."

She smiled again, her face radiant. "That was fun. Maybe we can do other things now?"

A pounding at her door forced them apart and had him on his feet.

Worst timing in the history of man. "Who is it?" Larissa called out.

"Michael," came her brother's voice, loud and pissed with an undercurrent of scared, enough to remind her she never called her brother after being taken away from him to let him know she was all right.

Oops.

Terak looked at the door as if the thought of punching through it to get to the man on the other side was a good idea. She should probably prevent that. Larissa rubbed her hand over his chest. "He always did have the worst timing," she murmured.

His eyes blazed with more than interrupted lust. "He took you to the Guild. He allowed you to be harmed."

Warmth seeped through her over his fear for her, but it would do no good to allow this anger at her brother. "He didn't know what was going to happen, and he would never have knowingly allowed something to happen to me."

"It does not change the fact that he lost you."

The banging on her door started again. This was an argument they were going to have to have later. "He's my brother and he's not going away, so no matter how mad you are, you need to play nice, and you need to change into your human form."

CHAPTER TWENTY-SEVEN

As soon as the door opened Michael grabbed Larissa by the upper arms. "You couldn't be bothered to call me? I was out of my head worried over you!"

Before she could reassure him, Terak came forward and pulled her away from Michael, placing her behind his now-human form. Great. Just what she needed, another overprotective male.

Now Michael's expression was turning thunderous as he stared at the male who would dare involve himself in family business. If they started a pissing contest, she was kicking them both out. "Michael, I'm fine. I'm fine."

He paid no attention to her, all his focus on Terak. "Who the hell do you think you are?"

Terak straightened at Michael's tone. If he had been in gargoyle form, his wings would have flared out. "I am her protector, and you will not touch her in such a way again."

"Terak," Larissa whispered, placing her hand on his back. "He was worried about me, and he didn't hurt me at all, I promise. You won't find a mark on me."

Michael had to step up the tension though. "Oh yes, the oh-so-great protector my sister loves to talk about. Got a question for you – if you're such a great protector, why couldn't my sister get hold of you today?"

Terak stood his ground. "There seems to be a problem with the magic. Though it should never have come to that, in the end it matters not. I would have returned soon. You should have waited for me. It was foolish of you to take her alone to meet with Guild members."

Michael's hands came to his hips. "I'm a cop, who the hell are you to talk to me about going into danger? Besides that, I don't try to control my sister."

Larissa would have snorted at that if she wasn't trying to keep attention away from her.

"So instead you willingly lead her into danger?" Terak bit back.

"Guys!" Larissa stepped out from behind Terak to get between the two males and pushed them apart. "Stop posturing. What's done is done. All we can do is learn from this and decide if we'd do something different next time."

Michael looked like he wanted to say more. Actually, he looked like he wanted to punch Terak. Probably the only thing stopping him was the fact that even in human form, it looked like punching Terak was more likely to cause him to break his fist than cause any damage to Terak. "I need to talk to my sister, and if you don't mind, I'd like to do it privately."

Terak crossed his arms over his chest. "I will not leave her."

It was a stare-off of epic proportions. Neither was backing down, and she was the chew-toy between them.

Then Michael's eyes flickered, and he stared hard, taking them both in – her hastily donned clothes, Terak's too-small shirt, her had-to-be swollen lips and lovemarked neck. As if a light switch had flipped, Michael now appeared a little green around the edges. "Did I interrupt something?"

Why did she feel like a teenager caught necking? Oh right, maybe because that was darn close to the truth. "Michael, that is none of your business."

He scrubbed his hands over his face, reeling away from them. "Oh gods, I did."

Well, this was awkward.

Terak stiffened behind her. When she turned his eyes were closed and his brow furrowed. "Terak?"

His eyes opened then, at first unfocused before returning to awareness. After he came back to himself he gave Michael a hard stare – which her brother handily returned – before he pulled her into the doorway of her bedroom, still in Michael's sight but beyond his hearing range. He put his mouth to her ear and whispered, "Malek has called me. There is need for me."

Terak looked none-to-happy. "Is anything wrong?"

His mouth thinned. "While I was not given details, there must be. Malek would not call otherwise."

Michael had the good manners not to try to listen in to their conversation, but he didn't leave their line of sight and his glare was focused on Terak.

She didn't want Terak to leave. Selfish, yes, but after the night she had she didn't want him anywhere out of her sight.

And after what had been going on not ten minutes ago, she wanted to finish what they had started. She was wet and achy, and thoughts of his mouth on hers and his cock pounding inside her took most of the available space inside her brain.

But his people needed him, and as much as the upcoming conversation would suck, she really needed to speak with Michael. "I promise I won't leave. You need to go and learn what's happening with your people."

He shook his head. "You are not safe here alone and I will not risk you again."

"Terak, your people need you."

"I need you to be safe."

The war was clear on his face. That he placed her welfare on the same level as his Clan humbled her, enveloped her in a warmth much gentler and sweeter than the inferno he had ignited in her minutes ago. "It would hurt me to know your people did not have you near when they needed you because of me. Go."

His mouth opened and closed several times, but no sound came out. His hands reached down and enveloped her face and he brought his forehead down to hers.

She brought her hands up to cover his. "Come back to me when you can. I'll be waiting."

His head lifted a little, his eyes opening and looking into hers. His gaze was clear and he allowed her to look at everything in him, past his barriers. It hurt, this gift of himself, but it was a welcome pain. "I will always come for you, little human. Never doubt that."

She nodded. "I know. Go."

In a shaky, stilted movement so unlike him, he turned from her and went out the front door, never stopping and never looking back, not even that last moment as the door closed behind him.

Even though he would be back, having him out of her sight had her heart crumpling. They were on the verge of something, and this interruption couldn't have been timed worse.

Michael cleared his throat. His patience was admirable and unexpected, but it was time to deal with him. "Michael, I was wrong to not call you as soon as I was safe, and I'm sorry. But you have no business talking to him like that. He saved me."

He looked at her, question in his eyes. "I'm confused, Ris. Who is this guy to you? First I thought he was a boyfriend, then an acquaintance who for some reason was guarding you, and now I have no clue."

She sat on her couch, looking around her room as different ways to tell Michael about Terak formed and were discarded. Her coat was lying by the balcony door. Funny how she didn't remember taking it off, but every second of Terak tearing off her shirt was seared into her brain. When she was ninety and rocking away in a nursing home, she'd still remember that moment.

"I told you once, he is special and I'd never regret that he had been in my life. That's still the truth. As for anything further, I'm not going to talk to you about it when we haven't even discussed it."

Michael sat down next to her. "I don't like it, but that's fair."

"How did you know I was back in the apartment?"

"When you were kidnapped I brought my unit in to help get you back. I had people everywhere, including watching here. My CO called me and said you were back. It might have been nice if he warned me about the guy with you, though."

Wait, if they were watching, wouldn't they have seen Terak with her? Why wouldn't they have been more worried about the appearance of a gargoyle and given Michael all the details?

But maybe they hadn't seen her enter. Maybe they simply saw the lights in her apartment go on, and called on that alone.

And maybe the little knot in her stomach was pure nerves and this sense of uneasiness was simply a remnant of a horrible night best forgotten, nothing more.

Maybe.

CHAPTER TWENTY-EIGHT

Nalith stood out from among the crowd who were waiting, striding toward Terak even before his feet hit stone. "What is this, you imprison the future *Meyla*?"

His council member was walking a dangerous line. "You will not question me in such a way," Terak said. "I am sure you have heard of her crimes."

Larissa did not need to know this was the reason he was called away. Malek contacted him through the same magic means as the silver ball he had given Larissa, to tell him Nalith was inciting discord and close to advocating open rebellion, placing blame on Larissa and questioning why Terak was with her.

Nalith's voice rose in contemptuous rhythm, so all the surrounding warriors could hear. "I heard no crimes, only how the future mate of our Clan Leader was fulfilling her responsibility to us, in looking to make treaty with those who can assure the future safety of our Clan. You say we should not question you? I say the time for questioning you has been left for far too long. You have abandoned our Clan, instead concentrating all your time on a human female who is unworthy."

His people were watching this battle. None seemed to be active in their support for Nalith, but many of their faces held a shadow of doubt.

Terak had made his decision this night. His decision – *his choice* – was Larissa. His Clan would either walk with him on this path and make their way together among the New Realms, or he would forge his own path while gargoyles stayed in the shadows and hidden in their keep.

Either way, the Clan's future would be decided tonight.

That didn't mean he would give up without a fight. "You would have as my mate one who would defy the desires of Clan and Council? Valry is no longer my Intended. She lost that privilege by conspiring with vampires. So careful Nalith, or I will think you were in league with Valry in her betrayal. Do you wish to be inside the prison as well?"

Nalith straightened to his full height "Is it so wrong I wished to hear how our people could be more powerful in this realm?"

"So do you admit you contacted the vampires with Valry?"

"With pride." Nalith's eyes blazed, his lips peeled back from his teeth. "I served to the best of my ability our strong *Meyla*, not our weak *Mennak*."

"Then in front of all the warriors assembled, you admit treason and dare try to make it appear noble? Did you see treaty with the necromancers as the way for the Clan to gain power, or for *you*?"

"You would have us bare our throats to humans and the Guild. I would have us rule over all."

"Except we would not." Terak raised his voice, a whiplash against Nalith's pathetic excuses. "We would be nothing except servants to necromancers, existing at their whims. I would rather ally and learn to live in this world than be nothing but cowed in front of the necromancers and a bully to all other races."

"You are like your father before you, too weak to walk in real power."

"What you call power I call cowardice – an inability to move forward and meet this realm and its challenges. I will not ally with evil because my own fear." He nodded to Malek. "Take him away."

Before Malek could step forward, Nalith brought out a short sword. "You think you are such a great leader? You call me a coward? I call you the dog of a human. I challenge you."

"You would fight me with a magical weapon for the challenge?"

Nalith smiled, a vitriolic twist of lips. "It is not forbidden, *Mennak*." The title dripped contempt as Nalith circled him, the sword before him.

For a coward, his hold on the sword was surprisingly good. There had been practice with this weapon. "Drop the sword. You will not be forgiven for this."

"Once you are dead and the pathetic leadership you have displayed is no longer in effect, I think I will not only be forgiven, but I will lead this Clan to a new age of gargoyles."

Nalith swiped at Terak and kept moving. Terak stayed away. Nalith was not a warrior, even if he could handle this weapon. A mistake would be made soon. Terak had to keep Nalith off balance and angered. In anger, mistakes were always made. "You think to be leader? If our enemies see you charge into battle the only way they would be hurt is by falling down in laughter. Younglings have more skill in battle than you."

"Spoken like a true savage. You have no skills save for your prowess on the battlefield, and you would demean those of us who truly rule the Clan."

Nalith lunged again, but his arm was overextended. That was the opening Terak needed. He grabbed Nalith's arm and wrapped his tail around one of Nalith's ankles. Nalith pulled back but overcompensated, and with Terak's tail still around his ankle, he could not right himself Nalith fell, and Terak grabbed the sword.

Several warriors came and restrained Nalith, taking him to the dungeon even as Nalith screamed about the mistake they were making in following Terak.

Malek approached Terak. "Is the human well?"

"Yes. She is unharmed. I saw her emerge from a side door during the assault on the club and collected her." Terak placed a hand on Malek's shoulder. "The attack was executed flawlessly. You did well. Were there any problems?"

"No. There were no injuries on either side, and everything went according to plan." Malek looked uneasy then, his head dropping a few inches. "The Oracle came up behind me. She told me you had the woman and asked if I could retreat because she wished to get her nails done."

"She is indeed a being unlike any other."

"That is one way to phrase it."

"Mennak." Krikus's voice cut through the low rumble of the remaining crowd.

Terak looked away from Malek. Krikus was striding through the crowd in battle armaments that gave reminder to his days as a great warrior before he became a Council member.

"Yes, Councilor?"

Krikus came to stand before him, metal bracers reflecting the light around them. "Was there any truth in Nalith's words?"

His people stood silent as they witnessed the second great clash of the evening. "Let us be plain. What is it you wish to know, Krikus?"

"Your Clan deserves to know the truth of the situation regarding the human."

The crowd had grown around him, wave upon wave of his people. There could be no more subterfuge. He would be the leader that would make his father – make Larissa – proud, or he would not be leader at all.

"I have only always wished for the good of my people. It has been what has guided me from the moment I have been born. However, Nalith has spoken some truth. I am lost without my little human. She is my mate, my *Meyja*," Terak said, ignoring the gasps that surrounded him. "And I proclaim her so in front of all of you. I will live at her side, and if the Clan cannot accept her as my mate, then I will leave the Clan."

Krikus alone seemed unsurprised by Terak's proclamation. "And to accept the human is to accept living among the other races of the realms, is that not true?"

"We no longer have the luxury of isolating ourselves."

Krikus stared him down, something the older gargoyle had not done since Terak was a boy. "You have given the Clan much to consider. You must allow Council and Clan time to discuss."

Krikus's words might say *consider*, but Terak knew. He had lost his Clan this night. They would not follow Nalith or Valry, but damage had been done and they would follow him no longer. He was strong enough he could hold on through sheer force, but no, that was not the leader he wished to be. If the Clan no longer wished to follow him, he would honor that wish.

Surprising, he thought it would hurt more. But Larissa's face blazed bright in dark places, and this decision was the easiest he had ever made. Terak nodded at Krikus and watched the older gargoyle depart, leaving him alone except for Malek. There was nothing more for him here, and he spread his wings for flight.

"*Mennak*." Malek stopped him. The younger gargoyle looked vulnerable at that moment, a rare expression from Terak's second-in-command.

Terak gripped Malek's shoulder hard. "Calm, Malek. We both know how this will play out. You are ready for this role. I would not have selected you otherwise."

"I am not capable of being half the leader you have been, Terak."

"No, you will be greater. I will always be there if you have need of me. Be a good leader for our people. Guide them well. I am sorry I am leaving you with such a heavy burden, but none I have more faith in than you." With a final squeeze, Terak opened his wings to their full span and he took flight.

Malek's voice followed him. "Is she worth the loss of the Clan?"

She is worth everything.

CHAPTER TWENTY-NINE

She was sleeping, his little human, her eyelashes soft shades under closed eyelids. Her lips made a little pout as she slept, as if she was waiting for a kiss. That was one request he would always grant.

He ghosted his lips over hers, bit by bit applying more pressure with each pass, until she woke. Those eyes opened, the room too dark to see their full color, but after the focused on him they relaxed, losing the lines of confusion and settling into happiness. "I'm sorry I fell asleep. It's been a long day."

He pushed her hair back from her cheek, the petal-soft skin sensitizing the nerve endings in his fingers. "Yes, it has. I wish I had the willpower to let you sleep as you need, but I could not wait that long to hear your voice again."

"You need to be careful saying things like that. A girl could get used to them."

"I am afraid I am unable to speak anything but the truth. I hope you can forgive me my bluntness."

She pushed herself up with one hand while her other hand stroked over the contours of his human face. "I guess I'll have to learn to manage."

He gathered her into his arms and laid her head against his chest. "You are very good to me, thank you."

For several minutes she stayed still in his arms, resting against him and occasionally rubbing her cheek against the spot over his heart.

She broke the silence. "Your heartbeat is different than a human's."

"Gargoyles have two hearts. No matter my outside appearance, I am not human."

She pushed back against his arms, giving herself enough space that she could look up into his face and meet his eyes. "Even looking at you now, seeing you in your shifted form, I'm very aware you are not human. I am here with a gargoyle, and I would have it no other way."

A weight he had not been aware of broke free inside him at her words. He swallowed hard to tamp down the shout of joy that threatened to escape. "In our creation myths, it is said gargoyles began as creatures created of magic. The first of us were created by wizards to be companions to humans, to be used however the humans desired. But the wizards made us too strong, and soon we overcame our masters and created the first of the Clans."

Her eyes widened, and he saw the scholarly part of her nature come to the fore. "Is that true?"

"How can anyone know the truth when magic is involved?" He could not help but smile at her chastened look. She was adorable, and brave, and sensual, and all his.

And he would wait no longer to make her his mate.

Terak lowered his voice, and was rewarded by her eyes half closing and her breathing becoming labored. "I know not. What I do know is gargoyles and humans are *compatible*."

He covered her mouth with his, a deep invasion that gave no mercy. She would have no doubt to the meaning of his words.

She met him stroke for stroke, his little warrior. She rose up on her knees so their mouths were level and brought her arms around his shoulders as she dug her nails into his back.

She was wearing a flimsy shirt and the same underwear she wore before. Her scent, that same scent that made his mouth water in desperation, wafted around their sanctuary and held him in thrall.

She was aggressive, crawling up his body for better leverage. She pushed into him, her tongue attacking his mouth. As she dominated him from above her hips worked on him, moving in the sensual rhythm he had seen her use many times as she danced while he watched from afar.

His hands wrapped around her hips, not to stop the little movements she made, but to encourage her to bring them closer, let him feel every delicious torment her body delivered to his. She obliged, and that sweet warmth between her thighs settled over his cock. At the desired sensation his hips shot forward in instinctive reaction. Without the fabric of her panties, he would have been inside her.

This unseated her, and she fell forward, her momentum startling him enough that he fell backward on the bed while she landed atop of him.

Her head picked up, embarrassment clear in the lines of her open mouth and wide eyes. But after a few moments she started laughing.

No sound was more dear to him, save her moans and cries when she came. "What is so funny, *Meyja*?"

Still chuckling, she ducked her head, discomfiture still evident. "We're both virgins. This situation might be hopeless."

He rolled her over so she was now on her back while he loomed above her. He nuzzled her behind her ear, making small moans erupt from her throat. "I may not have done anything yet, but I have imagined you naked and beneath me too many times to count." He leaned up and took off the shirt that hid her from his view, her bare breasts now visible to him. Her shocked gasp ended on a low moan, and her lower body started moving again.

With one finger he circled her tight nipple, the skin there pebbled and rougher than other areas of her body. But would she taste the same here, at this little pink area? His tongue laved over her, dampening the peak and tightening it further.

His teeth scraped over the nipple and he was rewarded with a low wail. He rolled it in his mouth, loving her taste here as everywhere else.

The only place she tasted better was between her legs.

One hand wandered over the gentle slope of her belly to delve into those little curls. She was panting, her legs coming apart to give him complete access. "Believe me when I say this, little human – I might not be perfect this night, but I won't stop until I have you coming apart in my arms."

She was wet and warm and perfect, as she had been earlier. "Terak, take off our clothing. I need skin."

Never would he deny her anything. Her undergarments were pulled from her body, followed by his pants, pulled with such haste he heard a rip as they came off him.

What did it matter? It didn't, not when she lay bare before him. "Spread your legs, *Meyja*. Spread your legs and let me feast."

Meyja. There was something so intimate, so sensual about the word. It rolled off Terak's tongue in a deep rumble, and her body went hot at the sound of it.

She had been half-serious in her conversation before about their experience, but the heat and conviction radiating from Terak indicated there was nothing to worry about.

His body was stunning, almost seven feet of thick, hard male, all hers for the taking.

She ran her tongue over her bottom lip. He seemed to like that, if the bobbing of his already hard cock was any indication. Gods, he *was* huge, as big as her imagination supplied that long-ago day.

It might take a little getting used to, but she was sure she was up for the task.

He climbed onto the bed, lowering himself between her legs. "There will not be any more interruptions from your family, will there?"

Poor Terak. What he suffered for her. "No. Michael has no desire to come anywhere near this place for quite a while."

He ran his fingernails up and down her thighs, raising goosebumps in his path. "Good. Because I do not think I could stop myself from killing the next person who interrupts me, a member of your Clan or no."

"I won't stop you. If I had a gun, I'd shoot him myself."

His fingers kept up their lazy glide until he grabbed her between her thighs and spread her legs, using his shoulders to hold them apart as he settled between them. "I am glad we are in agreement. Now, I wish to put my mouth to other uses."

Her hand shot down to push back on his head. "But you've already done that. Don't you want me to return the favor and do things to you?"

Not moving from where he rested, Terak grabbed her hand and gave each finger a kiss, nipping the littlest finger when he reached it. It was a quick pain, sharp but quickly forgotten. "I wish that very much, but not tonight. Tonight I want to gorge myself on you to convince myself this is not another dream."

"Well, how can I refuse?"

His mouth gave a quick curl into one of his almost smiles, but this one was different than others, the sensual cast reserved for this intimacy. "You are most generous. I thank you."

Those stormy grey eyes locked onto hers as his head lowered, his heated breath covering the damp flesh between her legs. His tongue peeked out, broad and flat and oh-so-talented. Oh yes, she would never forget how talented he was.

He gave a long swipe over her clit, the *zing* of sensation racing up her spine with only that little movement. "I wish to drink you down, but it would be best for you to remain wet. Therefore, I will only play here to make you come."

That sounded like a reasonable plan…and then thought processes ceased as his firm lips closed over her clit and with soft, sucking motions he brought her deeper into his mouth.

Her hands found themselves in his hair again as she held on while he played with her. His tongue would press into her, only to flick away when she pushed harder into him. She wailed, "Don't tease me."

Only for him to do it again.

Amidst this teasing one finger entered her, slow and gentle, a tentative stroke that sensitized her far more than it should. "Another finger."

He did, and now she was being stretched. She licked her lips, absorbing the newness of his actions, and in response Terak moaned. She opened her eyes to see Terak fixated on her face as he worked her body.

With his monstrous control he could do this to her all night, and that wasn't the area she wanted him to exert his control in. "Terak, I love this, but I want you in me. Please."

He let her go, rising above her and bringing his lips back to hers. The kiss was firm but his lips trembled. "You have not come yet."

"I'll come with you in me."

"But I have read it is difficult for a woman to achieve satisfaction that way."

He was so unsure, her warrior, looking down at her with anxious eyes. All because he wanted to please her. How did she get so lucky? "You read up on human mating habits?" she said, only allowing the most gentle tease into her voice.

Even at that a blush graced his cheeks. "I want you never to regret this."

"I never will. Now, come into me."

He entwined his fingers with hers as he settled between her legs. His skin was warm and rough, fine sandpaper against hers, and he squeezed her fingers as his hips pushed into hers.

It was fullness more than pain, a stretching no fingers could duplicate. His pace was slow, coming into her in small degrees until he seated himself fully in her.

"Larissa?"

It was only after they opened that she realized she had closed her eyes. "I'm fine. It feels nice and strange, but nice."

"I am not sure *nice* is the word most males wish to hear at this moment."

Her laughter bubbled forth, her gargoyle's sense of humor becoming ever more prominent and showing up at the most unusual times. She squeezed his hand harder, loving that he was here with her and that he was hers.

She raised her head and brushed her mouth against his, needing connection with him in every place her body would allow it.

Terak deepened the kiss and started to move within her, the pace slow at first.

Nice was also falling by the wayside, forced aside by the rekindling of the fire they shared earlier, a fire that had been banked by nervousness and the interruption of reality.

His moan told her he was experiencing it too. Their entwined hands he brought to rest on the bed by her head. His other hand he used to wrap her leg around his hip, giving him leverage and providing a different angle to thrust.

"*Holy hell!*" Dear gods, what was that *spot* he was hitting now, the one that had every pleasure center in her body sit up and start singing hallelujah?

His mouth went to her neck, kissing under her ear while his hips kept a steady rhythm to her moaning pleas. Those hips bucking into her were relentless.

The pressure was building in her, the same pattern Terak forced from her earlier in the evening. "Terak, I'm coming. Move, faster, move faster by *gods* move faster."

His mouth covered hers, his hand coming to bury itself in her hair as he did as he was instructed, burying himself to the hilt in her over and over in ever-quickening thrusts.

White was all she saw behind her eyelids while her body pulsed around him. She could feel every vein of his shaft as she squeezed him with the force of her orgasm.

Terak's low, pained groans sounded in her ear as he joined her, binding them together.

CHAPTER THIRTY

Larissa was dozing on his chest, her hair splayed over his chest in a cascade he could not stop running his fingers through.

She stirred, her eyes opening to show him that glorious blue. After taking a moment to focus, a small smile played over her lips. "Hi," she said.

"Never have I seen anything more perfect than you at this moment."

She blushed deep red at that, her eyes refusing to meet his. "I think you are beautiful as well."

"My human form or my gargoyle self?"

His tone was more hesitant than he would have wished. At his words, her gaze came back to his, all signs of embarrassment gone. She clasped his face between her two small hands. Such a soft prison. "Don't you know? Both. I find both so beautiful."

He kissed her, and everything – his love, his devotion, his *soul* – was in that kiss, hers for the taking.

They strained against each other, their bodies eager for a continuation of the pleasure of the night before. He stroked over her round, firm bottom and squeezed. She broke off the kiss, laughing and blushing. "I'm a little too sore for anything right now."

Instantly he sat up. "What do you need?"

She grabbed his arm, bringing him down. "I need you to cuddle me. Unless gargoyle males have as much a problem with that as human males apparently do."

"I do not ask my fellow warriors such things, but I always wish to be surrounded with you."

She cuddled against his shoulder. "Tell me a secret."

You are my queen, you are my love, and I gladly leave my Clan for you. He said, "My parents loved each other."

She raised her eyes to his. "That's a secret?"

"Remember I told you that the Clan Leader does not marry for love, he marries the strongest female for the sake of the Clan?"

She nodded. "And you told me the first night that you inherited from your father your title."

"In the Magic Realm, gargoyles were not one great Clan. There were several smaller Clans who were allies but did not answer to each other. My father was a great warrior, the Clan Leader of the largest and strongest of these scattered Clans. His Intended was the strongest, as was our custom."

"And your mother?"

"My mother's Clan was one of the smallest Clans. They were also a Clan with a greedy and unjust leader. His avarice caused the downfall of that Clan and the loss of many lives. The survivors sought my father to ask for admittance into his Clan."

Larissa went up on one elbow to look down at him. "What happened?"

"My father told me he took one look at her and knew he wanted no other female. But she was not deemed suitable."

"Why not?"

"Her mother was human."

Larissa's eyes went saucer wide. "Your mother was half-human?"

"Gargoyles can mate with humans, as well you should know," he added, leaning up to kiss her where neck met shoulder.

She giggled, squirming under his mouth. "Yes, but I didn't realize that there could be children."

"Perhaps there is more to our origin myth than merely a story to tell around the fire. Any child created in such a union is born a gargoyle. While not common, it is also not unheard of for a gargoyle to take a human mate."

The last humor left her face, and she worried her lower lip between her teeth. "But are such unions frowned on?"

"No more than a gargoyle taking as mate a gargoyle from another Clan. Until they prove themselves loyal to the Clan, they are regarded with suspicion."

"But you said that your mother was not accepted as worthy."

He brushed her long hair back, the multiple hues of blonde caressing his fingers. "What is acceptable for an ordinary Clan member is not always acceptable for the Leader of all. Is it not the same for humans?"

Her gaze lowered, her generous mouth turning down. "Yeah, I guess it is."

He lifted her chin so she would meet his gaze. "My father defied his Clan and married my mother."

Her expression could not settle on one emotion and flickered between hope and trepidation. "Were there any consequences?"

"My father was too strong for anyone in the Clan to take his title, but he was never seen in the same light again. When my mother died, he lost himself, for she was his world. That led to more talk about how he had been weak to mate with her. He died not long after."

Larissa stroked his face. "I'm so sorry."

He accepted her gentle caring and pushed his face into her hand. "It was long ago. But while I planned to return to my Clan's tradition and mate with the strongest female, I never once believed when they said loving my mother made my father weak. I saw him with her. I knew better than anyone – loving her only gave him strength. I always envied that he could mate with the female he loved while I could not."

"Then why go back to the old ways?"

"After the Great Collision, the various Clans needed to band together if we were to survive in this new world. This was not an easy process. While the Clans had always been allies, this did not mean the various factions were friends. In order to bring some stability to the Clans, I needed to make clear my intention of honoring the old ways."

She stroked his cheek with the back of her fingers. "Like I said, a good leader."

He rolled her over underneath him, kissing her. "Terak-"

"You are still sore, little human. This does not mean I cannot kiss it to make it better."

She was sighing as he kissed down her body. "Tell me secrets of yours," he said, before licking a nipple.

"Mmmm," she groaned in appreciation. "Let's see. I'm allergic to peanut butter."

"I'm very sorry to hear it."

"I'm double-jointed in a lot of areas."

"This explains much of what you did last night," he said, spreading her legs and anchoring his shoulders between them.

"And I was…oh *gods,* Terak. Do that again."

"I am yours to command."

CHAPTER THIRTY-ONE

Terak leaned her over the bed. The sheet was cool as it slid over her nipples but behind her, he was an inferno, his thighs behind her, his cock rubbing the valley between her thighs...

A knock sounded at the entrance of the teacher's lounge and Taneasha Jackson stuck her head in. "Miss Miller?"

Maybe fantasizing about her sex life during the school day *wasn't* the best idea ever, even if she was on a break. Larissa drew in a deep breath and hoped her voice was steady when she said, "Yes?"

Taneasha looked nervous, her eyes darting to the side before coming to meet hers again. "I was wondering if I could talk to you?"

The girl's worried tone was enough to shake off any vestiges of embarrassment. Larissa motioned with her hand. "Of course, come in."

Taneasha made sure the door was closed before walked to stand before Larissa and started talking again. "Miss Miller, I need to talk to you about something important. But before we start, I need you to promise you won't get upset with me."

Oh no. Was Taneasha pregnant? On drugs? Larissa took her hand. "I promise I'll never get upset. I always want you to feel like you can come to me."

Taneasha nodded, licking her lips. "Miss Miller... I'm studying magic."

It was so far from what Larissa was expecting that full comprehension took several long moments. "Excuse me?"

"My mom forbade it, but I love it so much. I have a gift for it, my Master – that's what you call your magic teacher – he told me so."

This was not good. This was very not good, and Larissa's stomach dropped as horrifying possibilities for the girl in front of her flitted through her mind. "Taneasha, this is serious. You can't practice without the proper guidance. Magic is regulated for a reason, and it is always forbidden within the city."

"I know, but I couldn't pass up this opportunity to learn. My family would never have permitted it if I asked them."

No, Larissa knew enough about Taneasha's family to know it was not even the remotest possibility. She ran her hands through her hair. She was bound by oath to report this, but if she did, this girl would be severely punished. "Taneasha-"

Before Larissa could finish, Taneasha broke in. "Miss Miller, I told you this because something bad is happening to you."

That caught Larissa's attention. "What?"

"My Master says that once you start learning magic, you begin to feel when things aren't right with the people you care about and...well..." she blushed and looked away, then brought her attention back to Larissa. "Anyway, I've been having a bad feeling about you, so I've been casting spells, on my own and with my Master's help. They are meant for your protection and your welfare. And I've discovered some things."

Taneasha looked around, and then, from her backpack, she brought forth a globe. "Don't touch this, just look into it."

Larissa did. She was looking from someone's point of view, though whose was anyone's guess.

The mystery person walked into a large grove. From the looks of the grounds it had to be sometime in summer, early autumn at the latest.

As soon as the mystery person laid eyes on the female in the distance, they stopped.

It was the Oracle. She was wearing more than what she wore at the club, but not by much. A diaphanous white gown, with a square neck but high slits running along both thighs. She wore a gold collar and large gold cuff bracelets.

"Very punctual, Clan Leader of the Gargoyles."

And Terak's voice answered, "I am grateful I can say the same for you, Oracle."

Larissa was seeing through Terak's eyes.

She wasn't going to invade Terak's mind like this. About to pick up the globe and give it back to Taneasha, she paused when she heard the Oracle say, "Her name is Larissa Miller."

"And what care I about a human woman? Gargoyles are not bodyguards, nor are we your lackeys."

"I am not asking you to watch the woman for my sake, Clan Leader, but for you and for your Clan."

"What do you mean?"

"She is connected to the future of your Clan. Guard her well." With that pronouncement, the Oracle turned to leave.

"What do you mean?" Terak called after her. "How is she important? What am I to guard her against? I demand answers."

The Oracle looked over her shoulder and smiled. "Feel free to make an appointment. I believe I'm free in a few years."

The scene shifted, and now as Terak Larissa was looking upon many arguing gargoyles. Valry stood. "Have we sunk so low as to bow before the Oracle?"

"The Oracle has never been wrong," called a voice from the back.

"How can she be, when she makes such vague pronouncements? Merely by the act of being observed, this human becomes important to our Clan as she has taken our *Mennak* away from us for long periods of time. We have no use for the outside world, especially for a woman such as this, one who lives in the confines of the *human*-only city. Think she cares about gargoyles?"

Loud agreement followed the words, with shouts and stomping of feet. Malek stood. "While I will not say I am in complete disagreement with Valry's words, I am not so eager to cast off the words of the Oracle. I would wish to observe the human for a period of time. What can that hurt?"

Larissa-as-Terak stood. "I have heard all your words. All of it wise counsel, but I must choose a path. I choose to watch the human. While I do not trust the Oracle, I will not ignore her for no reason other than pride."

The scene faded, replaced by other. Now the scenes sped up.

Her. It was Terak watching her, before they had ever met.

She saw the seasons change. How long had he been watching her – two, three months?

And then the bottom dropped out of her stomach.

The building across the street. The protective presence she sometimes wondered about, always attributing to an overactive imagination.

Stupid. Stupid woman. Why the hell didn't you ever question anything? Why did you never question Terak?

Because everything had always been going so fast. There never seemed to be time to sit still and think.

Terak hadn't shown up as some good Samaritan who happened to pass by. He'd been watching her for a long time.

"Don't cry, Miss Miller." Taneasha covered Larissa's hand with her own. With her other hand, Larissa put her fingertips to her cheek, shocked that tears covered the surface.

"I'm so sorry, but you have to see one more thing."

Again she was looking from what she assumed was Terak's point of view. This time he was looking at a man.

Red eyes. No, not a man – a vampire.

They were in a wooded area, the light dim but not yet full dark, so it had to either be at sunrise or sunset. The trees contained the full spectrum of color, which meant this hadn't happened very long ago. The vampire spoke first. "We need her and her alone. To possess her we would be willing to pay a very high price."

The vampire had to mean *her*. He was talking to Terak about her.

"How high?"

No, no. That can't be. Terak was setting him up, there was some kind of trap being planned at that exact moment. He could not be asking what this vampire would give in exchange for her.

"When we return the Magic Realm to its former state, gargoyles will rule over all, second only to the necromancers."

Any moment, a band of gargoyles would jump out and trap the vampire. Any moment.

Any moment.

"I need time to consider my options. How do I contact you to reopen negotiations?"

The little ball went white.

The heater in the school room kicked on, blowing hot air directly overhead. Outside the door the five-minute warning bell rang, indicating that class would be over soon. A couple doors opened, and a low hum of voices drifted on air currents.

All so normal. How could everything be so normal? Shouldn't this much pain be heralded by some change: a blizzard, a volcanic explosion? Shouldn't something happen in the world when her heart shriveled in her chest?

Terak had betrayed her.

He had been watching her for months, planning to give her to the vampires since the beginning. Helping her? He probably was keeping her safe to get better terms for his Clan.

Taneasha wrapped Larissa's hand with her own. "Miss Miller, I know they're watching you right now. I can cast a spell to get you out of here without them seeing. Do you want that? I can take you to my Master and he can help."

"Yes." She'd use Taneasha's help to get away from them, then she'd go home. She'd tell Dad everything and let him figure out the next step, because she was done. She was finished being terrorized and bullied and made love to…

A sob escaped her throat, and Larissa put her face down into her cupped hands. She dug her fingers into the skin of her face and forced herself to calm down. This was not the place to fall apart.

Taneasha stroked her hair. "Right after school, meet me at the gym. I'll have everything ready, and we'll get you to safety."

CHAPTER THIRTY-TWO

Taneasha dragged her through the back gate behind the gym. Larissa didn't ask where she got the key when only the gym teacher was supposed to have it. Wondering about that was for later, after she avoided Terak and got to Taneasha's house.

A car idled at the curb, and Taneasha got in without hesitation, her hand wrapped around Larissa's wrist in a death lock. Larissa was pulled in, the door shut behind her, and the car took off, tires squealing as they peeled away from the curb.

As they rode, Larissa's mind became a jumble. Images of Terak from last night overlapping with the conversations that little ball showed her, and always present were the eyes of that vampire, glowing red as they bartered her life the same way someone would for a piece of meat.

The car went over a bump hard enough that Larissa was jostled in her seat and her mind came back to the present. She looked out the window, unable to place where they were. "Taneasha, this isn't the way to your house."

"I couldn't take you to my house. Too many questions." Taneasha looked around as though to assure herself that they weren't being followed. "Don't worry, Miss Miller. They'll take care of the gargoyle."

Unease trickled through Larissa. "Who are *they*?"

"My Master's other students. They were told to look out for the gargoyle."

"You never mentioned anything about that."

Taneasha looked out the side window, her attention away from Larissa. "I'm getting you to safety, so don't worry about anything."

Maybe it was because she was in the *very* unfamiliar position of being out of control around a student, but Larissa's spine began to tingle, waves of warning electrifying her nerve endings and making their presence known. "Let me out at City Hall, Taneasha. There are people there I know can help me."

"None like my Master, though."

"Yes, your master is very kind to offer…his?…services, but I want out."

"We're already where you need to be."

At that the car stopped and Taneasha started to open the door. Larissa put her hand over Taneasha's arm to stop the girl from leaving. "Taneasha, where are we?"

"We're going to meet my Master."

"I want to go home."

Taneasha's face changed, and the bright, studious, shy girl Larissa knew from class was replaced with this sly creature before her. "But Miss Miller, it took so much to bring you here."

Taneasha jerked her arm away and left the car.

Stupid. Stupid, stupid, stupid, stupid, stupid. How stupid could one woman be? Gods, she never thought Taneasha could betray her, but she should have known better. She should have called her brother.

Larissa drew in a deep breath, using the exhale to center her thoughts. She looked around, but could see nothing in here that could be used as a weapon.

"Come out, Larissa Miller."

The voice was male, though not as commanding as it wanted to be. She didn't want to be in the position of having someone or something reach in and pull her out, so Larissa exited the car.

It was the vampire from the sphere, the one who offered Terak power in exchange for her. Taneasha was at his side, a little puppy awaiting praise.

Without taking his eyes from Larissa, the vampire ran his hand over Taneasha's long braids. "Excellent, Taneasha. You have done well."

Taneasha preened under his praise, her eyes almost closed and her neck arched back so now the puppy was asking for a scratch under its chin.

"Larissa Miller, I am Garof," the vampire said. "You have been a very difficult woman to find."

The driver's side car door opened, and a young man came out. Probably human, but his size and the gun at his shoulder said disregarding him would be a mistake. Larissa focused on the vampire. "Can't say I'm sorry about that."

"No, I don't suppose you are."

Breathing helped center her. She had power, meager as it might be at this moment. These *things* needed her alive for some reason. They had not gone to all this trouble and suffered all those losses to kill her now.

The vampire held up a ring. "I need you to hold out your hand, Miss Miller. I need to try something on you."

"Don't think you're coming anywhere near me with that."

"You can hold out your hand and I shall put this on you in a very simple process, or you can resist and I shall use force to make this happen. Is this truly the time to make your stand?"

When put like that, no, it wasn't. Larissa held out her hand, fingers spread wide to let him put on the damn ring.

Without touching her he slid it over her forefinger. Only when darkness hit her vision did Larissa realize she had closed her eyes against whatever this ring was supposed to do to her. She opened them and saw a plain silver band resting on her finger, comfortable and quiet and so innocuous a vampire should not have it in his possession.

But while the ring looked innocuous, the smile on the vampire's face was anything but. His sick joy radiated out from him, and a shower would be nowhere enough to make her feel clean again.

She ripped the ring off her finger and threw it at him. "There. Whatever you needed to know, you know."

"Yes, I do, Miss Miller. You are perfect for what we need."

"Shove it, I'm not helping you. I know what you are trying to do, and I will not take part in that."

The vampire sneered at her. "You think not, a pitiable excuse for a human like you?" He laughed, contempt in the sound. "You amuse me. You espouse such grandiose statements, but at the first pressure you'll break. All your kind do."

"Go fuck yourself. No matter what you do to me, I'm not helping you." Brave words, but the more he spoke, the smaller she collapsed inside. Gods, she wasn't a warrior. How was she going to stay strong?

The vampire smirked at her. "You think we'll hurt you? You are mistaken. We would not touch you. We need you. This one, though," and he grabbed Taneasha by the hair, making her cry out as he dragged her beside him. "We do not need her."

There was no sly creature here. Now all that was before her was a scared girl who had tried to break away from her family in the stupidest way possible, and was now confronted with the price.

Taneasha held out her hand toward Larissa. "Miss Miller!"

"Get away from her!"

The vampire regarded her coldly. "If you do not do as I say, I will skin this girl alive before your eyes. And if that does not make you change your mind, I will capture another of your students and do the same thing tomorrow. And the day after. And the day after. And I will continue until you agree to help."

Taneasha was screaming, spittle dripping down her mouth. Cold sweat broke out over Larissa's skin as nausea threatened with every breath she took. "I'll do it. Please don't hurt her."

"That easy?" He threw Taneasha into the arms of a waiting male. "And here I thought you weren't going to help us. So you'll sacrifice the entire realm for a few pathetic brats. Or maybe you'll sacrifice the realm to appease your own conscience, so instead of feeling like a murderer, you can cry and wail about how you were tricked." The vampire smirked. "Pathetic."

To the men, he said, "Get ready."

CHAPTER THIRTY-THREE

Wulver strode down the corridor to the meeting room, stopping inside the doorframe as Fallon's raised voice filtered into the corridor. "Next time I see the Oracle I'm going to take one of those spiky shoes she likes to wear and nail her in the *throat*!"

Fallon and Aislynn were both present. Aislynn noticed him first, shaking her head as well as a small shrug to her shoulders, a *What can you do?* move. For her part, Fallon was standing in the middle of the room, hands on her hips and posture as aggressive and aggrieved as it got outside of a battlefield, that sword of hers looking as if it was practically vibrating on her back. He might need to order her to the sparring rooms tonight. Maybe Rorth would be brave enough to partner her.

Wulver leaned against the door. Might as well get comfy while dealing with the seething swordswoman. "Kyo's not too happy with the circumstances, either."

Fallon's gold eyes were hard behind narrowed eyelids, her mouth a compressed line so tight there was no delineation between lip and jaw. "Then he should have had the balls to deny the Oracle. Larissa Miller was here. We had her safe, we could have figured everything out, and instead we had to play games."

In her naiveté, in her constant fight against the powers surrounding them, this was where Fallon's weakness lay. While Wulver had a few moments when he envied her fight, times like this weren't among them. "When don't we play games? When aren't we at the whims of this god or that force? You talk like this is a rare occurrence."

A muscle ticked at where her jawline met her throat, but she didn't answer. Aislynn jumped in, no doubt to calm the negative energy vibrating in the room. "What are we going to do about Larissa Miller now?"

Wulver shook his head. "We are not to go near her unless it's a direct order from Kyo."

That started Fallon up again. She threw up her hands in a violent motion and started pacing again, though this time she kept her focus fixed on him. "Fuck, Wulver! She needs to be here! I don't know how the hell she fits into their plans, but they want her bad. I don't want to be sitting here while she plays ga-ga eyes with a gargoyle!"

He'd already had enough crap dealing with Kyo this morning. He didn't feel like going through everything again because Fallon couldn't accept reality. He growled as any alpha answering a challenge would. "It's over," he said, and even to his own ears his voice was deeper, with an echo of a wild animal running through it. "And you will not touch her. Am. I. Understood?"

Fallon's jaw worked as she stared down Wulver. Something flickered behind her eyes. It reminded Wulver of a lizard, that inner eyelid they had that would close and reopen. It was so fast it barely registered in the conscious mind, but it left him unsettled. Abruptly, Fallon relaxed her shoulders and took a step back, her arms coming to hang beside her body. "Yeah. I understand."

Wulver breathed deep, relaxing his own muscles that locked during the argument while he struggled to control the alpha roaring in his head to pin her into submission, bare her throat and feel his teeth digging into the soft flesh, taste blood on his tongue. He turned his attention to Aislynn to help gain control. "We have other problems to deal with now. Merc took the job and the spellbook is under his control."

Aislynn's calm acceptance went a long way to help him regain control. Her jaw tightened for only a moment, but her voice was even when she spoke. "This is unhappy news, but not a surprise. It was a matter of when, not if. What of Rhaum and the Dream Crafter?"

Fallon must have decided to keep a lid on any more emotional displays to keep tension levels at bay. She replied, "Inara tells me that he expects to have her in a couple weeks and to be ready for his mini-majesty's summons when the time comes."

If Rhaum said he would have her, it was as good as done. "I'll want you and Laire to meet with her and explain the situation."

Fallon's mouth quirked, but her eyes still held that unsettling flicker. "Sure. Why not? I always enjoy playing puppet master to someone's life."

Before the conversation could go any further, the building shook violently motions, which had the three of them scrambling to stay on their feet. "What the-"

The shaking stopped and deep bellows sounded from the corridors, followed by the clang of sword on sword and high-pitched screams of pain.

Wulver spun away and ran toward the sounds of fighting. Before him, orcs and goblins overran every free inch of space, their mottled green-skinned bodies blocking exits and using swords, axes, and bows to strike down anyone who came out to fight them.

As soon as he was close to the main section Wulver leapt. The shifting pain within was dim, far away, easily ignored. Bones lengthened and teeth sharpened and senses magnified. With a hungry growl he crashed into the largest of the orcs. His jaws clamped over the creature's face, tearing away skin and bone before he ripped into the thing's throat, disgusting sludge coating his tongue and sulfur clogging his nostrils.

Aislynn's arrows whizzed by his head as the archer stayed back to rain down death. Fallon took up position beside Wulver and in concert they destroyed their enemies. Orc after orc stepped close to the fighting Fallon, only to have Aislynn's arrows bring them down. Fallon twisted Tenro and plunged the sword into the chest of the creature in front of her. Before she could yank her sword back out an orc attacked from behind. She kicked back to hit the creature in the knee, bringing him down. Freeing Tenro, she sliced the orc in half and used the momentum to get the orc who came at her next.

Aislynn's arrows flew past, striking some of the orcs in the distance. Pandemonium erupted across the control room. For every enemy brought down, three more took its place.

Darkness swirled across the floor and Shadow rose to join the fight, taking out a goblin at Aislynn's back. The elf tipped Wulver a quick smile but did not stop her assault on the advancing hordes.

A ball of fire erupted in the middle of the latest group of goblins, creating piles of flame and ash and the explosion knocking down several nearby.

Fallon turned. "Dammit Laire, what took so long?"

Laire shrugged. "Had to find my shoes." Motioning with her fingers, she brought down bolts of lightning from the ceiling and fried the orcs in front of them. "The whole place is in chaos. Everywhere needs help."

Laire began to say more, but a large orc came behind her. Fallon grabbed a long dagger from her waist and threw it, piercing the orc in the eye. The dead creature would have crashed into the mage if Fallon hadn't pushed her to the side.

Undaunted, Laire looked at the dead orc and shivered. "That would have been ugly."

"That's why mages stay at a safe distance. How are you on spells?"

"Medium."

There were still large groups of enemies. Fallon hefted Tenro. "Stay back and save power for the big stuff. Tell us what happened while I'm kicking some ass here." And with that, Fallon charged back into the melee and dragged a goblin away from a young female healer who was being pulled out of a nearby room. "How the fuck did they get past the barrier?"

Laire crossed her arms and leaned against the wall as Shadow vivisected a particularly ugly specimen ten feet in front of her. "Suicide onslaught. There were so many who hit at once the barrier was overwhelmed."

Aislynn frowned before she let loose an arrow that brought down a hanging screen, killing several things that were under it. "It would have taken hundreds to do that, perhaps thousands."

Laire's expression was uncharacteristically somber. "Yeah."

Aislynn shook her head in disbelief, risking a glance away from the battle toward the mage. "What are they after? What can they expect from this?"

A fresh batch appeared in the doorway, and Laire groaned. "Gods, how many are there? Can't they stop coming? Hang on. Fallon, at the entrance!"

At Laire's scream, all eyes turned toward the gathering across the room, to see Larissa Miller in the middle of the pack of enemies. Fallon yelled, "Time to use magic. Laire, get her."

Laire created another ball in her hands that looked like an overgrown soap bubble. She aimed it and threw it at Larissa, hitting the woman dead center of her torso.

Nothing happened.

Laire stared at her hands, then at Larissa. Laire's mouth moved, though no sound came out. Then her eyes widened, and all color fled to leave nothing but a chalky residue behind. "Oh gods." Laire voice was low and terrified.

"Laire?" Aislynn's voice held uncertainty, seeing their normally unflappable mage become this upset.

"She's a null. That's why they are after her. She's a *null!*"

Fallon got knocked over and fell to the ground. Before the orc could land another blow, she flipped over in a handstand and brought Tenro up to slice the orc between his legs, from crotch to brainpan. Without pausing she pivoted to bring the sword down and cleave another orc in two.

Aislynn let loose several more arrows to take down the creatures around Larissa. The arrows struck true, but as soon as one orc fell, another took his place. Whatever Larissa was involved in was their primary goal. "Laire, what do we do about Larissa? What the hell is a *null?*"

Backing into a corner, Laire muttered to herself before crying out, "The vault! They're using her to get into the vault!"

Aislynn could see it wasn't orcs and goblins that surrounded Larissa. A necromancer and his acolyte were behind her. They made their way to the elevator that led to the vault, unconcerned with the battle that raged around them.

Laire darted across the battle scene, her focus on Larissa and the necromancer.

"Laire, *wait!*" Aislynn cried out. The mage didn't stop, so Aislynn followed. An orc appeared in front of her. Aislynn jumped onto its shoulder, aiming an arrow and firing into his forehead before catapulting over him.

A troll tore across the floor and headed straight for Laire. She turned and cast a quick barrier in front of her, but the troll threw himself against it and hurtled the mage across the floor.

Wulver jumped on him, his claws tearing a hole into the troll's chest. While the creature was trying to throw Wulver off, Aislynn drew back and shot an arrow into that hole. The troll howled in pain, and Aislynn fired off several more.

Suddenly, as one, the orcs and goblins lifted their heads. The next moment they disappeared, magic letting them escape the building faster than the speed of thought, leaving blood and chaos and the bodies of their dead behind.

Wulver turned back into his human form, blood-drenched and eyes blazing as he came to stand before Laire. "What the fuck happened?"

Aislynn helped a shaky Laire onto her feet. "Laire, what were you saying before?"

"The vault." Laire brought her hand up to her bleeding head and winced. "They wanted the vault."

Wulver and Fallon took off, while Aislynn helped Laire before they went down to the vault as well. The mage and the elf entered the vault area in time to hear Wulver yell, "*Gods damn*, how could they have done this?"

The vault door, one of the most magically protected items in the entire world, was hanging off its hinges. Items were scattered in sparse clutter while row upon row of shelving was empty. While not everything was taken, even someone with no knowledge of the contents could tell it was sacked.

Wulver hit a comm panel. "Tec, talk to me."

A posh British accent replied. "Fully half our people are damaged, over fifty confirmed casualties, which includes several of our healers. I've made the call for back-up, but that will not be a quick process. I'm compiling what has been taken from the vault and will be finished shortly."

"Get down here as soon as you have that list." Wulver turned to Laire. "How did they get into the vault? A hundred mages working together shouldn't have been able to break it open, and a lone vampire waltzes in here and does just that?"

"Larissa Miller. She's a null. Magic has no effect on her. Walking into that vault was as easy for her as walking into a grocery store." Laire began banging her knuckles into her forehead. "I should have caught it. I should have thought."

Fallon grabbed Laire's hand. "Stop the crazy. How could you have known?"

"She was born at the Great Collision. I concentrated on the fact that magical powers never materialized, but the ability to not be affected by magic is also a power. It's just so much rarer I overlooked it."

"But you put a shield on her and that worked," said Aislynn.

"No, I didn't. I put a shield *around* her. She only affects magic she comes into contact with. If I bothered to look into it, I would have found dozens of examples of how magic items broke around her."

"And she didn't know this about herself?" Aislynn asked.

"She lives in the most perfect place to *not* know it. Think about it. The least amount of magic they can get by with, no interest in pursuing magic, and while powers materializing would have made an impression, how do you figure out you cause the absence of something?"

"Yet the vampires knew about her when we didn't." Anyone who knew Wulver knew that tone of voice did not bode well for anyone in his path.

Before any response could be made the elevator opened and Tec walked out, his gingery curls sticking up at all angles. "Three-hundred and forty-seven items," he said, the list in his hands grabbed by Laire before he came to a standstill.

"Almost half gone," Wulver said, voice low. He scratched his cheek, fingers curled against the angry-red scar. He stopped and he looked up, his eyes on Laire. "They didn't spend all that effort to get her solely to break into the vault. They need *her* for something very special. Search the list. What is big enough to start the rip and specifically needs a null?"

Laire was the embodiment of concentration, her eyes flying over the list. Her eyes stopped their movements and she jerked back, her mouth forming an *O*. "What day is today?"

"Tues-" began Ais, but Laire pulled out her phone and scrolled through the calendar function. Her teeth ground together when she found what she had been searching for.

"*Well?*" demanded Wulver.

Laire's eyes were wide, horrified. "They have the Stone of the Four Souls and the Dagger of Kerith Tay. They're going to use her to release the Four Demons."

"The demons the gods themselves had to band together to trap?" Aislynn's voice shook. "There is no way a necromancer could control them. Not even to rip the realms asunder would they chance bringing them into this world."

"I might not have any love for fangboy," Laire said, her lips giving a little twist. "But I can admit how powerful he is. If any necromancer ever had the ability to control them, it would be Reign."

"And he's arrogant enough to be willing to try," Fallon finished. "When?"

"Tonight," responded Laire. "Tonight is a blue moon. It has to be tonight, when the moon is at its zenith. It's the only time."

Aislynn spoke. "It's impossible to go against them tonight. Even if we knew where they are. Our forces are decimated. The mages used most of their spells to fight the invasion, the healers are overwhelmed, and our warrior strength is cut in half."

"We can discover where the ceremony will be held." Shadow stepped through the wall and pulled someone behind him. It was an acolyte, the one who walked with Larissa and the vampire, his hands bound behind him. "I caught him on the way out. I've already blocked his link with his master."

"I do love that freaky shadow magic stuff you do," Laire said, normal smart-assy coming back into her voice. Shadow tilted his head toward her, the only concession he heard the praise.

Wulver's lips turned up. He turned to Fallon and arched his eyebrow. "That only leaves making some new friends to help us out tonight. Can you handle it?"

It was in the form of a question, but there was an undeniable order underneath that. Fallon nodded. "Of course. I'm always up for making new friends."

The acolyte watched them, a fervent gleam in his eye. "What makes you think I'll talk to you and abandon my Master?"

"Trust me. You don't have a choice," said Wulver.

"But I think I do." And the acolyte stuck out his tongue and bit clean through. The pink fleshy nub fell to the ground and spurts of blood squirted from his mouth.

Before the tongue hit the ground Fallon pulled out a knife from a sheath on the outside of her thigh. "Laire, *fire*."

Laire complied, and Fallon's knife went red-hot. Fallon grabbed the acolyte's head with her other hand and forced his mouth open, bringing the knife against his gushing tongue, burning lips and cheeks and any other skin that lay in the way and sent the smell of burning flesh wafting through the air.

The man flailed and wrenched and shrieked, but in long moments his wound was closed

Wulver watched. When it was done, he turned to the mage "You need to bring Kyo. You would be fastest."

Laire's face tightened and a hurt, almost betrayed expression crossed her features for a brief moment. But then it smoothed into a mask, and she disappeared.

Fallon still had her hand wrapped around the acolyte's jaw, and she pulled the man close, her fingers digging into his skin, making him wince. "A necromancer wannabe not able to kill himself? I'm ashamed for you." She twisted his head, studying the work of her knife. "You should have kept your tongue, because now the Psy Master is going to *rip* into your mind."

He whimpered. She loosened her grip and leaned close to whisper in his ear. "Don't worry. If you're still alive after he's through with you, I'll take pity on you and kill you. I have enough compassion that I won't let you live like that."

CHAPTER THIRTY-FOUR

Terak searched Larissa's apartment. Each pass plucked the ever-tightening string of fear that wound around his heart.

They had her. Somehow they had used a magic even he was not immune to and could not see through and had taken her from her books and her children. He spoke to Olivia, who informed him she had not seen Larissa since lunch. Olivia called Larissa's father and brothers who also did not know Larissa's whereabouts, and reported that information back to Terak.

It was now, when his mate was in danger, Terak understood the value of Clan, the slice-cut of being alone. He had no one to turn to who could help him save her.

Larissa's door opened, and Fallon entered, cloaked with her customary assurance. Her sword hilt shone bright above her shoulder and her movements placed her where she could draw freely.

The quick-rise of anger flooded his muscles, expanding them with desire to destroy the warrior before him, but long-fought-for control held him still. "If you have her, I'll kill you."

"If I had her, I wouldn't be here." She took a step toward him, still out of reach, still with her sword at the ready. "Did you know why they wanted her?"

Assured Fallon was, but there was a harsh tension in the lines of eyes and mouth and shoulders that not even battles with orcs and wargs had engendered. Something was out of her control, something frightening, and Fallon was readying herself for a life-altering battle.

The string around his heart pulled tight in a snap and severed the organ in his chest, the destruction leaving him unable to breathe. "Where is she?"

Fallon made no comment on the weak and pitiable sound, but her head tilted as she studied him. "She's a null," the swordswoman said after long moments. "They brought her in and used her to tear through our security. Years of magic cast by the greatest of mages, and tissue paper would have given her more of a challenge."

"Nulls are beings of myth."

"Really? Maybe you should tell that to my *dead*." Fallon's body shifted in her anger, but within a moment she was back to her original stance. "There's more. They're sacrificing her tonight to raise the Four Demons."

Sacrifice.
Sacrifice.
Sacrifice.

He rushed at Fallon and grabbed the swordswoman by the throat. "Tell me where she *is*!"

Fallon's eyes bore into his, molten gold surrounded by fire, and under his hand a peculiar warmth, a current of power traveling over her skin. "Get your hand off me or lose it."

His hand loosened but did not let go. "*Tell* me."

"Will you fight beside us for her and for the protection of this realm? Will you order your Clan to come to our aid?"

Terak stepped back. He did not break eye contact. He would never be ashamed of his decision, though at this moment he regretted it more than he ever contemplated. "I have no Clan. I gave them up for her. There are no others that can help."

Fallon's eyes lost their fire, though her body still had the brittle tenseness that spoke of upcoming battle. "Well, hell. Looks like I owe Ais ten bucks."

Thwup. Thwup. Thwup.

Both looked toward the balcony to see Malek and a half-dozen other gargoyles on the landing. Malek walked in while the others waited outside. "*Mennak*, the Guild has contacted us and told us what happened."

Confusion flew through him on hummingbird wings. "Malek, why are you here?"

"To rescue our *Meyla*."

"What are you speaking of? I am no longer Clan."

"No." Malek cut him off, his wings flaring out with the strength of that word. "That is unacceptable. We have cut ourselves from the Clan as well, because we will follow none but you. The old ways are unacceptable. We trust you to lead us in a new Clan, you and your mate."

Terak shook his head as sorrow seeped into the cracks of his battered heart, the parts that broke when he flew away that last night. "I did not want this. I wanted the Clan to be strong and united."

Malek placed his hand on Terak's shoulder. "Perhaps it was inevitable. We were never a single Clan before, perhaps it is not our way. All we know," he said, gesturing to include those behind him, "is we follow none but you. We trust you with our lives and the lives of our mates and children. We go where you lead."

"And if my first order is to place you in danger to protect my mate?"

"We live and die for our *Mennak* and our *Meyla*. It has always been so."

Terak drew him close and touched their foreheads for a moment, mixing gratitude and acceptance and relief. He pulled away. "How many warriors to follow me tonight?"

"Sixty."

Terak turned to Fallon. "Will that do?"

"Is there another choice? Now let's go kill some necromancers."

CHAPTER THIRTY-FIVE

So here was where it ended, in a maze of caves far away from her home, a sacrifice to release powerful demons who were going to destroy this world and rip the realms apart.

Larissa huddled deeper into her jacket. Earlier, above the clang of metal on metal and the screams of those hurt and dying, she had heard Laire's voice.

She's a null!

Before today, she'd never heard that word, the reason for all these weeks of pain and worry.

The reason Terak had come into her life.

Larissa glanced through the bars to where Taneasha lay in the other cage. The girl was quiet now, curled in on herself, but earlier she had been alternating between screaming at the vampire to let her out and begging Larissa to forgive her, swearing that what had been shown her was real, Terak really said those things.

It didn't make sense. Nothing made sense. Had it all been a lie? Everything they had talked about those long evenings, the battles they had fought together?

Making love?

How could that have been a lie?

Shivering, she stuffed her hands into her pockets. Stiff leather brushed against her fingers, and she grabbed the unfamiliar object, pulling it out.

This was the book the Oracle had given her. *The Mating Habits of Gargoyles.*

The Oracle. The woman who had started it all, if those images were indeed true.

Guard her well.

He did do that. He held her and protected her and he was so warm. If he were here right now, she could be curled up against that chest that could double as a furnace.

She pushed the confusion over Terak away and flipped the pages open. Knowing what she knew of the Oracle, this book promised to be…interesting. But it wasn't like she had anything else to do while waiting to be sacrificed.

It was written in English, which was good. But instead of salacious, wonderfully purple prose, it was written in academic speak. Well, that took some of the fun out of it.

Still, she kept reading, until one passage knocked in her chest and pushed all breath from her body.

"The ultimate physical expression of love for a gargoyle is the wrapping of their wings around their 'mate'. It is an instinctive gesture and one that the paranoid and isolated gargoyle cannot force and cannot compel, as it leaves the gargoyle's only true vulnerable spot on their body accessible to the one who is enveloped. Even couples who have been mated for years – decades – sometimes have not reached this level of trust."

Terak wrapped her in his wings that first night as she had sobbed against the castle floor. She was the one who forced him to let her go.

A photo album of memories flipped open through her mind, and time after time Terak stood with her, his wings either completely enveloping her or half around her as they stood together. He blocked out the world and let them remain in their own little world together with those wings. He hugged her tight to him that last night. It had been the most exquisite feeling of safety of love when he enveloped her, a feeling not even the embraces of her father and brothers had ever touched.

She felt loved.

And it was because he loved her.

None of it had been a lie, and she had been an emotional *idiot* to believe otherwise for even a moment. She knew Terak. She *knew* him. He was good and honorable to the point of being a stick-in-the-mud. That she could doubt him was ridiculous.

There was a reason he had been speaking to that vampire. It didn't matter what it looked like, she was a jerk to have lost faith as she did.

Gods, she had made a real mess of things.

Revelation sparked through her body and demanded movement. She stood, regaining her fight and her momentum.

Terak loved her, and he would be here for her. Of course, that didn't mean she should wait to be rescued, but knowing back-up was fighting like hell to get to her, well, that pumped the spirits up.

She had a student to save, necromancers to thwart, and a gargoyle to make amends to. It was going to be a busy night.

CHAPTER THIRTY-SIX

The magical shield around the mountain pulsed in bright arcs underneath the hand of the Battle Mage, the glow illuminating her almond-shaped eyes and small, straight nose as she talked to Fallon, Terak, and assorted other warriors. "We can create a pocket in the shield for a short time. If everything goes well, the pocket will stay open long enough to allow eight to twelve people to get through before the barrier seals itself again. Then we'll have to recast the spells, which will take at least ten minutes per casting. The first waves are going to be deep in the shit and sans back-up. First wave should be ready to go in three minutes."

Fallon nodded, her calm expression telling all that the mage's words were exactly what she expected to hear. "How many waves can we get in before the start of the ceremony?"

Laire looked up at the moon. "Three at most, and that's if the casting is perfect with no problems." She waved her hand toward a group of haggard beings chanting in front of the wall. "As you can tell, perfect might be hard to achieve."

Fallon looked over at Aislynn who stood at the edges of the group. The elf was on lookout, her bow at the ready. "Any signs someone has seen us?"

"None so far. The invisibility spell the wizards cast seems to be working."

The shield started to flicker and break. It wouldn't be much longer. Fallon turned back to Laire. "What about inside? Any clues what's going on there?"

"I can give guesses, nothing more," said Laire. "They suffered major casualties today, but they know they did damage to us. Even if they suspect we're here to attack them, I wouldn't be expecting huge numbers of guards, but the guards they do have will be fresh and ready to fight. As for the mages, a lot of spell power has been used today to get ready for the ceremony. They won't be at full power any more than we are. But there will be at least one vampire in there, and a half-tapped vampire is still a powerful enemy."

Terak clenched his jaw, keeping his snarls behind teeth instead of roaring out his displeasure. It was of no matter how many stood guard or fought tonight. They were dead, and he would get his mate back.

"Gargoyles." With a snap of her fingers the mage brought before them a glowing map in the sky, pointing at a little x marked far away from the squares and circles that dominated the bottom. "This is where you guys are being teleported. The cave has an entrance that is high in the mountains and goes down. Impossible for anyone not winged or otherwise flying-abled, which is probably why they didn't put a barrier there. Bad news is we don't know exactly how easy it will be to travel that path. No dwarves we know had anything to do with the construction of these caves. At best, you're going to arrive T-minus fifteen minutes, putting you somewhere between the second and third wave. At best."

Terak shook his head. "I will be in the first wave through the barrier. The rest of my warriors are to be transported."

Malek came, putting his hand on Terak's shoulder. "We will retrieve our *Meyla*. Do not fear."

Terak placed his hand on Malek's shoulder, returning the gesture. He looked over at the warriors who stood ready to fight. "No matter the end of this night, we will teach the vampires to fear the gargoyle."

Laire flicked her fingers with clear impatience. "As heartwarming as this all is, gargoyles who are going to be flying need to gather together. Teleporting this many beings is not easy, and I'd like to get you somewhere close to the entrance and not Siberia."

Malek let go and stood at the head of the group of gargoyles. With a wave, the mage made the gargoyles disappear.

The mage swayed after they disappeared, and Fallon went over in front of her. "Laire?"

The Asian woman waved her off. "Long day. We all have to push past, right?"

Fallon smiled, and for the first time Terak could see friendship in the expression. "Right."

"Thirty seconds," called one of the wizards working on the barrier.

Laire clapped her hands and motioned toward the entrance. "If you're stupid or suicidal, please step up to become the first wave."

Fallon gave her a slit-eyed glare as she hefted her sword free. "That wasn't directed at me, was it?"

"If the heavy-ass sword fits."

"Ten seconds."

Terak walked to the barrier behind only Fallon. Fallon gave a quick glance towards him. "Well, Gargoyle, let's do this."

The barrier opened.

CHAPTER THIRTY-SEVEN

The door opened to Larissa's cell, and Garof walked into the room, followed by two human men. Their eyes were lowered so no clue if they were red or not, but based on their demeanor they didn't seem much above garden-variety whipping boys.

Taneasha was crying in the corner. She stood, only to moments later fall on her knees before the vampire. "Master, please," she begged.

The vampire crouched down in front of Taneasha, taking her chin in his hand. "Hush, girl. Think of the glorious part you will play in the ascension of the necromancers to their true position in a reborn Magic Realm. Your death will have so much more meaning than a child like you deserves." He motioned to his followers. "Grab the child. I will transport the null."

The men each grabbed one of Taneasha's arms and dragged her out of the cell.

Garof turned to Larissa. "I have no need to drag you, do I?"

"No." Larissa stood. "I would prefer you didn't. I am capable of walking myself."

"Good. I prefer when things are kept dignified, do you agree?"

They walked for several minutes until they came to a room where two stone altars stood next to each other, about ten feet apart with a fire pit between them. Floating above the fire was an ornate dagger and a large red stone, both items she had grabbed from the vault.

Taneasha was already chained to the altar on the left. Garof grabbed her upper arm, but Larissa pulled away. "I said I wouldn't make a scene. Don't touch me." She walked to the other altar.

Manacles. The stupid bastards were going to chain her down. She bit the inside of her cheek to keep the relief that pulsed through her from showing on her face. The cuffs were older but in good condition. They also glowed red, which meant they were enchanted.

Which meant the vampires probably placed most of their trust in the magic of the chains and not the physical strength of the chains themselves. That seemed to be the theme of the day.

And there were no manacles for the feet, which meant she had a chance of making at least step one of her plan succeeding.

Too bad she hadn't formulated step two yet.

Larissa lay on the altar and put her arms up. Garof shackled her. "I am impressed, human. It is rare to see such a display of obedience."

"Hate to break it to you, but compliments from you don't really do it for me, so I wouldn't bother."

The vampire inclined his head. "As you wish." He stood between the two altars and motioned for the two followers to kneel at the foot. "Start the casting."

Not even a minute after the two men began to chant, a shrill scream filled the room. The two acolytes stopped chanting, only to have Garof say, "Do not stop, no matter what!"

Another human in a robe ran up to the vampire. "Master, we are being attacked."

Garof stepped away, though not before Larissa saw his lips form a snarl. As he walked from the room, she heard him say, "They must be delayed until the spell can be completed." Garof and the robed human left.

The only bad guys left in the room were the two chanting.

No time like the present. The cuffs were tight but nothing compared to what her brothers put her through. She freed her hands with barely a scrape.

The rhythmic chanting was rising in volume, and the cave walls started to not so much shake as *undulate.* Both the dagger and the jewel were glowing, the dagger red and the stone blue.

The commotion outside the cavern was growing louder as well, echoes of multitudes of footsteps intermixed with the clanging of metal on metal and screams – which abruptly stopped.

And then came the call. *"Meyja!"*

Terak! He was here, yes, he was and no way was she going to be some sort of sacrifice for these idiot vampires. She had a gargoyle waiting who she was going to kiss until her lips fell off and then mate with him and live wherever they could be together – her world, his world, or a world they would create on their own.

Dumb and Dumber down there on the floor were oblivious to everything outside their chants. And in front of her, right beside the fire pit, was a decent-sized and solid-looking cauldron.

Never had she been quieter than she was at that moment, not even when she had been taking pictures of her brother Christopher getting to second base on their sofa with his high-school girlfriend.

A couple of well-aimed conks later, both men were unconscious. If they got brain damage, oh well.

Taneasha rattled her chains, her eyes pleading when Larissa looked at her. "Please, Miss Miller, don't leave me here. I'm so sorry. I never thought anything like this would happen. They said they wanted to talk to you about helping with a spell. I'm so sorry."

Maybe she was. And maybe Larissa understood how this could happen with a girl as shy and sensitive as Taneasha was. That didn't change the fact this was Taneasha's fault and there would be consequences for her actions. "I'm going to free you and get us out of here. Everything else can wait until we're safe."

Knocked-out acolyte number one had the key, and Larissa freed the girl from the altar. Now, where to go? Terak's voice had come from the main door, but that was where the necromancer had gone. To run out there would be to run straight into them.

Looking around the cave, there was one small side door behind the altars. It could lead anywhere, or it could lead nowhere at all, but it was the only other door. "We're going through there. The front door would be too dangerous with that battle going on."

Taneasha nodded, staying close to her.

"I need you to stay a bit away from me."

Taneasha looked at her with hurt eyes, but understanding dawned moments later when Larissa grabbed the stone and dagger. "I don't know what these things would do to anyone not magically immune, and I don't want to find out by watching what happens to you."

Taneasha nodded, staying a small distance away as they ran through the doors.

CHAPTER THIRTY-EIGHT

Terak clawed through another orc, dismembering the beast before throwing the carcass to the side.

There were fewer enemies than expected. The earlier attack on the Guild must have taken most of their resources. The first wave made good progress as they tore through the underlings, but it was too soon to gloat over easy triumph – the necromancers still awaited them.

"Doing okay over there, Gargoyle?" Fallon's voice could be heard above the cacophony. Her sword clanged as metal struck metal in her own battles.

He didn't bother to answer. Instead, he threw his head back and yelled, *"Meyja!"*

A blast of power hit Terak in the chest and threw him back into the wall, the stone jabbing into his body.

"Pity gargoyles are resistant to magic. That would have made a satisfying spectacle of carnage." Garof's voice penetrated the daze Terak was shaking off. He rose to see the damned vampire standing before him. "Originally created by necromancers, at least that is what the myths say about your kind. My brethren did perhaps *too* good of a job."

"Where's my *mate*?"

"You should have taken me up on my offer. It would have worked out much better for you."

The vampire raised his hand and cast another blasting spell, but Terak rolled out of the path and only dealt with the flying debris behind him.

Out of the corner of his eye, Terak saw Fallon finish her fight and rush toward the vampire. The vampire saw it as well, for he waved in Fallon's direction and a wall of rock shot up between them and the rest of the battle. "I'll deal with Fallon later. I want to finish killing you first."

Terak growled and lunged for the vampire, dropping them both to the ground. But the vampire twisted his body, using momentum and a strength Terak was not expecting to throw Terak into the opposite cave wall.

Terak regained his feet to see Garof already on his. "Don't underestimate me, Gargoyle. You are indeed a warrior beyond compare, but I am Vampire. You are nothing to me." The vampire stilled then, his head cocked to the side and his eyes wide in alarm.

Terak used the chance to run into the vampire again, slicing into his neck with his claws.

Flesh parted, but no blood came out. Instead in a blink the skin knitted itself together, and Garof punched Terak in the chest so hard he couldn't breathe for a second. The vampire kicked the side of his knee, and Terak fell before him. Garof kicked Terak in the face and he crumpled into the ground. "As entertaining as this has been, Gargoyle, I believe I will finish this after the Magic Realm has been returned to us. You will be a fitting sacrifice."

A thread of worry was buried in the vampire's tone, and hope pulsed through Terak's muscles, granting strength and pushing him to his feet. If the vampire was worried, it meant his little human was well and was causing problems for the damned necromancers. Of course she was. His mate was more than a match for a legion of undead.

Garof was not quick enough this time to throw Terak when the gargoyle landed on his back. They wrestled as Terak landed blow after blow.

The blows had little effect and the vampire freed himself. He grabbed Terak by the throat and repeatedly punched him in the chest. Terak's bones fractured under the prolonged force, and his entire torso became a mass of pain.

Garof dropped him and grabbed a sword from the ground, an evil-looking blade with serrated edges. "I've heard of the gargoyles' formidable healing abilities, so I best end this now." He raised the sword high...

...and *screamed.*

Frantically, Garof tried to reach behind him. Terak stared as the vampire twisted, revealing an ornate dagger hilt protruding from his back. Larissa stood behind the vampire, her arm lowering from driving the blade into the undead. Terak reached for her, but his wounds were not healed enough yet that he could move much.

Larissa stepped back from the vampire as he fell to the ground. The wound was smoking, and his skin was starting to crackle and blacken.

The vampire was a repulsive sight. Larissa's face held a sick horror as she watched the disintegration of the creature. "Larissa," Terak called, to break through her fascination as much as for help.

It worked. The most beautiful smile lit her face and she moved toward him.

Tremors rocked the mountain, knocking her to the ground, as well as a young girl behind her that only now Terak noticed. The tremors stopped, and Laire's voice magically echoed through the caverns the way a PA system would. "Attention, good guys. You did great because I'm getting readings the ceremony was stopped. But bad news anyway. This mountain is magically booby-trapped so if the ceremony doesn't go through, the mountain will implode. We're holding it together the best we can, but we suggest getting your tushies out here ASAP if not faster."

Larissa turned to the girl behind her. "Run out now!" The girl did not have to be told twice and escaped, and though he would have told a child the same thing, a momentary shiver of loathing hit his gut on how easily the girl ran from those who had helped her and left them to their fates.

His bones were already knitting together, so he pushed himself up. Since he could yell at Larissa to run all he desired and she would never leave, he needed to push past the pain and get them out of here.

He took a step forward and hit a shimmery blue wall. A force cage. Terak punched into it, but he could not get through. Larissa stood on the other side, her eyes wide.

The vampire still lay on the ground, black smoke still rising from his all-but-decomposed corpse. A rusty laugh escaped from a now-lipless skull. "It was a good fight, Gargoyle. I think it only fitting we die together. It's not a very strong cage. The weight of the mountain bearing down will pierce it, and you'll be crushed to death. I'd say this battle is a draw."

No. This couldn't be happening, this couldn't be real. She had been the target, and now she was safe and sound. This was supposed to be the end of it. She was *not* supposed to see the male she loved trapped in front of her, waiting for a mountain to crush him to death.

"Leave me!" He was bloody and bleeding in the cage, his arm hanging at an odd angle. "This place will soon be destroyed. Go!"

He was trapped. She could travel through the force field, but she could do nothing to free him. This power that had necromancers hunting her was worthless when it mattered.

"*Meyja-*"

"What does that mean?" she interrupted, her eyes clear on his. "You swore you would tell me once this was over. What does it mean?"

His eyes were intense on hers. "It means *Beloved above all, even above the Clan.*"

And if there was any question of what her choice would be – which there wasn't – that decided her beyond any doubts. She pushed inside the force field.

His arms and wings came around her as if he could not help himself, even as he said, "*Meyja*, I don't want you here. Think of your father, your brothers. They need you. I need you to live. I need you to leave."

She snuggled into his embrace. "For once, I'm only going to think about what I want and not consider them. I'm not going to ever leave you, Terak. If this is where it ends, I'll face the end with you."

He sunk to the floor, keeping her in his arms, kissing her face, her hair. "Love you, *Meyja*. I have always loved you. Forgive me for not telling you before this day."

She nuzzled into him. "You did. I didn't understand." The rumbling was louder now, the heat building. She curled into Terak's arms. "Love you, my Gargoyle. My warrior."

Love you.

Shadowy arms wrapped around her, and Larissa was pulled down through the floor.

CHAPTER THIRTY-NINE

"Hi there, Sleeping Beauty."

So I've died and gone to hell. It was unmistakably Fallon's voice, and the swordswoman wasn't on her favorite persons list. Considering Fallon's general attitude, there was no way she was on anyone's favorite persons list.

But Fallon had come to free her. And she had fought with Terak. And she did look cool carrying around such a big sword.

Okay, maybe purgatory.

"Take your time waking up. It's fine. It's not like we have anything else to do except sit around and stare at you."

Awareness came in short spurts. Grass scratched her cheek and arms, and the earth was solid underneath, solid and cool, but warmer than it had been when she had been forced through it like a ghost, insubstantial, weightless, *wrongness*. Her skin prickled at the sense memory, and she shuddered with the renewed cold. Did Terak feel...

Terak.

"Terak?"

"Here," and strong, rough fingers grazed her chin. She forced her eyes open to see his beloved face. He was sitting to her left, looking as if had just risen from beside her.

"What happened?" Because last she checked, she and Terak were about to get crushed under a mountain.

"Shadow," Fallon answered as Terak helped Larissa into a sitting position.

The world's rotation was observable, but Larissa took a few deep breaths to get the dizziness under control. Once that was accomplished, she looked to the area where Fallon pointed, to see the dark warrior on the ground, a healer above him. Shadow looked greyer, like a faded copy instead of the original.

"Is he okay?"

"He will be. Mostly," Fallon said. "Don't overthink it. It's what we do."

Larissa looked at the various Guild members. No, they weren't nice and they weren't good, but while she would happily live her life if she never met up with them again, that didn't mean they weren't needed in these days.

Days that would only get darker during this period that the necromancers could destroy all.

She reached for Terak, needing skin contact. He meshed his fingers with hers, his eyes dark and bright. "Thank you all for saving Terak and saving me."

From out of a giant purse Laire pulled out a small, black velvet bag. "I'll tell you how you can show your thanks – hand over that little bauble you've got with you."

Terak's fingers tightened on hers. At his nod Larissa fished the jewel from her pocket. "What would this have done?"

"Pray you never find out," Laire said. She held out the opened bag. "Drop it in there, please."

Larissa did as asked, and Laire spoke a few words in an unidentified language before tying the bag off and tucking it back in her purse. Laire looked her over, and the term *X-ray vision* floated through Larissa's brain. The mage asked, "The dagger?"

"Buried in Garof's back, if you want to go back for it."

For one moment, fear flickered over Laire's face, but the Asian woman closed her eyes and turned away, heading back for her companions. Fallon exhaled in an explosive blast, and Larissa decided to not ask any questions.

And now to the other problem of the night. "Taneasha?"

"We have her, and we know her part in this."

Fallon's tone might have warned against asking any questions, but Larissa couldn't let it go at that, no matter what the girl did. "What's going to happen to her?"

"We're not going to kill her, if that's what you're worried about." Never let it be said Fallon tried to soften news. "But you're not going to see her in class again."

Before Larissa could even begin to process her conflicted feelings about her former student, from the sky dropped several gargoyles. Terak rose but kept her in his arms, beneath his wings. She curled into him.

Terak called out, "All have survived?"

"Yes. We looked for you, but the mountain was crumbling too quickly and we had no choice except to leave."

"I would have it no other way, Malek."

Larissa squirmed a little. When Terak looked at her she arched her eyebrow and tilted her head a tiny amount. They really were a couple because Terak read her wants perfectly and set her down, though he kept her close. She spoke to the assembled gargoyles. "Thank you for coming to my aid. I am grateful to all of you beyond what I can say."

Malek shook his head, his arm casting aside her words. "You are ours to protect, *Meyla*. It is duty and honor to come to your side when we are needed. We made that promise when we followed your mate away from the Clan."

Away from the Clan. Larissa looked up at Terak. He stared straight ahead as if he had no idea she was looking at him, but the tick in his jaw gave him away. "What do they mean, *away from the Clan*?"

He took a long breath before he gazed down at her. "I made a choice."

"No." There was no way she was going to let this happen. Not his Clan. "I'm not worth it."

His gaze became fierce and he brought himself to his full height. "You are worth everything," he said, the tone brooking no argument. "I would give this realm for you, so do not talk to me of leaving the Clan. They cannot accept you, so I will have no more dealings with them."

"Your people-"

"My *Meyja*."

Before she could continue, noises above made everyone turn their attention to the sky, in time to see a contingent of gargoyles descending in front of them.

An older gargoyle stepped forward, and Terak moved to meet him while keeping her behind him. "Krikus, how did you know of this place?"

"The Guild transported us here once the danger was past. I informed them the need to see you was urgent." The old councilor looked past Terak and straight at Larissa. When their eyes met, he gave a bow. "Forgive me for not introducing myself earlier, *Meyla*. I am Krikus."

Terak went still at the title. "You call her *Meyla*?"

"Why would we not? She is the mate of our *Mennak*."

With those words, as one, the gargoyles dropped to their knees in front of Terak. Malek smiled, and he and the warriors joined in the display.

The wondrous confusion on Terak's face cracked Larissa's heart. Her beloved gargoyle was so exposed for all to see – his desire for what they were offering warring with the disbelief it could be happening.

Krikus waited for Terak's attention to return to him before he spoke again. "It will not be easy. We still have doubts, and some will never be convinced. But you are right – our Clan must be united to survive. We choose the path behind you. We will follow as you create this new place."

Terak was still speechless, so Larissa came up and placed her hand in his. "I hope," she began, and gave Krikus the smile she had perfected when she convinced her father to let her go on her first date, "This means you will help me in learning how to best serve my Clan."

Surprise lit the old gargoyle's face before a wide smile split his face. "I would be honored, *Meyla*."

Terak's eyes were soft on her, adoring, and Larissa basked in the force of that gaze. Her gargoyle, her mate, her *love*. Still, a little tease wouldn't hurt. "There is one last thing to conquer."

Terak's visage turned wary, and he glanced around. "What is that?"

"You need to meet *my* family."

CHAPTER FORTY

He heard her coming toward him, the *clack-clack* of her shoes heralding her arrival on the stone embankment long before her words reached his ears. "Why are you in that form?"

Terak turned to face his mate as she approached him, wearing a long coat belted at her waist. "I thought you would prefer me to meet your family while I was in my human guise."

Her mouth was tight, little frown lines between her eyebrows. "As you told me, no matter what you look like, you are a gargoyle. I didn't fall in love with a human, I don't want a human with me as I introduce the male I love to my family. I want the Clan Leader of the Gargoyles, my mate, by my side tonight."

His heart became more hers at those words, if that were even possible. Still, he shook his head. "They will only see me as a monster and try to take you away. I do not wish to fight the family of my mate, but I will not let them keep you from me."

"Terak," she sighed, coming over to take his face between her hands. "That won't happen. They already know everything and know what to expect when they meet you."

"Are you saying your Clan is happy with your mate?"

"I'm saying they don't have a choice in the matter."

He brought up one hand to cover hers as it lay against his face, warm and soft. "Why would you believe that? Your father is anything but weak-willed. He will not accept so easily any mating of yours, but especially to one who is connected to the New Realms."

"My dad has to accept it, because I told him I love you the same way he loved my mother, and I asked him if anything in this world would have kept him from her side. When he admitted nothing would, I asked him what lengths he thought I would go or what I would give up to stay with you. I can't say he's completely happy, I won't lie about that. But you left the Clan to be with me. Do you think you mated with someone who does not have the same level of commitment as you do?"

"Never, little human. You awe me with all you have given up already to be at my side."

"Then prove your faith in me, and turn into your true form." With a naughty smile, she started to remove the long coat. "I'll make it worth your while."

Her reveal was a punch to his chest, stealing his breath away as he took her in. Her dress emphasized the soft swell of her breasts, the skirt was very tight and very short, and on her feet were shoes with spikes that made the lines of her legs into works of art.

He reached out to touch her, but she backed away and waggled a finger at him. "*Tsk tsk*, I don't see your gargoyle form yet."

Putting aside his own fears, he took a deep breath, closed his eyes, and changed into his true form.

When he opened his eyes again, he saw her gaze moving over his body, taking in every inch. "Now this is what I want."

"Then give me my reward, mate."

She smiled then, walking toward him with her hips swaying, the sight of it making his body hard. Once she was before him again she lifted herself onto her toes and took his bottom lip between her teeth, giving a soft bite she knew would drive him insane. "Out of the two of us, I'm the one who should be worried."

"Oh?" he said, enjoying the feel of her.

She licked the spot she had just bitten. "After all, I'm only a puny, insubstantial human. I can't defend myself."

He moved his mouth to graze over hers. "A gargoyle who is not strong enough to defend his mate does not deserve to live."

She lowered her mouth to nuzzle under his chin. "I have no claws."

"I disagree. I feel your claws when you rake them down my back," and he groaned as she proceed to show him how good her claws felt as they traveled his front.

She nipped the underside of his jaw. "I can't fly."

His hands cupped her face, locking their gazes. "I will always carry you."

That beautiful smile that defined his world lit her face. "Show me."

He was undone. He lifted her into his arms and jumped into the air before them, taking flight.

He thought he loved flying before, but holding Larissa in his arms remade the experience. She kissed his earlobe, worrying the flesh between her teeth before she bit down. He struggled to keep his eyes open against the sensual assault, but when she licked the shell of his ear he shuddered, losing momentum and dropping a few feet.

She giggled. "Am I having an effect on the mighty Clan Leader," she teased, blowing into his ear now.

"Larissa," he growled, but she paid him no mind. Putting her mouth to his ear, she whispered, "Wrap my legs around your waist."

He groaned. "What are you doing to me?"

"Me? I'm enjoying the flight. You concentrate on keeping us in the air, I'll take care of the rest."

She slid her leg down his torso. He should stop her, yet somehow, he found himself settling her as she wished.

Once she was secure, her hand reached down between her legs to the fastening of his pants. "Larissa," he tried again, but even as he spoke her name her hand curled around his aching shaft, freeing him from the fabric. "Gods, I love the feel of you," she breathed, stroking as far down as she could. "I want you all the time. I think of you inside me all the time." She wiggled down his body, bringing them into intimate contact.

It took all his willpower to stay aloft. He had no reserves for speech, so he could not tell her to stop. Otherwise he would…and then she stroked him against the wet warmth of her pussy, laid bare to him.

"Where…are your undergarments?" Sweat ran down his spine, pillowing in the hollow of his back as his hips instinctively flexed toward her.

"Oops, guess I forgot something." Nothing in her voice suggested she was sorry for this.

She would pay. She would pay for doing this to him, for robbing him of all sanity right as he was going to meet her Clan. As soon as he could think again, she would pay.

Larissa gave him a quick, hard kiss, her eyes hazy with lust. "I wish I could taste this right now, but I've learned adaptability is key to survival. I'll get back to that later." Using her legs, she worked herself on him, but without leverage there was little friction, only the delicious feel of her wetness over his tip. Her nails dug into his back right above where his wings attached while the pointy spikes of her heels speared into his thighs in the most pleasurable pain he had ever known.

"Terak," she cried. She was pink and tousled, her pouty lips parted in frustration that she was not able to take him deeper and bring them both the pleasure they craved.

Below them was a deserted park. He needed to end this or he would lose his sanity.

He landed with a hard thud, his usual grace absent as he stumbled. Wasting no time he fell to his knees, placing her with gentle care on the ground on her back before he fell above her, his wings flaring out behind them.

Larissa's breaths were jagged as she watched him. He plunged into her, the tightening of her body against the sudden invasion bringing him to near climax.

No, not without her. He fought against every nerve in his body begging him to plunge again, to race toward climax. Instead he stroked inside her with small, even movements, movements that made her breath labored and her back arch.

"Yes, yes, yes," she chanted, her hips squirming against his, pushing him harder inside her. Using her heels, she pulled him in. "Deeper, Terak. Get as deep as you can in me and make me come."

Her words broke any restraint and now he only knew her, to pound inside her and pour himself into his mate, to mark her so deeply no one who beheld her would ever doubt to whom she belonged, and her cry of satisfaction while her body clenched around him signaled her acceptance of that claim.

His head fell back as he came inside her, growling and cursing at one of the strongest orgasms of his life came over him.

Long moments later when their breathing normalized, she looked up at him. Her eyes were dreamy. She lifted her hands, delicate human fingers stroking over brow bone and pointed ears, pulling strands of his much thicker hair. "Why would I want to be with anyone but you?"

He leaned down, kissing her mouth, letting her sureness overcome his doubts. "We are supposed to meet with your father soon. I doubt he will be happy if I bring you to him in this condition."

"We'll stop at my apartment to get cleaned up." She smiled, a light teasing cast to her mouth. "Don't be overworried about making a bad impression. No matter what you do, Dad's going to hate you on sight."

Terak reared back. "I thought you said that he would accept me."

"Oh yes, he's going to accept you. He has no choice on that. But that doesn't mean he's going to like you. You are taking away his baby girl, after all."

"Is it always like this with humans?"

"Welcome to the family."

CHAPTER FORTY-ONE

Zemar waited outside, silent and still, a living statue hidden in the ragged shadows cast by the building.

The acolyte arrived, oblivious to his presence. The boy's focus was on the pouch he carried. He stroked the pouch with a hand that trembled with the slightest touch, the way others would caress a lover. The boy was laughable in his overt desire for power, a power he could no more wield than a toddler rule a nation.

Would the boy be foolish enough to run with the dagger? It was a powerful temptation, promising untold power to one who could master it.

No, no running for this one. The sheen of sweat coating his face even on this cold autumn night, the wide eyes and shallow breaths answered the question as the boy approached the door. He coveted, but he would obey.

The boy was right to let his fear triumph over any ambitions he might harbor. The dagger would only destroy him.

Zemar melted from the shadows to enjoy the panic of the boy before he registered who stood before him. The boy bowed, holding forth the weapon for Zemar to take. "Master," was all he said.

Zemar spoke no words to him. The blade now in his hands, he went into the building, taking the elevator to the penthouse.

The apartment was an expansive space, leather and chrome shaping the interior. The far wall was made of glass, and from this dizzying height the effect was the city laid bare, showing its soft underbelly in submission.

A couch was situated in front of the window and Zemar approached it. Reign sat in the middle, his arms draped over the back of the couch, the drained body of a young woman on the ground, her red hair a blanket over his feet.

Reign did not bother to take the dagger, merely continued his observation of the city. "Fallon?"

"She is still alive, my Lord."

Reign's rich laugh filled the air. "As if she were ever in any danger from the fools that were present." His eyes darkened to black-red. He murmured, "The only one who will take Fallon is me."

Zemar watched his Master stroke his hand over his lips while his gaze stayed on the window. With a negligent movement, Reign reached out his hand. Zemar obeyed, handing the dagger over.

Reign studied the blade, twisting it in his hand to go over every inch with his gaze. "How many did she kill?"

"Dozens, my Lord, until her sword was dull with the blood of her enemies."

Reign stroked the edge of the dagger with his forefinger until a drop of blood was drawn. The blood absorbed into the blade. "Only that? I will see her bathed in blood before me."

"And what of the Oracle's prophecy?"

Fallon snorted. "The usual crap she pulls. Of course Larissa was important to the Gargoyle Clan, she's going to be the wife of the Clan Leader and make future heirs to the throne. Is it me, or is using untold powers to play matchmaker a little beneath her?"

"The young enjoy getting into mischief. She will grow out of it."

"That's an interesting statement. Tell me, how old is she, and how much younger is she than you?"

"Nice try. Back to the gargoyle. Do you truly believe you can trust him?"

Fallon was resting her head on the back of the chair, her eyes closed in tiredness. "I believe we can. Strange to think of gargoyles as allies, but he truly does love her, and the other side wants her dead. As long as that's the case, he'll fight like hell for us."

"Any male fights like hell for his mate."

"Oh? And what would you know about that?"

"Fallon, who are you talking to?"

Aislynn's voice cut through the air, startling Fallon so she jerked upright in her seat. "Ais, I didn't hear you come in." Fallon rose, bending her neck to the side in a deep stretch. "Talking to myself, as usual. Just trying to come down from the last few weeks. What do you need?"

Aislynn shifted, motioning behind her with her thumb. "Wulver has called us. No rest for the wicked and all that."

"What's up?"

"Tec is giving us a complete list of missing items, with Laire providing commentary on how much chaos and destruction each can cause. We need to strategize about Merc and the spellbook, and it seems as though the Master of Monsters will be returning."

"Great, I can't wait to see Wulver start humping the furniture again. Something to look forward to. Anything else?"

Aislynn pretended to think for a moment, pressing her forefinger against her chin. "Don't expect to use your vacation benefits anytime soon?"

"Figures." Fallon made an *after you* gesture with her hand, and the two females left the room.

"What do I know of mates? Wouldn't you like to know..."

The End

STONE EMBRACE

CHAPTER ONE

Now was the answer. The question? *If there was* one *time you wished you were an unashamed alcoholic, when would you choose?* Forget the knife, the tension here could hide a pack of werewolves amidst its layers.

They were at the dinner table, Terak at one end and her father at the other, with her and Michael on either side of Terak and the other three brothers in the middle. Michael didn't look happy, but unlike the rest of the Miller clan, he had no obvious issues with Terak being there.

Terak was in his human form. After an aborted first attempt at meeting her family – where Jack Miller made damn sure to let her know she wasn't off the hook for bringing over her mate and in the same breath made damn sure she knew he wasn't happy about it – Terak refused with the full-force of that gargoyle stubbornness to meet her family in anything but his shifted state, saying he would give her family time to know him. The problem with that – *THE problem? Try problem number seven-hundred and twenty-three* – was illuminated the moment Jack Miller's eyes took in the tall human next to her. Confusion ruled her father's face for a long moment when he saw the man beside her, but the detective's mind pieced together recalled information at lightning pace, and when Jack got *it* – that everything she told him was true, gargoyles could shift into humans, and so many things Jack had believed since the Great Collision had been a lie – suppressed and impotent fury wrote itself deep into the lines of a face that never once showed those emotions in this home.

Larissa's tongue was numb from all the times she had bitten it tonight, and she reached for a glass of water more to feel the cool liquid slide over the abused flesh than because of thirst. Under the table she stroked Terak's hand, the fist the only outward sign of the gargoyle's own distress.

In their bedroom earlier, it had been he who insisted they come today. "They will never accept me if they don't come to know me, *Meyja*. You expect too much, too soon."

She sat on the bed with her back against the headboard and legs stretched before her. Her gargoyle was putting a shirt over his now-human chest, the sight as impressive as always, and an irrational wave of anger overlaid her already rational anger at her father. Because her gargoyle was trying to cater to her father and gain favor, she was going to be denied the sight of that chest all evening. Stupid parental figure. "I *expect* my father to respect the male I have chosen to join my life with. I expect him to not act like a *jackass*."

Fully clothed, Terak came to sit beside her legs and took her hand in his clawless one. "He will. That he did not betray my secret – betray my Clan – to the human authorities tells me he will. But you are asking him to go against the core of his beliefs in taking me as a mate. It is unfair to ask him to make that transition in an instant without giving him time and space to adjust and to grieve."

"Grieve?"

"Yes, grieve," Terak affirmed. "Grief over what he feels is a betrayal of his oath as the leader of the police. And this also lays bare once again his grief over the loss of your mother."

Terak's now grey eyes were direct on her, no hint of shading to tell her he was minimizing his own concerns to make her feel better. Her chest hurt, unable to contain the swell of adoration this male evoked in her, the pure gratitude that she had been blessed enough to have him come into her life. She stroked down the sharp plane of his cheekbone. "There's a very small, vindictive part of me that wants to tell him he can't use her as an excuse for his actions forever. But I never will, because the instant after that impulse occurs, I imagine my life if something were to happen to you, and I know for him it's not an excuse. And afterwards, I want to hug him in apology, because I'm in awe he survived as well as he has."

Strong arms pulled her against a hard chest, and thank gods in this form that smell of newly-cracked stone and undefinable male remained, the smell that was only and forever Terak. She held tight, dragging his warmth and strength into her, both for tonight and for banishing that momentary terror the thought of losing him always evoked.

Of course, now facing her father in the dining room of her old home as he was blatant in his disregard of Terak, the earlier council of giving her father time and space was heading into the territory of *don't think so* and a down-and-dirty yelling match became more inevitable by the minute. "Dad," she said, trying once again to engage Jack in a way that didn't involve him staring a hole through Terak, "How are things at the precinct?"

"I'd rather not talk about it." *In front of him* rang through Jack's tone and down the center of the dining table.

That was it. Larissa near sprang from her seat as she locked gazes with her dad. "Can I see you in the study for a moment?" Damn straight her teeth were clenched – so were her hands, her stomach, all the way down to her toes. No more of this.

Jack rose, defiance in the slow, steady movement. "Yes. Let's go." And he walked ahead without waiting for her to come beside him, like he usually did.

She brushed off Terak's hand and went after her father. The door click was still echoing in the room as she said, "*What* is your problem? We talked about this already."

"We didn't talk," her father shot back, restrained fury in his tone. "You waltzed in and informed me you were marrying a creature. Wait, that's not it, you *mated* a creature. You left not five minutes later while I was still stunned. How is that talking?"

A tiny tremble of guilt fluttered through her stomach, but she wasn't going to let that derail her from setting Dad straight. "It doesn't matter what word is used. He and I are together forever and are *it* for each other. Words are meaningless."

"I am your father, and you can be damn sure it isn't meaningless to me if my daughter is married or not!" Jack paced around the desk, hands on his hips and fire in his eyes. "You didn't talk through *anything* with me. You leave me in the dark while you are in danger. You trust strangers over family. And when it's all over, you leave it to Michael to tell me everything – you can't even face me and explain what was going through your head!"

"I'm twenty-six years old! I don't owe you explanations, Dad!"

"Is that right, baby girl?

Deep breath...deep, deep breath. Her father had a point, and yeah, he was owed an apology for that. "I handled things poorly, and I'm sorry about that. But Dad, if anyone can understand the kind of confusion having your life upended like that can cause, it's you. People and creatures coming at you, and this terror of something so much bigger than you, and you can't tell friend from enemy. The aftermath of all that was chaos, and somehow in all that Michael got hold of me and told me about the panic over me and Taneasha, but I couldn't get away so I had to trust him to handle it." Larissa paused, bringing breath deep into her lungs to calm the panic even the memory of that time could instill in her. "I am sorry. It wasn't how I wanted to let you know. At the time it seemed the only way and looking back, I still don't know how else I could have done it. But I waited until I could tell you about Terak myself. I never wanted you to think I was ashamed of him, because I never will be."

"Then why did you come in here and tell me and then run?"

"Because I don't know what the hell I'm doing?" She threw her hands up in the air, needing physical movement to dissipate the tension building. "You think I don't know how it looks to you, or that I *like* you're not happy about who I love? Of course I want your approval. Never thought it was a possibility I'd ever be without it."

They were toe-to-toe, prize fighters eyeing each other from their corners, each breathing a little hard as if they had gone a round. Long, still seconds, and then Jack broke off the stare, plunking down into the leather chair behind the desk, a long, low exhale accompanying the movement.

Larissa pushed her hair behind her ear, watching as her father let his head fall back against the top of the seat. His age was showing, lines and grey hair somehow more pronounced than they were even a few weeks ago.

How would Laura Miller look now, if that hellish moment never happened? How much grey would streak her hair? How deep would the lines around her eyes be? Would her mom feel differently about Terak, defending her daughter's choice to her stubborn husband? Maybe it was self-interest talking, but something deep inside Larissa warmed, and there was no doubt in what her mother would say. Laura Miller knew all about love – great, deep, abiding love. She experienced it with this stubborn, ornery man sitting behind a desk. Laura Miller would tell her without reservation to stand beside Terak.

Larissa stood before her dad and held nothing back. "I know how I feel. What I feel is eternal, and it's only him. Part of the reason I love him is *because* he is a gargoyle, and that honor and nobility he possesses because of it, the way he'll stand between me and anything that would come after me. I find him beautiful, no matter what. But that doesn't mean I know how to explain *this*. This love, this attraction, how I went from being a sheltered girl and a low-level teacher to being the mate of the Clan Leader of the Gargoyles, responsible now for this Clan that isn't even my same species. It's too big sometimes for me to think about. I realize you have doubts, Dad, and I understand why, because looking at it from the outside, it's impossible."

Jack hunched forward, his elbows resting on his thighs while his hands hung loose between his knees. Whole conversations took place behind his eyes, his mouth tight while the debate as to what he should say played in his head. "I don't doubt you when you say you love him. I see it, Larissa. And if I was young and idealistic, I would send you off with blessings and pretend that was all that was necessary. But you have to know somewhere inside you, this situation is wrong." He leaned up then, a fierce resolve playing over his features. "You cannot stay with him. It's only going to end up bad for you. And if that truth isn't enough to make you walk away, then the fact it will end up bad for him should."

"Dad, we discussed-"

"You discussed like two people in love discuss, which means jack shit." His words cut across hers like a sharp blade. He stood then, facing her fully. "Do his people really want you there? Don't bother to answer, because we both know they don't. They wouldn't want you there, as the *mate* of their leader, even if you had grown up with them. You think they're thrilled a human is wandering their compound and in charge of them?"

No, they weren't. Malek, a few others were openly supportive and true friends and allies. The majority were reserved with her, still judging and waiting. Then the final portion, a vocal minority, and their contempt could be felt through the grey walls of the keep.

It wasn't the easiest situation, but being with Terak was worth it. If he was worth dying for, he was worth fighting for.

And she had already proved he was worth dying for.

"It doesn't matter what they think. They asked for Terak to be their leader knowing I was part of the deal. They may not be joyous over me, but they'll accept me."

"You think so? You are a *risk* to them. With this weird power you have, you'll never be safe from the necro-" Jack's voice faltered, stuttered over the word that was the greatest threat to her safety. For one moment his eyes grew round and haunted, the knowledge of what the death of a beloved truly meant stark in those eyes, before he cleared his throat and continued. "You will always be targeted, and you will always represent a risk to their safety. If things heat up like this Fallon woman claims they will, what do you think the gargoyles will do in order to protect their Clan? What do you think they'll do to Terak if he tries to stop them?"

Goosebumps. One tiny portion of the goosebumps dotting her skin and the shivers descending over her body could be attributed to worry over herself. But Terak...was her father right? Would they force her removal, and what would they do to Terak in order to accomplish that? "They wouldn't have invited us back..."

Jack's hard voice cut through her weak protest. "They probably hoped he was going through a phase, an obsession with something foreign to them, and that he would grow tired of you and set you aside once he came to his senses."

"He won't."

"Maybe he will and maybe he won't, but do you really believe they are not going to force his hand? I raised you smarter than that."

And as she opened her mouth the door swung open, and Terak stood in the doorway.

CHAPTER TWO

With almost forty years on the force under his belt, Jack Miller could claim – without pride, without ego – that he knew how to read people. What he saw of the male before him almost had him taking a step back before he remembered himself.

Terak's human face was almost pleasant as he looked at Larissa. She walked to him, and with a light, steady hand he cupped her face, brushing some hair behind her ear. "I'm fine," she said, answering an unspoken question.

"I think it is time your father and I converse. Please, let me be alone with him. Please," he added again, when Larissa's usual stubborn nature reared its head and it looked like she was going to argue with him. And then his gaze left Larissa's face and came to rest upon Jack.

The quiet menace in that gaze was real. This was not some act put on by a stupid little shit who would piss himself if he ever saw real action. This was a warrior's gaze and a warrior's resolve.

That was fine with Jack. He was ready to have it out.

Larissa left without looking back, and a pang spread through his chest. His little girl didn't even check with him. For her, all she needed was the words of this male to make her decision.

The unexpected loss put Jack on the attack. "I'm assuming you heard most everything. Tell me I'm wrong. Tell me some bullshit how it's going to be fine and your people won't revolt and betray her the first moment danger comes around them."

Jack himself paced with strong emotion, a habit Michael had picked up from him. In contrast, Terak grew still, though the look in his eyes was anything but calm. "You speak of things you know not."

"I may not know everything about gargoyles, but I notice you're not denying my statement," Jack shot back. "It might be called human nature, but its primal nature. It's the core of us that's going to survive no matter what. Her existence threatens your people. Do you think they'll allow that? A woman from a race they consider inferior, who had the gall to marry their leader so he isn't married to a gargoyle girl like he should be?"

"I am not so weak I cannot keep my people in check." Now Terak advanced, his fingers curling inward. What would that sight look like if

Terak was in his gargoyle form, where instead of nails there would be claws? "I am very aware of *every* danger to Larissa. I have already taken the needed steps to care for her."

Jack scoffed, holding his ground. "Against your own people?"

Terak stood before him, his stone-grey eyes hard and flinty. "Against *any* enemy. A strike against her is a strike to me, and do I seem one who will not defend myself? You are her father, so I will make myself clear. Any who seek her harm I will kill. I will rip into them with claw and teeth and separate skin from bone from heart. An enemy, a friend, from within either of our Clans – it does not matter."

For the first time in eons, a shiver ran down Jack's spine as he took in the male before him. The will behind those words was absolute, the venom and the truth unassailable. "And if you are gone?" Jack forced the words through a closed throat, and swallowed to loosen the muscles.

Terak backed away, his voice quieted, but that venomous truth in no way diminished. "I have already made my deal with your devil to protect her no matter the circumstances. She is mine, Jack Miller. I fought against feeling for her, but my heart will have none but her. So I will claim her, and I will protect her, and any who become her enemy? I will destroy."

Shards of a long-ago conversation flittered through Jack's mind…

"She made her choice. If Laura Campbell had told me to go away and not bother her, that's what I would have done. It wouldn't have changed the fact I'd love her forever, but I'd never take what wasn't freely given. But she chose me, and eighteen is legal. So I'm going to marry her and keep her with me, and old man, if you can't accept that, don't expect us to come into your home ever again."

…and he took in the male before him with new eyes. There was nothing to like here. Even if he believed those two loved each other – and dammit, he did, he really did – that didn't change the fact this was a bad match. Larissa was in danger by being with Terak, and as much as Larissa pushed to the side any objections to Terak being a gargoyle, that was no small difference.

But before him Jack saw the same look he was sure was on his face when he confronted Bill Campbell about marrying Laura – flinty determination and the willingness to set the world afire if that was what it took to accomplish his objective.

Bill Campbell was probably chortling in heaven even now, looking at his son-in-law being put through the same hell he'd given as a young man.

After long moments, Jack spoke. "I can't give you my blessing. There's too much wrong here for me to do that. But I can't change your mind and I can't change hers, and I *can't* lose my daughter. So I will say I'll try to understand and keep my fears to myself." And here Jack put the full force of his will in his gaze, on this one point he would not back down on. "But in return you agree to keep me in the loop. You agree I'm going to know if anything is a threat to her, and you'll let me and my boys protect her when we can. Do we understand one another?"

Terak nodded. "We understand one another."

"Good." Something inside Jack relaxed then, something that had been twisted tight since the day Larissa had gone missing from school. With that release it was time to lay some ground rules for his son-in-law. Bill Campbell would approve. "But here's one last thing to understand. You may be some fearsome creature, but I'm her daddy. You hurt her, there aren't enough stone walls to keep me away from you and prevent me from mounting your head on a pike. You think you're a mean sonovabitch? Next to a father who's listening to his little girl cry, you're nothing more than pottery."

CHAPTER THREE

A peculiar energy emanated from Terak, a vibration that had Larissa on edge, had done so ever since he emerged with her father from the study.

The night hadn't lasted long after that, a perfunctory finishing of the meal and giving the expected thanks and parting words. But even as they left her childhood home and arrived back to their Clan and their bedchamber, the weird mood Terak was in didn't abate.

It wasn't safe – *he* wasn't safe – but even as her mind acknowledged, her body remained calm. If there was one truth to her world, it was she never had anything to fear from Terak.

However, it did prevent her from asking what she wanted most to know, about what their talk covered, about where *all* their relationships stood right now.

The tense lines of his now gargoyle form were as bad as when they were fighting for their lives. As wound up as he was, she doubted he'd be going to bed for a long while. "Are you going to go out on patrol?"

His eyes met hers in the mirror. "No. I would not be effective."

That was obvious, not that she'd tell him that. "Do you wish to talk about it?"

"Did he convince you?"

And this promised to not be good. Silly her, thinking maybe the actual dinner itself would be the worst part of the night. "What do you mean?"

"Your father," and the word *father* in that tone was a blasphemy. "Did he change your mind about your place here?"

"My father didn't change my mind about anything. I am where I want to be."

"Are you sure?" No physical change took place, but somehow she could swear Terak wound tighter and tighter, drawing himself in as he unleashed what he had held back earlier. "He did not tell you how you were in danger here? About how you did not belong amongst the Clan? About how *gargoyles* will betray you the moment first possible?"

"He doesn't understand, and you yourself told me to be patient with him. He'll get to know you and he won't have such prejudiced views."

Terak went on as if she hadn't interrupted. "And did he not tell you about how you being here was to invite my death and put me in danger."

Here she paused, the echo of her father's warning rampant in her head no matter how hard she pushed down. The momentary silence was a mistake, as Terak honed in on the stutter. He turned away, the muscles so tight she could almost believe a hard poke would shatter them. "Terak, whatever Dad said tonight, no matter what he brought up-"

"So you believe his words?"

"It doesn't matter-"

"Do you?"

"I'm not saying I believe them, but he might have brought up a good point."

"What point?"

"Terak, quit *this*. We'll talk tomorrow, after you've calmed down."

He came before her, his eyes hot and unwavering. "What point?"

"That I'm a danger to you." And tears fell, as they'd been wanting to since her father thrust the thought at her. "That you're in danger because of me. That they're going to come after me again. Maybe they can't do the spell they wanted me for back then, but what I can do is so rare, they have to come after me again. That I'm selfish to be here with you."

She met his gaze, thick lashes surrounding her stunning eyes, that cornflower blue which would now and forever be the color he associated only with her. In those eyes was a violent swirl of pain, and fear, but what loomed largest when she looked at him was love. Always love. She spoke again, and her words rocked against him with their unexpected force. "I would have died with you."

Ripping pain punched through his chest at the return of those memories, those moments when she had looked at him with such calm intent as the mountain began to crash around them. He cradled her face in his hands. "Never again, little human," he said, his voice roughened. "You must live. That is my one truth in this world. You must live, even should all others die."

She shook her head, an instant negation of his words. "But I can't live without you. I don't want to. And I'm terrified to think I might end up being the cause of your death."

With cat-quick feet, rage began to overtake pain. She could not...*she could not...* "What are you suggesting? That you leave? *Me?*"

His hands prevented her from turning her head, so she settled for closing her eyes, the circles beneath them a blue-black smudge against her pale skin. "I'm not saying that – don't put words in my mouth. But it still hurts, that my selfishness endangers you. I love you so much, I can't bare-"

"No!" How could this evening have gone so horribly wrong? His woman, his *mate*, thinking of leaving him? Never.

Never.

She had taken him into her heart and her body, had pushed past all barriers and filled the empty places within him with laughter and warmth, and now she talked of taking that away? For what? Pathetic fear? Fear for *him*? No, she should fear for any enemy who would dare approach her, fear the pain and death he would bring to them.

He was gargoyle. Skin and marrow and bone he offered for protection, a path awash with the red tide of enemy's blood.

Instinct, ancient and demanding, hot and molten, flared within him.

He was gargoyle. Tonight, his mate would learn *exactly* what that meant.

CHAPTER FOUR

Before her, Terak's wings flared as they did in battle, and the sense of danger she'd been experiencing all night increased a hundredfold. "Terak?"

"You think me so weak I cannot protect my mate?" His voice was a low wash of sound, a growl which caused enemies to tremble in fear.

She was trembling. But fear? No. No, it was something else in her responding to the vibrations of his tone, a deep feminine instinct to this side of him – a side she had often seen in battle, but never here in their bedchamber.

He loomed over her, huge and hard, a male in his prime, a leader who bowed to no one. A warrior god, and she stood before him a sacrifice.

How had she ever forgotten how overwhelming he was? Those hands, strong enough to crush her, stroked the length of her throat in slow, deliberate movement, the light press of calloused fingertips scraping against her flesh accelerating her heartbeat.

He stepped closer, engulfing her, surrounding her, and now his claws, light and sure, running over the thin fabric of her shirt – over her arms, down her back, the slow strokes prickling the skin underneath which strained towards his touch. "This is mine," he said, his voice low and rough. "I will lay low any who seek to separate me from you."

"Terak?" Was that her voice, so high and unsure?

"Take these off," and dark warning threaded itself through his words. "Or have them ripped off."

His face was inches above her, the hard glint in his eyes assuring her nothing he said tonight was for effect. Without conscious thought trembling fingers came to the buttons on her shirt, and one by one she undid the fastenings, all the while his eyes followed the movement with fearsome intensity.

The shirt skimmed her arms and fell from her body, and now her bra…and here she paused to take in the pure possession in his face, which only grew as his gaze rested on the slope of her breast, still covered in sky-blue satin.

His arms shot out, gathering her wrists above her head in one hand, and his mouth descended over her nipple. The rough wetness of his tongue could be felt through the thin material, and Larissa groaned, head falling back and eyes shutting against his ministrations.

His mouth was firm and warm and wet, giving her small, firm nips through the material between the long, firm stroke of his tongue.

Marking me. He's marking me.

This was so unlike him. He was always gentle with her, touching her as if she were fragile glass. *Gentle* was not the word she would use now.

Rip of fabric, and cool air hit her wet nipples. Now his mouth covered her, the nip from his teeth sharper, the pull in her belly deeper now that there were no barriers, only his mouth on her.

First on her breasts, then he lifted his head so his mouth covered hers, a controlled plundering where he dominated, forcing her mouth wide, the smallest scrape of fang eliciting a gasp and a swirl of heat through her belly.

Her wrists were released, and claws traveled down her back, dragged her jeans down the length of her legs in an explosive burst of movement, leaving her in front of him in only her underwear.

Without warning he turned her, moving her at his pleasure. She leaned against him, her back to his chest. His mouth was hot where neck met shoulder while the tips of his claws played with her nipples, the tiny nip of pain tightening them to pointed tips. His tail curled around her calf, warm and strong and supple, massaging the sensitized length of her leg.

"Are you mine, *Meyja*?" His voice was urgent, rough. "Will you leave me?"

Reason prodded against the murky swirl caused by the myriad of sensation in her body. *That's* what this was about? He was scared she might leave? "Never, I swear. Terak, I'm yours."

One hand left her breast to run across her stomach, never going low enough for her. She canted her hips upwards, but he remained in control, not allowing her any relief. She tried to rub back against him, but he held her away, his hold firm.

His tail moved up her leg, moving against her in sinuous rhythm, urging her legs apart, a demand she eagerly complied with, and she sobbed in relief as finally, *finally,* he rubbed against the edge of her clit.

Wave after wave of sensation crashed through her. Terak brought his wings in front of them and surrounded her, enveloped her. Her senses were filled with him, the sharp point of his teeth against the back of her neck while his hands continued to play with her breasts, pinching just to the point of pain, before rubbing over the hard nub in pure sensuous caress, and during all this his tail firm and strong against her, making her tense in near release and then it would still, slow, let the mounting sensation abate and leave her to cry out in frustration.

"Are you mine?" came the dark velvet whisper in her ear.

"Yes." Her answer was a sob, a supplication. Anything to have him *finish.*

One final hard press of his tail, and then the wings opened and the tail withdrew, and he bent her over the bed and thrust into her. It might be the position, or it might be he was so overpowering, using her as he wished, but he felt huge inside her, almost uncomfortable as her body adjusted to him.

There was no gentleness. His hand against her shoulder blades bent her deeper into the bed, tilted her hips higher, and his body owned hers with each forceful motion of his hips.

The clamp of his teeth on the nape of her neck pushed her over into orgasm, her body shaking so hard Terak faltered for a moment before he resumed his motions, hard and firm and fast, working her body for every last shudder of pleasure.

Even as her body came down from the high, Terak still moved, still pushed into her with his full strength. There was no respite. Her body barely had the final tremor of pleasure when he pulled out and flipped her onto her back, gathering her legs over his shoulders and sliding into her again.

He bent low over her, his mouth capturing hers again. Her nerve-endings were so sensitized it was too much – his mouth, the heat of him, the thrust of his body, the scrape and slide of skin against hers. Her mind was pure white, any rational thought quieted. All that remained was primal longing. Her mate fucking her, using her, forcing her to submit, burying himself in her and marking her with sweat and come.

He pulled up and took her legs from over his shoulders and pushed her knees to her chest before parting them. She followed his gaze and gasped to see herself so open, see in full measure his cock sliding in her, disappear into her and his pelvis crushed against hers for a moment before he slid out, his skin slick and wet and shining from her. He groaned above, and as if her gaze spurred him on his hips moved even faster, and he asked "Are you going to come again, mate? Do you wish me to let you come again?"

Where had this dominating male been hiding inside her gentle gargoyle? He owned her, and with every word he showed he reveled in it. She raised her arms, curled her nails in the hard mass of his biceps. She licked her lips, and would have smiled at the answering groan if she wasn't panting. "Yes, mate. Let me come."

"If I do, will you take my cock in that hot little mouth and swallow me down?"

Oh *fuck*. It was too much, and once again her orgasm surprised her, shook through her body and tightened every muscle as if an electric current was flowing through her.

He slowed, kept working her through every aftershock, as her body bowed and shuddered under him. He moved until she let out one last low groan and relaxed.

Only then did he withdraw, letting her legs fall back on the bed. Only then did he gather his cock in his hand and moved up her body, moving to her side and presenting it in front of her mouth.

She took it eagerly as she lay there, swallowing it down in one long stroke. The taste was pure eroticism, her taste strong at first but then the smell and sensation that was pure Terak coming through.

In this she answered the question he had been asking her all night, by her total submission to him and his needs. Her tongue stroked over the hard flesh while her throat massaged him in the deepest way possible.

His groans grew louder with every moment, and it wouldn't be long before he would come. She worked harder, wanting him to come so she could swallow.

His hands wandered over her face, worked through her hair, his fingers flexing to grab hold of the curls. He grabbed tight and guided her movements, held her close while he pushed his cock down her throat. The movements were slow and deliberate, controlled enough so no harm came to her, but insistent, dominating. His voice was dark and rough, velvet scraping over rubble. *"My mate. My love. Mine."* And then his growls, the most erotic sound in the Realms, as his back bowed and his wings flared, and she drank him down, greedy, hungry, wanting every part of him.

When she gazed upwards, it was to the site of his head thrown back, his chest rising and falling in deep movement. As if sensing her eyes, his gaze came down to meet hers, but it was not completion in his face. Instead, it was sharper, fiercer, the hunger in him not yet satisfied. He glanced down her body and his lip curled, a snarl emitting from his throat.

She followed his gaze, and a heat that came from embarrassment crept through her body. Her legs were sprawled open in wanton invitation, the curls between her legs noticeably damp. Before she could close them his hand was there, his fingers invading her, pushing inside her receptive body.

"Terak," she said, voice a small plea.

In swift movement, he gathered her two hands in his one and pressed them above her head. The continued domination had the same effect as it had all night, making her grow wetter around his thick fingers. "No, little human. For all of tonight, you are mine."

CHAPTER FIVE

She woke to Terak's claws raking through her hair and her body deliciously sore, well-used in the best sense.

His strokes were gentle and bordering on hesitant. So her gargoyle was back to himself, having left the demons which drove him last night to the darkness. She shifted so she was lying on her back, looking up towards Terak.

His eyes were hooded, and he wore no smile on his face. And when he voiced a somber, "Larissa," she knew what was going on in his head – and she was going to put a stop to it.

"You didn't hurt me. Everything we did last night was something I wanted."

"I was too rough-"

"Did I say no? Did I say stop? Go away? I don't want this?" With every question she awaited his acknowledgement, waited for him to shake his head, and after he had done so, she continued, "If there is one thing I know, I know you would tear off your wings with your own hands before you would ever harm me. You are my *mate*, Terak. You are my love and my beloved. And you are a gargoyle. So if that means things get a little..." and here Larissa faltered, images and sensations pressing against her, cutting off the righteous indignation and reminding her how wanton and carnal she behaved last night. Heat traveled over her body, a mingling of renewed desire and embarrassment.

Strange, but it was this reaction that seemed to finally relax Terak, more so than her verbal defense. His body lost the taut gravity, replaced with smug satisfaction. "So my mate enjoyed what I did to her last night?"

"Don't get cocky," she shot back, not giving him the satisfaction of looking away, no matter the burn in her cheeks meant there was a good chance she looked like she had a sunburn. "I'm not here to stroke your ego."

He bent down and brushed his lips over hers. "No," his voice a deep, wicked whisper. "You stroked other things, did you not?"

Last night he was in charge, but now she was back in the game. "I think it was you who was doing the stroking. All I had to do was open my legs, and there you were, every part of you, rubbing over me to make me wet and make me beg." She leaned up, giving his earlobe a gentle bite before whispering, "I was begging my mate to let me come. I begged him to make me feel like only he can. You're so big all over, and only you can fill me. You like filling me, don't you? You like pushing into me when I'm wet and dripping for you?"

"Yesss." It was almost painful, how he sounded now, and unlike last night, he was at her mercy. Time to flip him over and ride him like a bucking bronco.

Which is what she did. She barely had to push before he was on his back, and their mingled groans when she lifted her hips and joined with him told how ready they both were for this.

Last night was dominance, was pushing fear away with physical mastery. Now was recommitment, as his hands on her hips steadied and lifted her, as her hands on his chest moved in caressing strokes across his skin while she accepted and loved him in the most primal way a female could with a male.

Larissa took him deep, relishing each slide of flesh and the groans that came from deep inside him, telling of how much of a hold she had over him. Her gaze locked with his, and she willed him to see everything – love and devotion and that she would never *falter*, would never, to the end of her days, leave his side. He was hers, and she was his, and nothing would change that.

His breathing became ragged and her body responded, everything in her tightening to match his quickening rhythm. He pushed her back against him faster, harder, and her nails scored his chest as her body was abused in the most pleasurable way imaginable.

Terak surged upwards into her, once, twice, and a loud, long growl erupted as he emptied himself into her, her muscles tightening around him as she found her own release, her cries lost in his.

Collapsing against him, Larissa drifted, only peripherally aware of the cooling sweat on her skin and her labored breaths in the still morning air.

"What you do to me, little human." The voice was rough, though the humor was unmistakable.

"And I plan to keep doing it to you for a very long time, because I'm not going anywhere, and neither are you." Larissa pushed up, looking down at her lover's face. "I'm scared, Terak. I'm not ashamed to admit that. We're in the midst of something big. I hate that you're in danger – I'm allowed to hate that, I'm allowed to hate I'm a danger to you – but I can't leave you. So I listen to my warrior mate when he tells me how to stay safe, and I take every precaution to make sure I never do something stupid that puts you at risk."

The look in his eyes – adoration, gratitude, devotion – kept her enthralled. "I will gladly take every danger known to keep you at my side. Never leave me, Larissa. Not even to protect me."

Her beautiful gargoyle. She leaned down, bestowing on him the most gentle, most loving kiss she could, willing every emotion she felt for her protector to be expressed through breath, lips, skin. "You by my side, and

I'm at yours, and we'll never leave, no matter what else happens in this world. Right?"

His fangs brushed against her lips, his claws raked down her back, and his tail wound around both their ankles, binding the two of them together. *"Right..."*

The End

THE CAGE KING

CHAPTER ONE

It was in the alleys she had discovered his fear of the dark. As they huddled together, rats unseen but heard scurrying in corners, so dark not even a sliver of moonlight penetrated, he shook. Her big brother shook, tremors he tried to hide by holding her tighter, and all the while he swore, *he swore*, he was going to get them to a place light and open, where you could take a breath without the stench of garbage and shit.

And where had he ended up? A coffin – small, confined, deep in the deepest dark of the earth, crammed in with so many others, the gravestones not a hands width from each other.

The bump of magic across her skin brought Nalah back to the now, where she was not in a graveyard on the day of her brother's funeral but wandering familiar and loathed streets. This ability to know magic was the one constant in her life, a life that saw her and her brother moving from shelter to shelter. It was a crawl of heated sensation with a dancing, jagged edge – deep warmth with sharp little teeth.

Ahead of her, the pawn shop. A week ago Nalah came here with the only thing of value they owned, the ring her mother could never let go of, had worked three jobs and yet refused to sell. It had been her mother's mother's mother's, and maybe further back than that. Mama had died too young to tell all the stories, but the one she'd never failed to tell – as she'd wrapped her daughter's and her son's little hands around the golden band with bright red stones and pressed so hard the ring left an impression on skin – was of how special that ring was, how they must never lose it.

To protect her brother she was going to sell it, went into the shop willing to face her brother's wrath and her mother's heartbreak.

The pawnbroker offered fifty dollars. With greed bright in his eyes and drool a speck in the corner of his mouth, the pawnbroker looked at her worn clothes and shaking hands and would not offer a dollar more.

And when she refused...he took it anyway. He took it and threw the fifty at her as she lay dazed on the ground and dared her to reclaim it.

She was going to tell Jac, after. After the fight. After one last time to convince him of something of which he would not be convinced.

But there was no after.

There was only a coffin in the ground.

Her ring was there in the shop. Her mother never told her the ring was magic, but as she grew older, when she realized the strange sensations she always experienced was an ability to sense – *feel* – magic, the knowledge her ring was more than a mere decoration occupied many hours of play, where she imagined all the different possibilities of what her ring could do.

Magic protected this building. Nothing as easy as a rock through the window could help her. Magic separated her from the only item that had any worth to her now. An item that had been stolen, taken from her because she was too weak. She was going to have her brother get it back.

But now her brother was dead.

There was only being alone in the dark.

Her heartbeat pounded in her ears as her temperature rose, the tips of her ears starting to burn. Hatred, *pain*, darkness and the grave and all alone in this world, and she fucking *pushed* against the magic, the ugliness inside her free and battering against this *piece of fucking shit spell*.

Crack!

It wasn't audible, but the break sounded against where she had been pushing…whatever…outside of herself.

Crack! Crack! Crack!

A faint glow surrounded the building, the magic visible, dancing white and airy with cracks throughout. It was unraveling like a thread pulled from a knitted sweater, starting small but soon missing large chunks, until not a hint of magic remained.

"Holy crap, that was *awesome*!"

Nalah spun around before her mind processed the possibility of threat. Short bursts of information. Two women. One tiny, Asian, colorful. The other tall, redhead, all in black.

Then her breath punched out of her, and her body gasped to bring air back into itself.

Dear gods, the *magic*.

It was from the redhead's sword, of which only the hilt was visible behind her right shoulder. There was nothing soft or tiny about this sensation. It was inferno, clawed death and black wings, oppressive yet…compelling.

Come closer…

"Wouldn't do that if I were you." The Asian woman spoke, the same voice as the original statement. She stepped forward, as if to shield the sword behind her, but since she didn't reach the redhead's shoulder, it was wasted effort. "Keep your power to yourself. You're too weak to be messing with Tenro. Then again, I'm pretty sure a huge chunk of the gods are too weak to be messing with Tenro." The redhead smirked at that, but said nothing.

"Tenro? Power?" Nalah's voice was strained, broken, to her own ears.

"Tenro's the sword, and power – you don't know your powers, do you?" The Asian woman's eyes brightened and she turned to the redhead. "I got a great professorial outfit I could change into – or, wait, maybe I just have the schoolgirl outfit, but I know I have glasses-"

"Laire, focus." The redhead's manner was resigned, as if this type of conversation was normal. "Please explain before she rightly assumes your crazy level. What's your name?"

That last question was directed at Nalah, and even as emotional exhaustion threatened to topple her, instinct and long habit made sure her mouth remained closed.

Laire waited a beat before she went on. "Okay nameless girl, you are a Magic Breaker."

"*Magic Breaker?*" Nalah never heard of such a thing, though around here magic was of the low-level, thug life variety. Anyone powerful moved up and out in quick time. "I can't cast any spells

"I didn't say you were a caster, I said you were a breaker. Much rarer and a whole separate classification. That little demonstration?" Laire twirled her forefinger as she pointed at the building. "Tells me you are untrained but have a hell of a gift."

Gift? Being a wizard was a gift. If she could cast spells, she could've saved her brother. This was useless, even if it did have a name. "I thought only wizards and mages could undo magic."

"That's usually the case, which makes finding someone like you all the more fantastic."

The redhead spoke for the first time. "Why did you break that barrier?" she asked, lifting her chin to indicate the pawn shop, and the question of why these women were here – two women who belonged far, far away from this cesspool – formed deep in a sorrow-fogged brain.

Nalah could run, but what would be the point? The Asian woman's magic was subtler than the blast that emanated from the sword, but the more she remained in the woman's presence, the more the woman's pure power became clear. Both of them were strong, and she...she was tired. And if this conversation ended badly, well, that could be okay too. "He stole my ring, and I wanted it back. I didn't know I could do that. I got angry and it happened."

"Oh, okay." The redhead began to walk towards her...and then past her, to the front door of the building. Muscles relaxed that she had no clue were tensed as the redhead passed by her. Pulling on the door handle, the redhead called over her shoulder. "Relied on magical reinforcements. If I knock too hard it'll fall in."

Laire pursed her lips and rolled her eyes. "Swing the damned sword, Fallon. We both know you've been wanting to all day, and he's a creep who deserves to lose everything."

"True," returned Fallon, pulling the sword free before Laire had finished talking, and with the sword unsheathed the magic was clearer, barreling straight for her...

Smell of War, acrid and disgusting sweetness
Screams of the Fallen
Blood, Red, Permeating Everything

Pain, pain, so much pain, ache to the bones never to depart
DragonFire
…and Laire covered Nalah's eyes with small, delicate fingers, the skin the softest Nalah had ever known. There was enchantment there, a shielding, and Laire said, "You really are sensitive, aren't you? We'll train you to develop your own barriers. After all, too much exposure to strong magic has been known to drive people insane, and we don't want that."

An explosion, but no ringing in her ears, no debris, no shaking of the ground underneath her. Laire removed her hand, letting Nalah see the sight before her. Tenro had been returned to its place on Fallon's back, and the pawn shop was nothing more than a collection of rubble and twisted metal collapsing on itself. Fallon turned her head. "Your turn."

Laire gave a negligent flip of her hand, and from the rubble a huge safe emerged. "Magical," she said when it landed before them. "Withstands blasts and fire, the usual. I'll handle opening this one myself."

A moment later the door on the safe disappeared. Laire rummaged through, throwing aside money and valuables without pause. "There it is," she said, and picked up a plain grey ring box and opened it.

Red gleamed and Nalah's heart started, a pinprick of joy threading through the day's loss. "That's my ring. That's the one he stole."

Laire and Fallon gave a quick glance toward each other.

This is what they came for. No, no she wouldn't lose this, *she wouldn't lose this*, and Nalah snatched at the ring.

The effort failed as Fallon's hand clamped around her wrist, and several pulls proved Fallon was immovable as stone. The redhead waited until Nalah was still, and asked again, "What's your name?"

Fallon's eyes were a molten gold. Unbidden Esh's eyes surfaced in her memory, a similar color, except his always had a dancing flame within them. Nalah had scoured every book in the meager library, but she could never find that eye color as a characteristic of any known race.

He laughed, told her not to worry about it, he looked human and besides, he would never claim any race that abandoned him anyway. But she wanted to know, just for herself, because she loved his eyes, how they heated and the fire grew when his emotions did, before a fight or when he lowered his head to hers…

She slammed down that memory, buried it. Never again. "My name is Nalah, and that ring is mine."

"Nalah." Fallon repeated her name, as if the swordswoman could decode the bleak history and uncertain future within the sound. "And how old are you?"

"Seventeen."

Fallon glanced over to Laire, whose face scrunched up in thought for a moment. "A little old, but she's so freaking strong. I don't think it'll be much of a problem."

Nalah pulled at her wrist again, more as voiceless protest than with any real hope of getting away. "What are you talking about?"

The two women did some voiceless communication with their eyes, and then Fallon turned her attention back to Nalah. "Would you like to escape this place?"

"Escape?" This conversation couldn't get any weirder. Everything tonight was off-balance, a funhouse full of mirrors with no exit sign.

"Come with us. Join our group. We'll teach you to use your power, and in return, you'll help us save and protect this Realm."

What group? The offer was too glib, too good-to-be-true. No one got offered a ticket out of here without a hell of a cost. "That easy?"

Fallon gave a chuckle, her smile bright but her eyes hard. "Do either of us evoke *easy*?"

No. Fallon didn't bother to pretend to be anything other than a warrior, and while Laire tried to hide her own power and strength under an outfit reminiscent of cotton candy and a girlish voice, more than a moment in their presence gave lie to *easy* in any sense.

What group were they part of?

Did it matter?

"And my mother's ring?"

Laire had deposited the ring in her pocket and made no move to take it out. "That's a bit of a problem. That ring should never be allowed in the general population, kind of like Fallon when she's in a mood. Or really ever."

"What Laire *means* is you've felt the magic. You know something altering can be found in that ring, a power that shouldn't be used."

Bitter bile rose in her throat. Of course. What the hell else had she expected? Since when did *justice* figure into anything? "What is it the ring does that's so bad I can't have it back?"

"Can't tell you, sorry." Fallon shrugged her shoulders and gave the most insincere apologetic smile Nalah had ever seen. *Sorry? What sorry?*

Fucking bitches. They were strong and she was weak, and it didn't matter if you lived in this shithole or not, the strong kicked you to the side and maybe fed you scraps if you were useful. Fuck them. She'd join her brother before she'd take their offer. Nalah spoke, the same anger churning through her that caused the breaking of the magic. "For all your talk about your superiority over that douche, you're as much a thief as he was," she said, pointing at the rubble. "We both know I can't fight you, so go back to your group and shove your offer up your ass. I'll never be that desperate."

Shocked silence reigned for a moment, before Laire doubled over in a peal of laughter. "Ah hells, we've just been schooled. Thank gods Aislynn didn't see that."

"Yeah, we'd never hear the end of it," Fallon said, voice low and without any of the humor Laire saw in the situation. She released Nalah's wrist. "Fine. Let's modify the offer. You come with us, and after we teach you, after you understand what that ring is, if you still want to take it, it's yours. You take it."

"You won't let it go."

"Just said I would."

Nalah stepped around this mental minefield with careful movements, feeling for the trap that had to exist. "That easy?"

This time there was no chuckle, and Fallon's eyes were hard enough to pulverize stone. "Taking the ring would be easy. Living with the consequences, not so much."

Nalah bit back a retort, the anger flooding her veins giving her a kick, but the undertone of weary and numb remained.

Why not? The question kept circling her mind, despite the ping in the back of her mind that said making any decisions now would be a bad idea – and said in the voice she often used to try to stop her brother from making an insane decision. Now, she used it on herself.

Because she was alone.

Well, there was Es-

NO! Not him. Never again him.

She was alone, and why not? Get out of here, train in her power, maybe be useful in some way. Why not?

"Why not?" Nalah said.

Laire came over and patted her hand. "That's what I like to hear."

CHAPTER TWO

"Please, Nalah, please! They'll kill me. Gods honest truth, they will rip me apart. Nalah...please, you gotta convince him!"

SNAP. The crunch of bone carried loud and clear through the stands, the sound still echoing when the corresponding roar of pleasure rose up. Men of various races on their feet, cheering the carnage. Almost all men, and the few women who were without a male escort were limited to the groupies and the ring workers. And her.

Five years she'd been away from this crap, since that day she walked with Laire and Fallon, neither telling her where she was going. Five years, and seeing the fight now, it was as if not a moment had passed, as if she had just risen from her ringside seat, cheering *him* because of another win, consoling her brother over a loss or draw.

She'd grown up with the matches in all their forms, from midnight fights behind garbage bins to private fights in rich people's mansions. Since joining the Guild, there was the thought, the expectation maybe this was no longer her world. Tonight proved that wrong. Wherever her life led her, this would always be where part of her belonged, and that part would be comfortable nowhere else.

Not that she was comfortable here, not with this job. She should go back and tell Fallon to shove it, though fat chance the words would work. No matter what the swordswoman said, there had to be another way than this path that had her skidding down memory lane and breaking through all the *STOP* signs along the way.

A whiff of rank body odor hit her full force, and Nalah shrank further into her seat, wrapping her coat around her in a doomed-to-fail bid for invisibility. A couple of guys eyed her with interest, their leers and comments growing louder with each additional fight, each additional drink. Not that she couldn't put them in their place if necessary, but who needed yet another level of annoyance?

And then a different sensation, a charged energy raced over the crowd. Everyone quieted, their gazes and rapt attention on the fighting cage in the front. Nalah straightened and looked at the ring.

He was in the cage, bigger now than the last time she'd seen him – any gangliness of body or baby fat in the face gone from this version. Here was sculpted muscle and hard edges as he walked the ring, not showboating to the crowd but projecting his confidence, his superiority all the same. No shirt, only worn light-denim jeans, scuffed black boots, and a chunky silver-linked bracelet around his wrist.

She couldn't see his eyes from this distance, but the dark brown hair was shorter, a bit spikier on top rather than the mop from her memory, and his skin was the same sun-warmed brown it always was. She had placed her hand on that chest, marveled at the firm muscle and enjoyed the contrast of their skin, how he was a few shades lighter than she. The melding of tones looked perfect together.

More noise signaled another man entering the ring – tall and blacker than she was, bigger than his opponent but nowhere near the same presence. The crowd burst forth with an equal amount of cheers and boos at this entrance, as well as quite a few catcalls.

"Destroy the King!"

"I'm going to spit on your grave, you dumb fuck!"

"Beat him and make me some money!"

The announcer came forth, a short, fat man with a too-tight T-shirt, strutting around like he thought he had the same build as the fighters. Maybe once upon a time, but that time was now long ago. He started to talk, too high of a voice, but before she could even begin to focus on the words *his* head shot up, the direction of *his* gaze coming straight at her.

She ducked. No. No, no. This wasn't…She wasn't ready to face him, was still entertaining daydreams of telling Fallon to stick Tenro somewhere impossible. Besides, there was still the smallest of chances this assignment wouldn't be necessary. She was here to watch him fight and go back to her apartment and completely and absolutely not talk to him.

The crowd was on its feet, upping the energy with smack talk while last-minute bets were made hand over fist.

She shouldn't have come. She wasn't ready yet. She'd never be ready, but now was stupid, when there was still a chance she wouldn't need to convince him.

Time to go.

She rose from the seat, keeping her body low and tight to hide from that damned gaze of his. Growing up, she had always been exposed before his eyes, secrets laid bare and willpower gone, and the fire that lived in his eyes danced because the bastard knew it. When she was a child the fire had an affectionate, familial warmth, and then she got older and the cast changed, hunger and desire replacing unassuming and comfortable. Now was a different time, and she was a different woman, older, harder, but still, she didn't want to test if she was immune to his eyes.

A meaty hand wrapped around her wrist. "Hey little thing, where ya goin?" a slightly slurred voice asked, and dammit, she really wasn't in the mood.

She kept her voice even, the same way she always spoke to drunks. "Need to use the bathroom. Can you watch my seat for me?"

The hand pulled her toward its owner, a middle-aged man who was all potbelly and faded glory, the type she'd seen thousands of times at the fights. "Nah, you don't need to leave now. How bout after this match we go ta my place? You can use anything you want there."

"I really do have to leave unless you want a big mess. Can you let me go?"

"Told ya no." His voice got determined, mean, and Nalah glanced around for *anything* she could use as a weapon.

It was too easy. A twist of her arm broke his grasp and in quick turn she had his arm pinned behind his back. A jerk upwards wrenched his arm enough that he yelled in pain, falling away from her and onto his knees.

People turned at the man's cry and took in the scene, though no one stepped forward to help. A part in the crowd gave her a clear view of the ring, and *he* stared at her, eyes burning bright and as intense as she had ever seen.

Five years fell away, and it might as well have been yesterday when she saw him last. The sweat that beaded off him had the same effect it always had, the desire to nuzzle into him, the desire to stick out her tongue and follow each individual droplet down to wherever it led.

She stepped back to fade into the crowd. He started to follow, but his opponent took the opportunity to throw a punch, and as if someone had called out *action*, everyone turned their attention back to the ring and to the fight they had come to see.

As she ran, in time with her heartbeat, the name she had not allowed herself to think of for five long years beat itself in her brain.

Esh, Esh, Esh...

CHAPTER THREE

Four. Five. Six...

Safe in her apartment, Nalah counted off the locks as she engaged them, the pattern calming, bringing her down little by little until the last one clicked shut and her heartbeat approached something close to normal.

Her head fell forward, resting on the door. Safe. Safe now, from the stupidity she had – no, *Fallon* had – inflicted on her.

"The Cage King is im-*pressive*. How did you manage to walk away from that again?"

Speaking of..."Why are you in my apartment, Fallon?" Long practice stopped the irritation from coloring her voice, but only just.

"Is she asking as a serious question, or is she angry?" And there was Laire, of course. It would be too much to allow Nalah to deal with the memories on her own terms.

Fallon's voice again, pitched higher to make sure everything she said was heard. "I'm going with rhetorical."

As much as this situation begged for alcohol, Nalah needed her wits about her, so tea would have to do. Walking into the small kitchen, she said, "The briefing is tomorrow, and I like my privacy. I don't belong to the Guild."

Once in the kitchen, Nalah looked over the small island to the living area, and sure enough, sitting on the arm of her sofa was Laire in a yellow dress that fell to her ankles, but with random cut-outs along the sides, showing patches of pale skin. Her black hair was the same length as the gown and had thick streaks of yellow running through it, and on her feet were yellow shoes that consisted of two thin straps and seven-inch platform heels.

Fallon stood next to her in the usual black leather, the long coat cut to suggest her figure without being skin tight. "Don't try that line around Kyo. Trust me, Bossman makes sure it never ends well for the speaker."

"I'm not speaking to Kyo, and you don't need to be following me around and entering my house uninvited."

Tenro gleamed in its usual spot above Fallon's shoulder. Five years of training, of familiarity with the sword, and Tenro still battered against

Nalah's magical shields. Fallon continued, "I needed face-to-face time to make sure you're in the right spirit for this job."

Always the job, though she had just seen Esh the first time in five years and was still shaky. Fallon never let up.

And then it was too much. "I can't do this *job*," Nalah said, slamming the kettle on the stove.

Neither Fallon nor Laire so much as flinched, and gods damn if that didn't make her feel a foot tall. Inhale, exhale, inhale again. For several moments she played in the kitchen, readjusting the kettle and turning on the heat. "I can't do this job," she repeated, making sure the right amount of apology came through in the tone.

Nalah twisted to grab a cup from the cupboard and shut the door only to find Fallon so close, the fine lines around her eyes were noticeable. While there was nothing overt in Fallon's manner, Nalah's urge to flee went into overdrive.

Fallon spoke, her voice a deep freeze. "Three weeks ago, twenty people I called *friend* died. So did dozens of others who all went to their death on my watch." She tilted her head, lowering her voice, clipping the words. "I can't bring them back. All I can do is try to make things right. So while I realize this is the guy who makes the demons in your head run amok, the fact remains you are the only one capable of doing this job, which means you're *going* to do this job. And I *really* don't want to hear any more crap."

A bubbling cauldron of emotions roiled in Nalah's stomach. Shame was there, guilt as well, because while she hadn't lost any friends during the break-in at Guild headquarters, she had seen the aftereffects. But there was also anger that Fallon dismissed with such ease her memories that had been brought back this last week in the form of sleepless nights and crying jags.

Displaying an emotional maturity rare for her, Laire came over and motioned Fallon back to the living area while putting her arm around Nalah's shoulder. "Forgive Fallon. It's still raw for us, but the truth is you are the only one who can do this. Besides," and here Laire squeezed Nalah's shoulder before retaking her own seat, "I think you'll want to when you hear this."

"What?" Not that Nalah thought Laire could say anything to convince her of that.

"The item we need you to retrieve is your mother's ring."

The cup shattered on the ground, the sound echoing in her head. "It was in the vault?" She'd never been able to discover why the Guild found the ring so valuable. Every once in a while she asked to study it, but the magic was as confusing to her now as it had when she'd started her training, the last time being a mere three months ago.

Dumbass. Of course it was in the vault. Stupid she hadn't realized that before. "Are you going to tell me now what's so special about it?"

Laire shook her head. "Really, you shouldn't know, because you don't need that info to find it. Plus if you get captured and tortured, they won't be able to get any answers from you." Any emotional maturity Nalah had ascribed to Laire in the kitchen now withered and died on the vine with that little statement. Always a smooth move to mention torture before sending someone on their first mission.

Fallon shook her head, though in the uncomfortable three-second silence that followed, she didn't gainsay the mage's words. Fallon's own emotions were under control again as well, because her voice was neutral when she spoke. "The good news is Beylor doesn't seem to know what it does. He bought it to have a pretty ring that came from the Guild to put on his latest blonde. It's a brag piece to him, nothing more, so we hope that means his security won't be too tight."

Nalah put aside her own hurt for the moment and made an overture to the swordswoman. There was logic in their conclusions, whether she liked it or not. "I'm not trying to piss you off, Fallon, and I know what you lost. You understand, though, this is hard for me. I left with the intention of being gone forever."

Fallon drew a deep breath and softened her stance, though her posture was still dominant. "Do you hate this guy? As in, *really* hate him and what we're asking is impossible?"

Go straight for the vulnerability, that was Fallon's way. How to answer that question, though...how to answer. "I don't." And damned if that answer didn't surprise her almost as much as Laire, if the slip of emotion that appeared on Laire's face was any indication. "But that doesn't change the pain of what happened. It doesn't change the fact my brother's gone."

As usual, Fallon's gaze bore the weight of someone who was searching for the soft underbelly. After a few moments, she gave a slight nod. "I sympathize, I do, but you're not stupid. You see the chain of events. You know the ring's signature, you don't have to worry about your abilities not working if we're right and this is a blackout zone, and you can get into the Underground Tour in such a way that'll give you the freedom to look for it. Maybe if we had more time we could set people up, but the Tour is already gathering the fighters. We're pressed."

"But I'm not Blackguard. I don't have any thieving or sneaking ability, and I certainly can't get into a safe. Someone like that would be more useful."

"Someone like that will be there and will work with you." As if she heard the protest rising in Nalah's mind, Fallon pinned her with a stare she usually reserved for fighting orc invasions. "You are the one who will find the ring because he can't, and he'll steal the ring and get it out – because you can't. Both of you are necessary. He's already there and will meet up with you at the Tour."

"And the best way to get you to the Tour is the Cage King, and may I say, *meow*," Laire supplied, sounding supremely unconcerned about any objections and pushing her long hair over her shoulder. The urge to pull it hit Nalah hard. She resisted, but damn, it was close.

"What if Esh has no interest?" There was the desperation, and *damn* again, because she really *really* wanted to get through this conversation without sounding whiny.

Laire made a rude sound, waving her hand in airy fashion. "We saw him at the match. You were running away so you might have missed it, but that boy was interested."

"It's been five years."

"Yeah, but you still have that ass and it's obvious he's an ass man." Laire gave a firm nod before laying down her pronouncement. "I have a sense about these things. Plus that was where his gaze was locked."

Oh *hells* no. She was not getting sexually harassed by some damn canary. "What is wrong with you?"

"We're still figuring that out," Fallon answered, with the same long-suffering look that Nalah remembered from that first meeting.

"It was a compliment," protested Laire.

"Oh sure, I understand. I can see why someone as flat as you would be overwhelmed."

Laire's scowl was immediate, and indicative that maybe not many people responded to her in kind. "I'm perfectly proportioned."

"Yeah, for a board."

"Can we catalog physical traits another time?" Fallon said, reaching out and pushing Laire back down into the couch when it looked like she was going to do a takedown. To Nalah she said, "You need to contact him as soon as possible."

Nalah rubbed her arms to bring some warmth to her now cool skin, a swamp of memories chilling the flesh in an otherwise warm apartment. "You don't know him. He's not going to agree to this. He didn't-" her voice cracked and she paused, clearing her throat. "He didn't help me with my brother's situation, even though I asked him to. So all this arguing and angsting is over something that's not going to happen."

"Maybe not, but let's say we tried, huh?" To Laire she said, "Time to go."

Without a word – another rarity for the tiny mage – Laire rose from the couch and walked toward the door with as much dignity as a banana could muster.

The door slammed shut the same moment Nalah spied the long yellow scarf. "Dammit Laire, pick up your shit," she said under her breath, grabbing the item and heading to the door to stop the two Guild members. As she opened the door her gaze slid across the multiple locks.

Four. Five. Six...

And she swung the door wide to see *him*.

CHAPTER FOUR

Esh's massive body dwarfed the doorframe. His fire-lit eyes held her attention as they always had, not allowing her to look away, to back away – not allowing her a moment to think or reconsider or remember why shutting the door right now and pretending she had not seen him would be a very good idea despite the conversation not two minutes ago.

"Nalah," he said, his voice good-whiskey-smooth and going down just as easy. "Let me in."

"No." The word slipped out, but there was no intent behind it. No closing of door, no backing away from temptation.

Not that either of those actions would have helped as he said, still calm, still easy, "Let me in or I'll rip this fucking door from its hinges."

When put like that... Nalah stepped back and Esh stepped forward, his presence too large in the tiny apartment, filling every corner and nook.

His eyes never left her, as if he was afraid that by looking away, she'd disappear again. She, on the other hand, did her best to look everywhere but at him, no matter that she felt his gaze on her, hot as flame.

Once again a hand wrapped around her wrist, but this time no disgust crawled through her at the sensation. The stroke of his fingertips over her inner wrist had her heartbeat go staccato and sparks flick along nerve endings. "How did you find me?"

"Had someone follow you from the match. How the fuck could you be so close and I never knew it?" His other hand wrapped around her neck in a gentle caress, and using his thumb he forced her chin up so their eyes met. "Why are you defenseless?"

"I can take care of myself." The rejoinder was automatic even after the space of years, but the annoyance of that familiar argument was not enough to dull the return of sensations that were raw and deep and sharp.

Instead of answering, he began to stroke along her neck, his fingers taking in the curve of her cheek, the small cleft in her chin, his eyes drinking in every spot his fingers passed over. His head dipped lower, the temptation of those lips – *gods*, that talented mouth – coming ever closer.

Nalah jerked back, the motion so forceful it left her dizzy for a moment. No, no this was not what she wanted, no matter how her traitorous body responded. Five years ago, she left, for reasons that still existed.

She cleared her throat and turned to go into the kitchen, for space rather than overwhelming thirst. No time to think how to play this...this thing. And now Esh was here, and if there was one thing she could never do with him around, it was think.

"Why did you come to the match?" He had slipped behind her without her notice, bending over her, his large frame enveloping hers, hot breath in her ear.

She grabbed the counter in front of her to have something solid beneath her fingers. What made her think she could ever do this? Time hadn't dulled a damn thing, not that she ever thought it would. "I wasn't thinking when I came to the match."

He closed in, his arms brushing the sides of her breasts, his hands resting next to hers. "Why did you *come*?"

She clenched her jaw hard so the groan wouldn't escape. Five years, and it was as if not an hour had passed. She moved so no part of her body was touching him, though he was still so near. "I work for the Guild now."

His body stiffened and his tone lost its seductive undertone. "Fuck you mean, the Guild? How could you be involved with them?"

Touching him was always a risk, but she pushed past his arm as quick as she dared to get away from the heat, the smell of him. Willpower was overrated. Safer now, leaning against the arm of her couch, Nalah said, "I needed to leave and they offered to get me away."

Esh had always been able to read her. He knew when to back away, when to bring her in closer. That ability was intact as, instead of crowding her again, he placed himself across from her, leaning against a wall, a vision of strength. "Tell me everything."

There was the old commanding tone, and she was grateful for it because now anger was coming forward, pushing back the sexual awareness of him. "You know everything. You were *there*. You were there when Jac got in trouble, and you were absolutely there when you left him to his fate."

"And he made his own choices," Esh replied, his own voice calm in contrast to her rising one. "I told him several times to stay away. I told them those matches were shit. He's the one who went anyway."

"One fight could have saved him."

"You're not stupid," he said, his own anger bleeding through. "It's never one fight with pieces of shit like that."

"We could have figured it out after he was safe!" The urge to bang her head against the counter hit hard. It was always his way. Make the decision and to hell with any further thoughts. He never listened to her. She exhaled, some of the fight going with it. Calmer, lower, she said, "We could have figured it out."

"Except I don't – get – *involved!*" Every word he spoke was salt rubbed deeper into the wound. "I don't get mixed up, and I don't put my neck out. Jac knew that when he made his choice, and he needed to see it through."

She saw it all, as clear as that day. Her brother bursting into their little apartment, the nicest one they'd ever lived in. The fear on his face, in his voice. Falling to his knees, begging her to talk to Esh.

Esh's face – hard, unyielding. Refusing the fight, no matter that her brother had been his best friend for years, no matter that her relationship with Esh had been venturing from schoolgirl crush to hot-and-heavy. They'd only kissed and petted, but five years later those moments were still the hottest sexual experiences she'd ever had.

But their relationship hadn't mattered. Still he refused. Still her brother fought. Still her brother died.

"Since you didn't come to the match because you wanted to see me, why did you come?" His face and voice were now as inviting as a brick wall. There would be no more talking about the past, at least not now.

She was alone in this world, but she had two things she could be proud of and cherish – the work she did and her mother's ring. The Guild's inner workings, well, they made the crime lords she grew up around look like cuddly stuffed animals in contrast, but because of them her life and her gift had meaning. And her mother's ring was every good memory in her life of her beloved mama. Mama left too soon, wasted away from illness, but until the end she read to Nalah before bed every night and never once snapped at her when she asked once again *"Mama, why?"*

The past wouldn't change, and today proved her damned sexual attraction to this man wouldn't either. Neither mattered though, not compared to the importance of reclaiming the ring. It was what Fallon had been telling her today, and the message at last had made it through. "I was there on Guild business. A situation has developed, and we need your help. I want you to work with me on an assignment."

Not Happy was an understatement if his darkening countenance was anything to go by. Esh's fingers stretched wide before curling in a loose fist and with measured movements he stepped away from the wall, began circling her little apartment. "Five years not a word, but once I'm a useful thug, all is set aside and you'll bother with me again? Did you bring a leash as well?" He was still walking, still too calm.

The flinch that struck her body hit hard, as hard as if he'd laid hands on her. That tiny piece of guilt she'd pushed far back in her emotions wiggled free now, reveling in its moment. No matter the justification for leaving or the importance of the mission that had driven her to see him again, it was the truth. Before the break-in at headquarters and her subsequent assignment, she...well, she'd always thought about Esh and kept up with his exploits through the grapevine, things not even the anger could get her to stop. But going to see him, approach him? No. Before the break-in, that part of her life had been dead. "If anyone else could be here, I would never have brought this back in your life."

Esh's voice was mocking. "But of course, out of all the Guild, you are the only one who could come, and the fact that the woman I loved needs my help isn't a manipulation to get me to agree."

Loved broke through her, her body flinching at the past tense. Unbidden, images rushed through her – a first kiss when it had been pouring rain, Esh's mouth so soft on hers when nothing else of him could ever be described as soft. Looking up from a book only to find his face inches away, and his smile saying he'd been there for some time, only she hadn't noticed. A ten-year-old boy glaring at a gang of bullies as he stood over a seven-year-old girl, protecting her and making her safe in a way her brother could never quite manage.

She shoved them away, brought her mind to the present. That was over, and only what happened next mattered. "We both know it is, though given our history, I told them not to count on it being an effective one." She held up her hand to stop the words he began to voice. "No, let's not go over it again. Let me tell you the job, and we go from there."

He spun on his heel and went to the kitchen, finding her stash of whiskey in an upper cabinet on the first try. Much as she wanted a drink herself, she said nothing as he belted back a shot. Once done, he licked his lips, and she could almost feel those lips on her neck, traveling downward as his teeth came and nipped along the path.

Nalah turned away before he caught her staring. Not good to give him any ammunition. From behind her, he spoke. "Okay, clear your conscience."

She did her best to keep any emotion out of her voice. "The Guild has discovered Beylor has purchased a very important magical artifact, one the Guild wants to get into our possession. Word is he doesn't realize what it is or the power it possesses, so the main focus is to get it back before Beylor finds out what it does."

"The Underground Tour. You want me to get you in," Esh said, grim humor in his voice.

Grateful she didn't have to explain further, Nalah fell silent to allow Esh to work it out in his own head. In the underworld of cage fighting, the Underground Tour was legend, the match all fighters dreamed of. Only a few ever made it, and Beylor, the operator of the Tour, was by turns revered and feared by most.

Except Esh didn't have any interest, though he received an invite for each Tour. *I'm not a dog to bark on command.* He never trusted it, and as he once told her, he wouldn't be part of anything where he couldn't see all the pieces in play. And if anything was shrouded, it was the Tour.

The fact that his continued refusal made him a legend and had people coming from all over to both fight him and see him was an unexpected side effect.

After long moments he spoke again. "Why can't the Guild show up and force the return?"

She turned to face him. He was still holding the glass, giving it the occasional slow spin so the liquid arced and rolled within the cup. "Too many things are in play. Politics, for one. The Tour draws a lot of important people. Beyond that, Beylor is slippery. The Guild has bits and pieces of information, but they've never been able to get enough to pin a location down until after the Tour has moved."

"No wizards can magically find him? That much power in one place – don't know how it could be missed."

"Not that simple. The theory is Beylor operates the Tour in what are known as blackout zones. No magic works in or escapes those areas."

He cocked his head in question, ready to learn more, like always. While Esh had never read on his own, he'd brought her every book he got his hands on – though how he got them she never asked. And at night, he'd listen for hours as she discussed whatever she'd learned that day. "He protects himself by sticking to areas where magic is useless and he's surrounded by fighters and warriors. Man's not stupid." He drained the glass and set it on the counter before coming to stand in front of her. Anew, desire shaped itself low in her stomach as the scent of sweat and leather and that something that came to be labeled *Esh* in her mind hit her, but Nalah dug deep and refused to back away. She wouldn't concede any ground to him. "Why are they sending you, outside of the very important reason they're hoping you'll convince me to get you to the Tour? Did you turn into a master thief while you were away? Because if you aren't, can't see how you going matters."

And here it was, the moment she'd been dreading. Laying herself bare in front of the one man she wanted to be shielded from. "Remember when I was a kid and always talked about feeling things? We thought maybe I had some magic in me but I never passed any tests and we decided that wasn't the case."

"Yeah, except for that old fortune-teller. She always said you were in contact with the spirit world. I don't know how the hell anyone took her seriously when she smelled like a bar." And for one moment he smiled, open and free and emotionally intimate, and it was the three of them again, making a scruff of their neck escape and laughing about it once danger had passed, and the jolt that passed through her chest when Esh turned that smiling gaze to her.

"Well, anyway," she said, not responding to his smile, breaking the moment, and his face settled back into harsh lines, though he didn't back away. "I can't cast magic – I'm not a wizard, that's true – but I can sense magic, and I can break it. I can *unwind* it, reverse the spells, make it like they never existed. It's known as being a Magic Breaker."

Esh's eyebrows rose, though no other signs of hesitant disbelief appeared on his face. Considering she'd never heard of Magic Breakers until the Guild entered her life, she wouldn't have blamed him if he laughed outright at the thought. "You can't cast spells?"

"Nope," she said, popping the *p* at the end.

"But if you come to a house that has a magical lock on the door..."

"I can open it, twist the handle and go right on in. It's amazing how many people will lock up their houses with layers of magic but not use a ten-dollar deadbolt."

Esh crossed his arms over his chest and breathed deep, as if settling everything he'd learned inside him. "So the Guild thinks Beylor, what, lives in one of these magic-free zones you were talking about and they expect you to walk in and grab this piece of jewelry?"

He looked skeptical, and she didn't blame him. "Not quite. I'm not going to be alone. There's a thief I'll be meeting there. I need to find the item, and they're going to steal it."

His hands went to his hips and he widened his stance, and damned if she was going to admit the dominating aura did anything to her insides, because like hell she'd ever give him that type of ammunition. "If they got a thief, why do they need you?"

"Beylor is known for making multiple fakes of his valuables. Multiple fakes in multiple vaults, so I'm needed to lead my contact to the correct item."

"And it's got to be you because you're a Magic Breaker?"

"Exactly. A wizard would be useless, but what I'm able to do isn't the same, so I'll be able to function."

His stance was still aggressive, those large hands resting on trim hips. "That's all well and good, but you're not a warrior. Beylor'll have an army of thugs wandering around."

"I'll deal with it."

Wrong thing to say, because he went from calm to pissed, veins in his neck raising beneath the skin. "Like *fuck* you'll deal with it! You think I'll let you just walk into that shit? Beylor has access to the best fighters, and none of them would have a second thought about hurting a woman."

Ten minutes after walking in the door, and he thought he had the right to an opinion? Like *hell*. "What makes you think you have any say in my life? I've been doing just fine."

"And if I don't help you?" he challenged.

"Then there's plan B," she responded, flinging her hands up in frustration. "They might have determined this to be the best plan, but I guarantee they'll have someone else I can travel with. I don't need your *help*."

She turned, but his fingers wrapped around her upper arm stopped her from leaving. She twisted to face him but didn't get a chance to speak before he claimed her mouth, his lips on hers and his tongue demanding entrance.

Familiar yet new. So many times he'd done this, evoked fire in her body, flames that started low in her belly and spread to engulf her whole body. He dominated her, taking possession with his mouth, forcing her to receive pleasure as he deemed to give it.

Only white existed in her thoughts. She was all feeling, all senses. His touch, the calloused hand rough and tender as it slid along her back. His scent, sweat from the match still on his skin, woodsmoke, and the musky male undertone that was pure Esh.

Nalah's hands were weak, trembling, as she pushed at him, breaking free enough to whisper, "We can't. Esh."

He groaned as she said his name and retook her mouth, a languid conquest where he drew out sighs and groans from her against her will.

It was his hands sliding down to cup her ass that brought back damned reality to the forefront. This time her push against him was harder and caught him off guard, enough that she was able to escape.

The clench of his jaw and the heavy breathing told of bringing himself under control.

They studied each other for several moments. He would do this in the cage, this focused deconstruction, those few moments before the match started, and Nalah would swear that these were the moments he was most dangerous. The fights might be more spectacular, but this was where Esh figured out his enemy – how they were weak, how to strike, how to break.

Yes, anyone with sense would fear him most in these moments.

And never let it be said Nalah didn't have sense.

When his body relaxed, that was when Nalah's guard went up. "I'll do it," he said. "I'll accept my leash and take you to the Tour." And just as she was about to breathe out in relief, he added, "With conditions."

Of course there were. "What conditions?"

Esh crossed his arms over his chest in a way that stretched his T-shirt over his chest, every muscle defined under the cotton, and her mouth watered a little. "The only reason a fighter would bring a woman was if she was his, so for the duration of the Tour, you're mine."

"What do you mean?"

"What I said."

He was arrogance personified standing there, and damned if that wasn't a good look on him, the bastard. "Pretend I'm stupid and spell it out."

His eyes burned as they raked over her body, as strong as a physical caress, and the sensations that hadn't dimmed since their kiss burned brighter. "No fucking," he said. "I'm not going to fuck you until you beg me. Everything else, that's allowed."

"Everything else?" she asked in spite of a very dry mouth, needing and dreading clarity for that statement.

"My mouth on yours," he started, and began to walk toward her, slow and steady, winding and hypnotizing like a snake before it strikes. "My palms trailing over your breasts. Teeth biting into your skin, marking you for everyone to see. My cock rubbing over your ass. Tongue on your clit, and my fingers deep inside you as you come all. Over. *Me.*"

He was in front of her now, their gazes locked, both breathing heavy. "That's what you agree to give me if I do this. From now until you get your item, you stay by my side, and I have the freedom to claim you as *mine.*"

CHAPTER FIVE

"You know who you called."
Beeeep
"Warm and fuzzy as always."
Throat clearing.
"I want to be clear, since you left so fast last night. While I get I have to pretend to be yours, what you said isn't going to happen. Yeah, for realism some things...yeah. But ummm...not like you said. You and I aren't there."
Pause.
"Just want to be clear."
Click.

He had to bring the motorcycle.

All sleek chrome and purring engine, and there Esh sat, the king of his world. His legs were splayed to keep the bike steady, the tight jeans a nice showcase for what lay underneath, highlighting both muscles and length. Over his T-shirt? A worn leather jacket that was near enough a second skin, buttery soft and inviting. The urge to stroke it – stroke *him* – was as sharp as ever.

"I don't like motorcycles anymore. Death traps, you know." Her resistance was token, but she couldn't climb behind him without the attempt.

"Get on," he replied. The problem was she'd never had any older women in her life to advise her as she was growing up. Older women would give out good advice, like never tell a man who wanted to get into your pants that motorcycles and black leather made your thighs tremble, and your biggest fantasy was sex on top of one.

After hearing things like that, men tended to use that sort of information against you.

She could do this. One leg over, scoot back as far as possible, hold onto Esh with only her hands. Simple.

Except the moment her butt hit the seat Esh reached behind him and curled his hands under her thighs, pulling her forward until she was flush against him, breasts and belly against his broad back, her thighs spread wide to cradle his hips.

The gasp couldn't be stopped any more than breathing could be stopped, her arms reaching around him, and then the motor gunned. She held tight as the bike took off.

The wind made conversation impossible. In jagged bits her body began to relax, to settle into both Esh and the bike. The vibrations of the bike rumbled through her skin. Esh's back protected her from the worst of the whipping wind, and she burrowed into him, pressing closer to move with the bike, relaxing into the turns and absorbing the bumps in the road.

The sun was warm as it beat down on them, a nice complement to the bite of the wind. There was nothing like the freedom of a bike, pushed close behind your man. He wasn't her man, not anymore, but a moment, just a moment, she could disappear into memory and enjoy.

After almost an hour of travel, he pulled onto a side road that led deep into a wooded area. "I think serial killer movies start this way," Nalah said, loud enough to be heard over the engine.

"Yeah, but I'm around. You should be more scared for them."

Stupid comeback, but the smile curled her lips anyway, and she ducked her head and placed it against his back as if there was a chance he could see it.

They came to a large clearing filled with mostly motorcycles and beat up trucks. The spacing was haphazard, leaving Esh to park in a loose circle of racing bikes.

Nalah pushed off, and as soon as both feet hit ground her trembling thigh muscles refused to support her weight and her legs buckled. Only Esh's quick reflexes stopped her from falling against the motorcycle.

"It's been awhile," she said as warmth bloomed in her face and she avoided his eyes. Nice thing being darker-skinned was blushes were a lot harder to see, but Esh was close enough that if he was observant, he'd notice it – and Esh was nothing if not observant.

"I'm not going to complain knowing that," he said, voice low and tone possessive, the same one he'd used when he'd told Jac they were leaving and she wouldn't be back until morning. Her stupid brother had only smirked and said to have fun.

Thoughts of her brother brought her into the present, dissipated the blush and made sure the only reason her thighs trembled was because of the reality of riding the bike and nothing to do with the man in front of her. She met his eyes now, and whatever he saw had his mouth thinning, had him giving a small nod and grabbing her elbow for support only as they walked a small path through more trees to what she assumed was the fighters gathering area.

Steps one, two and three, they were enveloped by trees, but with step four a large gathering area opened up. A rough guess would place the number of people before them at about a hundred or so. So far all of them were human and the vast majority were men. They moved forward and joined the group.

Esh's palm was a brand where it lay on the small of her back. Men only had to glance at it and then at Esh before they averted their eyes from her and became interested in other sights.

Women took it more as a challenge. More than one looked at the hand, looked at her, and then smirked before they gazed at Esh with half-lidded eyes and pouty lips. And any fantasy she had about ripping off those fake lips? It had nothing to do with Esh. It was because they were being rude.

After the third such display, Esh's fingers tightened on her skin. "No fighting before the tournament, right, Nalah?"

The unconcealed humor in his tone focused her ill-defined anger from the bottle-blonde to him. "I don't know what you mean by that statement." To further make her point she stepped away from his touch.

The crowd was loud and getting louder, the people here not used to patience and not enjoying it. The paper Esh had received after he'd agreed to participate in the Tour had only coordinates along with a date and time. No other information was given, and it looked like people weren't happy about that fact.

There were a few faint magical signatures, suggesting items such as magically enhanced brass knuckles or other weapons, but they weren't impressive. As for the quality of the fighters – something was wrong. Yeah, there was always the one or two who didn't look like they could take you apart until they exploded in the ring, but there was usually a *something* – in the way their eyes always scanned the surroundings, how their bodies always had a faint edge of tension, on lookout for the next attack, an inner spark – a *something* that drew eyes to them, that set off warning lights inside and said, *This person. Watch this person.*

Moving amongst this group? Nothing lit up inside her. They were ordinary people, not the caliber one would expect from people entering something as legendary as the Tour, none who would last more than a minute with Esh in the cage.

"So you feel it too." Esh had come beside her as she studied the crowd.

They were alone enough that as long as she kept her voice pitched lower she was comfortable speaking her thoughts, so she said, "It can't be this easy."

"It's not." Esh's eyes flicked back and forth, stopping a couple of times to study something in more detail. "There are two other true fighters here."

"So what's going on?"

"Multiple entry points and times. They don't want us to know our opponents before we meet wherever we're going. Also keeps us from fighting now."

"And the rest of the people?"

"Some old ladies," he said, squeezing her side. "Some friends. Some support staff. Some told they were going to the Tour but aren't."

Before she could respond a magically projected voice boomed around them. "*Fighters!* Welcome to the Underground Tour! The winner will receive everything in this life he wishes. To everyone else – there is no second place."

CHAPTER SIX

Magical transportation. Sure, it was quick, but as Nalah oriented herself to her new surroundings and suffered the two seconds of vague panic that zinged through her until she focused on Esh, Nalah decided she'd rather take the motorcycle everywhere.

One moment they were in the clearing, the next she and Esh and half of the crowd were standing before the gated entrance of a small town. The gate opened and everyone moved forward.

It took only a dozen steps for Nalah to realize, yes, this was a blackout zone. The Guild's intelligence was right about that. It was…dull. Flat. No bursts of iridescent color combining in the corner of her eye, no almost musical twisting and twining wound tight around her skin.

"What's wrong?" And only with Esh's words did it register her feet had stopped and her body was stationary, while people flowed around them.

As attention was the last thing she needed, she got her feet moving again. "Sorry. I was taking it in."

His face creased lightly in disbelief, but he didn't call her on it, and they continued forward as they were directed.

The set-up was impressive, especially when you added in most if not all of it had been built without magical help. In rather hilly land, a large tract of forest had been cleared to build a little town. The structures on the edges were shoddily built, their quick construction evident with a glance, but the further in you got the nicer, bigger, brighter everything became.

Esh must have seen something in her face give away her thoughts, because he said, "Outside houses are for staff, the rank-and-file security."

"Where will the fighters be housed?"

"Close to the middle. Easier for the guards to keep an eye on us."

As if his words conjured them, the guards became more noticeable. The prevailing theme was big and mean-looking, and armed with bladed weapons. No bows or staffs – no, all of them had knives and swords in easy reach.

They traveled through the town, the buildings in the middle looking less like barracks and more like condos. From here the houses built up into the hills were noticeable, and Esh said, "The guests. The ones who are watching the fights."

"Beylor?"

"My guess? His house is whichever one looks like the most money went into it."

That would be the one right in the middle, and it was a monstrous celebration of excess without thought to good taste. Somewhere in there, her mother's ring was waiting, and a sharp pain lanced through her chest, for a moment the loss of something so precious to someone like *that* unbearable.

On the opposite end of town from where they entered was a huge building, built abutting the forest. The closest she could compare it to was a coliseum, except this had a roof. "The fights will be held here?" she asked.

Esh nodded, nothing much more to be added to that observation.

"Fighters." This voice had no magical enhancement, instead relying on an antiquated speaker system. It took moments to locate the source, a man who was standing on a scaffold on the outside of the coliseum. His long, pointed nose and lack of a chin had Nalah thinking cheese and mouse traps. "Fighters! Welcome to the Underground Tour. Congratulations. Only the finest are offered a spot here. You are all to be commended to have made it this far. I am Beylor."

A natural public speaker he wasn't. His voice wasn't squeaky – surprise, that – but he did have the faintest lisp that made any authority he tried to project into his voice a lost cause. Still, the large amount of jewelry, the finery of his clothes, and the fact that he was surrounded by scary looking goons made sure everyone gave him their attention.

"There will be three days of fighting. At the end of the first day, we will have our final sixteen. At the end of the second, eight fighters will be left standing. And on the third day, the King of the Tour shall be crowned."

The crowd responded to this, loud cheers following suit. Beylor held his hands up for quiet. "You are allowed no weapons, but apart from that, there are no rules. You will fight until one of you can fight no more, and the one left standing is the winner. Are you *ready*?"

More catcalls, more yelling with now the stomping of feet added. "Between the fights you are welcome to whatever you wish, wherever you wish to go, with again only one rule – there will be no fighting outside of the Tour. Is that understood?"

All around them the guards raised the various weapons, and the cheering was more subdued from minutes ago. Beylor retreated back into the building, and women came forward to start leading the fighters to their rooms.

Well, that and to get harassed. Several fighters were brushing against the women, speaking to them. Nalah couldn't hear the words, but the pinched look on the women's faces said everything. She crowded closer to Esh. Esh, who had noticed as well and was taking it in without a sound, only wrapped his arm around her shoulder and waited until a woman came forward for them.

They were shown to their apartment, located in the smallest of the cluster of buildings that seemed to be the fighters housing. The rooms were well appointed and spacious and a far cry from what she had been expecting. Nalah started searching room to room, holding her finger to her mouth when he would have said something. Shrugging, he lay on the bed, hands beneath his head as he watched her work.

Finally she nodded, and he spoke. "What was that?"

"Remember I said most people put seven different security spells on a building but wouldn't bolt their door? Well, this was the opposite. There's no magic here, so I was looking for old-fashioned methods to listen or spy on us."

"Any?"

"None, which is kind of shocking. Paranoia is Beylor's defining characteristic. I can't understand why he wouldn't be keeping an eye on the fighters. I put up some countermeasures in case he gets the idea in the future, but right now, zilch."

"I'm not surprised. There are several other ways Beylor keeps an eye on us, and someone finding a bug in their room wouldn't be good for his business. That's a line most of us wouldn't accept being crossed, especially for those who bring their women. Speaking of," he added, patting the bed beside him.

He was intent on her, focused on her in a way he was nowhere else, not even within the ring. His words from that night pounded in her brain, the beat upping her heart rate and bringing warmth to her skin. She couldn't let him get the upper hand, not so quickly, but inside her still lived the ten-year-old who looked up to him like he was a rock star and the seventeen-year-old who loved him as only a teenager was capable of, and they were both demanding she snuggle with him on that bed.

Straightening her spine, she did the only thing that came to mind – stall and hope it worked. "I'd like to get cleaned up, look around a bit, check out the fighters."

"Later," Esh said, and his face was settling into lines that promised a battle should she fight him on this.

So much for that plan. Nalah took off her shoes, debating a moment. If she tried to stay on the opposite side of the bed he'd come after her. There was nothing to do except cuddle into him, so she did, positioning herself so her face lay on his shoulder and her arm rested over his upper waist.

He snorted, but didn't say anything, instead tightening his arm so she was comfortably crushed to him.

His fingers moved in lazy circles over her upper arms, sensitizing every square inch of skin and leading her mind to latch on one question – *Where will he touch next?*

And the small disappointment when it became obvious the answer was nowhere else, that he was content holding her in his arms and stroking the skin of her arm? It was because there were better things she should be doing right this moment.

Yeah, right, said the seventeen-year-old. Not wanting to examine her thoughts or motives all that closely, she closed her eyes and let her mind drift.

The first time she was in his arms in a romantic sense was right after their first kiss. It was her first kiss ever, though Esh couldn't claim the same – not that she ever pressed him on that.

The kiss was so soft. Of all the words that described Esh, *soft* never once entered her mind before that night, but that was the only word that fit. His lip was split, but he didn't hesitate to press them to hers when she lifted her face, the faintest aftertaste of blood lingering. His fight swollen hands roamed feather-light over her skin of her shoulders and arms, going only a moment to the stretch of skin over her tummy her too-short shirt revealed, before tugging the material down and returning to the neutral areas.

He laid her on top of him that night, not making any allowances for the various bruises the fight left, but he pushed her no further – soft kisses and soft strokes were all that were given that night, until she fell asleep in his arms.

"Why do you want to check out the other fighters?"

"Hmm?" It took a moment to be brought out of her hazy lassitude. "Oh, I want to see if any of them are innate."

"Innate?" he asked, voice curious but still calm.

"Yeah, I should be able to feel if any of them have powers by magical means." She glanced up to see him studying her, his face calm confusion.

"Didn't we just go over how this place isn't magical?"

She straightened, sat up on the bed to look down at him. "Magic is...weird." Wow, that was a lame way to start. He smiled but didn't say anything. "I know, I know, really helpful. I'm trying to think how to explain."

"Start by speaking. I'll ask questions along the way."

And there was Esh, pragmatic and straight ahead. "There is no one way magic behaves. There is no one truth. It makes dealing with magic difficult." He still looked confused. Taking a deep breath, she tried again. "All right, say someone casts a spell to light a fire. The magic is in the spell. The fire, though, the fire isn't magic, even though it started that way. Right now we're in an area that doesn't allow magic, so if someone cast a spell to light a fire, it wouldn't work. But if someone cast a spell to light a fire outside of this dampening area, and then brought the torch with the fire here, the fire wouldn't extinguish the moment they crossed into the zone. But even though the fire isn't magic, if I looked at it, I'd be able to tell the fire was started by a spell instead of a match. It would still carry its beginnings."

Esh face was open, questioning. "So what do you mean *innate*?"

"When we call someone innate, it's because they have powers that are magic, but are not subject to the same rules as straight magic. Their powers can't be dispelled – at least, usually they can't – and they could still use them even in a magically dead area."

"Such as?"

"Such as a werewolf's ability to shift. It doesn't matter if that ability came into being because of magic or not, it's now part of them. Same as a gargoyle's ability to fly, or a shadow stealer's ability to blend into shadow, or in theory a dragon's ability to breathe fire."

"Too bad there are no dragons to ask if that's true." Long experience told her the lines between his brows and the thin lips meant he was rolling her info in his mind, absorbing this new knowledge.

"Innate type magic is more intricate and harder to place. It can get lost in noise pretty easily." At that, sledgehammer to her face couldn't have surprised her more, and the *ohh* fell from her lips without conscious thought.

That's what she'd been feeling from Esh, this itch that overcame her. It was light and, added to the storm of other feelings being around Esh engendered, near impossible to suss out.

Innate. There was something in him innate – buried, buried deep, so deep he probably didn't know of its existence. The part of him responsible for his eyes, maybe his superior strength and fighting as well.

"What?" he asked.

She shook her head, continued on. Not until she thought this through would she mention it to him. "I want to make sure I at least try to see if any of the fighters have that advantage. I don't want you caught off guard."

"You mean like this?" he asked, and rolled her onto her back, trapping her beneath him.

CHAPTER SEVEN

Those gorgeous dark-brown eyes of hers were wide with surprise as he rolled her under him. No reason why they should be. He told her this was where she was going to be for the duration of the Tour.

"Esh," she started, and in response he pushed his hips against her pelvis, rubbing hard against her.

Her mouth parted. A long, deep breath met the movement while her eyes went half-lidded. Her hands went to his shoulders, her fingers half digging into the muscle, her arms both pulling him closer and pushing him away.

His Nalah was conflicted? Well, he was going to put an end to that real quick. By the end of the Tour she was going to be back in his bed and standing by his side, where she belonged now, and where she'd belonged these last five years before she'd run away.

To the Guild. Of all fucking people, she had gotten involved with the Guild. He growled, the need to mark her as his and not theirs growing in him, and he lowered his mouth to her throat.

She panted and moaned as his lips and teeth ravaged the sensitive skin below her ear, the sounds tightening his belly and ratcheting up his arousal. He wanted her to make those sounds all night, he wanted her hoarse tomorrow and embarrassed because everyone would give her a knowing look each time she spoke. He sucked the dark skin into his mouth, wishing the small bruise would show.

How had he lived without this these last years? She even smelled the same, summer nights on the beach. He told her that after their first kiss, and she laughed, saying they'd never been near the ocean in their lives.

Didn't matter. That was what she reminded him of. Her scent was always a mix of citrus and salt while her eyes and skin glowed under moonlight. She was wondrous, his escape from a shitty life, and always had been. Her eyes alight with pride as he fought in the ring, making him a hero and a warrior instead of a thug. Or how she never stopped teaching him or acted like he was too stupid to be bothered with.

He nipped her, a little harder, teeth a little deeper into her velvety skin, and her answering moan had his cock beating against the zipper of his jeans, demanding to be let out.

"Esh, let go," she whispered, those long fingers still digging into his upper arms.

She wasn't saying anything he wanted to hear, so he concentrated on licking the tang from her skin and listened to that tiny hitch in her breathing.

"Warned you." And before his brain processed, Nalah shifted, using her leg to dislodge him while those fingers twisted his body and had him on the floor.

She got off the bed and now stood above him, hip cocked to the side and fists on them, her eyes sparking in an all-to-familiar way, one that used to mean he was sleeping on a couch that night. "Damn woman, who taught you that?"

"Who do you think? I might not be a warrior, but do you think I'd let myself be totally vulnerable?"

She *was* vulnerable. Any of Beylor's men could have her on her back with either a sword in her belly or them crawling on top of her in five seconds flat. But right now, with her foot that close to his balls, he wasn't going to point that out. Instead he rolled and got to his feet, watching her watch him the entire time.

There was appreciation mixed with the earlier anger, the way she followed the bunching of the muscles in his thighs and his arms. Nalah wasn't immune to him any more than he was to her. "Why'd you stop me?"

"Again, why do you think? I'm not here to be your personal amusement. Already told you."

He snorted. "When have you ever been that? If that's all I considered you good for, do you think I'd be here?"

That stopped her, her mouth closing, her face scrunching up in a *V* of confusion. She collapsed on the nearest chair, her arm draped across the table. "You and I need a little clearing of the air. Cards on the table?"

Yeah, that didn't promise a good time. He shrugged, going to sit across from her.

She waited until he was settled before she began. "Why did you agree to do this?"

Talk about denial. He met her gaze, held it, until she was near fidgeting but still didn't look away. "You aren't stupid. You know why. I'm not changed."

At that, Nalah did look away, out a window that overlooked the nearby forest. "It's been five years," she said, her voice as low as he'd ever heard from her.

"So? Fuck does five years mean? You're it for me, always have been. Knew it as soon as you looked up at me with those big brown eyes and I told you so back then. Told you the same before we came here, though you wanted to pretend that wasn't what it meant. If it won't change in fifty years, why do you think five years is some magic number?"

She swallowed, the movement doing little to hide the slight quiver of her chin. "'Cause I haven't been around."

He snorted. "Yeah, like that changes shit."

Now she turned back to him, her chin square, her eyes dead set on his, hard in a way they rarely were back before. "Because Jac is dead."

"And?"

As if she had been touched by a live wire, Nalah jumped from the table, pounding her hands hard against the wood surface. "What do you mean, *and*? You could have stopped it. You *should* have stopped it."

He rose to her challenge, stepping toe to toe with her. "Why? So he could turn around and do the same stupid shit the next year, the next month? He knew and he chose to do it anyway. He did it knowing I wasn't going to get involved."

"Oh yeah, you and your famous *I don't get involved*." She flung her arms wide, the movements wild and her voice loud and angry. "That's why they thought it was safe to target him. Because there was no worry over retribution. The Cage King's best friend, and they killed him, all because you *don't get involved*."

"So what're you saying? You blame me for his death?"

That shocked her still, her voice and body going slack for a moment. She looked...she looked like she wanted to argue, and she wanted to cry, and she wanted to bang her head on a table and not stop...all of it, rolled together.

Her arms wrapped around her waist, one hand stroking along the length of the other arm. "I'm not saying- That night, when I disappeared, do you know why I went with the Guild?" She didn't wait for him as she dove into the answer. "Because I didn't care. Whatever they had in mind for me, I was okay with it. I knew what they said they wanted, but if it was something else? I'd just lost everything and I was so tired. As long as the pain ended, I was okay with it. "

Gods, why didn't he have a fight now? He needed to hit something, feel bone break and flesh part under his fist. "What the *fuck* am I supposed to do with that? Why are you putting that on me now?"

"I'm not telling you to worry you, not even to punish you. It was five years ago, and there is nothing of that feeling left." With effort, she unhooked her arms from around her, let herself open up to him, her neck and body exposed as any prey hoping to appease a predator. "I'm telling you so you understand. I am not the seventeen-year-old you knew, not even close. I'm still attracted to you – hell, probably ninety percent of the women and twenty percent of the men in the New Realms are attracted to you – but whatever was between us... It's not there anymore, not like it was, because I'm not like I was."

She said it like it was some big revelation, and while he wasn't going to convince her of anything right now, not with all the emotions running high, he also wasn't going to let it lie, let her have the last word and think he believed what she was saying. "You aren't telling me anything I don't see. So what you're not seventeen, the core is still you. What we feel for each other is still real. Doesn't matter how attracted you are to me, you wouldn't respond if it wasn't."

Nalah's stubbornness came out full force as she shook her head. "That's muscle memory. It's part of the reason I'm here. I wanted to get some closure to move on."

If he ever got the asshole who thought up that word in the ring... "I hate that fucking word. What, you're supposed to put a bow on us? Closure doesn't exist."

"No, I know that. I do. But the way it was before, how I left, that was wrong. Too many open wounds for both you and me are left from it. Yeah, I agree, closure doesn't exist, but what it is now … Five years later, and it's still bleeding. I want the bleeding to stop. I want the scar to form so I can go near it without constant pain."

"And you think us here will accomplish that?"

"If anything can, it's this. Not that this is a relaxing vacation, but outside in the world, there would be too many questions of me being in your life, people maybe remembering me from before. This way it's as blank a slate as us two can manage."

"Cards on the table?" he echoed her earlier words. She nodded. "You might be going for your closure, but the only thing I'm working for is you back in my life and my bed. I warned you before, and the words are still the same. While you're here, you're mine, and all I want is for you to never leave me again."

CHAPTER EIGHT

Nalah rubbed her neck where Esh had marked her yesterday, once again holding her head high and refusing to acknowledge the smirking looks directed her way. Damn Esh. Because of him she looked like she'd been attacked by a vampire and total strangers thought they had a right to comment on her private life.

"Where are you going?"

Startled, she stopped short in front of one of Beylor's men, the shitty attitude and weapon in hand both giveaways to his identity. "I'm just looking around." *For innates and a magic ring*, but he didn't need to know the end of the sentence.

"Women need to stay in the lodge unless there's a match. Turn around."

For one brief moment, a wish that Fallon was here to deal with this sexist idiot bloomed bright in her heart, but she turned and took herself back to the lodge without complaint. Underground matches were not a haven of sexual equality, and women talking back, well, not so much. She wasn't going to bring scrutiny to herself, no matter how good flipping him off might feel.

A few dozen women milled around the common room a few other guards pointed her toward, the overall mood cautious but still welcoming. Before she finished even a handful of brief introductions, in came the blondest, boobiest woman she'd ever seen in person, wearing about two pounds of make-up, ten pounds of jewelry, and a few ounces of clothing.

No magic ring, but if this woman wasn't Beylor's plaything, Nalah would get a makeover from Laire.

A slavering entourage surrounded the woman, high-pitched giggles in response whenever Blondie spoke. Definitely the queen of the compound.

Blondie gazed around until her eyes locked with Nalah, and she came over, all blinding white teeth in a horsey face. "Omigods, you're the Cage King's woman! How did you get him?! Omigods! Oh, I'm Tiffany, and you're Nalah! I'm so glad to meet you!"

She pulled Nalah to sit beside her on the plush pink loveseat, three other women taking seats wherever there was room in the circle. Needing to get into Tiffany's good graces and taking a chance due to Tiffany's own pink ensemble, Nalah opened with, "I'm so glad to see other women here. I've been waiting for a chance to get away from the fight talk. By the way, I *love* this room. You should give a bonus to whoever decorated it. It's so cheery."

As Nalah suspected, Tiffany's eyes lit up. "I did! I told Bey that women needed a little color! He's so involved in all those fights, he forgets we're not all dark and dreary like the boys."

Tiffany continued to speak in exclamation points, and Nalah endeavored to nod at appropriate places. Unless Tiffany was putting on a hell of an act, she was, perhaps not the brightest of lights, but genuinely friendly and enjoying the female company – as well as her place as the alpha female whom everyone else sucked up to.

Finally, Tiffany leaned forward in the universal pose for conspiratorial gossip sharing. "Soooo, you and the Cage King? How did you get him? He is soooo hooottt... Like, we were all talking, and there is no one better looking on the circuit. Honestly, you should keep an eye on some of these women. I wouldn't trust any of them alone with him."

The other women nodded, and from the flash in the eyes of a couple, perhaps one or two of the women Tiffany was worried about were sitting right here.

"I'll remember that," Nalah said, "but I trust Esh. He knows how I feel about straying."

"Honey, they *all* say they know, but it's really 'Don't ask so you won't be told.'" Tiffany waved that away as if it was a known quantity, and continued. "But when did you get together? I only heard about you when Esh accepted the invitation – and gods, that was a complete surprise! Bey near had a heart attack when he got word!"

Figured there would be gossip. If luck prevailed, Beylor wouldn't think about how the Cage King accepted an invite after so many years and brought a new woman no one had ever heard about. If he did, and then realized how it coincided to the acquisition of the ring, she might be screwed. "I knew him when we were younger. My family moved a lot, so we got separated, but not long ago I walked in on one of his fights. When I realized it was him, I met up with him just to catch up, and one thing led to another..."

Nalah trailed off, gave a half shrug. The less detail, the better, and the best would be to let Tiffany and the rest of the girls create their own drama from those few sentences. Judging by the giggles and the half-friendly/half-envious nudges they were giving her, they were concocting some serious stories.

This was all well and good, and making a connection with Tiffany was a lucky chance, but training time was waning and she needed to check out the fighters still. Nalah slapped on the most false-feeling simpering smile she could manage, and said, "I'd really like to watch Esh, surprise him a bit. You can imagine how hot it is to see him during practice."

Waggling eyebrows and lewd comments met that statement, but then Tiffany gave a small frown. "Bey said we're supposed to stay here. He said the women aren't safe on the grounds."

"I know, I know," Nalah cut in, quick words to stop the conversation from derailing. She lowered her voice and leaned in. "But just finished from training, dripping sweat, those muscles all defined..." And she gave an exaggerated wink, full of false sisterhood.

Giggles became shrieks and grown women fanning themselves, and Tiffany looked around, her gaze locking on where the guards stood, very bored and very not listening. When no closer guards were found, Tiffany whispered. "The back door never has many guards, and they change shifts for lunch, so they won't be looking for anyone. But if you get in trouble, you didn't hear anything from me."

Nalah crossed her heart. "You are innocent, I swear."

Leaving was easy after that, the guards not worth the name, and in quick work Nalah approached the first training area.

There were three training areas located on the outer edges of the compound, not much more than a large ring and basic equipment. None of the fighters would do any serious fighting before the tournament started tomorrow, so it was more for keeping limber and sticking to whatever their exercise regime was.

"Hello, pretty lady."

Crap. Nalah spun around, off-guard as she looked for the owner. The voice was more force of nature than mere instrument of communication, and as she located him, she took an instinctive protective step back while elemental flight-or-fight primed every cell.

He was part orc, features less misshapen than the full-blood version but no one would ever call him even average-looking, his body massive compared to a human's, his darker-toned skin with the slight undertone of green.

"Are you lost?" he continued. There was no magic around him – not surprising, since orcs as a general rule had little magical talent – but his presence hit her as hard as Esh's always had. He would give Esh a hell of a fight.

She cleared her throat, threw off some *I'm not to be screwed with* attitude. "No. I wanted to watch my man and get some air."

"Maybe give them the fuck-off for telling you girls stay in the house?" Her face had to show the shock she was too late to cover up, and his laugh was deep and genuine, regardless of the coughing edge that made her think he didn't do it too much. "I know a few women who would have shoved pointy objects up Beylor's ass if they heard the rule about staying in the quarters, and you have that same look about you."

She shrugged, taking a step closer. "Can't say the thought didn't cross my mind. Esh in this area?"

"You checking out your man's competition? Sizing us up?"

"No need for me to. Esh will win." She gazed around with what she hoped was an unconcerned air.

No Esh in sight, and when her gaze came back to him he was nodding in approval. "Good woman. Every man needs one like you. Keep treating your man right, and make sure you can say the same about him."

"What's your name?" She needed to ask Esh about him. Something about him wasn't sitting right. He was a warrior, but he didn't belong to the Cage. He didn't give off that vibe. Which, if that was the case, why was he here?

"Rorth. And you'd better get back before the guards are out in more force. Hate to think of you in trouble." With a smile that looked very wrong, given the number of sharp protruding teeth in his mouth, Rorth left.

As if his prediction had brought about the change, a large number of men appeared, most ignoring her but some stopping to give her a blatant once-over.

And that was that. Innate hunting was a bust for today. There would be other ways to find out the information she needed.

But even as she turned to face the apartments there was a tickle, a tease, a dim thrum to *come look, something here, come find me* grabbing at her...compelling her.

She walked past the edge of the training center, down a path a little more overgrown, a little less trampled than the others. The feeling tugged at her, twisted along pathways in her mind.

At the sighting of the figure in the distance, she stopped, even with the magic pulling on her. It was...*wrong*, like a saccharine sweet scent over rot, the disharmony inciting rebellion in her.

The fighter appeared to be an albino, bright and white and so large, a mountain of snow against an evergreen background. He was shirtless, the loose white pants darker than his skin. He had been shadowboxing, but within moments of her arrival he lifted his head, scented the air, before turning bloodshot eyes in her direction – not the true red of a vampire, but the unwavering stare unnerving all the same.

Further back, from behind him, evil magic...*crawl of fetid flesh*
slice of the blade into decayed muscle
deep, feral joy at the pain yet to be visited upon them, on all of them...
Nalah's pulse jackrabbited in her neck, cold sweat a clammy reality at her hairline. The only time she'd experienced anything close to this feeling was those first moments exposed to Tenro. Tenro was savagery, war, bloodlust, mixed with the last moments of the damned.

This... This was...
Pure *madness*.
And a cold, crazed love of death.

Something clamped down on her upper arm – large, with a grip that *hurt*. *"Get off!"* Her fist came up to hit at whatever had her. "Get off me!"

"What are you doing here?" He caught her fist, blocking her with less energy than she would use to swat a fly. Bad, but... Her pulse slowed and comprehension flowed through her. He was a guard who caught her breaking rules, not a servant to that madness. And he was *human*, large and mean in that generic way all the guards around here were, as if they'd been selected for that exact reason.

Her pulse normalized, and as she came back to herself and the evil faded, now something from this guard teased her senses, beat against her skull. He wasn't connected to what she had just felt, but this guard was innate, and she didn't recognize this power.

Did Beylor know? Was the guard selected because of that, or did he hide it from his employer?

She had to get away and regroup, with the least amount of trouble possible. Clearing her throat, she went for a tone of Tiffany oblivious. "I was trying to find my boyfriend."

No, he didn't buy that at all, as his fingers gripped even tighter. "You don't seem in too much of a hurry to find him."

She jerked once, twice, finally free though very aware it was because he allowed it. If oblivious didn't work, time for attitude. "The set-up is interesting! No law against looking, and don't fucking *touch* me again if you don't want the Cage King crawling all over your ass for manhandling his woman!"

The look in his eyes was dissecting her, trying to decide her place here. She couldn't do anything else but go all in, and she crossed her arms over her chest and glared at him, pure put upon.

He blinked, those eyes too sharp in his big dumb face. After a few breaths of stand-off, he waved someone else over. After the prompt appearance of another guard, he said, "Here, whatever we say is law *is* law, and the law is you stay in the main house with the women. Got it?"

"Got it," she said, putting as much pouting attitude into the words as possible.

The other guard motioned her to start towards the house, and she turned and began walking. It was a minute before the guard at her side spoke. "I would've thought Fallon would send someone sneakier."

Nalah would have tripped if his hand didn't come out and stabilize her. Before she could look at him, he spoke again. "Keep looking straight ahead. You already brought enough attention to yourself."

Damn! Here was her contact, and she hadn't checked him out earlier, too intent on looking at her tormentor. "You're acting as a guard?"

"Low-level, mostly patrols of the ground, meaning I keep an eye on the women and the house." Which was perfect for their needs. Had he requested that, or had the Guild known exactly how to position him to get him into the right spot? "I wasn't expecting you to make a scene."

"It was necessary for me to get out to do my job. And I'm sorry, but if Fallon told you about me, she must have brought up my distinct lack of sneaking ability. I'm doing my best."

"She did. I was hoping she was underselling you."

"Gee, thanks."

The sigh was more felt than heard. "It doesn't matter. We'll work around it, as long as you can find the artifact."

"That I can do. Do you know where it is?"

Another set of guards was walking toward them and her contact shut up until they were well out of earshot. "Beylor always has multiple safes in his home. How close do you need to be to feel where the artifact is?"

The last time she had held her mother's ring, it was like it started singing to her the moment she entered headquarters, the sound as welcome to her as her mother's laughter. "Normally, entering the house I could lead you to it, but I don't know how being in a blackout zone will affect my range."

"Then I'll need to scout and find where the safes are. We're only going to have one chance with you in the house, and I don't want your magic not working like you think it should." His voice was grave, and the weight of what they were doing fell on Nalah. It wasn't her and Esh and their baggage anymore. This was a mission. This is where she or Esh or the man behind her could die.

Dread pooled through her extremities, leaving her fingers icy numb. She'd never taken lead before. She'd been on missions before, but she was always in the back as support, and even if there was fighting she'd been surrounded by so many others, the possibility of being hurt almost didn't exist. Now, she was in an unknown place, allied with a guy she didn't even know what he looked like.

They were nearing the apartments. Another minute tops before they had to separate. He asked, "The Cage King – is he a tool or part of the operation?"

Esh would hate to be called a tool. And though she tried to convince herself in the beginning that he was only a cog... "He's part of it. He doesn't know how to find the artifact though. That is only me."

And there was the door. In a whispered rush, the man said, "The artifact is most important. I'll try to escape with you and the Cage King, but if I must leave either or both of you to secure the artifact's safety-"

"I wouldn't expect anything else. Don't worry about it."

He opened the door, and as she entered he gave one final warning. "Watch for Lian. You are in his sights now. You were before, as he has an obsession with Esh. He will report you to Beylor. Beylor has a severe underestimation of women. Lian does not, and Beylor will leave it in Lian's hands."

"I'll watch my back," she said, but the man was already gone.

CHAPTER NINE

"The illustrious Cage King. Truly an honor."

The tone said it was anything but, a sentiment Esh had plenty of experience with. "Fuck off," Esh said, not halting his work on the bag, the give of the fabric not even close to the density of skin and muscle underneath his knuckles, but all he had for now.

The voice lost the insincerity and now held only resentment. "What, you're too good to even speak to the rest of us?"

Jealousy, loud and clear. With a glance, Esh took him in. A guard, not a fighter, so maybe he lost money on a betting against Esh. Or maybe he was a fighter on the outside, one unable to get into the Tour, and now he was taking it out on the man known to have turned down several offers. Whatever the guy's background, his tone was personal, and the guard had a hard-on for him specific, not fighters in general.

The bitterness was seeping out of the man, but there was cunning as well. This man wasn't stupid. Too early to tell if this guard would harm Nalah to hurt Esh or not, but guard-boy needed to be watched. "I'm in training. What do you want?"

"There was a small problem with your female companion today. I found her wandering the grounds."

"Is that all?" Esh began on the bag again. "She's not a dog. Let her go where she wants."

"That's not the rules."

"Right, since we're rules followers here."

Malice dripped from the man's words. "So you're okay with others sharing your woman?"

Esh quit the bag and turned, and the guard lost the smarmy smile. "Let me be real clear. My woman is *mine*. She is not to be touched, and I don't care what your *fucking rules* say, I don't care if she's breaking them or not – if anyone touches her, I will rip their ribs out of their chests and beat them to death with 'em. And if any of you dumb-fuck guards get in my way, I'll break so many bones no healer in the New Realms will be able to put you back together. Are we understanding one another here?"

The guard swallowed hard, but that was the only sign Esh's words got to him. "Just get your woman under control."

"I'll talk to her. You talk to everyone else and tell them what I said."

The guard got himself more under control, enough that he now gave a sneer. "Because you're the Cage King, and we all jump when you speak?"

Esh went closer. The guard was his height, a little broader, but the man still cowered, still had that sneer. "Because I'm the Cage King, and you know what I can do when I want. Don't you?"

"Yeah." In a strange reversal, Esh's words seemed to give the man determination, strength, because he straightened, meeting Esh's gaze with a lot more fire. "Yeah, I know."

"Heard you had an interesting day," was how Esh greeted Nalah as he entered their apartment, and the sight before him slammed into his chest and stopped him short.

Nalah was doing nothing more than sitting curled in a chair, reading a book. It was how he'd often found her, always reading, her face mobile as she absorbed whatever words lay before her – frowns, smiles, sighs of pleasure, all normal and expected.

And he *missed* it, maybe more than anything else, because it was the best part of her and showed who she was – smart and sentimental and willing to let their reality go and keep searching for something better, never settling for crap and saying there was no other choice. More than anything, she was what had kept him going those early days. He never wanted her to lose this part of herself, would protect it with whatever he had in him.

"At least I made some new friends first. Tiffany and I are now besties," Nalah said, not looking up from the book, but bringing her hand up, her first and middle finger twining together.

Gods, this fondness, it bubbled up inside and damned if he could stop the smile overcoming his face. "C'mon. We're going walking. Beylor ain't going to say shit if you're with me."

The bookmark went in and the book went down, the movement quick but protective. "Yay! I almost feel like we're out of the Middle Ages."

With a quick, "Stow it, smartass," he ushered her out of the building and in short work they were walking around, her hand engulfed in his, the low-level warmth bubbling within him as they walked and talked like they had before she left.

They weren't the only ones out, and Esh let Nalah take the lead so she could get whatever she needed. She studied everyone and everything, but there was never any look of real interest on her, nothing to say she felt anything more than he did. For that, he was grateful. They had enough dealing with this item she had to collect. He didn't need any other headaches.

"Have you met Rorth?" Her voice was quiet, careful not to carry.

"Yeah, this morning. Did you get something from him?"

She shook her head, which was what he'd figured. He'd never heard of an orc being anything magical. "Not like that. We spoke for a minute though."

"And?" Nalah wouldn't have brought him up if there wasn't something.

"Does he seem like he belongs in the Cage?"

Course she would pick up on that. Nalah was as connected to the fights as he was, even if she hadn't ever stepped into the ring. "No, but damned if he's not a fighter. He's one of the few who'd made me take notice."

"I got that, but that doesn't translate to participating in the Tour. The timing is suspicious."

He didn't get that from the orc. Yeah, she was right, there was something more that had him here, but Esh wasn't worried about other fighter. But what she was saying did bring up a question. "How many know about Beylor having this item?"

"I don't know. It's a recent development, but it wasn't exactly a secret transaction."

Esh swallowed hard against the spew of curses rising up. Why did the Guild send her in here without information? This was supposed to be some all-important magic, but the person trying to find it was flying blind. "The Guild ain't impressing me much."

"I met my contact." Nalah's voice was so low it was barely above lip-reading, but he caught it.

With a quick look around to verify where everyone was, he pulled her to the side of a building and pushed her against the wall, bending low so her face was inches from his. "Tell me."

"A guard. I don't know what he looks like, and we only had a moment."

"When do you meet again?"

"We didn't have enough time to decide on one."

"So not impressed with the Guild." Even he heard the pissed-off growl in his voice.

But Nalah laughed, her eyes clear and easy in a way they hadn't been since before. "Contrary to rumor, they don't know everything. Well, maybe Tec does, but he's too busy with online gaming in his off time to tell them."

"Who's Tec?" Pissed off *and* jealous. Great combination.

"Not my boyfriend," she said, which was the most important information to him after all, and her smile said she knew it.

Hmmm. Wasn't this a cozy spot to explore that smile, somewhere she couldn't get away easily unless she wanted to make a scene.

Her eyes widened and her body shifted for flight, but he bracketed her head with his forearms. "Not fair, Esh."

"So?" he said as his mouth lowered. "Think of it as keeping up appearances."

He brushed his mouth over hers, playful and light, and she began to relax, pushed herself up on tiptoe to meet him.

It became a game, one of them pushing into the kiss, trying to deepen it while the other held off, then a sudden switch, the roles reversed. No matter which, Nalah's smile held, her lips satiny smooth against his.

And then she froze, her mouth hardening, and her head whipped to the side so fast a few braids flicked against his chin.

Following her gaze, he saw the albino fighter. He hadn't met the man earlier. While the other fighters played at introductions and good wishes, the albino had been there only long enough to see the competition, then had gone to the forest.

Rorth was one of the fighters Esh was keeping his eye on. This guy was another. "Did he speak to you today during your travels, like Rorth?"

His gaze never left the albino, but he saw the quick shake of her head from the corner of his eye. "Worse."

The pale fighter's stare never wavered from them, and under his hands Nalah began to tremble. Inside him, something kicked, fought free to take on this thing, this being who didn't feel right, even without anything in him like Nalah had.

She pulled on his arm, and he looked down to find Nalah staring up at him. She blinked, her eyes going from fearful and confused to determined. "We need to get back to the apartment. Please. You can't fight him here. They'll kick us out of the Tour."

Yeah, he had to get away. Her hand tugged on his, and without further comment Nalah led them back, quicker on the return trip than they'd been going out.

The door had only shut behind them when he said, "What did you feel? There's something magic with him."

Nalah was pulling herself back together. "I don't know if it's from him, but there's dark magic connected to him, strong enough that even here I feel it full blast."

"But magic doesn't work here."

"*Most* magic," she corrected, pressing the heel of her left hand against her forehead.

With that gesture, he went to a cabinet, grabbed medicine, and gave it to her with some water. Her startled expression morphed into thankfulness, and she downed the offering. "It's strong enough that it's giving you a headache?"

"Yeah, pretty much."

"Do you recognize it?"

"No. It's evil. It's connected to death, but I've never felt anything like it, not from any necromancer or vampire I've ever come in contact with."

Esh swallowed hard, the casual sentence confirming every fear he'd had since that first night when the name of the Guild had been brought up. "You've been near necromancers?"

The pause of her body told that she realized what she revealed, but she went on the offensive. "You had to know. I'm Guild. At least for me it was only in contained situations. I was never in any danger."

Contained? Being near things that used torture and death like foreplay before they did so much worse, and now Nalah and he might be facing that here? "Yeah, well this situation sure as fuck ain't contained, and you're telling me something here's so strong it's messing with you inside a place that's supposed to stop magic? This stops now. We're gone."

Her long fingers curled around his forearm as he started past her to pack their belongings. "That won't happen, and the days of you telling me what I will and won't do never existed, so don't think they start now. This is what I have to do."

Underneath her pissed-off attitude existed something else. It was there in the shaky way she held herself, in the pleading mixed with the attitude. She was desperate to remain. "Why do you have to stay? We get out, you tell the Guild everything you know to this point, maybe it's enough they can get other people in action. They got a thief here already."

"And he needs me."

Her attitude was pure stubbornness, something she always had in abundance. "What's going on? What are you hiding from me? And don't lie or I swear I will go to Beylor now and drop out."

With those words, her body half crumpled on itself as she sagged forward, her hands reaching out to steady herself on the kitchen table. "What Beylor has…it's my mom's ring."

She couldn't mean…? "What?"

"The one with the red stone. I always wore it on the chain around my neck." She swallowed, looked very obviously *not* at him. "The one I wanted to have as my wedding ring when I got married. That's what Beylor has."

"You're telling me your ring is some big-time magical item? What does it do?"

"I don't know," she said, and as he was about to lash out, she looked up and held out her hands in a pleading gesture. She drew a deep breath, went into what he always dubbed 'story mode'. "I never got a chance to tell you, but the ring got stolen by that pawnbroker on Third right before Jac died. When I went to get the ring back I met the Guild. They were there for the ring, and they were the ones who told me it was magic. Said if I wanted it back I had to train with them. What it does is still a mystery to me. I haven't gotten strong enough to break through its magic."

"Doesn't make sense they'd send you after it without telling you about it. And that still doesn't explain what Beylor's doing with it."

Her fingers wiggled, like she wanted something she could write with to illustrate her point. "The biggest protection for any magical item is no one knowing what it does. Because the possibilities are near infinite, people can spend years on even a medium-level item trying to find out what magic it contains. But once you know what an item does, it's only a matter of time before you control the item. The Guild can't take the risk of that information getting out, so since I don't know already, they aren't going to enlighten me. As for Beylor-" She broke off, looked him straight in the eye, serious and strong and with nothing of the little girl in her he always strove to protect. "If I answer that question, this has to remain between us."

"You have my word."

A nod to acknowledge him, and pleasure buried itself in his bones with that quick acceptance. Even with everything that lay between them, she still took him at his word. "Not long ago, Guild headquarters was attacked. When that happened, beyond killing a lot of people, the attackers broke into a vault that held the most powerful magical items in the Realms and stole a good number of them. The Guild counterattacked not long after and got some back, but you can imagine in that chaos how many items were bundled off by different lowlifes. They were able to track my mother's ring to Beylor."

"And that magic tonight? It's after the ring?"

"I think it's a very likely possibility. Whatever is out there is strong, and by definition anything in that vault is going to interest powerful people. Besides, what else could they be here for?"

"If they're that sick, it might be they want to watch the Tour and let albino boy tear through the fighters."

The odds of that were pretty low, but Nalah went slack-faced at his words. "What do you mean? As in killing them? Beylor wouldn't allow that. They'd be disqualified."

Esh had kept her from the worst parts of the fighting world, but she couldn't be that naïve to not realize that was a possibility. "You're kidding. Half the people here are for the bloodshed."

"No, I thought…it's about prestige, the best of the best fighting. I was never told…" Her eyes were wide and horrified. She collapsed into the chair, wiping her hand over her mouth, her brow furrowed as she absorbed the words. "I would never have asked you to come if I'd realized."

"Like I have anything to fear." But Nalah didn't move, the vague horror of her expression not changing. "Seriously didn't know?"

"Of course I *didn't*." Vague horror turned to indignation. "I don't lie."

"No, you run."

Fuck if he meant to say those words, but now they were out and he was glad, meant or not.

She shot him a filthy glare, jerking up from the seat. "I don't want to talk about that. We have other things going on now."

"Convenient. I thought you were all about the *closure*." The words were tumbling forth, unstoppable. "It's only closure when you get to tell me how fucked up I did, right? Not going to hear my side?"

Nalah smiled, her mouth sharp-edged and ready to tear through him. "What is it you're going to tell me? You're upset he died? I *fucking know* that. He was your best friend. Didn't stop you from turning him away when he needed help."

"You got *no clue* what I went through, because I kept everything away from you so you wouldn't worry or see what an ass he was." Memories bombarded, the love and hate for Jac that were so mixed up in him, those last few months, when his soul brother kept fucking up and he kept trying to stop it. "Do you know how many hours I worked with him to make him better? How many times I stepped in when he couldn't work a fight? How many fucking times I *begged* him to *never* get involved with those assholes?"

"Then why didn't you do it one last time?"

She just never fucking gave up. "Because if I stepped in it would have put you in danger, and as much as I loved him, there's nothing in this world that would ever make me sacrifice you."

"*Me* in danger?" Her lip rose, nose wrinkling as if the statement was so dumbass, she had no idea how to process it.

More than anything, it was that look that pissed him off. That look that said she had no clue his actions were from anything except pure selfishness. "Fuck *yeah,* you in danger! What do you think would have happened if I'd bailed Jac out? They would have known it wasn't because of Jac – I'd already said I wasn't covering any more of his losses. They would have looked to his pretty little sister and wondered why I'm suddenly helping Jac out of a fucking mess and why I'm never with any other woman but her, and they would have pieced it together. And if they'd pieced it together, known I'd helped him to protect you? Your life would have been *forfeit.* You wouldn't know peace again."

They were both breathing hard. He turned to look out the window, watching the evening sun shining over the tops of the trees. "And then you were gone. Nothing. No one knew shit. You left me without a whisper, and all I had was a dead best friend and my woman missing. Do you know how scared I was? Do you have any fucking clue how scared-" and for the first time his voice broke, choked up, and he gritted his teeth hard, pushed air down through the constricted muscles of his chest and back so he could take a deep breath, because fuck if this was going to control him.

"It wasn't on purpose." Her voice was soft, tentative, all edges gone and pure sorrow throughout. "It wasn't to hurt you. I wasn't myself, and I couldn't think or consider anything, not even what you might be going through."

He swallowed the rough emotion, the swell behind his eyes. "Letting me know you weren't dead? That would've been too much?"

"At the time? Yes."

A short snap of humorless laughter escaped him. "And yet I'm the asshole."

"When I came to myself later, I was going to tell you." An unsteady hand brushed his shoulder, the touch unsure of its welcome, while the voice that accompanied it pleaded to be heard. "I really was. I would never have left you like that. But when I said I wanted to contact you, Laire told me she'd taken care of it and let you know I was alive and taken care of. Maybe it was the coward's way, but I didn't press after that."

"Three days after you disappeared, I got a note. At the time, I thought it was from you. It made it clear you weren't coming back."

Her hand left him and her voice grew faint, a note of begging twirling around her words. "I'm sorry. I am so sorry I put you through that."

Esh pushed away from the window, not looking at her as he set for the bedroom. "How's that closure working for you?"

CHAPTER TEN

The first fights were starting, and Nalah wasn't there to watch Esh.

It had been by mutual, unspoken decision, come to as they'd worked around the apartment with awkward jerks and split-second stops so to not touch each other. For the first time, her presence would be more hindrance than help, and Esh couldn't lose in these first rounds. Beyond the toll it would take on his reputation, it was only after today's fights that the real festivities would begin, where Nalah would have access to Beylor's home and Tiffany would start wearing the brag-worthy pieces of her collection.

Once again, she was with the other women, a surprising number of whom weren't going to watch their men.

Tiffany snorted. "Why would they? It's boring. I only go on the last day because it's expected."

They were alone for the moment, Tiffany wanting girl time with Nalah. Nalah picked up the drink Tiffany had brought for her, the smell of alcohol strong even this early in the morning. "I love watching Esh fight."

Tiffany near purred before she took a big gulp from her own glass. "I'd definitely make an exception if I was cheering him. But if that's the way it is, why aren't you there today?"

"He told me not to bother, the real fights don't begin until round two anyway."

"He's right. Most of the guests don't go until second round either. I asked Bey why he doesn't cut it in half, but he said day one is good for the bloodlust crowd and he makes a fair amount in bets."

Tiffany rattled off the explanation like it was no big deal. Why hadn't Nalah realized in asking Esh to fight, she was asking him to put himself in the way of people who wanted not just to fight, but to kill him? Or that he might have to kill in order to keep himself protected? He was a fighter, and she had no doubt he'd kill if he had to, but that wasn't his nature. It was one of the reasons he was so careful in choosing his own fights, to prevent that. How could she have been that stupid?

Because Esh always kept you away from the worst. You might talk big, but you still have this almost romantic version of the fights. Fucking traitorous inner voice, making her feel smaller than she had last night and so young. She'd always felt old, starting even before her mom died when she was seven. But these last few days, she felt young and stripped, facing all her poor decisions and coming away shamed.

A chill wind of magic blew through, a hint of power, subtle, amorphous. Nalah pulled herself from her thoughts, looking around in what she hoped was a nonchalant fashion to find the source.

Through the room came a being more porcelain doll than flesh-and-blood woman. Her silvery-white hair was pinned up in the front but the near knee-length mass flowed down her back in perfect curls, falling over shoulders bared by her red corseted gown, her skin almost the same color as her hair. Refined features, a little rosebud mouth, an aristocratic, pouty slant to her cheekbones and jaw, and her eyes...

Pure midnight black, save a pinprick of white in the center. They didn't reflect the surrounding light; they absorbed it, turning all to darkness within them.

Tiffany shivered and Nalah fought to prevent herself from joining in. The newcomer was touched with the same magic the albino had been. Whatever evil was present here, she was part of it. The magic was building at the base of her head, pounding into her shields like waves rolling into breakers.

The woman didn't look around, but Nalah had the gut deep certainty she was being studied. No one spoke or moved until the woman left the room.

Conversation began after several minutes, low and halting, as if everyone were waiting to see if the doll-woman came back. Nalah leaned over and spoke to Tiffany in similar low tones. "Who is that?"

"Everyone calls her The Pale Lady." Tiffany spoke the name with reverential terror, and Nalah could hear the capitalization of the words. "Bey says he doesn't know why she's here, that she's never come to any of the Tours before. I don't think he's happy she's here, but he never says anything out loud."

She wasn't vampire. The magic was close, but not quite.

More worrying was the fact that this was her first Tour. Even as Esh put forward the theory last night that maybe the dark magic was here to satiate bloodlust with the Tour, she could tell by his tone he was doubtful about it. But with Tiffany's info, doubtful became not applicable, and that meant this Pale Lady was after the magic ring.

Nalah was about to make an excuse to leave when one of the Tiffany clones bounced in, excitement in every overexaggerated feature. "Omigods, you'll never believe it! Nalah, you missed your man!"

Nalah began to say "What did I miss?" but excitement girl began talking in rushed sentences before Nalah was even half-finished. "Esh's turn, right? And he looks at the three other fighters in his block, and he goes and says, 'I'll fight them all at once. They aren't worth any more of my time.' *Like*, he really says that, he's just going to fight them all! And everyone's yelling, and those other fighters were so pissed, and they said sure."

Tiffany put a hand on the woman. "Sweetie, sweetie, slow down. Esh fought three other fighters at the same time?"

"*Gods* yes! And they all ganged up on him, because of course they would, he so insulted them by doing that, *and. Esh. Won!* Can you believe that? Three fighters at once, and then he just left without saying anything."

Nalah was out the door and down the stairs and across the uneven pavement and back in her apartment before thought caught up to her. Only when she saw Esh sitting in the chair, his head leaning back across the top and his eyes closed, did she remember last night and why he might not be happy to see her.

Esh's eyes opened and he moved his head to the side to see her, though he didn't lift it from where it rested. "News travels."

"You're the talk of the women." She stepped in front of him, his gaze and head following her. "Everyone is very impressed. I'm sure you're going to be stalked tonight."

"You know me, I live for the limelight."

Each of her twenty-two years mocked her for her inexperience right now. As she stood before him, Nalah catalogued the lines and scars and the bone-deep *something* each plane of his body displayed, all of which told how he lived on the front lines.

She didn't know what she was doing, but it was time to take steps forward, make experiences, no matter if they were ultimately mistakes.

Her body trembling, Nalah moved forward, one step, then two, until she was before him, until she climbed onto the chair with her legs straddling his, until her face was close enough that mouths could meet and tongues could tangle together.

His skin bordered on fever-hot, kindling a matching fire in her, a desire to burrow into that warmth and let it engulf her. Strong, calloused fingers stroked over her jaw and throat, turning her head so he could deepen the kiss, meet her eager mouth in the longer strokes she craved.

Nalah may have been on top, but Esh controlled, only letting her move where he allowed, deepen the kisses and touches to where he desired them. She growled, and in defiance twisted her hips, the movement grinding her ass against his rock-hard cock.

"Fuck!" The exclamation was torn from him in a pained outburst and his hands shot out around her hips, halting the movement.

Not that it stopped her. She changed from twisting to a rolling motion, and his stuttered groan told he might even like that one more.

"*Don't do that.* You are not making me a minute-man."

A giggle burst from her, because right now his hair was in disarray and he looked both horny and pissed with a good bit of amused thrown in, and this man right here was the one she thought she'd spend all her life with, and it was *so good* to see him again.

He grumbled, but his own lips turned up in a smile before he leaned up and began attacking her neck, pressing against her those open-mouthed kisses that got her going but had everyone snickering around her the next day. She pulled his head back. "Nuh-uh, no marking."

"But I like you marked." As if to support his words, he made for her neck, only her hold keeping him back.

"Then mark me in other ways." Nalah meant it to come out sexy, but her voice still had that breathless laughing quality, and Esh's eyes lit up.

"That's a challenge I'll take any day," he said, a wide grin, the first she had seen since they reunited, giving his face a near-boyish quality. Her heart stuttered to see that look on him again. "Let's see, where to begin…"

He worked the buttons of her shirt, ignoring her slapping hand and her, "Hey! I didn't say you could do that!" To distract her – the cheating bastard – he stretched up to capture her mouth in another kiss, and what a happy discovery to learn you could still kiss reasonably well through giggles.

In retaliation she went for his chest, which didn't have a shirt covering it, but instead was left bare, and wasn't it great that Esh had sensitive nipples? With a firm stroke she rubbed her thumbs over the hard brown points, eliciting another growl and the loss of a few buttons as her shirt was torn from her.

He tangled her arms in the sleeves of her shirt, the fabric trapping her and not…letting…her…touch, damn him. His grin was unmistakable against her skin, where he currently was enjoying the swell of her breast above her bra.

"Think that's funny?" If his hands were trapping her arms, that meant they weren't on her hips any longer, and Nalah always loved to dance, to move her hips in abandon. Today's music was the growls and groans and sighs and laughs of the man beneath her, and she was going to take full advantage of the concert.

And what a sound spectacular it was. With each grind he answered with a groan, with each hitch of her breath a corresponding growl emitted from his own throat, the sounds scaling from a high, surprised gasp to the lowest rumble from the center of his chest.

"Nalah," he said in a deep, desperate groan, and that was the sound she would take with her if she was allowed to remember only one sound from her life. His voice, saying her name as if the word contained every good and wanted and desired thing in this life.

Her hands now free, she encircled his neck with her arms, and his own answered by clamping around her waist. He rose, and as he did her legs came around his waist.

With quick movements he placed her on the bed, pulling off her jeans and shoes until she lay before him in her underwear. He rid himself of his own pants, and unlike her, he was naked, his cock hard. He didn't shield himself, let himself be studied as she wished, but his eyes lost the mirth from before as he waited for her next move.

Strange. When she approached him, she expected to have a moment's hesitation sometime during their play, a voice that would tell her this wasn't a good idea. Right now was a perfect time for that voice to show up, but her body only thrummed. She leaned up on her elbows, giving him an exaggerated once-over. "That thing looks more dangerous than what you show in the cage."

And with that, the mirth was back, and all hardness in him was due to desire. "Wait until you see it in action."

"Well, for that, I think you need to come closer." And she wanted him closer. They'd never gotten this far before, and this was the reality of what had only before been fantasies she'd spent years creating in her mind.

He prowled over her, skin rubbing over skin, his muscles skimming over her softer curves and those gorgeous, otherworldly eyes aflame as they roamed over her body. "I don't know where to start first," he said in low tones, but his gaze came back to hers, and he started with another of his panty-melting kisses.

Well, maybe not accurate, since his fingers pressed against her clit and the panty was still in the way. Esh didn't let that stop him. The panties were more than damp enough that the fabric didn't irritate and instead worked her even higher.

"Esh, good, so good." Nalah couldn't tell when they'd stopped kissing, but without Esh's mouth on hers, the words flowed forth, unstoppable with his fingers against her, and coming out faster, breathier when his mouth replaced his fingers, when her panties were pulled to the side and his tongue buried itself in her body, stoking the fire he built inside her to new heights.

Esh pulled himself to his knees, their lower bodies aligned, his cock ready to plunge into her. "Nalah?"

He waited, but the voice she'd been expecting took over, at least a little, because she froze, couldn't nod, couldn't give him that final permission.

After a moment, Esh looked back to her exposed pussy. With the head of his cock he pushed on her clit. He started slow with only the tip, but soon came longer strokes, and now the underside of his cock slid against her, using her own moisture to lubricate the flesh.

The pressure was unrelenting, building in her body a terrible need. It was the sensations he invoked by the press of his body to hers, yes, but it also built by watching him between her legs, the hungry cast of his face as he took in her body, the visual of his hands and his hips directing his cock over her. It was that hard length of flesh on her, an instrument for her pleasure. The head moved to lay against her opening, the faintest press in, before it disappeared and moved up, bringing slickness and warmth and friction with it.

Inside, the sensation climbed, tightened, and not for anything could she keep her eyes open any longer. Instead, her head fell back as pleasure burst through her body in long, loud sweeps, leaving trembling muscles and shivering skin in its wake, and as she came back to consciousness her own whimpers met her ears.

Into this Esh's own groans mixed, and spurts of warmth hit her pubic hair, trickled against the wetness of her lower body, a welcome brand against her skin.

CHAPTER ELEVEN

The party to celebrate the end of the first round of fighting took place in Beylor's home. The décor of the huge pile of bricks was loud, ostentatious, obnoxious – in short, exactly what Nalah had expected.

Of the sixteen fighters left, one was Rorth. The huge half-orc stood in the corner. He was quiet, watchful, not disrupting the party but not part of it either. Esh might have dismissed him as a threat, but she still couldn't shake the unease.

Yet Esh was Esh, and he went straight for that corner, calling out, "You're still alive."

"Not surprised to see you either," the not-literally-but-almost-a-giant replied, giving a smile that showcased teeth with a slight tuskish quality to them.

"Wasn't going to get beaten and lose the opportunity to fight you."

Something in Rorth's eyes shifted, and his smile went from genial to almost approving. "So, you're that."

Damned if Nalah could make out the meaning, but Esh only smiled a rare smile, his tone conspiratorial as he replied, "Hells yeah."

"Well then, you and I, we'll give them a show."

"Would have it no other way."

With a half nod to Rorth, Esh grabbed her hand and left the half orc to his corner. The moment they were out of earshot, Nalah asked, "What was that about?"

"Finding common ground."

"Don't be cryptic. What did you two mean?"

A man gave Nalah a once-over, and Esh scowled at him, pulling Nalah close and putting his arm around her shoulder. "It means he's like me, even if you don't see it. That's why I'm not worried about him. The reason he fights is the reason I fight."

The reason Esh fights? She always thought it was something he fell into and was the only thing he could make money from that was at least a little aboveboard.

Esh's statement crystallized something in her, a back-of-the-head musing that started with their reunion. She didn't know Esh, not really. Yes, in some ways she knew him better than anyone alive – meeting at seven and ten and then spending the next decade in constant proximity assured that.

Still, because of that, she became lazy and assumed so many things about him, assumptions this re-meet challenged on a daily basis.

Tiffany bounded up, breaking into her musings, her smile wide and white and directed at Esh. "I heard all about what you did today! For the first time I actually wished I was at a fight! I'm Tiffany. Me and Nalah have been hanging while you boys do your fighting thing!"

In other times Esh's dumbfounded expression upon being confronted with Tiffany would have Nalah doubled over, but her attention was focused on the ring on Tiffany's finger, bright red, the color looking foreign and wrong against the paleness of Tiffany's skin versus the warm brown tones of her mother.

Tiffany must have noticed her focus, because she asked, "You like the ring, Nalah?"

"It's stunning," she said, at least she thought she said it. The ring held her enraptured. She shouldn't stare, shouldn't give so much info away.

"I've never seen you wear jewelry! You totally should. Your man should have enough winnings to get you a piece or two!"

The ring called to her in a way it never had before. Its magic was sharper, clearer, a song that she had forgotten the lyrics to, but if she kept humming the tune, it would come to her. She would know everything.

Beylor was approaching now, his eyes going first to the deep cleavage Tiffany was displaying before coming to look at Esh. "Quite a display, Cage King."

"Didn't want to waste my time." And Esh, the magic in him was growing as well, slow and subtle, and now his magic jumped in the presence of the ring. His eyes grew more alight every hour, and Nalah still did not know what to attribute it to.

The ring was singing again, and Tiffany kept talking. "With your coloring you just need deep, rich colors, like emeralds or sapphires!" As Tiffany went on with a fervency that would make a street-corner preacher proud, all Nalah could see were the exclamation points that surrounded each of Tiffany's excited utterances. The woman didn't seem to know how to speak in anything less.

The ring sparked, the song lyrics became clear, and magic around it grew and enveloped, ran through her...

Here was sunshine and humid air, all lush foliage and earthy scents, a haven of comfort. It was green and good and warm, rich soil, the scent of which perfumed the air, earthy with a hint of floral.

Here was desert. Here was arid, a dry that cut deep, that sucked out the moisture through your pores and a dry you could not get rid of, no matter how much of the very precious water at your side you drunk.

Here...dear fucking gods...here was an abomination. This ground, this wasn't soil – this was flesh. The desiccated flesh under the mortician's knife, the dry flesh of death not yet decayed. This was tendrils of evil masquerading as life, as foliage, of...of...

"Nalah?"

Esh's low, worried tone broke through, and the magic receded, quieted, the song waning. Her focus came back to find everyone looking at her. "I'm sorry. What?"

"We lost you there for a minute," Tiffany said. Her smile was tentative, the lack of her usual exuberance telling how lost Nalah must have appeared.

Training took over and Nalah pasted on a smile without thought. The magic still sent an occasional pang through her. Even in the warmth of the room shivers ran through her body, and Nalah huddled a little closer to Esh to disguise them. She couldn't unpack this, not yet, not in front of them, so she had to keep marching through. "I'm so sorry. So much has gone on these last few days, I think it caught up with me in a serious way."

At least Tiffany accepted the excuse, because her voice and movements grew loud again. "I know! Us too! Oh, and you didn't hear this, it happened after you left, but we found out one of the guards was actually a thief, can you imagine? How scummy can you get, coming here to steal from us! Isn't that low?"

Tendrils of ice slid down Nalah's spine, freezing her as she stood before Beylor. Esh's voice, low and hard, carried through the air. "He didn't do anything that could hurt the fighters or those with us, did he?"

Beylor scoffed, raised his hand through the air in a dismissive motion. "Don't be ridiculous. He was after our guests and their wealth. What could the fighters have that would interest a thief?"

"Wanted to make sure," Esh replied. "I'm not leaving Nalah alone if your security is so shitty."

That caused Beylor to go red, and Nalah swore she could hear his blood pressure raise. "My security is top-notch. He was found, wasn't he?"

"Think I'll go to my apartment, look around to make sure." Esh's hand landed on her shoulder. "Come on, Nalah."

"Night, Tiffany." Nalah's parting was automatic, but Esh didn't linger for any reply. With quick steps he took them back to their apartment.

The next several actions happened in blinks. *Blink* and she was sitting in the chair in their room. *Blink* and she had a blanket over her lap and a water glass beside her. *Blink* and he was crouching in front of her, his eyes steady on her. He raised the glass and pressed it in her hand. "Drink. You still look in shock."

She grabbed the water, aware of a disconnect between her body and brain, but not quite able to break through and correct it.

Taking the glass away after she had a sip, Esh set it on the table beside them, then fisted his hand through her hair and pulled her head up for a hard kiss.

One moment, two, and then fire raced through her body, shattering the ice and she kissed him back, tasting whiskey as his tongue battled hers.

Another minute before Esh pulled away. "You with me now?"

"Isn't a slap across the face the usual way shock is handled?"

He smirked. "Smartass reply. Glad to have you back." The smirk disappeared. "Probably your guy, huh?"

"Probably." She didn't know what else to say about that. Beylor had him killed, no doubt, but she didn't even know his face. "I'm horrible. I'm more upset I have to figure out how to do this without him than the fact that a man is dead."

"He wasn't your friend and you're amongst enemies. You're thinking how to get safe. The mourning will come later." He spoke with full certainty, and even if it was self-serving, Nalah hung onto the words and let them comfort her. Esh continued, "Even before we found out about the contact, you were acting strange."

"Did you notice-?"

"Tiffany wearing the ring? Yeah."

Distant notes played through her head. The ring calling for her, or the memory of such strong magic. "Tonight the magic revealed itself to me. I know what it is."

Taking the ring would be easy. Living with the consequences, not so much. Words she once thought were only an excuse to thieve the one physical item of value to her, but now she knew their prophetic nature.

Esh remained silent, waiting for her to elaborate. "It's called a Realm Jumper. It's rare. In fact, I never thought they really existed."

His eyes never wavered, and no, she hadn't been mistaken. The flame in them was more intense, more defined, even from this morning. "What is this not-myth Realm Jumper?"

"The Great Collision came about because two Realms collided, and instead of destroying each other, somehow they merged together. Well, that old bitch librarian always called them dimensions and not Realms when I asked her any questions about it. You remember any of that?"

His level stare told her what he thought of her question. "I'm not the brain you are but I know that."

"Sorry, I never knew when you were listening or not. I only got your attention for sure if it was connected to fighting." She drew a deep breath, loosened her shoulders to try to fight the tension. "Anyway, when you think about it, if there were two Realms, there's got to be more out there, right?"

He shrugged, small annoyance across his face. "I guess yeah, makes sense…" Esh trailed off and the annoyance faded, his gaze locking on her throat, the spot where once a red ring rested upon its chain. "You called it a Realm Jumper."

She spoke quick and short, wanting to get it out before he could interrupt. "There are eight known Realms beyond this one. It's mixed what you find on them, but a couple of them, the phrase *hell on earth* couldn't be more fitting. They're a necromancer's wet dream." Pictures of the last world the ring had showed her skittered across the front of her mind, and now that she knew what she was seeing, that it was *real*…

"Nalah." Esh's voice was a whip crack, hitting and banishing the image for now. His hand cupped her cheek, forced her to stay present. "Finish telling me. What can this ring do?"

"Magical travel is possible between the Realms, but accomplishing it, we're talking multiple high-level mages and very exacting conditions and even for the most powerful, it's a dangerous spell. With a Realm Jumper though, it still requires powerful people, but so many of the variables won't matter, and it'll be much easier to access the other Realms."

"And? So some necromancers get to take a vacation. Why's that matter?"

She shook her head, trying to dislodge the scenarios that were fighting to bury themselves in her brain. He never saw…he didn't understand. "It's not them leaving. Don't you see, what's terrifying is what they can bring *here*."

CHAPTER TWELVE

Round two began in one hour, a two-part extravaganza where the real fighting started.

Esh stretched, limbered up. He wasn't fighting either Rorth or the albino today, and none of the other fighters worried him. He wouldn't underestimate anyone, but those were the only two who had his palms itching.

Still, he worked his body, more to get the mental game going than the physical ready. Everything was turmoil in his life right now, and not shaking it off could have him lose real quick.

He'd gone from the high of tasting Nalah for the first time only to plummet, learning about the ring and having their contact here get captured. If Nalah thought she was horrible for not mourning the guy, he better not tell her all he felt was pissed the idiot got caught.

Back to Nalah. They weren't alright, despite yesterday's making out and last night's holding onto each other. Nalah pressed herself close to him even in sleep, like she trusted him to keep the boogey-men away. It was nice, it was flattering, but it wasn't quite real.

He understood her, though. Nalah was a creature of black and white, and he'd introduced a lot of grey into her world. She never took change well.

Closure his ass.

He ran his hand over his face, through his hair. On top of all that, he had himself to deal with. There had always been a burn in his gut, a flame that rattled its chains trying to get free. He didn't know what it was and never tried to find out. He never even mentioned it to Nalah. She was obsessed with finding his heritage, that's what she called it, and he had no interest in that.

He wished he looked into it now, though. Whatever it was, it was getting stronger here. The proof was in his eyes, in the strength of his body, the quickness of his reflexes. He had been stronger last night than he had been yesterday morning, and today he was stronger than he had been last night. His body was his weapon, and even though it was improving at an astonishing rate, he didn't like not knowing what was happening with it.

The heavy steps announced Beylor's arrival before he came into view, the loudmouth guard from before with him. "Esh, how goes it?"

"All right." He kept himself neutral, not welcoming, not threatening, and hoped Beylor would go the hell away.

"Good to hear. I'm expecting a great fight from you."

"Won't disappoint."

Beylor puffed himself out, showing the gold around his neck. Esh supposed the smile was meant to be fatherly, but all he saw was full of shit. "Esh, a man like you, you can do so much better than the circuit. You're young and with so much ahead of you. If you chose the right paths, of course, paths I'd like to help put you on."

And there it was, five years of avoidance gone to waste. Here was the offer that Esh knew would be made the moment he'd set foot into the Tour.

It wasn't the first offer he'd received, but it'd be the hardest to turn down. *If* he could turn it down. Offers from people like Beylor weren't meant to be turned down. Otherwise, the people who made them tended to get mad.

The guard next to Beylor looked at Esh with ill-disguised hatred. And there, proof even if he did accept, he'd have someone waiting to end him from the inside. Yeah, this offer was cocked from all sides.

"I can't think about that right now. Need to concentrate on the Tour."

"Absolutely," Beylor agreed. "We'll talk after. For now, I know my guests want only the best, and they've been waiting for the Cage King such a long time."

The excitement of the fights fell over Nalah, a wave she hadn't experienced in five years, her one fight the night she'd reconnected with Esh not counting. The rush of adrenaline that was transmitted from the fighters to the crowd, and how the crowd fed on it, in turn hyping up each other. She was almost nauseated, and she caught her hands clenching and unclenching in nervous excitement without her directing them.

As the crowd cheered and the announcers made small announcements until the fighters came forward, Nalah looked around the stands. No magic so far, either in the ring or out of it.

With nothing else to do, Nalah waited. Esh's fight was next, the last before the mid-day break. Rorth won his first match as did the albino. She hadn't watched them, and once she heard what the albino had done in his fight, she was grateful she'd missed it.

She was sitting in the front, the space reserved for whoever the fighters wanted. Behind her were the cheap seats. It was above, in the boxes, where Beylor and all the wealthy and powerful watched.

"And now..." came the announcer's voice, restrained and theatrical excitement in those two words. The crowd quieted, and Esh moved towards the fighting floor, that innate *something* in him glowing brighter than ever.

The groundswell grew until it included even the highest of the boxes. Yes, Esh was a draw, no doubt about it. His legend rivaled the Tour, and it took little imagination to see Beylor's preening face over this turn of events.

Esh was dressed as always – no shirt, jeans, boots, and he needed nothing else to incite the noticeable hum of appreciation from the women in the audience. And if that hum brought a smug grin to her face because she knew how *good* he was with his tongue, well, any woman would agree that was allowed.

Next into the ring came his opponent, a man she hadn't run across yet. He looked to be human – a statement you could never be positive over – but this man was almost as big as Rorth, both in height and body mass. Like Esh he was shirtless, his chest a landscape of ridges and curved muscle. Take out the palpable excitement for blood, and this could be a photo shoot for some fitness magazine.

He passed by her, and magic tickled the edges of her mind. Not connected to the death magic, but he was innate of some type. It was vaguely familiar, one she was sure she knew but learned long ago amid her studies. Damn, damn, damn, and then there was no time, because the bell rang, and the men circled each other. No weapons, only the damage done with legs and fists and heads.

Fists met body, the accompanying spray of blood reaching the first seats, the onlookers crying out in horrified delight at the feel of the liquid droplets. Flesh absorbing blows, the rippling of skin showing the savage path of pain. The crunch as bone connected to bone, and underneath it all low rumblings of the crowd.

Then a hard echo of magic, clear as a sun flare. The other fighter activated some type of power, and Nalah stood, hoping the magic left a physical change on the man.

Esh struck the fighter hard in the side but frowned, clenching and unclenching his fist as he backed up, rechecking his opponent.

And then Esh on the defense, twisting to avoid a heavy blow to his skull, not moving fast enough and a punch to his chest brought him low, had him rolling away.

After several more turns of Esh doing nothing more than dodging, the crowd around them booed, not here to see the Cage King skulking and avoiding the fight. A kick to his ribs had Esh skittering across the ground.

Every muscle went jittery, and her mouth went dry as parchment. This was bad. She'd seen Esh get hit before, but this was nothing short of being dominated, and Esh's opponent was out for blood. If she couldn't help him soon, there was a chance Esh might be brought down.

She'd spent years perfecting her magical shields, but now she tore them down, lay herself bare to any magical power around her. She opened herself in complete abandon to any energy around her, her concentration complete and only on Esh's opponent. Past the layers, down to the…skin?

Concentrate, study, no shields. Skin, skin, something in the skin, concentrate, what is it, what is…he?

No, *it*. There weren't different sexes among the Skin Dwellers.

Skin Dweller. Shit.

Not necromantic magic, but dark enough. She dug through memories of the training she'd received on the various races, so numerous most of them had disappeared days after she'd learned of them.

Their skin could harden until it was more akin to armor. Also, it was poisonous, enough a normal human could only endure two or three contacts before beginning to fall ill. Esh wasn't normal, but how long before it was too much for his system?

Their weakness, they did have one, but…what was it…base of the spine. *Yes.* A couple hits there started the process of weakening the skin, turning it back to normal, which led to other punches hurting them. Once the cycle started, as long as the poison didn't kill you, the Skin Dweller could be defeated.

Now, how to tell Esh? There were no rounds. They fought until one collapsed, and the one left standing was the winner. She couldn't go up and say she had to speak to him. They'd kick her out if she tried to interfere.

Somehow Esh had to come to her…

Nalah glanced around and zeroed in on the man on her right. He was already drunk and had propositioned her as soon as she sat down, though he did back off after she told him she was with one of the fighters. Still, she'd gotten a familiar vibe from him, one that had her leaning as far away as possible.

Please let him be as much of a jackass as I think he is. Nalah stood up at the next hit to Esh, a not-entirely-feigned gasp of shock pouring from her mouth, and put her ass in front of his face.

The vibe was right. He didn't go for her ass, his hand went straight for between her legs, and a completely not-feigned shout of outrage left her mouth as she turned. "What the *fuck* do you think you're doing *touching* me, *asshole*?"

It took only moments before she was lifted out of the way, Esh beside her and trying to go after the guy.

Never let it be said she didn't know her man.

As nice as watching the prick get beaten might have been, there were more important matters. Nalah wrapped her arms around Esh's neck, trying to make it look like she was burying herself in his grasp for comfort as she spoke in his ear, his blood seeping against her mouth and flavoring her words. "Your opponent is a Skin Dweller. Skin is poisonous and like armor. Kick him instead of hitting him, keep skin contact minimal. Base of his spine, hit it enough and the armor goes away. You can beat on him then."

Hands gripped at Esh and dragged him back, shouts of outrage that he left the ring. Esh was yelling at the ref, up towards Beylor, gesturing at her, and the guy who touched her was dragged out. Hope that she was correct on how to beat the Skin Dweller, that Esh had heard her message and would act on it, curled in her stomach and lay heavy there.

After a few tense moments Beylor nodded, and the fight was resumed. The fighters once again circled each other, and this time, when the Skin Dweller lunged forward, Esh twisted so he had a clear shot at the back of the man and kicked hard into the base of the spine. The Skin Dweller crumpled, and when he righted himself and stood, surprised fear was plain for all to see.

Esh had heard and she was right, and Nalah breathed for the first time since that flare of magic, because it was going to be fine.

Esh would never lose a fight.

After the initial blow, the Skin Dweller faded in quick order. Esh owned him, and at the end Esh used his hands several times to deliver the final, body-dropping blows, but didn't seem susceptible to the poison.

The Skin Dweller fell and didn't rise, and Esh was proclaimed winner. Without thought or intent, Nalah ran to the ring and threw her arms around him, light-headed and happy, pressing kisses over his face.

He stopped the small kisses and captured her lips in a deep, drugging kiss, and the catcalls and rude remarks faded from her ears, and all Nalah knew was Esh, alive and whole and victorious.

And then he pulled his head away and turned, growling at something. Nalah followed his gaze, and there was Lian, his hand on Esh's arm and a cruel smile on his lips. "Beylor wants to see you both."

CHAPTER THIRTEEN

This must be how being called to the principal's office felt.

Not that she'd know firsthand since she'd never stepped foot in a school, but there was a vague sense of dread compounded by exasperation she was put in this place to begin with.

Beylor was in full-on rant, which he'd been doing for several minutes and still looked nowhere near done. "...and I'll have you know a fighter has never stopped and stepped from the ring! Where the fuck was your mind? I should kick your ass out for that."

Esh hadn't spoken since Beylor had started, but now his voice, cool and bored, came through. "Go ahead. Kick me out."

"Esh," she protested, though hopefully Beylor assumed it was because of her not wanting him to give up the Tour.

Esh's look to Nalah said *Let me handle it*, and though rebellion ran strong through her, she shut her mouth and sank into her seat.

After watching her a moment, Esh turned to Beylor. Esh's voice was low and sure and sharp enough to cut through steel. "Let me get something straight. I'm here for the prize, but I can say fuck you and walk away and not think twice, and if you think I'm going to let some limp-dicked asshole touch my woman and not tear off his face so I can have the *privilege* of being here, you never met me. Now, kick me out of the Tour, or let me recover so I can give a damn good fight this afternoon."

That was the longest she'd ever heard Esh speak at once, and even she didn't want to upset him any further and bring that buried wrath in his tone down on her.

And the way Beylor made an abrupt change to his tune, his hands coming up to placate though he strained to keep his voice firm, he must have agreed. "Fine, I can understand. I would never let anyone touch my, ah, Tiffany." The little stutter before the name didn't bode well for their long-term relationship, and Nalah hoped Tiffany's next rich boyfriend was nicer and did legal things. Beylor continued. "But she's banned from the second match today. I can't have a repeat."

"That sounds reasonable," Esh agreed, and she was about to voice her opinion when he added, "But she's at the final match."

Beylor gave a quick nod, probably deciding the final match was safe and that he didn't want to push Esh again. "Fine." He turned away, the move obvious dismissal.

Esh led her out and put her on the path towards their temporary home. "Get back to the rooms." He leaned down and gave her the softest kiss possible, and when he would have pulled away she held on to him.

Something had shifted in the ring. She was the one who helped him, protected him. Because of her training, Esh escaped with little damage.

Giddiness suffused her, had her pressing deeper into the kiss. She had been valuable to him, and in return, he protected her from any consequences. Inside her some heretofore unknown part unfurled, opened up to him, and basked in the glow he provided.

They separated, not easily, but he brought his head back and smiled down at her, a half-smile that still had her heart pounding in that airy way he introduced with the kiss. "We'll talk, and I might have to thank you too."

"Damn straight." And she winked, because she could, and the widening smile on him was everything she'd hoped.

Esh breathed through his mouth, broken nose useless for the task. Cracked ribs, shoulder that had been dislocated and shoved back into place, stomped on foot… all in all, not too bad for the night.

The roar of the crowd started to penetrate his fight-fueled brain, going in seconds from the light buzzing of a fly to a volume wave that could knock him over if he didn't take care.

He stood and stretched, and his eyes gave another involuntary once-over of the front seats for Nalah. Not that he wasn't used to that. Five years apart, and he always looked over the crowd for her.

Well, it worked, didn't it? It was why he'd seen her that first night.

Beylor came up to him, unearned swagger in his walk. The fuck annoyed him more every time he saw him. Every negative thought he'd ever had about Beylor didn't add up to the truth of the pissant.

"Excellent show. Will you be well enough to attend the dinner tomorrow?"

"Yeah, we'll be there." Great, he got to be on display for the guests. It was supposed to be a night of relaxing before the final fights, but it was a freak show for the rich and powerful to look over the fighting beasts before they bled their last.

Nalah would want to be there. Good chance that Beylor's blonde would be wearing the ring again. After all, when else would Beylor have a chance to show everyone his victory over the Guild?

Not that he knew what to do even if the woman was wearing the ring. Fucking Guild. For all Nalah's talk, there wasn't any plan B he could see. She kept assuring him something had to be planned, but the lines that appeared between her eyebrows when she said the words spoke volumes. Still, all Esh could do at this point was keep moving forward. Outside of a body bag, there was no way he was getting out of the end of the Tour.

Lian kept close to Beylor like always, his beady eyes not leaving Esh for any other. Once things were settled, he and Lian would need to have a discussion with their fists.

From the ring, Esh walked straight to their apartments, doing his damndest to keep any hint of limp out of his gait. He didn't need Lian or anyone else going for him, thinking he was weak. Yeah, there was the rule of no fighting outside the ring, but strange how easily that could be forgotten by someone when they saw easy prey.

Nalah was sitting on the sofa, once again reading. She glanced up with half-smiling eyes that widened with worry as she took him in. The book was down, she was up, and he was sitting in less time than it took to open his mouth to explain. "I heal fast," was all he got out before the gauze was brought out and her fingers skimmed over his skin with healing intent.

Touch was always good, and if he had to sit around and accept it, sure, why not?

"This is worse than from your fight with the Skin Dweller."

He shrugged. "Guy knew how to fight. That thing didn't, relied on his armor. What is a Skin Dweller, anyway?"

"It's probably more accurate to call a Skin Dweller an *it* than a *he*, and they're small league baddies, more a race that follows orders than does anything on their own."

It was hard to concentrate on mundane conversation when she was so close and smelled of comfort and sunshine. His body still buzzed with adrenaline, and though he was beaten enough it was muted, it along with the promise from that earlier kiss had him ready for other activities. Long experience taught him, though, that until he was patched up, Nalah would not let herself be distracted. "The ring?"

"Yeah. The only question I have is if it's connected to the evil I've been feeling or if it was sent from someone else."

"I really wish the Guild had given you a clue what was going on. I'm going to have a serious talk with someone." Her eyebrows rose to her hairline and though she didn't comment, it was plain what she thought about that possibility. Esh continued with the earlier conversation. "Once I got the armor out of the way, it had no defenses and nothing was left but destroy it."

A soft, wet cloth was run over his skin, and he stayed still, obeying her to turn this way and that. "Lian give you any grief today?"

"Yeah, he was watching me."

"I wish I knew what that was about." Ointment was rubbed into his knuckles, her touch tender and sure. "In our one conversation, the contact said Lian had an obsession with you even before I stirred up trouble, but he didn't elaborate. Don't know if he didn't know or he ran out of time to talk."

"Don't worry. Guarantee he's not the only one. The title brings lots of those types to my door."

She hummed in vague agreement as her hands continued to work medicine into his skin. The buzz was getting stronger, harder to control. He loved that she wanted to heal him, but right now, healing took second place to getting his hands on her and getting her under him. He needed the taste of her again, wet and ready against his tongue.

She picked up the bandages and started to place them over various cuts. "Beylor took it easy on you."

Her tone picked up at the end, giving the statement a hint of question, and of course her brain would pick up the talk went smoother than it should. "He wants me as one of his men, spoke about it before the fight. He's not going to run me out until that's settled."

Nalah's face showed no change, which meant she'd already considered that. "I'm so sorry."

"Don't be. Knew it would happen if I accepted their invitation to come."

That caused her head to jerk up, eyes wide with a hint of confusion. "And you came anyway?"

"Yeah."

Her eyes shifted back and forth, like she was reading from an invisible book for answers. "But why?"

The truth of what she was to him still didn't register with her. He'd hoped that kiss earlier meant it did, but they weren't quite there yet. "You were going to be here. No way you were coming without me."

She huffed, grabbing up the supplies and moving to put them away. "I've been taking care of myself for a few years now."

"No, you haven't." Before she could interrupt and make a retort, he hurried on. "You've been back-up, or you did research. This is different. This is you in the front lines, and not where you should be."

There was only one area on Nalah that darkened when she blushed, the tips of her ears, and right now they had the red hue that spoke of her embarrassment. "I've still been on my own."

"Don't take it badly. Doesn't mean you aren't brave as hell. Always were, even if you gave me and Jac heart attacks sometimes. You never ran when we told you to run."

"That's not fair!" She tossed the basket of supplies on the table and went into her hands-on-hips pose. "I couldn't live with myself if I ran and you two were hurt. If I could do something, I wanted to be there to do it."

"We'd rather of been hurt than see you be a human punching bag – or worse." Memories crowded his head, him and Jac passing a beer and bitching about yet another group beatdown they'd fought through because of Nalah's mouthy *help*. "We probably got into twice as many fights because of you, cause you wouldn't run and instead defended us. Took on groups no other dumbasses would've."

"I was so young," she murmured, gave a small snort of laughter. "I never meant that. Attitude took over when someone insulted my two favorite guys."

"Fuck it, don't worry on it. It's probably why I'm able to fight so well. Good early training and all."

Nalah smiled, the sun and moon and stars in that smile which contained only the good and no bad from their shared memories. He had to protect that smile. He had to get that ring and get her out of here.

And if once they were out she decided they should separate again? No, fuck that. Wasn't going to happen. He'd convince her, somehow.

She went to move away, but as she passed he caught her hand and brought the palm to his mouth, placing a small, biting kiss in the center. "Esh, stop that. Your nose is probably broken."

Definitely broken. Pain didn't matter. He'd been through worse before and would be through worse again. "No worries. It'll be fine tomorrow."

"Then we'll do stuff tomorrow."

He growled and pulled her into his lap. "How about we do stuff now. Kiss and make it better."

Her hand was gentle as she pushed against his chest in a playful smack. "Oh, is that what I'm doing? Should I go put on a nurse costume?"

Oh hells yeah, once they got away from all this. But for now... He pointed at his nose. Her squinty-eyed glare was not effective when paired with her lips curling up. Finally, she gave a deep, dramatic sigh, and with that, Nalah leaned forward and with the lightest brush possible, touched her lips to the broken nose.

That worked, so next one. He pointed to his shoulder. This time was less hesitation and a bit more pressure, but light enough to express his injuries still worried her.

Changing tactics, he pointed to an area on his chest with no bruises, scrapes, or bloody patches. The squinty-eyed glare was replaced with a half-open mouth, the tongue touching the corner in a gesture that was pure habit and hell on his rising cock.

Her soft mouth descended on the unbroken skin, and Nalah no longer needed direction. For every bruise she found, her tongue came out to run over the skin, leaving a trail of heat behind. She looked up at him through her eyelashes.

"Adorable and fuckable," he murmured, and her ears went red. "What are you going to kiss next?"

The brush of her palm over his cock. "Does this hurt?"

"So much." And that was the absolute truth. He was vibrating, anticipation rushing through him in a great wave, leaving him breathless in its wake.

She nibbled her lower lip, the movement reddening her mouth and bringing a groan to his lips. "I think you might be taking advantage of my medical care of you."

He took her hands and pressed them to his cock through the jeans. Her fingers moulded around him, working him through the fabric, and the sight of those long, dark fingers had sweat beading at his hairline. He needed to see her skin on his. "Never," he got out, his voice little more than a croak. He cleared his throat. "I just want everything checked."

Those gorgeous, wondrous fingers undid the zipper, letting his cock spring free, hard and ready for her. His earlier hopes were answered as she curled those fingers around him and gave a long, lazy pull. "No underwear?"

"Didn't want to slow you down." Her stroke was feather-light, barely-there, yet to him it was a brand.

She slipped off his lap, her expression sensual and mischievous all at once. Her head dipped, and that pink tongue slipped out, and, oh fuck... She licked him. She licked him like he was an ice cream cone and she'd just discovered the treat. Little licks, but nothing tentative about them. They were sure and often, and the came all around the head, driving him fucking nuts because it was too much and not enough, and she was going to kill him.

Her mouth surrounded the head, the first pull of suction eliciting a groan. With slow, sure strokes she went deeper, swallowing more of him, pulling him further and further into her throat.

His hand came to rest on the back of her head, directing her, and he fought with himself not to force her down, and to put all of his cock in that incredible wetness. But he didn't have to, because she deep-throated him in one smooth movement. And she did it again. And again. And again.

And between how she worked him with her throat and the long-desired sight of her sucking him off, he came quicker than anyone older than fourteen ever should, his head thrown back and his vision gone white.

When he came to, her head was in his lap, and she was stroking his cock, petting it like it was a kitten. Or a pussy. Petting a pussy sounded like a good idea. He made to pull her up. "My turn."

"No." She was adamant, pushing him back when he would have risen from the chair. "Nothing else tonight. You heal."

"I'd rather bury my face in your pussy and see how many times you come in an hour."

Instead of crawling on the bed and opening her legs, she bust out laughing. "You have a broken nose. Do that and you'll suffocate."

"Worthwhile way to go."

"You're cute when you're trying to be naughty." She got up and kissed him on the top of his head, and it warmed him in a way not even the feel of her lips on his cock had done, the warmth more valuable than any sexual heat ever could be to him. "I'll make dinner and we'll turn in early. Tomorrow will be interesting, and I want us both ready."

"Nalah." She paused from getting out a pan and looked at him, her eyebrows raised in question. "From here on out, if I tell you to run...run."

She blinked once, twice, long slow blinks under furrowed brows, and he was grateful she was taking it seriously. In the end, she said, "If I did that, I wouldn't be me, would I? Besides, where could I go? It's together or not at all."

And even with the fear that churned his gut at the thoughts of what could go wrong, that didn't sound too bad at all.

CHAPTER FOURTEEN

Esh was gorgeous in the basic white tailored shirt and black pants combo, and the complete boredom on his face as he talked with the various guests made him better looking, not less. The women certainly thought so. Or maybe they just took it as a challenge. Either way, Esh was surrounded.

Not that Nalah didn't have her own gaggle going on here. Tiffany grabbed her and dragged her from group to group without letting her do more than sip from her drink between sessions. If Nalah could have gotten away with it, she'd give them all an Esh-level scowl and huff off. All the women talked about were clothes and make-up and hair. Gods knew at this point she'd take Laire over any of them. Sure, Laire usually talked about clothes and make-up and hair as well, but at least she threw in the occasional story about blowing something up.

Fifteen minutes later, Esh was still surrounded but she saw a chance for escape and took it. Free of the women, she breathed deep and gave another look around. The Pale Lady wasn't here, but Nalah would place money every other guest was.

Tiffany was wearing the ring, and every sighting of it poked at Nalah, mocked her because she had no idea what to do, other than smack Fallon the next time they were together for not sending a better thief. There had to be a back-up plan. Esh's disdain and her own frustrated grumbling aside, the Guild always had a contingency strategy in place. All she could do was keep her eyes open and be ready for when it appeared.

Well, that, and hope it was sooner rather than later. Not only were they now dealing with Esh being in Beylor's crosshair and a psychotic guard obsessed with both of them, but the dark magic around here was battering the hell out of her magical shields. She hadn't felt this exposed since those first days of training, but now was worse. Now, she knew what it looked like when someone's mind was torn apart because their shields fell. That her shields were crumbling and she couldn't quite keep them shored up was a terror she had to keep to herself, because Esh would make them leave.

It wasn't because of the ring that she was determined to stay, either. She wasn't so naïve that Esh could hold the truth from her. Once Beylor made that offer, Esh was either leaving here as one of Beylor's men, or he wasn't leaving, unless the Guild stepped in. If he tried to get her away now, Beylor would take that as open season.

She wasn't going to risk him like that. She'd deal with the shields, keep them up somehow, but she wasn't going to give him yet another reason to make himself a target.

A new woman approached her, a clone of Tiffany except her hair was dark and wavy and her eyes such an electric green they had to be fake. Unlike Tiffany, there was nothing of genuine feeling in her smile, and when she spoke, her voice was malicious regard. "You're Nalah? I had to come over and meet you. I never thought the Cage King would get a woman. I know women who've been trying for years and there's never been the suggestion of anything outside of him bedding them for a night."

Really, that was appropriate? But she pushed down the urge to take out her earrings and gave the most obvious fake smile in return. "Yes, I'm Nalah, and yes, I came with Esh. Who are you? I don't remember Tiffany introducing you."

The woman didn't bother to answer and gave a negligent wave that highlighted her manicure. "How did you get him?"

This woman was pushing every one of her buttons with the attitude. "I wish the story was exciting, but it's pretty boring. We knew each other as kids, and we reconnected as adults."

The woman leaned closer, eyes sharp and looking for any weakness. "And you weren't scared off by his violent reputation?"

"He fights in the cage. So do many others. Doesn't make him a thug."

Stroking the rim of her champagne glass with one red-tipped finger, the woman smiled with malicious delight. "You can't tell me you don't know the rumors involving him and Vitto. Why, if you don't..." she gave an exaggerated shudder. "You might feel differently about him once you hear the truth."

All the blood fled from Nalah's limbs, leaving them icy cold in the wake of hearing her brother's killer's name. She'd blocked that name for five years, never let it be heard even in the deepest recesses of her mind.

But, what were the rumors she was speaking about? Esh never fought for Vitto, not before her brother died, and there was no possible way he fought for that man after what happened with them. This woman was talking crap, and Nalah was done. "I'm not interested in rumors. Excuse me."

The woman grabbed her arm and forced her to stay, and as Nalah's hand balled into a fist, from the corner of her eye she noticed Esh turn towards her. The woman continued. "He's a murderer. They say he single-handedly destroyed Vitto's organization. They say he killed Vitto himself."

Nalah was rooted to the ground, buzzing in her ears as the woman's words ricocheted in her head. That couldn't be true. Esh would have told her if he did something like that.

A large, calloused hand wrapped itself around hers, and the back of her mind registered Esh coming beside her, glaring at the woman and pulling her away, leading her out of the party and towards their rooms.

The buzzing in her head quieted until other sounds could penetrate. The soft hum of the refrigerator, the radio she had left on from earlier, a jazz song playing, low and mournful. "We keep leaving his parties. Beylor's going to get a complex."

He retreated to the wall, leaning against it and staying silent. He looked like a mistreated junkyard dog, watching a new arrival and just waiting for the blows to start.

The tension stretched between them, the weight of that last week – the week that started with her brother falling to his knees in front of her and ended with his body being lowered to the ground – crushing them underneath. "Is it true?"

"It's true I killed Vitto. That his organization fell afterwards wasn't on me." Esh's voice was clear and steady and neutral. It was a statement of fact, concise, the way he approached everything.

"Why didn't you tell me?"

The question hung, suspended in the air. He lifted his chin, like fighters did when they were daring their opponent to take a hit. "It wasn't meant for you to know. I didn't kill him for you. Unless it's convenient for you to attack me with, you seem to forget Jac was my best friend. Vitto was an evil bastard who killed my best friend, and by doing that, destroyed my life." In a sharp motion he brought his hand to his hair, clenching the strands between his fingers before smoothing the hair back. "Why would you think I wouldn't kill him after that?"

"Because you don't get involved. Because doing that marked you."

She didn't mean the words as an attack, but the way his body tensed told her he took them like that. "Well, maybe you weren't the only one who didn't care what happened afterwards, as long as the pain ended."

No. Gods no, she never thought Esh…she never wanted him to be in that dark place, with nowhere to turn and no one to believe in him.

And she had put him there. She didn't mean to do it. She was thoughtless, mired in her own pain, but even in her darkest times she never wanted Esh to hurt.

His gaze was sharp, defiant. "Got anything to say about that? Like, it was what I deserved? Too bad it didn't work out that way?"

Standing like that, for one moment he was the little boy she'd known, standing rebellious and daring everyone to judge him, daring her to put him down once again for his choices, but underneath the attitude was fear. Fear he would be rejected. Fear he'd end up alone again.

The thought of him going off alone, it struck her hard on her breastbone, crushing her chest and making it impossible to breathe. Any mistakes he made were the same kind she had – thoughtless, maybe prideful, but never malicious.

No, never malicious. She never told him she knew that, when they were starving in the streets, he would give her his portion of food, telling her he'd eaten earlier. Or he made sure she was blanketed even if he faced the cold nights in nothing more than a thin T-shirt. She'd watched him work long into the night with Jac giving Jac the only help her prideful brother would ever accept, help on making himself a better fighter, even nights that Esh had watch and wouldn't get any sleep afterward.

A street kid who managed to hold onto that goodness would never let his best friend go into a fight that would kill him, no matter what consequences faced them. She'd been so wrong to put so much blame on him.

All because she didn't want to rail against Jac. Her brother had been so reckless, so careless, so *weak*. Weak that he'd get himself into these situations without care of the cost the rest of them were always paying.

No, her brother wasn't malicious either, but he was weak, and in those last days, she had begun...

She'd almost started...

Gods help her, those last days, she'd *hated* Jac.

"Nalah." Esh's voice was concerned, his thumbs brushing over her cheeks, and only with that did the wetness on her cheeks register in her memory-dimmed mind.

Five years they'd been separated, but as she looked to see his gaze on her, she saw what she always had – love, concern, happiness that she was near him. He was so easy to read, at least to her. Five years and nothing had changed. Not for him.

Not for her.

The bands she'd unknowingly placed around her heart snapped free, and with their destruction all the love and affection she'd been holding back burst forth, flooding her with warmth and contentment and *joy* because she was back where she belonged, with the boy who protected her and the man who challenged her, and both of them always, *always* loving her.

She lifted her head and placed her mouth on his, and in that kiss she let everything she felt run free. As she licked at his lips and was allowed access to go deeper, she poured everything running rampant inside her into that kiss. Adoration, joy, hopefulness, and above all the love and happiness she'd denied herself so long, in a misguided attempt to punish herself.

He'd stiffened for a moment, then wrapped his arms around her, crushing her to him as he took over the kiss, drawing from her everything she offered and leaving himself open in return. His kiss contained awe, wonder, and a bone-deep promise to always stay at her side.

Esh lifted her in his arms, never breaking the kiss, and headed for the bedroom. Once there they were naked within moments, with Nalah only having a vague impression of tearing cloth and buttons flying.

The sheets were cool against her back while the man above her was hot and hard, the glide of his skin on hers sparking a deep desire that had her heart rate soar and brought a sheen of perspiration to coat her skin.

"I'm going to devour you," he growled when his mouth wasn't otherwise marking her breasts and the valley between them. "I'm going to get between your legs and not leave until you forget your name." And then he headed down to make good his claim.

She watched that skillful tongue come out to make a light pass over the outside lips and clit before it delved deeper, entering and tasting her, lapping up the wetness and creating more.

She watched the dark curls move as his head turned this way and that to taste every inch available. There wasn't a patch of skin that hadn't experienced his lips and tongue on it, and his expression was of a man savoring every experience, committing it to memory.

She watched as his fiery eyes lifted to meet hers, and not breaking their gaze, his tongue and lips found her clit and began to work.

His teasing had worked her up, made her muscles jump and her skin crackle with electricity, but it was his eyes that ratcheted up her arousal, had her wet beyond all reason and desperate to come. Those gorgeous eyes watching her, taking his cues from her body and without words, pressing harder here, sucking a little more there.

A rolling hunger swept through her, and in quick decision she grabbed his hair and pulled him up. "Not like that. I'm coming with you in me."

His eyes closed like a man in pain. "Are you sure?"

In answer she spread her legs wider, opening and making herself vulnerable, willing him to understand everything in her heart with what she was offering.

He lowered himself over her, taking her mouth again, and she accepted greedily, tasting herself on him and loving how they combined. "Esh, I'm yours."

He surged forward, burying himself in her. She wrapped her legs around his hips, holding tight as he rode her, long perfect strokes that had her already primed body coming apart in minutes.

As her orgasm began to end he came, groaning in her ear as his body emptied in hers, and she held him tighter, holding onto him and vowing in her heart she'd never let him go again.

CHAPTER FIFTEEN

The final day of the fights. Esh was going against Rorth in the first round, and Nalah had accepted Esh at his word that she didn't have anything to fear from the half-orc.

She *did* fear the albino, though, and her heart beat a mad rhythm whenever she considered the possibility the final match would be between him and Esh.

All in all, fear held her in its grip, though she did her best to dispel it and keep moving forward. It was too insistent though. Today was the end, and all she saw was disaster. She didn't tell Esh, but she was beginning to question what was going on with the Guild. There was no indication she'd received about anyone else being her back-up or coming for her, and that combined with the albino and Beylor's looming *offer* had her downing antacid and hoping she wouldn't be sick.

She'd seen Tiffany earlier at breakfast. The woman had been wearing the magical ring and talking her usual mile-a-minute about nothing in particular. Before she left she gave Nalah a hug and a wink and said how glad she was they were joining the "family". That made Beylor's expectations pretty clear.

Esh was already at the ring. After breakfast she'd come back to their apartment, but it was about time to head out and cheer him on. There was a knock at the door, and before she could answer Beylor walked in, followed by Lian.

"Hello Nalah," he said in that high voice, and strange how being alone and defenseless made the usually pitiful tone suddenly menacing.

"I'm about to head to the ring," she replied, though from Beylor's smug, sure face, there wasn't anything she could say that would change what was about to happen.

"I hope you understand we don't want to harm you. We just need to give Esh the proper incentive to make the right choice."

Lian moved towards her, and his power rose in him, a beacon shining from within. In his hand was a gold cuff, and as he fastened it around her wrist, his power surged forward, branding her and making her hiss at the repugnant sensation. Her hand jerked in automatic desire to get rid of the loathsome shackle.

"Don't touch it," Lian said. "I have a gift, you see. Take it off, and it will poison you. Move more than five feet away from me, the same thing will happen."

Nalah prodded the magical item. Lian was telling the truth, the magic circling the band giving light taps to her skin before pulling itself back, and one tiny thread rose from the band and split apart, pinning one side of itself to her shoulder and the other latching on to Lian.

Beylor made a motion with his head, and Lian grabbed her and jerked her upright. Beylor continued. "You'll be fine as long as Esh makes the right choices. So quit whining. Gods, women are such a pain."

Beylor left, muttering something about Tiffany starting to get on his nerves. Lian kept her still in the apartment, and after Beylor was long gone, spoke to her. "So you understand your circumstances," he began, his voice perfectly pleasant. "You are dying today. If the fights don't kill Esh, I'm going to kill you in front of him, and then I'm going to kill him. Of course, if you run from me, you're dead that much sooner, and I'll simply throw your dead body in front of him."

"You can't do that! Beylor said-"

"After I kill Esh I'm killing Beylor, so I don't care what he said. That fool has been too lax in running his empire. It was time for it to fall."

Nalah studied him for any hint of what was going on. With everything else going on, they hadn't taken him seriously enough. "Why are you doing this? You're really that jealous of the Cage King?"

Lian's lips thinned. "I couldn't care less about that ridiculous title. What I care about is he murdered my brother, and it's time he paid."

"Esh doesn't murder anyone. If it was a cage match-"

"My brother's name was Vitto," Lian interrupted. "Ring any bells? It should. Your brother died in one of my brother's matches."

"Vitto didn't have a brother." This was madness. She wanted closure, right? Well, closure was slamming down on her hard, knocking her to the ground and gut-kicking her while she lay there broken and bleeding.

"'Half-brother might' be more accurate. While we might not have been close, Vitto was my blood, and I won't let his death go unavenged. So I'm going to kill Esh, then take over Beylor's operation and merge it with the remnants of my brother's that I was able to salvage. My empire will be one everyone will envy. You won't be around to see it, of course, but you'll be the one who starts the dominos falling. "

He grabbed her arm and pulled her to the ring. Instead of being up front, they were in their own little box, about halfway up. Nalah had a clear view of everything, including the ring, including Beylor, and including the Pale Lady, who was taking in the scene before her, and even at this distance the woman's magic was fearsome.

The announcer stepped up, and the crowd lit up. Nalah put her hand over the gold cuff and began working on it, fighting the Pale Lady's power beating at her shields and concentrating everything in her to figure out how to unwind this unfamiliar innate magic. Damned if they were going to use her to control Esh, and she'd make sure they regretted putting a hand on her.

Rorth lunged for him, but Esh shifted his body and had the half orc hitting the ground hard, the resounding *thud* echoing through the building. Rorth groaned in pain.

The match had lasted a while, both of them able to take a beating. They were worse for wear, but Rorth's face was now as distorted and misshapen as any orc's, and his skin had a decidedly green hue.

The half orc was an excellent opponent, but the way he moved told Esh he was used to handling weapons and defending himself against a large number of opponents, not cage fighting and not fighting one on one. Nalah was correct in what she saw in him.

The crowd's roar was beginning to penetrate his brain, and a quick glance showed bets being paid out.

Esh moved away from Rorth, waiting to see if his opponent was out or would try to rise one last time.

A few boos came from the crowd when it became apparent he wasn't going to go after the half orc when he was down, and a chant began, started from the upper boxes. "Kill him. Kill him!"

It spread through the crowd. *Kill him, kill him, kill him!* Fucking cowards, so willing to watch death but they'd piss themselves if they ever entered the ring themselves. He took yet another step back, to louder boos and louder chanting.

Finally, Beylor rose, lifting his hands for quiet. "Cage King, listen to the crowd. End the match."

"The match is ended. I won."

Beylor's eyes narrowed, and beside him, Tiffany began to twine her hands together, her face uncertain as she looked up to Beylor. "I said kill him."

The end game was beginning, and now he'd get through it the way he always did – he'd fight, and the gods take pity on anyone in his way. "I won't kill him."

CHAPTER SIXTEEN

"I won't kill him," Esh repeated. Raising his voice, he looked directly at Beylor. "I'm not your dog, so like fuck I'll kill on your command."

Beylor's rat face had a smug smile Esh couldn't wait to pummel off him. "You think you have a choice? Kill or die."

"Oh, I'll kill, don't doubt that." Esh enjoyed the loss of assurance from Beylor's face. The little piggy might pretend he was king of all, but he knew the truth, and that moment proved it.

Rorth rose behind him, the half orc shaking blows and soil from his body, and the movement had the smug look returning to Beylor's face. "You handful against my army? I don't know why, Cage King, but I always thought once you came here and saw the truth, saw what I would give you, you'd be practical and join me. I'm disappointed this isn't happening."

Nalah. He had to get to Nalah. He could waste his time hoping she got to safety, but she'd proven time and again she wouldn't run if he was in danger. It was left to him, to fight, to kill. The fire in him started its journey, the small flame that always flickered in his gut sparking, a slow inferno tripping through his limbs, burning doubt and fear and all emotions, burning everything save the one truth in his world – Nalah would live, and everything that tried to hurt her would die.

Rorth started laughing, the sound from not-an-enemy, therefore the reason for it not a concern. Beylor, though, frowned and said, "Disgusting orc, it was a mistake to bring you into the Tour."

"For more reasons than you can know, you pathetic piece of shit," Rorth replied in his earthquake voice. He looked up to the long, flat expanse of ceiling. In quick succession Beylor as well as those in the stands copied the movement, and even Esh's followed in automatic response.

A crack bloomed in the center of the ceiling, chunks falling in, once in a slow pulse, then a repeat of the action again and again, the cracks now with audible accompaniment. From the corners of his eyes Esh took in the actions of those surrounding him, Beylor's men shifting with confused jerks, and the sounds of movement and vocal mutterings from the stands.

An explosion blew the center of the roof open. Screams from the stands, shuffling became the thumps of bodies colliding, and something...*someone*...fell from the sky, landing in the middle of the ring, legs bent and back curled to absorb the shock, in one hand the largest, most impressive sword he'd ever seen, in the other a double-bladed axe three times normal size, the metal sharp enough to decimate stone with its edges.

The being straightened, revealing a tall human woman with long red hair. Her eyes alighted over the fighters. They paused on him and there was recognition, but then they moved to look past him and she smiled, wicked delight in what she took in. "What the four hells? You got beat? You're not seriously expecting to be my sidekick after that, are you?"

And Rorth flipped her the bird, though his tone and eyes said he'd expected this reaction. "He's the Cage King. Give me a break. If it was weapons it would have been different."

"No excuses. Expect some serious sparring time, Mr. Not-the-King," and after speaking she threw the axe underhanded to Rorth.

Esh looked back as Rorth took control of the weapon, spinning the weapon in his hand with practiced ease. The axe looked more an extension of him instead of a mere weapon. The giant half orc looked straight at him as he swung the axe a few times.

The woman turned and continued her perusal, the twist of her lips expressing her opinion about their worthiness as opponents. She then turned her face to the stands where Beylor sat. Beylor must have known who she was because he shrunk back in his seat, disbelief and terror on his face for all to see.

Instead of talking to Beylor, she turned back to the fighters surrounding them. Her voice carried, as cold and strong and immovable as her stance. "I've got places to be and things to do, so I'm giving all you underlings a choice today. Stay and fight, you'll die. Run away and I won't chase you, so you'll live until you make your next stupid decision. Any takers on running away?"

There was hesitation, shuffling in place, but Beylor had convinced himself distance meant safety because he rose, shouting, "Kill her! Kill them all!"

The slight hesitation the men experienced was lost at Beylor's words, and they rushed forward. The woman brought her sword up to the ready. "No one ever takes advantage when I offer."

Rorth moved beside Esh, drawing his attention away from the woman with the sword. "Go get your woman."

And now the reason for the man being here was so obvious. "You're Guild."

Rorth clapped him on the back. "Talk later, go now. We're fine here," he said before he ran toward the guards in the other direction, axe brought high and already falling to strike its first blow.

Esh wasn't going to argue, but then came the screams. Esh looked back to the red-haired woman, and took in the pile of bodies already at her feet and the blood covering her sword.

No, he wasn't going to argue, but with or without him, they had nothing to fear from Beylor's men.

Fallon.

Nalah shuddered at the magical signature, slamming against her shields full force. She'd never known Fallon like this, in the midst of war. Power radiated from her in waves, pulsing energy that threatened to topple all in the way, and with her training Nalah could only hold it off well enough to still function. Maybe it was the way Nalah saw the magic, but Fallon's movements were in slow motion, where light glinted off the blade as it fell against the throat of an enemy, or the swing of her hair suspended mid-air before falling in a stop-motion wave.

"Kill her!" Beylor called again, true fear in his voice. Not that his men weren't trying, but the swordswoman was cutting a bloody path through the surrounding warriors.

Lian's attention was on the chaos in the ring. Nalah took her eyes off the fighting down below and returned her concentration to the cuff on her wrist. The magic was fighting her, though whether it was because it was placed by an innate or because of the blackout zone, she didn't know.

There! The click, the wash of acceptance, the signal she'd broken the magic enough that it would abide her wishes.

Lian turned away from the ring and grabbed her upper arm, but before he could do anything else, another figure fell from the sky. This one landed on the upper stands. It was a female with long black hair streaming behind her, a bow in her hands.

One of the guards attacked the female, but her foot connecting with the side of his head knocked him out, and without pause she twisted and grabbed at her back, bringing the bow up and loading it with the arrow she retrieved. Aiming at the ring, she shot arrows in a quick succession Nalah could not follow, taking out guards in the lower stands.

The black-haired woman scanned the crowd, pausing when her eyes found Nalah. She jumped down to Nalah's level, landing on a bar that couldn't be more than three inches wide, and the agility combined with the inhuman speed had to mean this woman was an elf.

Please be Guild. While Lian was distracted watching the archer, Nalah clasped the gold cuff around the wrist of the hand that was holding her.

His grip loosened as he glanced away from the chaos and toward her, and with that opening, Nalah pushed him over the railing. The split-second look of surprise that crossed his features as he fell over was almost comical, and then he was gone from sight, the magical thread snapping as he disappeared.

The elf appeared then before her, and a faint memory of this woman seen from a distance at Fallon's side rose up and replaced Lian's face at the front of her thoughts. "Aislynn?"

"Yes. The Realm Jumper?"

Nalah pointed toward the now empty box that once housed Beylor and Tiffany. "The woman is blonde and with Beylor. She has no idea what she has outside of a pretty ring. But there's someone else, a woman with long silvery hair, she's gone too-"

Aislynn's hand shot out and grabbed Nalah's upper shoulder in a near painful grasp, restrained panic clear on her face. "Silvery hair, past her waist, pure black eyes and beautiful like a doll?"

"Yes, that's-"

Aislynn didn't wait but turned and hauled ass towards the box's exit. Nalah followed, running as fast as she could, which was nowhere near what the elf was capable of. The only reason Nalah could keep the elf in sight was because Aislynn had to dispose of the guards who finally figured out there was an enemy here. She used her bow as a melee weapon, parrying the edged weapons the men carried and striking out with it, spinning the instrument to fight the guards as they crossed her path.

They neared the box, and from a small hidden hallway came the echo of her mother's ring. "Aislynn, down that path," Nalah called, and pointed the way when the elf turned to look at her.

Aislynn swerved, and now there were no guards, but this time the elf couldn't outrun her because barely two dozen steps into the hallway were two bodies lying in the middle of the hallway.

Beylor and Tiffany, both recognizable despite the multitude of claw marks on their bodies and the chunks of flesh torn from their exposed torsos, expressions of horror still detailed on their faces. This wasn't a quick kill – someone took time slicing them both up. Bile rose in Nalah's throat, a thick lining she swallowed hard against as she stepped back and averted her eyes to the elf. Aislynn had no expression and didn't appear to be fighting the nausea like Nalah was. Aislynn's eyes wandered over the bodies before her gaze met Nalah's. "Is this the woman who had the Realm Jumper?"

"Yes."

"Her hands are bare. The ring was taken." The corridor branched off into five possible routes of escape, and Aislynn gave a quick glance around each exit. "I see no obvious sign of which path was taken. I need you to find the ring."

Tiffany hadn't been a friend in the strictest sense, and she'd made her choice when she'd taken up with Beylor, but the good-hearted blonde hadn't deserved this. Nalah had seen the aftermath of death, but not this type of desecration. Magic infused the corpses. There was an echo of joy attached to the bodies, pleasure in the pain and fear they'd experienced, even a shade of disappointment it hadn't lasted longer – sick joy that was burrowing into her, becoming part of her, past the feeble defenses that were losing ground by the second. The bile thickened, and Nalah pressed her hand hard against her mouth.

Cool, smooth skin stroked over her brow. "Nalah." The voice was understanding, with warmth, and love for life, all things opposite of the magic surrounding her represented. "The ring is heritage from your mother, a link to her goodness and love for you. Fight now, and protect it."

The weight of Aislynn's words penetrated, dissipating the evil, and Nalah breathed deep, blanking her emotions. She pushed her power out, searched the myriad of corridors the killers may have used, keeping all attention away from the bodies. "Down the farthest right."

They took off, but not ten more steps Nalah grabbed at Aislynn and pulled her back, hard enough that despite her superior strength, the elf stopped and turned in confusion. If only Aislynn could see, she would understand. Magic shifted in impossible ways, swirled through the air in violent streaks past her, a shredding of barriers that existed for very good reasons. "Aislynn – something's *wrong*."

CHAPTER SEVENTEEN

Aislynn made to bring up her bow, but Nalah didn't let go of her arm. "Shouldn't we wait for Fallon?" Even this evil didn't blot out Tenro's signature, a hard burn bursting against her and making Nalah's skin tingle, and no offense to the skilled elf archer, but nothing in Aislynn compared.

"I would love to, but there is no time. I carry nothing that can contact Fallon through the blackout zone and inform her of where we are, and as this development was not one we prepared for, I do not know when she will arrive." With that, Aislynn disentangled herself. If the archer felt any fear, it wasn't evident in her sure stride or steady hands. She went forward, keeping Nalah behind her and protected.

Whatever door once was now lay in ruined shards on the ground, letting the late afternoon light filter in. Aislynn tilted her head, and twenty-to-one odds the elf was doing it to listen for any traps before they stepped into the sun.

Either she didn't hear anything or she decided to chance it, because Aislynn pushed forward, slow and deliberate.

An unearthly giggle, and Aislynn's arrow flew toward a cluster of treetops. Rustling started at one end of the long line of trees and then moved, shaking branches straight down to the other end.

Then both giggle and movement stopped.

Another arrow in Aislynn's bow, and though the elf's head moved in small motions back-and-forth, her arms were locked in position. "Where do we go now?"

Nalah extended her senses. The other magic pounced as if it had been waiting for her, dominating her own meager powers as it began stripping her of her protections.

"Nalah, the ring?"

Ring, ring, what about a ring? There was no ring, there was, there was...there was dark, putrid magic, so cloying it clogged her senses and blocked even Tenro.

"*Nalah*, stay with me." A vague, floaty voice, but the other descended upon her, desecration, decay, bloat and the pure joy in – *only happiness in* – shred-the-soul suffering.

Dark, so dark, so cold, always cold, and she was falling. *It* had her.

It had her.

You're mine, Magic Breaker.

Esh threw the guard over his shoulder down to the lower levels as he made for Beylor's box. A woman descended from the ceiling and began shooting arrows, then went into the crowd. Since Rorth and the redhead hadn't moved to combat her, she must be Guild too. Which meant she'd go for Nalah, and Nalah would lead her to Beylor and the ring.

Beylor's box was empty, a door to a hidden hallway behind it open. Esh followed through the long corridor, sliding to a stop in front of the two bodies.

"Fuck!" They were brutalized, and Nalah was walking into the path of whatever had done that. Before him – *Fucking Shit* – five paths. Five fucking paths, and he didn't have time for a wrong choice, not with what these sliced-up bodies meant. The evil Nalah had been talking about had decided to make itself known, and Nalah was running toward it.

Nalah. Nalah, Nalah, Nalah.

Panic, blind and frantic, her name on a loop in his head. She was alone without him, alone with creatures capable of this, and he had *no fucking clue.*

The burn deep in his belly flared, orange-red flame winding its way around his lungs, his heart, heading straight for the center of him and *demanding* attention.

It was enough to break through the loop of panic and in unthinking movement, Esh hit out with the side of his fist against the wall, the jarring pain resetting his brain.

He had to get to Nalah. He didn't have time to search and hope he got lucky. How the fuck was he supposed to find her?

The flame flickered, drawing his attention. It was straining, stretching against binds that held it. It was offering, promising what he wanted, if he would give it what it needed.

It wanted freedom.

He wanted Nalah.

There was no hesitation. Esh dug deep inside, raced for the flame, concentrated on releasing every tie that held it back.

It wanted freedom.

And as long as Nalah was safe, he would give it.

The last tie released and the flame shaped itself as it stretched out, two wings of fiery plumage reaching for the sky, the neck arching, a red-orange beak, sharp and lethal, opening to cry a song of freedom, of joy.

It infused him, spread through his limbs, and knowledge lit within him, the ancient knowledge of what he was, and the strength to protect what was his.

Nalah.

CHAPTER EIGHTEEN

The wing of flame surrounded her, pushed back the dark, broke through the deep death magic that crept around her with stealthy paws. Nalah jerked, Aislynn's voice above her.

"Nalah, answer *me*." Aislynn still had the bow and arrow at the ready, dividing her attention between Nalah and whatever lay beyond their sight.

"I'm here. Someone's coming, to help us I think."

Aislynn's chest rose and fell in a deep breath, the only outward sign of any emotion. "I hope you are correct."

The words were no sooner spoken than that giggle again, and from the trees the Pale Lady emerged, and she wasn't part of the magic, she *was* *magic*, the wielder of such profane power – power as ancient, as brutal, as undeniable as Tenro, housed in this delicate woman before her. The magic manifested as a black sludge surrounding her, its oily tentacles floating in the air close to her body.

The bowstring drew taut, but no arrow was released. Then another giggle, a whisper of wind, and Aislynn's bow was broken in two in her hand, a clean slice through the center given by a sharp blade.

The Pale Lady gave a demure laugh, her hand coming to cover her mouth. "My little pet, so loves to play. The two before only whet the appetite." The voice was high, girly, and held madness the depths of which Nalah had never plumbed. "Elf royalty, a princess? Am I remembering right, or perhaps an ancestor of yours? Time, so little meaning."

One second the Pale Lady was alone, the next a child – pre-pubescent, twelve, thirteen? Boy, girl? – was kneeling next to her, shapeless clothing, black hair long and straight, covering its face except for the strip down the center, wide enough it showed the black eyes. Eyes that were lifeless, but not in a way that suggested zombie. No, there was no soul in those almond spheres. It was an empty container that existed only to please its master.

The child's face was blank, pure mask, and it was still as the Pale Lady ran her hand over the hair, its arms hanging at its sides, and on the end of each finger were sharp, thin blades, at least a foot long and too far away to tell if they were placed on the child, or part of the child.

"Where did – it – come from? Did magic bring it here?" Nalah asked Aislynn, who'd dropped the pieces of the bow and now held a short sword.

"No, it moved to her side, so fast I did not see until it stopped."

That was very bad news, considering how extraordinary elven senses were purported to be.

"Another demonstration, little Magic Breaker? So cute, how you kept fighting me and how you were *so overwhelmed* by all the *bad, scary magic.*" The Pale Lady pushed her lips out and scrunched her face in an exaggerated pout.

To Nalah's eyes, the child never moved from the silver-haired woman's side, but Aislynn cried out, a sharp sound she clamped down on. On Aislynn's chest, four long cuts were gouged into her skin, visible through tattered leather, and a slow seep of blood welled forth and darkened the brown vestment.

The mad woman gave a quick triple clap, like a little girl trying to capture her parents' attention. "Would you like to know a secret? I despise the color red. I wear it to announce what I am to those inferior, but I dream of the day it goes away, when it no longer splashes around me. Alas, my little pet loves it so, and loyalty deserves reward, don't you think?"

Aislynn stood, weapon at the ready, her face not betraying any emotion or pain from the ever-seeping wound. And though Aislynn tried to step in front of her, Nalah maneuvered to stand at the elf's side, though her heart thumped hard inside her chest and unlike the elf, her shakiness was easy for anyone to see. But she would stand, and meet her death without cowering.

Arms encircled Nalah, but there were no blades connected, and the arms were too thick, the chest against her back too broad, to belong to the child.

Within and without, wings of fire, strong in their magic, surrounded her and warmed parts she didn't know had gone cold in the presence of that mad woman. Nalah shifted, looked to her protector. "Esh?"

His eyes were a brilliant blaze, as if she was staring into the heart of an inferno. He let her go, turned to face their enemies, standing in front of her, magnificent and powerful. His back displayed four deep cuts in his back, cuts that were meant for her and were stitching together even as she watched.

"How?" she whispered, her hand moving to stroke the fast healing skin before she stopped herself. Power pulsated from him, and that piece of innate in him she'd sensed now twisted tight around him, mixed with him so completely it was no longer a separate entity but part of him. And it was *beautiful*, every shade of red and orange represented and a songbird's melody floating around him. "What is this?"

"Yes, what?" The Pale Lady asked, fake simpering in that voice. "I want to know."

The child next to the white-haired woman lifted its blade covered hands, and the woman's tongue came out to swipe along the edge. Her eyes widened in a sickening parody of awe. "Phoenix fire and phoenix blood," she breathed out, a smile without humanity on her face. Her gaze focused on Esh. "How exciting. I don't have that in my collection. This means we must play."

From beyond the Pale Lady the albino emerged. Before, he'd been terrifying, but now, with the vicious power flooding through him, Nalah quailed against the horrific onslaught of magic. She huddled closer to Esh. "He's been magically enhanced."

He looked down at her, the expression easy and sure. "I know. I can see. Don't worry."

He'd said that to her before so many fights, but he always meant it, and he always won. With that, belief in him calmed her, and with a smile to show her faith in him, she let him fight.

Watching Esh had always roused something in her. He was made to fight, his movements strong and deadly and so decided. There was fear for him, but it was a small undercurrent, barely noticeable amidst her admiration. Instead, she concentrated on the animal grace he exuded as he went after his prey, the muscles bunching with restrained strength and his body sinuous in the way it flexed and spun.

Now, with the phoenix, it went further. He fought as one with his flame, the new power giving a heretofore unknown power to his blows, the flame following each strike to deepen the wound, painting the albino in streaks of blue and black and red, breaking bone and crushing flesh.

The albino once terrified her, but now it was pathetic how it fell before Esh. Esh stepped back as the albino lay on the ground, the body releasing magical vapors. The phoenix lifted its head in a war cry.

The Pale Lady had an intense frown on her face as she stared first at the body, and then toward Esh. "I don't like this game anymore."

The black coils of magic surrounding the woman arced out with sudden speed, the ends morphing into the faces of snarling black dogs with rows and rows of white shark teeth, green saliva dripping from their fangs, magic that was visible only to Nalah, but all three fell to the ground as the dogs tore into them.

Pain was her world, but she fought to keep her eyes open because Esh rose beside her, his own magic coming to the fore, his magic in the form of the phoenix with wings beating fast, the beak sharp and ripping into the black magic, but the multitude of dogs clamped down onto it with fierce jaws, and the bird screeched in fury and pain.

And then...

and then

The world was no longer red or black, but a deep rich green shot with silver. It separated the magics and threw back the dogs. The dogs howled with rage, snapping and growling at the intruder but pulling back all the same.

A wave rolled through – so hot it froze all in its path or such a deep, deep cold it incinerated?

The black tentacles of the Pale Lady circled in long sweeps across the landscape, probing and pausing and when confronted with the wave, jerking back, hesitating in their path before they rushed forth, and the two opposite magics *collided.*

And Nalah's magical shields, battered and bloodied for so long, fell.

CHAPTER NINETEEN

What the *fuck*? The pale woman pulled back her attack, and now something else was entering the battle. Esh's flame settled in him, aware but still. This incoming second power must be connected to someone good, or at least on their side.

Beside him on the ground, Nalah tore at her braids and began screaming, bringing her knees to her chest and rocking her body.

"Nalah!" He fell to his knees, the elf coming to crouch beside her as well. "Was she hit?"

The elf ran her hands over Nalah's head, across her still screaming mouth. Nalah seemed unaware, still locked in her mind. "Strong magic can break the minds sensitive to it." The elf looked up to the pale woman, then around. "And the magics here are some of the strongest of this world."

Nalah's screams were interspersed now with sobs, her head moving back and forth. "What can we do?"

The elf shook her head. "I have no skill in this area."

Esh rose, ready to tear through the pale woman, but the elf grabbed his wrist. "Let *go*," he said, and the words were a snarl. She may be an ally, but he'd destroy anything to protect Nalah.

"Wait," the elf replied, and motioned with her head to the path that led to the building.

Down the path came the red-haired woman, the impressive sword in her hand glowing with blood and magic, a veritable inferno of escaping power. The skin of her sword arm was marked with red flames…no, not marked. The flames moved in the skin, reaching up past her shoulder to the edges of her neck.

Rorth moved at her side but traveled some steps behind, enough to let her swing that huge sword without hitting him.

The woman walked straight ahead and never took her gaze from the pale woman. The white-haired woman returned that look, her face twisted and without the previous maniacal glee. The child at her feet hissed at the swordswoman, but clung to the pale woman's skirt.

The redhead walked without stopping on her journey to the other woman while Rorth went toward the elf. As the swordswoman passed before him, the flame in him rose, and it *bowed* to her.

Beneath him, Nalah's screams turned to constant whimpers. Ahead of him, the redhead walked until several feet away from the other, the sword steady at her side and the other woman square in her sights.

The look between the two women was as familiar to Esh as the break of bone. It marked bitter enemies, those who would fight without the promise of money or glory, only to feel the pain and humiliation of the other.

The pale woman spoke first, breaking into a simpering smile. "Dragon Slayer."

"*A Rainha da Flor-Cadaver.*"

The pale woman cocked her head and pushed out her lower lip. "You always break up my funnest games. Why can't I have the phoenix?"

"You wanna play?" The redhead twisted the massive sword with a roll of her wrist, the flames in her skin jumping at the movement. "That's why I'm here."

The pale woman's face lost all artifice, and pure and simple hate shone from her as her eyes rose to the swordswoman's hair. "I so despise red," and the words were a curse, spat with deepest loathing. She held up her hand, Nalah's ring encircling one pale finger. "Tell Reign next time to come himself and not send anything as pathetic as a Skin Dweller to do his dirty work." And she and the child disappeared, Nalah's ring and all magic connected to her going with them.

The fire on the redhead's skin faded until her arm was bare, her power pulling closer, and once she sheathed her sword, Esh felt nothing further from her. She turned, taking them in. "Ais, what's the story?" She walked towards them, her gaze falling to the slashes across the elf's chest. "Immediate care?"

Aislynn shook her head. "I will be well soon enough, Fallon. There is nothing magic about this. That child would not poison the weapon with magical means or other, not when the purpose is to inflict pain."

Fallon nodded, then turned her attention to him. He stepped in front of Nalah in an instinctive move. Yeah, she'd saved them, but that much power – it was impossible to simply trust.

"Calm down, fighter boy. I've known her five years and haven't done anything more than subject her to Laire's fashion critiques." After saying that, though, she motioned to Nalah with her hand, asking permission with the gesture. He moved away in answer, and she crouched down to run her hand over Nalah's face much as the elf had earlier. Nalah continued to cry, the sound low and piteous.

"Fucking pale-ass bitch." Fallon's voice was low, the volume and tone suggesting she was more talking to herself. The next words were louder and directed at them. "Her shields are smashed and her psychic landscape is fried. I'm amazed she lasted this long, considering she's been dealing with the Pale Lady the entire Tour."

"And how do we *fix* it?"

After placing her hand on Nalah's forehead and sweeping her hair back, Fallon rose, all predatory grace. "*We* can't. Shields are too personal, and it's instinctive to fight against any attempt to mess with them. Only someone she loves could try without getting pulled into the chaos that's her mind right now. Which means *you* gotta go in and do it."

"I don't know if she-" Esh stopped the sentence. Fuck if it mattered if Nalah loved him. No one else was a possibility, and it didn't sound as if she could get worse. He was with her until the end. "What do I need to do?"

Fallon's eyes gleamed bright, and a jab of adrenaline lined with unease rode through him. He knew this look – it was what he'd heard snatches of conversation about, opponents talking how he looked through them and with that look, knew how they ticked. Then the look vanished and she was only a concerned friend again, and said, "Let the phoenix lead. Healing and resurrection is what it does."

"I don't know shit about the thing inside me-"

"It's been part of you your whole life. It is you, and it's proven it fights for you, so trust it." Fallon cut through his protestations with a no-bullshit tone.

Inside him, a song rose, fierce as the drums of war, but with a peaceful undercurrent, beckoning him to follow.

This was for Nalah.

So he did.

Down the path of fire he walked, and then it wasn't a fire, it was their old library in the shithole town they grew up in, Nalah's second home he and Jac had always called it. Same two worn and weathered chairs in the middle, the once-red fabric now a bloody brown and shelves of the most battered books that still managed to hold themselves together.

"Only good for getting out of the rain."

The owner of the voice walked towards one of the chairs, sat in the broken cushion. He was still wiry and compact, the white of his teeth and eyes blinding against his dark skin, his hair close-cropped to his skull. "Jac." The world spun the way it only had after he'd been jumped and kicked in the head by the group of boys when he was young, not able to right himself because of the dizziness.

"Sit down, man. You fall over, you'll embarrass me."

"You're here?"

Those dark eyes rolled in dramatic fashion. Yeah, Jac always had a larger-than-life edge to him. Strange, that Esh had forgotten. "She's my sister. You think I'll ever truly leave? Will you?"

"Fuck no," came the immediate reply, and Jac nodded in ready approval.

Jac was relaxed in the chair, the lines and tenseness that had been constant on the man the last months of his life gone. He looked good, like he did before being Esh's friend wasn't enough, before he had to prove he was somehow better than the Cage King.

"I didn't think you'd die." The words released on quick breath, the utterance not planned yet inevitable. "I thought they'd hurt you, and I wanted them to."

And maybe that was why he'd let Nalah go, why he didn't run after her, because how could he love her, make love to her, create a family with her, when deep in his heart, he'd wanted her brother hurt. Hurt bad enough, become scarred enough, that Jac wouldn't put them through any more shit.

Forget not interfering. That was why he hadn't taken Jac's place, and even as he said the bullshit excuse to Nalah, he'd known.

Jac laughed, and the sound was clean without any bitter taint. "That sounds like my son-of-a-bitch best friend."

Esh gave a half laugh in response, not as unencumbered, but less pain than he was used to. "What the fuck else could I do? I had to get it through your fucking head to not start shit anymore. If I thought for one moment they'd kill you, I'd of been there. I'd of taken the spot."

Jac shook his head. "Nah. Wasn't your place, and I was wrong to put it on you. Everything that happened that night was on me, so don't live with it anymore."

"Kind of hard not to."

Jac threw the chair pillow at his head. "My sister knows. She's just stubborn about shit. Lucky you always could outwait her. How many damn times did I catch you here watching her and waiting for her to finish? Well, you waited until she looked up from her book, and after that you hustled her ass out in seconds flat." The smile that followed had a hurt edge, the first showing of pain since he arrived. "Always hated that look. Do you know what it told me?"

"No."

"Told me I was going to lose my sister and my best friend and be all alone. And it was right." Jac rose and went to the astronomy section, the only section he ever looked at. It didn't surprise Esh the first time Jac did it, not with the hours upon hours Jac spent looking at the stars. He'd read the titles, studied the pictures displayed on the covers that faced outward. Yet in all the years they went to the library, not once did Esh ever see Jac pull a book from the case.

"You always had us. No way we would have left you."

"Wish I'd been strong enough to find something I could have given that look to." His hand ghosted over a spine, but he didn't grab the thick textbook. Instead he turned away. "You take care of my sister. That's all I want now, and if you think you owe me anything, do that and we're good."

The walls rattled, and outside dogs barked. Jac's voice became urgent. "Do what you came here to. Get her out of this."

There was no time to speak the other thoughts that lay uneasy on his tongue. There was now only movement, the library falling apart and a graveyard, dark and dank with a sliver of moon for light and a lone headstone in jagged silhouette.

Nalah stood over it, her face tear-stained but no active tears. "It's my fault."

He came to stand beside her, and the fraction she shifted away cooled the fire inside him by several degrees. "It wasn't."

Her body was bent, sagging under imagined weight. "I keep thinking about all the decisions I made that led to this. I should have done so many things different."

The inches between them might as well been miles. He was lost now, in a way he hadn't been since she came back into his life. He didn't know how to make things right, not with his own decisions mocking him. But that guilt was on him, not her. She'd always been the glue, strong and holding them together. She'd always fought to do things right. She didn't deserve to take any of this weight. "You always did your best, Nalah. Jac and I, we saw that. It made our lives easy, cause we could trust you. Any decisions you made wrong, they were made by a kid. How the fuck can you blame a kid for not knowing what they were doing?"

She shook her head, her expression saying *You just don't get it.* "Being a kid wasn't an excuse. I'd have made all those same decisions if I was an adult. I'd probably make them now."

"Like what decisions?"

The movement was subtle, but she shifted toward him now, and her lashes lowered to rest against wet cheeks. "I looked up and saw a boy who fought a whole gang to protect me even though he didn't know me, and right then I decided I was going to follow him wherever he went. I didn't know what it meant at the time. I only knew he would be my life, and I never considered where that would leave my brother."

Esh hadn't mourned for Jac when he'd died. Esh had been too pissed, and then too scared with Nalah missing, and after she hadn't come back all that was left was empty. Now, the back of his throat thickened and his chest went tight.

They'd all made stupid decisions. He and Nalah had been so wrapped up in each other they'd left Jac behind, and Jac let his hurt turn him bitter, leading him to make stupid, destructive choices that Nalah was always cleaning up after, until the one time Esh said no more, and that one time destroyed everything.

The dogs howled around them, mad, frantic barking that grew louder, closer, circling. Nalah turned to the sound. "They're almost here. You should leave."

"Without you?" Nalah met his gaze, and the vague mourning for Jac morphed into a cold pit that ate up his heart. She was ready to say goodbye. "*Dammit* Nalah, you're not a *fucking* liar. Don't say you're going to follow me and then let me *go*. I won't allow it. From here on, we go together."

Her unfocused expression pissed him off, like she expected him to accept her words and leave her to her fate. He grabbed her hand, placed it over his heart. "Do you know what happened to me when I saved you? Before you I hated what I was. I knew I had something different in me, and it was from assholes who threw me away to the streets. If I could have gouged it out with a knife, I would have. But you fucking smiled at me like I was a miracle, and that thing inside me sparked and lit. And I knew it was *for you*. That thing in me was a good thing, because it made me strong enough to protect you. For the first time I didn't hate what I was. I was *grateful*."

Beneath her palm the fire in him rose to greet her, the phoenix raising its voice in exultation. "This fire is yours, and if it can't be used to protect you,

I don't want it. I'll throw it away and walk by your side to meet whatever's coming. But what I'll never do is leave you again."

Tears fell and her lower lip trembled. "Am I betraying Jac? How can I have loved him if I want to live while he's dead, when his death is my fault?"

Take care of my sister, that's what Jac said. Whether him speaking to Jac was true or an illusion, the rightness of that statement sank into Esh. "If you asked anyone, they would say the same thing. *Jac loves his baby sister*, and you know that's true. Now honor him, because do you think the man who raised you would have wanted you in pain for five minutes because of him, let alone five years?"

Her face collapsed on itself, features stretched out with her sobbing, and she buried herself into him until not a breath of air could have found its way between them. Her tears broke something in him too. He'd never be totally right with Jac's death, he'd never forget it, but it was time for some forgiveness.

The black dog came into view, savage intelligence in its dark eyes, teeth sharp and exposed. He wanted to hold her until her decision otherwise, but the timing was out of his control. He bent over her head to speak low into her ear. "Nalah, do we fight, or do we submit?"

Her fingers curled and nails dug into the skin over his heart. Her head lifted, those dark brown eyes clear of the past, and gods were they beautiful. "We fight, because the Cage King always wins."

As if it had been waiting, the phoenix burst forth around them, its beak sharper, its flames burning hotter and higher than they'd been before, the colors more distinct and varied between reds, yellows, and even the hint of blue.

"So beautiful," Nalah said, awe in her wide eyes and open-mouthed half-smile.

The phoenix took flight, its song full of joy and wonder. It swooped low at the dogs, which cowed and crept back into the darkness, before soaring into the heights once more. It twisted and turned, cleansing the air wherever it passed and banishing the night, the graveyard, and now they were at a waterfall, lush foliage and sun sparkling above and about as perfect a place as Esh could ever want to be.

"Didn't know you liked waterfalls."

After all they'd been through it might not have been the most insightful comment, but Nalah started laughing, full-blown belly laughs that had her doubling over. "You kept sneaking the travel book that had this waterfall like I wouldn't notice," she said as she straightened. "I cut the picture out and kept it with me."

For him. This was *for him*. He lowered his head and poured everything he felt into the kiss he wrapped her in, and overhead the phoenix sang in approval.

CHAPTER TWENTY

Esh opened his eyes to see red hair and gold, gleaming eyes, a spark off the hilt of a sword. "Was it real?"

Fallon didn't ask for details. She was quiet for a moment, and if she pretended she didn't know what he was talking about, he might take a swing at her, Guild or not. "The knowledge is real," were her ultimate words. "So take it and move on."

Move on. Yes, that he wanted to do, and he got to his feet, walked to where Nalah was sitting up, protesting her treatment by Rorth and Aislynn. "Honestly, I'm fine. I'm good. My head feels clear for the first time in forever – better than it used to." His shadow touched her and she looked up, and a luminous, hesitant smile stole over her face.

Screw hesitation. He bent and lifted her, picking up the kiss as it had been by the waterfall, and her hands tangled in his hair and pulled tight as she kissed him back. It felt like their first kiss all over again, and in a way it was. They were as free of the past as they could be, and it was time to celebrate.

Whistling. It was whistling that broke them apart, and Fallon gave a close-lipped smile. "If you let us wrap this up, you can do that as much as you want and I won't bother you again."

"Fallon," was Nalah's small protestation, but she patted Esh in an unspoken plea to be put down, which he complied with. She looked among the three of them. "My mother's ring."

"I'm sorry, but it has been taken," said Aislynn, her expression pure empathy for Nalah.

"That…woman." Nalah shuddered and huddled closer, and Esh held her to combat the chill. She looked to Fallon. "Who was she?"

"*A Rainha da Flor-Cadaver* – the Corpse Bloom Queen. Pray you don't meet her again."

Esh never prayed – never a reason to – but if he ever started, that would be his first.

Fallon turned the conversation away from the ring and their recent enemy. "The Phoenix Clan will want to know about you. Do you want to meet your people?"

"If I have a people, why the hell was I running the streets?" Old hurt rode him even after the earlier cleansing, and bitterness still seeped through his tone.

"You don't need me to tell you the Great Collision destroyed a lot of lives, so don't expect me to coo over you because yours was one of them."

Before he could open his mouth to respond, Aislynn put her hand on Fallon's shoulder and said, "Perhaps at this point I should speak?" Fallon motioned her forward, and Aislynn took focal point of the group. "I do not know what happened to your family or why you were alone. What I can assure you of is the Phoenix Clan is small, and it values all of its blood. If the Clan knew of you, they would never have let you live out your life on the streets. And while in one way that would have been a great joy, it would have meant you would never have found Nalah or your calling in the fights."

"You think the fights are a calling?"

Esh's question was full of attitude, but Aislynn's response was not. "Some of us have the skill to fight, but we are not fighters. While I accept my place in battle, it is hard for me to exist there." The elf's blue eyes went flat in a way Esh knew from older fighters, those who were at the end of their time in the cage and ready to escape it – in any way necessary. His gaze flicked to Fallon, but she was speaking in low tones to Rorth and not watching the elf. "You, however, thrive there, and you enter and leave the same way, as a good man who upholds his honor. So yes, the fights are your calling. Whether they are in front of a crowd, or should our battle come to your door, beside us in combat."

They were Guild. Their existence was fighting. Kind of surprising, Nalah ending up with them instead of him. And if Nalah stayed with them? Then fucking positive the battle would land at his door, because she wasn't going without him.

"One day," Esh answered. "Soon, I'll meet with the Clan. Got questions I want answered anyway. Right now I want space."

Fallon had finished her discussion with Rorth and again took point. "Sounds reasonable. I'll let them know of your existence so they'll be ready when you contact them." She softened a fraction then, her eyes flicking to Nalah, who was still in the circle of his arms. "You did well. Not many could take on the Corpse Bloom Queen for even a moment. What are your plans now?"

Nalah glanced at him, love and desire and no ghosts in that gaze. He thought he knew freedom before, but this, loving and being loved, this was free. This was true happiness. "I am going to be with him and we're figuring out our life together, and I don't know how long it's going to take or where it's going to lead us." His heart stuttered in his chest over this final proof she'd forgiven him, and herself as well.

"And the Guild?"

"I don't know."

"Fair enough, but even if you choose not to come back, know you'll always be Guild. You've been marked by our enemies and you need to remember that, and if there is a question that only your talents can find the answer to, we will call on you. You're never truly free."

Fallon's response was reasonable. Still, flame bristled under his skin at the directive, while Nalah answered. "I understand. That means also if there is something only the Guild can help us with, we'll be sure to call *you*."

With that, Fallon smiled a wide, genuine smile. "Make sure you invite Laire to the wedding. She gets horribly depressed if she misses any occasion that allows her to dress up." In a smooth movement Fallon turned and headed back to the town, the other two following.

Let them clean up, or arrest people, or whatever else. He was done, and all that mattered was getting back home, getting his motorcycle, and bending Nalah over it as he'd been dreaming about for six years.

Speaking of, Nalah leaped into his arms and began raining kisses over his face. "I love you," she said, fierce and forever, and it seared itself onto his heart. "But don't think you're getting your way in everything. Five years is a long time, and we need to readjust to one another. So don't expect us to move in together right away."

He started kissing her neck. Not right away then. He'd give it two weeks before he moved her.

She was wriggling in his arms, her voice growing breathier as her body responded to his kisses. "And I'm not staying at home while you get in trouble. Even if I don't go back to the Guild, I need to use my talents and be productive."

There were handcuffs to keep her at home. Though by the bulge in his jeans, handcuffs were both a good and bad idea. Good because it would keep her safe. Bad because he'd never leave the apartment if she was cuffed to the bed.

"And why the hell do I bother to talk? You aren't listening to a damn thing I said."

"You said you love me. What else do I need to hear?"

And after her bright smile, as she leaned in to kiss him, she said, "You better stay very good in bed if you expect lines like that to keep working."

That, he intended to do.

CHAPTER TWENTY-ONE

The huge walls and domed ceiling of the hall told the story of a proud and powerful people. Guards stood at the ready with weapons while behind them tiled scenes decorated every square inch of stone, scenes depicting battles and victory and always, always, flame and ash and the burnt remains of those who were enemies.

Red and gold dominated, followed by rich earthen colors. A closer look revealed the decoration to be gold and silver, gems of all types within the designs. None entering could mistake this place as anything but the domain of one who should be looked on with awe or fear – or both.

The hall led to a room, large and forbidding. Everything from the wood of the floor to the fabrics that covered the scattering of furniture was rich and sumptuous, tasteful, restrained, and any Blackguard's mouth would water at the fortune contained within.

At the far end, in front of a huge picture window, the man stood, his shoulder-length red-gold hair alight from the incoming sunshine, creating a halo effect.

"No wonder your kind were looked upon as heaven's messengers. I can almost hear the harps."

He didn't start or look away from whatever held his attention beyond the glass. He answered, his voice the deep tones of culture and breeding. "And do you wonder about the workings of heaven, Dragon Slayer?"

Fallon gave a short laugh that edged into humorless. "Hardly. I have enough problems worrying about all the gods wandering underfoot down here. I'll leave heaven to its own. Lord Kyo sends his regards."

He turned to her, his eyes a simmering flame, red and gold mingled together, almost the same shade as his hair. The expression on his face was pleasant, the rehearsed pleasant that spoke of training to never let real emotion through. "I have been anxious to hear your account of our operation. I am pleased it was a success."

Fallon's eyes flicked to the side, her mouth twisting in one corner. "Depends on your definition, though Kyo agrees with your assessment."

"Yes, Lord Kyo and I are in agreement." His next words were a volley, a gentle probe against her defenses. "And your thoughts?"

The quirk of her eyebrow spoke that she knew what he was doing, but she answered anyway. "While I agree that Esh was our priority, I think I put a little higher value on the Realm Jumper than perhaps you or Kyo."

"The Realm Jumper has many advantages, yes, but it can accomplish nothing that a large group of powerful wizards could not."

"Perhaps."

"And your tone says you believe otherwise."

She smiled, a shading of amusement that he called her out. "I don't trust magic, so I'm always asking *what if*. The Realm Jumper can access all nine of the other Realms, but *what if*, just maybe, it can access more?"

"The Tenth Realm? That's a fable."

Her smile widened, and she inclined her head an inch. "More likely I'm pissed the best I can claim is a draw with the Corpse Bloom Queen."

He stepped closer, keeping a respectful distance but placing himself behind his desk and into the center of authority. "Ah yes, the Pale Lady. Unexpected, that."

Fallon put her hands in her pockets and leaned back against the wall, one knee bent and the sole of her foot propped against the vertical surface in a false façade of casual repose. "Was it unexpected for you as well?"

"Of course. When it comes to the necromancers, I would not leave unmentioned even a suspicion of their workings." There was a globe on his desk, done in browns and gold with very little primary color. His index finger stroked with lazy ease over a section changed more than any other because of the Great Collision, an area where necromancers ruled. "We now have in-fighting amongst the necromancers to consider in our future plans. Reign and the Pale Lady have ever been at odds, but this display means that she, at least, has decided no longer to keep it hidden from us. Open warfare has been declared in their ranks, and we will be drawn in."

"Necromancers not able to make friends with one another? Shocking," Fallon said with deadpan delivery.

"I would not take this so lightly. Of all in our alliance, she has an especial hatred for you."

"Let me lose sleep that yet another necromancer wants me dead, or undead, or whatever."

"Oh, she wants you dead. She wants you obliterated down to the mention of your name. She would not keep you around even as a trophy to display." The handsome lines of his face *sharpened*, and the predator flickered over his features for the briefest moment. "But it's not as if that is what all of them wish, is it?"

Fallon met his gaze straight on. "Beware taking that path, Phoenix Lord. I am not yours to poke and prod." She straightened, hands still in pockets but body more visibly ready for battle, Tenro glinting behind her shoulder.

The barest tilt of his head signaled the acceptance of her words, and he continued. "Do you have any word why Reign did not try harder to reclaim the Realm Jumper? Using only the Skin Dweller in such circumstances is almost pathetic."

"We came up with the same reason I'm sure you did – something better is out there that he wants and his efforts are focused elsewhere. We have Tec working on it, but…" Her words trailed off.

"With the theft of the items in the vault, too many variables."

"Too many variables," she agreed, her attention locked onto a ten-foot tapestry of a phoenix in full glory, its wings and its neck straining upwards. "Esh will come to you soon. He's still holding onto anger, but even if he wanted to leave his heritage alone, Nalah is too curious to let information go unclaimed."

"Of course he'll return. From the moment his fire awoke, that conclusion became inevitable. He is of phoenix blood. When the blood calls, he will answer, and he will stand beside us in all battles."

"Such good luck one so strong and talented came into his power in these tense times, when war is edging ever closer." Fallon's voice held a weary, far away note, her vision fixed on the phoenix.

"War is always close. Our existence is to hold it at bay." For those few words, the false pleasantness was gone, and pure determination and fierce purpose were all that existed. With a deep breath, he became again bland politeness. "Please thank Lord Kyo for his assistance in returning one of ours to us."

Fallon took her attention away from the tapestry and once again faced him, her face as devoid of true feelings as the Phoenix Lord. "Lord Kyo needs no thanks and is always ready to help his allies. He does ask that you share a financial burden that came out of this mission. It seems the Blackguards accuse us of not informing them of the true danger of this mission, which caused their man to get caught and killed. To smooth over relations, Lord Kyo has offered monetary compensation, which they have accepted."

"Of course. Should I include a note of condolence?"

"No need. The man killed was a violent scumbag who had no family. Personally, I think the world is better off without him and am sure he would have died soon enough, but…" she gave a small lift of her shoulder, the move shifting Tenro and causing her red hair to curl around the sword's hilt. "Politics and all."

"Politics is all." He bent over the desk and wrote something in elegant cursive. "To think, if this man hadn't died, Nalah would have accomplished her task in short order, and she and Esh may never have reunited, which would have meant Esh's power would not have manifested." Stuffing the note in an envelope, he handed the paper to Fallon.

She took it with quick flick of her hand, her gaze steady and unflinching on his. "Crazy to think how things work sometimes."

"Indeed. How do you believe *things work*, Dragon Slayer?"

She snorted, straightening up, her body language that of one ready to depart. "I don't care about gods or heavens or politics. I swing my sword and take down any in my way, and the moving of the pawns I'll leave to all of you who enjoy sitting behind the desks."

"As you say. Please give my regards to Lord Kyo," he replied, courtesy in every line of his body.

She inclined her head and turned to go. When she was halfway to the door, he called out, "And please give my highest respect to the Most Great One, Master and UnMaster of all."

Fallon spun to face him while walking backwards, still heading towards the exit. "I'm sure I don't know what you mean," she said, her voice and countenance amused confusion. And she spun around again and continued to the door.

He lowered himself to his seat. "Oh yes…"

Tenro's hilt gleamed against Fallon's coppery-red hair, visible only a moment before the swordswoman exited the room.

"I'm sure."

THE END

THE ROOFTOP

CHAPTER ONE

"So this is the Dragon Slayer? A human girl not even old enough to buy alcohol from the bar down below?"

It was windy here, on the top of the six-story building situated on the edge of the city, a strong enough wind to drive the cold through the leather of her black coat and settle it into her skin. The cold, though, had been a small price in return for both the view and the peace she had been enjoying, an enjoyment cut short by her visitor.

Fallon didn't need to glance towards the roof's edge to know who he was. He didn't hide his magic as he approached, a tsunami of dark power that threatened to topple her, and only the steady weight of Tenro at her back kept her upright.

He stayed on the periphery of her vision, but she refused to offer him the satisfaction of looking his way. He wasn't attacking – not yet, at any rate – so she'd let this play out. "Very perceptive, Master Vampire. Your legend is obviously earned. What next? Commenting in awe over the fact I have red hair?"

"The hair color is the one thing I approve of." He strolled into her line of vision, a confident walk of a man who owned all and was comfortable in that power. He turned to face her, the blood-red eyes of a vampire alight in the full moon, his near-black hair gleaming like the pelt of a wild animal.

The whispers now made sense – low, hungry words from men and women who should have known better than to be pulled in by physical beauty from such a foul creature.

Her fingertips itched, and not in desire to release Tenro.

"Don't be a fool."

Her spine straightened in instinctive reaction to the tone, the interruption of those words from deep inside her enough to break any fragile bonds the vampire wove.

Before her lay the enemy. The only end guaranteed if she forgot that fact? Death – or worse. "Strangely enough, approval from those who don't even bother to introduce themselves before commenting on my shortcomings...tends not to make much of an impression on me."

The corner of his mouth lifted at that, and then the swiftest, lightest furrowing of his brows, as if even he did not expect to give this reaction. "Forgive my poor manners. Please, call me Reign."

She shrugged, taking care to lift Tenro into his line of vision. "Of course I will, at least until the day I call you a dead enemy."

His smile at that statement was pure humoring. "And until the day one of us utters those words, what shall I call you?"

"Let's keep this informal vibe going, shall we? I'm Fallon."

"Fallon." He repeated the name as though he was tasting it, breathing it out to distinguish the subtle shifts, the various nuances. "It suits you."

"Don't expect me to return the compliment."

He was intent, no humor now but no anger either, his whole bearing the relaxed awareness that spoke of one who was relating the complete truth as they knew it. "It is who I am, and not even the Dragon Slayer and wielder of Tenro can change that truth. What are you, girl? Twenty, twenty-one?"

Moonlight poured over him, this vampire who was a legend in ancient times, long before the Great Collision. It highlighted the sharp planes of his face, making the predator stand out that much more. "I think this is where I tell you age ain't nothing but a number, and the only thing that matters is how hard I shove Tenro through your chest."

His features relaxed into a devilish smirk, and his tone became pointed, poking to find the soft spots. "Even younger then? Tenro must be desperate to choose such a champion. Are you allowed out so close to bedtime?"

Mama clutching her close.

My brave little girl.

My beautiful little girl...

She hadn't been young in a very long time, and she returned his smirk with her own, designed to tell him so. "Actually, I was sent out to get some exercise so I could get a good night's sleep. How about I pull my sword and we have ourselves a little workout?"

He faltered, the smirk fading as he studied her with more intensity than he had earlier. He must have reached some internal decision, for the intensity lessened though did not disappear. "You just may be a worthy adversary after all."

The fight inside her faded, at those words, at the beginnings of *something* which lit his eyes, announced itself in the tilt of his head. No, she didn't want to fight, and unease filtered through her nerve endings at that knowledge. Fallon shoved against it, hardening her voice as she replied, "But we aren't going to find that out tonight, are we, Vampire? After all, you weren't prepared to bump into me, and you wouldn't want to do anything that may cause disruption to your future plans."

No surprise showed on his face at her talk of plans. He either was an excellent poker player, or he long ago accepted that something of the magnitude of ripping apart the Realms could not be hidden. "There is something to be said for anticipation."

There was no innuendo in his tone, but that *something* in him deepened, sharpened, and her breath seized in her lungs as surely as if an enemy had landed a punch center of her chest.

He turned away, to go back the way he had approached. "We will see each other again, Dragon Slayer. Don't disappoint me."

He couldn't have the last word, not at this first meeting. "It would hurt my heart to know I didn't live up to your expectations."

Reign glanced over his shoulder, his gaze locking with hers. "No," he murmured, the sound only a decibel louder than the still swirling winds. "I think I need not worry about that."

"I knew I'd find you here."

"Are you saying I'm predictable? Bad habit for my line of work." Fallon answered as Reign came to stand across from her. Such predatory grace, the way he moved, sure and possessed, gentleman and jungle cat in seamless combination.

"Which would you rather I say? That you are predictable, or there is a part of you that no matter how hard you try, I still *know*?" The question wasn't meant to get an answer, it was meant to get under her skin. Damned if she'd let him see if it did. He only waited a beat before continuing, "I would think after the unfortunate event that occurred with the vault, Kyo would be more careful in letting his people wander alone."

She snorted. "Please. All that means is we now have a bunch of idiots waving around items to make themselves look cool, all the while having no clue how to wield them. I'm in more danger of getting hurt from looking at some of Laire's fashion choices."

Reign stood there, looking the same as he did at each of the handful of times they had found themselves together on this rooftop. Still beautiful, still dangerous, still possessing a power that threatened to buckle her knees under her – the only being who could claim that particular privilege. Sometimes she had come in search of him, other times he came to her, but it was as he said…they both somehow just knew.

After all the years, all the *war*, only that fact could stop her in her tracks and terrify her as no bloodshed in battle had the ability to.

He looked her over with blatant intent, his gaze containing an edge that had her swallowing hard before she could stop herself. "Do you know what I think?" he said at last.

"I live to hear such things."

He stepped forward, only a handful of steps, but enough that the full force of his gaze grabbed and held hers, enough that she could almost believe she could feel his breath, hear the beat of his heart under his chest. "I think I am done with anticipation."

In the longest, darkest nights, when she was pushed past exhaustion, almost past sanity, thoughts would occur, thoughts she would never allow herself otherwise. Now, Reign stood before her and, with only a sentence, battered against a door she did not acknowledge existed – and on the other side of that door, thousands of thoughts screamed and scratched to be let free.

A cry for help broke through the haze, and in instinctive reaction her head whipped to track the sound. "One of yours?"

She turned back to him. Reign's face held such repressed fury Fallon had to lock her knee to stop the urge to step back. "If it is, they'll beg for death months before I let them experience it."

The door was now safe, and she was not going to allow herself to go near it again. It was time to leave. "And here I thought Kyo was a tough boss."

Fallon walked to the edge, ready to jump down, only to be stopped by Reign's words. "We will not meet here again, will we?"

The truth of his words hit her, and loss came hard on its heels. No, they would not meet here again. The end game was in motion, and the strange neutrality that marked these meetings no longer existed. Looking into those beautiful blood-red eyes, she opened her mouth to speak, shaped her lips around the word, but the sound wouldn't come, the final affirmation refusing to let itself be uttered.

Another cry from below, and Fallon tore herself away from his gaze and went to help whoever was waiting. She did not look back.

She did not look back.

The End

NOTE FROM DANIELLE MONSCH

Peoples! Thanks for purchasing **Entwined Realms, Volume One,** a compilation of the first four stories set in the *Entwined Realms* universe. If you have a moment, please leave a review! Reviews are the way retailers decide which books are worth promoting, and reviews help authors so, *so* much – Thank You for the consideration!

Next up to be Released**: The Dream Crafter (***Entwined Realms,* **Book 2)** will be out **November 2014**.

For those of you who love Fairy Tale redos, ones that are slightly twisted, very sassy, humorous (as only I can deliver!) and promises you a Happily Ever After every time, please give my *Fairy Tales & Ever Afters* series a try!

And should you be interested in hearing about my other books and want to know as soon as they are released, please sign up for my newsletter! Newsletters are sent out only when a book is released or I'm giving stuff away, and your email is never used for any other purpose or sold/distributed to anyone else!

FAIRY TALES & EVER AFTERS
READING ORDER

Loving a Fairy Godmother
Loving an Ugly Beast
Loving a Prince Charming

LOVING A FAIRY GODMOTHER

Once upon a Time, in a Kingdom that was just a little twisted (oh yeah, and kinda far away), Fairy Godmothers Rule! Elf Kings drool, and a Knight was having a bad time with a Dragon.

Too bad he didn't realize the Dragon would be the least strange part of his day...

Fairy GodMOTHER. As in female - it's right there in the name. With those divine dimples, killer blue eyes, and hard muscled body, no one's going to be mistaking Tiernan for a female anytime soon, but due to a wish gone wrong, Tiernan is now the only Fairy Godfather in existence. Strangely, most Fairy Godmothers don't have a problem with this change in the status quo... all except the one Fairy Godmother he'd go and win a kingdom for.

Organized, efficient, logical - and happy with the status quo, thank you very much - Reina never liked that Tiernan was allowed in the program. After all, the FGs do not need a stubborn, infuriating, feckless male messing up tradition, and she wants him gone...like yesterday. Circumstances arise that might let her get her wish, but in a way even she never wished for.

Tiernan's employment status is called into question, and to prove himself worthy of being an FG, he is given the task of getting a woman named Cinderella a Happily Ever After. If he doesn't, he loses his position as a Fairy Godfather and becomes human again. Unfortunately, becoming human means becoming Dragon chow. So Cinderella will get to the ball and get her Prince if he has to dress her down to her shoes himself, and he's bringing Reina along to help. After all, who said only mortals should get a Happily Ever After?

ABOUT THE AUTHOR

Born to the pothole-ridden streets of Pittsburgh, PA, Danielle Monsch started writing in a time long ago, a time when there were not enough vampire stories to read and she had to write her own to fill the void. Yes, such a time of darkness did indeed exist.

Danielle writes stories full of fantastical goodness and plenty of action, but always with lots of romance (and a bit of woo-hoo!) mixed in. Vampires and Werewolves and Demons and Angels, Sword & Sorcery, Fairy Tales, Updated Mythologies and the like – if it's out of the ordinary, it's fair game for her stories.

Go to **www.DanielleMonsch.com** for one-stop shopping with everything to do with Danielle - there you can join her **Newsletter** (*highly* encouraged as it contains all info about upcoming books, plus random surprises) follow her on **Twitter**, and like her on **Facebook**. Just want to send Danielle a quick email? Easy enough, that's **Dani@DanielleMonsch.com**.

www.ingramcontent.com/pod-product-compliance
Lightning Source LLC
Chambersburg PA
CBHW020609270626
47155CB00022BA/338